Only Human

By J.D. Estrada

To my wife for inspiration, love, support and banana pancakes.
To my mom for swelling my chest with pride.
To friends and family for urging me to just do this already.
To the sea for she knows me better than I know myself.

Table of Contents

About the Author

About Only Human

Prologue

Prologue

Pitiful humans... How you parade and frolic in your false grandiosity. There you go again, constantly proclaiming your dominion of the cosmos, while remaining oblivious to an existence you barely grasp. "Masters of the Universe!" you boldly declare yourselves.

Please.

At best, you are the logical primate that has for some irreverent reason proliferated and become the dominant species; some malignant termite that through sheer force in numbers has climbed echelon after echelon in the evolutionary scale, until reaching the zenith of this world's food chain. If alive, your Darwin would be most unpleasantly surprised.

Plagues, natural disasters, epidemics, World Wars and still your societies prevail as a collective pest that not only survives, but thrives with reckless abandon, no matter what grave circumstances it may face.

If pressed for an answer, surely any of your kind would say that all this has been possible through the delightful virtue you call hope. I would counter by singling your resilience as the only true asset worthwhile of your kind. And no, resilience is not the same as hope. One is tangible while the other is almost poetic, metaphorical even. Still, no matter the adversity, as a whole you always manage to remain tick-like, refusing to be shaken off your carrier. Quite a useful quality, since you also represent the livestock of sustenance for other species.

How impressive that for however un-evolved and barbaric as you may be, you still manage to be the dominant race on this planet. Something to truly marvel at, because even hating each other and discriminating based on color, creed, race, and whatever other classification you so ingeniously concoct, the status quo of your quid pro quo ways remains. Flesh begets flesh while your souls result in nothing more than a mockery of the very gods you so doubtfully fear.

Yet now we must look to aid you in regards to the biggest problem humankind faces: itself. My kind and others in line must put aside our differences to rescue all world kind, no matter how close we have come to extinction at the hands of one another. For now, we shall forget our mutual aversions in the hope that we may all survive to kill each other some other day.

But the abomination that is humanity is the reason we unite, for it seems that in the enemy resides the solution to our common predicament. Quite interesting since like vaccines, it seems the cure is found within the disease. Let us hope that my instincts and judgment prove true instead of having failed me once again.

Chapter 1: Needle from the hay

High up on an imposing bell tower, a dark figure hovers deep in thought while contemplating the world from atop its stone altar. Veiled by darkness, cobalt eyes slice through the shade, themselves attached to a dim silhouette crouching in the gloom.

The shadow fidgets, making graceful checkmarks in the air as the next move in a mental chess match is plotted and played. Twenty stories below, the bustle of the restless city hums and beats as people traverse a busy intersection.

Midnight nears.

As the mental stampede rumbles between both temples, the eyes flicker back and forth, at times screening the crowd though often just searching for a thought that momentarily slipped the shade's grasp.

Mumbles and whispers seep from the shadow and occasionally spoken outbursts of apparently groundbreaking ideas appear. But they hardly last and before any sense is given to them, they melt into unintelligible clicks and hisses.

Time suddenly freezes.

The gaze no longer dances madly across the crowd and the shadow visually dissects something below. What once were dark blue orbs frost into white lightning.

Hawk-like, the gaze burns onto one point, one single crow within the murder. Its breathing picks up and transitions from a slithering four by four to an all out fugue. Its pulse mimics a child's when coming face to face with the largest Christmas parcel.

The hawk follows its prey with military precision while two hands break free from the vice-like grip each had on the other. They slither to the shade's center, tugging lightly on a thin gold chain that sparkles in the dark. A gold ring hangs at the end surrounding a multicolor glass that looks predominantly like amethyst. The golden trickle hangs in the darkness and the figure nervously inches the disc towards the white-blue orb on its right side.

"Please let me be right," rasped a man's whisper. "Let human hope shower atop the head of one of the condemned, as they would call me. Let me for once weep of jubilation instead of frustration."

The ever-changing lens leapt suddenly from his hand pressing against his right eye socket, digging and raking itself into arctic flesh that now showed under the glow of the lens. His broken breath signaled pain as all muscles tensed in unison from suppression, but there was no screaming. This pain was not new.

After a moment, only a thin gold trickle leaks out of the once sapphire eye. A myriad of colors begin parading phosphorescently unlike anything known to man. A heavy breath heaves as the figure adjusts to the new found vision and the deep raspy voice once again breaks the sky's silence. "Now, where is my little friend? He must still be around. He has to be."

The multicolored eye desperately scanned the scene, backwards and forwards over the crowd until finally the eye shrieked to a dead halt. The newly polychromatic cornea fixes on a young man who entertained himself with a half eaten pretzel. His brown hair was messy and his face was clearly sullen from fatigue.

The flesh and blood gargoyle became utterly fascinated by his newfound specimen and just barely, one could hear a whisper that counted in ascending fashion. With every new number a smile gleamed in the darkness until a twisted grimace not unlike that of a mad scientist glowed in the gloom. "At last, I've found some hope in this barren wasteland we call the present."

He then tugged firmly on the thin gold whisper that wept down his right cheek. A small groan escaped his mouth because of the effort. Through grit teeth, two exceptionally sharp fangs shine dimly in the moonlight. The lens finally slides free from the white flesh, dragging with it a single solitary ruby tear.

"I think I've found myself a date," said the shade as it caringly tucked the disk back into his shirt.

Afterwards, the shadow casually stepped off the ledge, plummeting and laughing madly for sixty feet until the darkness of an alley below swallowed him whole. His laughter echoed long after it should have logically ceased.

Chapter 2: The wicked invite

Nathaniel Runnels stood in the damp night perplexed by his current standing in life. His hair was a mess; his sunken eyes wore the strain of long nights and the painful hunger in his side was only slightly eased by a lukewarm pretzel alit with the decorative swirl of spicy brown mustard.

His coat had seen better days and so had his stomach. But on a writer-gone-reporter's salary, he was content to at least be able to break bread with himself.

Raggedy cuffs and a dimple of mustard were clear signs that at least for tonight, giving a damn was not particularly high on his list. He sighed every so often as conspiracy theories banged within his brain; or were those withdrawal pangs from the caffeine addiction he'd been nurturing for several years now.

'Hung over and exhausted... joy,' he thought to himself. 'I should have been a lawyer or a stock broker or some other profession that gives you high blood pressure from stress rather than the low blood sugar goodness that comes with a reporter's lifestyle.'

He stank of cynicism, self-loathing, brutal honesty and possibly too much gin. He recognized the life he'd given himself, fully knowing that the path he now walked was one he had chosen on his own.

He did not like the taste in his mouth as he remembered ingesting the false story of him only doing this as research for the characters in his book. A temporary job he'd convinced himself as he got ready to unleash the next great American novel, which for the past year and a half had grown to an amazing 26-page behemoth. In all honesty, he didn't have direction and wrote out of sheer determination every month or so only to sacrifice most of what was written to the apathetic and luckily non-critical fireplace in his studio apartment.

'Great job,' he thought to himself as his shoulders hunched with every new thought that did its best to shatter his morale. He finished his far-from-exquisite meal and licked his subway hands. He didn't care and it showed; it showed a lot. He mimed a tip of the hat to the street vendor and went on his way. At least he kept his manners.

Down the steps he went and his luck finally peaked. His teeth grit audibly as the subway made its way away from the platform. He knew he would have to wait an hour, enjoying the wonderful bouquet of urine, burnt rat droppings, and sewer water that would serve as aromatherapy during his wait.

He slumped down on the bench quickly noticing that there wasn't anything else open so he could purchase a savory candy bar or some gummy something to serve as a delicatessen treat after his half star meal. (The half star had come from the mustard, that's for sure.)

The deserted platform filled with his woeful voice. "Wonder how long I'll have to stay on the Ramen diet. Not too long before I get a stroke now... or hypertension; then maybe I'll be able to feast on hospital food. Mmm, mmm, mmm.... delicious hospital food. Jesus Christ, I'm a joke."

The lonely silence droned on and after a while, the young man was actually starting to enjoy it. So naturally it couldn't last. All of a sudden a violin weaved a terribly wicked tune that seemed to seep out from deep within the subway tunnels.

The young reporter stood up and looked both ways but was unable to find the source. His eyes fell to the floor and confusion set in. Abruptly, the rhythmic tapping of a boot began to accompany the morbid tune and upon turning to his left for a second time, Nathaniel saw an ankle peeking from a far off column. The boot bobbed forwards and backwards, clearly showing that the owner sat on the subway floor while leaning on the column. The ankle might have swayed lazily but the melody was anything but tranquil.

The frustrated young man sat back on the bench and faced the curious virtuoso that, as so many others he had seen, had chosen the subway corridors as his concert hall. On a dime, the song morphed into a gentle waltz that was just as magnificently morose as the preceding section.

"Do you like it?" slithered a voice into the young man's ear. There was something terribly offbeat within the words he heard. He was still unsure whether he liked the voice... or the music. "I wrote it some time back, and from your reaction, I can at least guess you are intrigued."

The young man did not respond, yet his attention was anything but absent. Unfortunately the wicked voice wasn't about to stop. "Cat's got your tongue? Pity, I rather fancied some conversation; even if it consisted of the rambling of a disgruntled writer playing at being a reporter."

A knot within the young man's throat was no larger than a grapefruit and no smaller than the same. His weak eyes leapt to life as he was not certain as to how a subway bum could know what he does for a living. A nagging sensation of danger drummed low in his gut.

"Oh my," said the voice in mock concern. "I've alarmed you. Don't worry though. I am no stalker but you do have a way of thinking aloud and I must confess it is quite entertaining."

His remarks were seasoned with a touch of condescension and a healthy dose of ego. Nathaniel replied with a slight snarl. Getting away from this annoying lunatic, regardless of his talent, was quickly becoming a top priority.

"I truly wish you would continue to think aloud," the voice said as it continued to jab at the young man as much as the bow struck the violin. "These walls hear far too much from me."

The ankle continued to tap merrily while the tune grew darker and moodier still. The shrill notes were the kind that tickle your spine and the ever hunching shoulders of the young man clearly demonstrated how tension could also rise to a crescendo.

"What do you want?" Nathaniel said. "Spare change?"

"So, it does speak," the violinist teased. "Progress at last."

For some reason, Nathaniel decided to reply. "Look, I've had a long day. Could you simply play and let me enjoy your fine music instead of your insipid thought pattern?"

6

"And it has vocabulary too," the violinist said while letting out a high whistle. "My, my... such big words. Please, do not cause yourself a migraine on my account".

Nathaniel closed his eyes and sighed. He was well aware that he had just guaranteed himself that he would have to spend a fair amount of his precious energy verbally fencing instead of having just minded his business. Having a car would be worse though. It would mean yet another payment he could not make.

"How 'bout eat me?" he finally spat out. "Is that simple enough for you? Please no talk. Play good. Pretty, pretty song, oh so nice." The young man's tone was harsh, disrespectful and clearly full of contempt, a reaction was more than due.

The ankle stopped bobbing and the music stopped on a dime immediately replaced by an evil rasp of a laugh. "I knew I liked you," said the creepy voice. Silence then hung coldly accompanying the electric drone of the faulty subway rail.

The young man stared perplexed at his present scenario. A long crummy day with no leads, no inspiration, a pathetic meal and now harassed by some madcap that knew how to play the violin far too well for even the best subway musician.

He fixed his eyes on the now static boot that had been so cheerfully tapping mere seconds ago. He didn't know if the guy had fallen asleep, died, or was simply waiting for the next comment that would never arrive. Since the ghoulish laughter, the absence of any noise was nerve-wracking, but finally it ceased to be quiet.

The young man's eyes jumped open as the faint scrape of a boot was followed by leather rubbing and grating upwards on a tiled column. The violinist had pushed himself up until his body was upright and neatly out of sight.

"This cannot be good," the reporter remarked listlessly. His pulse rate tripled. His muscles tensed and his imagination ran away with a series of potential headlines for when they found his body. 'Now I get inspired,' he thought to himself.

Silence reigned and he would much rather have the symphony of a crying baby, a Hare Krishna handing out the word of God while expecting a dollar in return, or even the old geezer that so often befouled one's ears with the huffing and puffing of an old out-of-tune saxophone only to receive money from people begging him to stop playing.

Hope then shone bright with the faint rumbling of a distant train. He had forgotten there was an express train that sometimes stopped here. The bad part was that this stop was notorious for the questionable wiring that would falter every time there was an arrival. He stepped to the platform to make as speedy an escape as possible.

Then it began.

Lights started to screw up and along with the holy train heralding his escape, Nathaniel saw a gloved hand extend four pillars away over the train tracks. It waved gleefully until pausing to extend four fingers.

The lights flickered and the hand seemed to teleport a column closer and a finger lighter. Three.

"What the hell is going on?" Nathaniel said.

Again the lights failed. Another finger down and another column closer. Two.

The train had rushed in and after a few seconds finally stopped but the hand had come one column nearer and only the middle finger stood cheerfully extended before the hand waved once again. One.

Two brilliant flashes of emerald were the last thing Nathaniel saw before everything went black. The subway doors opened and closed and only one person was in the train.

Sipping his coffee, the driver sighed and prayed he could get home soon to kiss his wife goodnight as the train made its way down the tunnel and away from the stop.

Chapter 3: Waking up from a dream called reality

The sheer darkness is static granite... black, cold and unflinching. I am lost in a barren landscape of unconsciousness. Black, upon black, upon black is all I see and the last thing I know is which way is up. Waves ripple slowly across the tar lake of my vision and small beads of light blink like stars in the oncoming night. They twitch, swirl and multiply until the void fills with shimmers. A horizon tears in the darkness and I am born to a dark, dimly lit room.'

Nathaniel had always insisted that he was an endlessly better writer the worse he felt. "I should have bought a car," he said out loud this time.

Though his thoughts were almost poetic, the young man's voice stung with remorse, fatigue, and strain. His face was even more sullen than before. Lips were chap dry and deep dark half moons beneath his eyes were indicative of the general malaise that seeped through every pore. He breathed deeply and his hands were the only thing holding his face from the floor.

"This is definitely not my millennia," he groaned. "Guess it wasn't enough to be starving, miserable, pent up and backed up; now I have the pleasure of being abducted by a virulently violent violinist... Ugh and I'm rhyming. Somehow I can hear mom and dad's I told you sos even from the grave."

He sat up and began to scan his surroundings while shaking off the last wisps of unconsciousness that still clung to his eyelids. His new accommodations seemed to include a large circular room with no visible windows and though he wasn't happy about it, the word cell came to mind.

Small candles lit the perimeter and he noticed he was lying on a circular pad in the center of the room. It was relatively comfortable, firm and slightly elevated. It was also weird as hell.

The room was around twenty-five feet across and the ceiling stretched beyond the reach of the fickle candlelight, so who knew if there even was a ceiling. The worst part was that he saw no door so naturally he wondered if he had been lowered into some strange pit. After this thought popped into his mind, he half expected to receive instructions to put the lotion in the basket so he wouldn't get the hose again.

Confusion boiled within him. It was made all the more powerful as it coupled with self loathing that battled to surge forth to the surface. He felt around the platform for any clue and later searched himself for any discernible wound he might have to worry about. With the exception of the headache slamming between both cerebral hemispheres, there was nothing to be alarmed about.

Again he chewed on his dry mouth, longing for something to rinse, drink and repeat. He concluded that this sensation was the result of a combination of dehydration and extreme exposure to pretzel salt. Something he would have remedied long ago if he hadn't been abducted. Abducted. The word hadn't sunk in when he had said it out loud, but now it rang in his brain as he tried to remember.

"What the hell happened?"

He knew what had happened. He just didn't truly know what had happened. He did his best to remember by talking out loud: "Ok. I had a crappy day and a crappy meal for dinner; if a pretzel can even be called dinner. Then I went to the subway and met the psycho. After the delightful exchange we shared, I walked to the platform to get on the train as quickly as possible. Lights flickered, I saw the finger countdown I would have gladly have that guy shove someplace else, and then I wake up in a circular room surrounded by candles. I'm assuming a parade of large and lonely inmates is planned for the next act."

His anger kept rising and the peculiar damp smell of the room infuriated him almost as much as the faint trace of a fragrance that still clung onto his clothes. He recognized the smell from just before blacking out. It was something like cinnamon crossed with sandalwood, if such a scent even made any sense. He also remembered two flashes of jade just before all went black.

He continued to scan his surroundings and noticed that the walls seemed unnaturally smooth, gliding across seamlessly, devoid of any imperfection, or openings. He was trapped. The surrounding candles cast ominous shadows all around him and just as fear was starting to creep slowly onto him, a hissing voice helped it all come in one big thump. "Awake at last? I was getting to think that my little bouquet had been too much and that you were allergic to any of the countless herbs used to render you unconscious. So good to see I was mistaken in regards to that."

One could swear the crashing of fear and hatred would have been heard miles away. In reality, barely a mumble came from the young man. The worst of it all was that he could not see where the voice was coming from, since it seemed to flutter about the entire room.

To his left: "Don't tell me..."

To his right: "... the cat has got your tongue again."

Above him: "It would be pointless to go through that once more."

To his left: "Just relax."

To his right: "Let's chat."

Above again: "No harm in that."

In front of him: "after all,"

Right behind his ear: "you're so entertaining."

Nathaniel stumbled forwards, but still saw no one producing those torturous words. Madness was looking like a more logical explanation with every second that passed. As if things weren't awful enough, something began to ring in his ears that ripped at his spine... the gentle tap-tapping of a boot.

Upon turning around, something finally broke the ethereal smoothness of the walls surrounding him: a large iron gate. His face fluttered with fear and confusion. How had he not seen it? Beyond it, he could scarcely make out the silhouette of something sitting on the floor. What he could clearly see though, were two grey orbs staring through the darkness; two floating host wafers looking for communion through communication.

"So, dear friend, how are we feeling?" the shadow hissed. The voice was raspy and male and a small giggle slipped after Nathaniel pulled his fists up to defend himself. "My dear man, won't you grant this poor beggar a few words to at least grasp that you are conscious. A fighting spirit is most welcome, but sentience should come first."

Nathaniel glared into the two floating eyes. He debated a second before replying, "What do you want?"

"Hmm... Basic question, yet it makes total sense. It obviously goes without saying that you have the right to ask and receive an answer. Yet I fear I shan't answer that particular question just yet. After all there are a few other queries you should be asking before that one."

Nathaniel focused on how much he was annoyed by the playful tone his jailer continued to speak with instead of the fear that welled inside him. "Fine; where am I then? Is that better?"

"Aww... Tut, tut. Don't get angry with us now. After all I must admit that's another formidable question. As a good sport, I'll even add the time and date since you have yet to notice that your watch is missing."

Instinctively Nathaniel patted his right pocket to call the bluff, but it was empty. The watch - his father's watch - was gone. Fear evaporated from his expression and unbridled rage seemed to have been cleared for ignition. His scowl bore through the darkness into the faceless eyes as three words just barely made it through his clenched teeth, "Where is it?"

"Listen now and I'll tell later," the shadow replied. "First on the list of things you should be asking yourself is where you are. The vague answer would be to say that you are not far away from where we first met. In reality we're less than 10 miles away from the city limits. Granted, access is a bit tricky to say the least but we also make a point of not giving any reason for humans to investigate. True, we may have a few strays now and again, but for now, no one has been sorely missed."

Nathaniel appeared to be listening, yet his mouth only moved to utter one phrase. "Give me my watch."

The shadow shifted as if making itself more comfortable and continued with its leisurely tone. "Mind your manners; you're interrupting. As I was saying, date and time should be a bit more shocking since midnight on Tuesday we met and almost Friday it is now. As I mentioned before, I was getting worried about your health. After all, we need you nice and healthy if you are to be of any use at all. My kind is counting on you."

Before Nathaniel began to speak, he stumbled on the last thing he had heard. "Your kind? What does that even mean? You're just some lunatic. Now give me my watch and let me out of here."

The shadow continued to ignore the human's orders, relishing the banter. "Ah... lunatic. Interesting choice of words given our nature. We dwell in the night and shy away from the sun."

Nathaniel's face melted into skepticism. "What are you? Some whacko with a scary movie complex?" His temper continued to flare but his tone was more desperate than angry. Fists clenched in tandem with his teeth and it was quite obvious he wanted to have a go at his jailer.

Unfortunately he was met by a calmly collected voice that merely continued to mock. "Whatever are you talking about, good man? I merely share the truth and these are my thanks. What nerve."

The last remains of control began to crack in Nathaniel and he yelled in response. "What truth?! What the hell are you even talking about?!!"

The shadow laughed again. "Poor man. Strain and stress don't do well I guess. Yet I must digress, it's hard to digest, so let me not idly jest. I shall do my best to inform and instruct and if you are in luck, the truth you will unlock."

Confusion ridged along Nathaniel's brow mixed with a heap of annoyance. "Great, I should have known it would be a cat in a hat who would kidnap me. What possible truth could you tell me about, you psycho?"

The shadow coughed up yet another laugh, "You silly human. You have no earthly idea of how little you know about anything. Let me sum it up for you: what would you say if I were to tell you that history, as you know it, is at best massively incomplete and more than likely quite false?"

Nathaniel sank deeper into confusion. Why had his captor called him human, as if they both weren't? Instead of focusing on this though, he took another verbal route to see if he could get any information. "I'd ask you to prove what you're saying since you almost seem determined to have me not think you are out of your mind."

The shadow breathed through what sounded like a smile. "Unhinged you may think me, but the truth is that I am not mad, I am not lying and I am not living a farce, unlike you. You would easily presume that humans are the first and only logical species on this Earth. In reality though, your lot is the most un-evolved of all free thinkers."

If only for a moment, anger had faded from his face. Nathaniel was just too damned baffled to be angry. "Who are you? Why are you telling me all of this and what am I even supposed to think that you are?"

"Don't think, my weary friend; know. I am a creature of the night, a mockery of death. In simple English: I am a vampire."

Rabbit hole seemed like a cliché thing to think in a situation like this, but that was the closest to a frame of reference Nathaniel could come up with. The problem was that he kept tumbling without reaching the bottom. Not that such a feeling would keep him from being skeptical. "A vampire? Right. And you wouldn't happen to hang out with Count Chocula or made some appearances on Sesame Street in an episode sponsored by the number 4? Like I said before, do you have a mental condition?"

Silence was the only response the darkness offered and the two grey orbs suddenly burned emerald green. Nathaniel remembered that color and for a second his heart skipped a beat and his lungs shuddered, unwilling to draw a breath. Then the eyes disappeared.

A strong gust of wind suddenly blew past the young reporter and he felt something brush against him. And as suddenly as they had vanished, the eyes returned to exactly where they had been an instant before.

"It seems a seed of doubt has been planted... Look at your hands."

The reporter did as told and suddenly a bottomless pit stood where his stomach once was. Both his hands were bound by a soft silk thread that gently but securely held his hands together. He also noticed that something had materialized within his closed fist, wrapped in a black satin scarf. He didn't need to unwrap it to know it was the watch. Cold sweat beaded on his forehead and a gentle tremble took hold of his hands.

The orbs cooled to grey but they still stared directly at him. "Now that I have your full attention, let us resume our conversation. I'd mentioned something about logical species. What I should clear up is that the world history you've been exposed to has various chapters missing in regards to what reality is."

"Myths and legends are often considered mere stories, but as with every story, there is some root stemming from reality. People revere numerous authors for supposedly creating their own microcosms within the pages of a book. You've surely read stories of dragons, goblins, and elves. What you don't realize is that these fictional characters are no less fictional than you or I. These stories are quite real and they have been passed down from generation to generation for over 30,000 years."

Nathaniel grimaced as if the number had just slapped him across the face. Surely his captor had been mistaken even if this was all a lie. "But written history and all archeological findings are no more than--"

The dark voice interrupted, "Forget human history and desist from convincing yourself that what you know is an absolute truth. Your kind's versions of history and truth are filled with politics, manipulation of information and utter lies. 30,000 years ago is a historical reality and in those times, four great races ruled the world.

Man might have existed, but you were far from alone. Oh, and if you're a good little monkey, I'll even show you all the proof you want."

Being called a monkey was clearly not to the young man's liking, but given his current situation, a nod seemed like the appropriate response.

"Good," the voice said as the shadow settled down. "As I was saying, there were four great races in the world. They each ruled their lands although peace was something less than probable. They were the Dwarf, Elfish, Goblin and your Human race."

This time, the look on Nathaniel's face was not of focus, fear or any of the other emotions he'd just experienced. He simply tried to control his laughter at what he had just heard.

A guttural growl boiled on the other side of the gate and the eyes vanished once again before another strong gust of wind blew into the chamber. This time however, the wind wasn't a momentary blast of air but a cyclone that batted against Nathaniel making him realize that his reaction may have not been the most appropriate.

A ghastly voice snarled through the entire room as the walls boomed and whistled from the hurricane stirring within. "FOOL!!! You dare LAUGH?! It figures that an ignorant representation of your species is what I might find. You damn primate!"

The voice growled ever louder, the wind howled harder and Nathaniel could barely breathe, but he could listen. "You do not even realize that phrases from your worthless society are rooted in the true knowledge of this world! Where do you think the phrase 'your fore fathers' came from? As always, you bastardize the truth and yet again proclaim yourselves all-knowing. I offer you one piece of advice human and I suggest you follow it: HOLD YOUR TONGUE! You've been warned and you should realize one thing..."

The aerial maelstrom howled harder still and just when Nathaniel thought he might pass out, a grotesque demonic face spat forth, mere inches from his, "... if it wasn't for that poor bastard of a train conductor, I would have fed on you by now!"

The demon mask vanished as suddenly as it appeared and the iron gate slammed shut, rattling on its hinges. Outside, a figure slumped to the floor in rage while the hurricane inside dissipated. All candles had blown out, leaving the young man in total darkness. The gale force winds were then replaced with heavy breathing that echoed off the walls. Nathaniel's mouth had been left cracked open. A scream wanted to burst forth, but it did not possess the will to leave the safety of his diaphragm. He could only respond by staying silent while his mind ranted at light speed.

The heavy breathing from outside the cell finally began to lighten and a voice forced calm spoke out. "I recommend that you listen well, boy. For the time being, your life is under my control. So let us delve further into the truth you so ignorantly mock. Do not apologize; do not say 'sorry', or 'my bad' or any other moronic attempt at an apology. Simply hold your tongue and listen. I mentioned the four great races and yes they did exist. They all existed at the same time and were quite similar to what you have read in the types of books I referred to earlier."

Nathaniel nodded from the platform. Although he couldn't see anything in the darkness, he was pretty sure his captor had no problem whatsoever in seeing him.

As if the terror he was feeling wasn't bad enough, something happened to make it worse with every passing second. Slowly, each candle lit itself to return the room to its original gloom. Within the shadows outside the gate the jade eyes had cooled to grey, and Nathaniel didn't need to be told that green was very bad, so he welcomed grey with open arms.

The shadow breathed deeply and Nathaniel looked on. "Those were true races that would not dare let a day pass without bettering their being. For their part, humans were tolerable. To be honest, your race has not changed much in 300 centuries. It insists on repeating the same atrocities over and over. You have always paraded about how great you are and I've always found it amusing that your most distinctive traits are double edged in nature and can just as easily spell victory or defeat."

Though Nathaniel had been sitting quietly on the platform, this time he could not hold his tongue, though he made sure to speak in a much humbler tone. "And what would those traits be?"

The two gray orbs tinged a little with a deep violet and Nathaniel wondered what this color meant before the shadow answered his question. "Love and hope," it said. "Although I may find it quite easy to understand your difficulty at grasping how these two emotions are reason enough for downfall or victory, ask yourself: how many people have lived and survived because they kept hope and love within their being? Concentration camps, the Black Death, and surely wars have made heroes of those who would not yield either of those sentiments. I'm sure you're asking yourself how these same gifts could ever be a reason for defeat. It's simple really. Just think of how easily emotions get twisted to the point where humans are blinded beyond all logical comprehension."

Although he was far from suffering Stockholm syndrome, these words seemed to strike true and make sense to the captive reporter. He accepted that hope could be molded into faith or fanaticism and that love could easily rot into obsession. "You have a point," he told the shadow.

The misty orbs then turned to a pale blue and the voice that followed seemed almost paternal in its sudden sympathy. "Finally, one who sees sense."

When the eyes cooled back down to grey, Nathaniel concluded that the creature had also re-acquired its composure. He thought for a second and then spoke up. "You said there were four great races. You mentioned Elves, Dwarves and Humans. So what's the last race and why are humans the only ones remaining?"

The eyes shifted a bit as the creature adjusted its position. "You seem wiser than your years. Well, to answer the first question, the last of the Great Four was the Goblin race. They are also the reason why the old world is no more. You see, the universe has a way of maintaining balance, always. It is definitely impressive that your race has produced some of the most marvelous thinkers of all world history. One of them even fully grasped that matter cannot be created or destroyed; only transformed. What I'm hinting at is that no matter what, the equation we know as reality shall always search for balance. Or at least that is how it's supposed to be."

"The three great races I've spoken of embodied intellect, inner strength and emotion. This fourth race is the chaos that brings out the best and worst in the first three and thus maintains the balance. Many living creatures have had the laughable notion that Goblins were stupid and incapable of being any real threat to the world. Such myths vanish with accounts of Agathoras, the Great City of Goblins. To understand its magnitude, take New York City, double its size, replace the majestic skyscrapers with cyclopean towers and citadels, fill the city with every vile thing you've ever thought or dreamt about and you start to get an idea of what once existed."

As absurd as it all sounded, Nathaniel found himself believing what he was hearing. It was almost too possible for him not to at least accept the possibility of it.

"I spoke of the Great Four but that doesn't mean that they were the only logical species on this Earth. They were merely the dominant ones. There were a number of other races but in comparison, they were mere packs numbering in the low thousands. The winged Hawkwind from the Asian mounts, the Equinox horse kingdoms from the Great Central Plain, and the Boulderian stone warriors to name a few."

"In the Great War, Agathoras was the last Goblin City and its siege began with the hopes of vanquishing the darkness that threatened to envelop all of Earth. All sides suffered greatly and when the end seemed almost certain, that was when the Human Factor arrived."

The last few words had been pretty much spit out, as were the ones that followed. "They of course aided the near fallen Elves and Dwarves and after making their gallant and quite fashionably late entrance, they helped deliver the final blows to the enemy."

Nathaniel could only look to the floor of his cell. "Almost like what Americans did in the First World War."

The shadow seemed to hum an approval. "A keen analogy, except that in your so called World War, Americans suffered much greater losses than in this particular one. With the Goblin race practically exterminated, two of the other great races faced similar outcomes. Elves took the few hundred of their kind that remained alive and gave a farewell to this world in favor to the dark side of the very moon we look at every night."

"It is said that some remained behind, but I'm not sure for what purpose. I'm actually not even sure if that's true. The last time an elf was supposedly seen was around 2,000 years ago. I heard of something about a man who stumbled upon a great tree that glowed from the inside, a vastly forgotten urban legend from England. For their part, Dwarves numbered in the low thousands and took to the Deep Underground. Surely you've heard that Everest and the Alps grow every year; well now you know the reason."

Before Nathaniel got the word tectonic out of his mouth, he decided against it. "I see. So those three races were eradicated and mine remained and proliferated."

The now icy blue eyes nodded. "Exactly. They cut their losses to a minimum and seized the glory. That is why both Elf and Dwarf kind were not known or even stated to be part of history. Always remember, he who wins the battle defines history."

The young man nodded in agreement. "It's like cowboys and Indians. The winner decided who the villain was."

The eyes pulsed brightly. "Good to see that you've taken what you've been taught with a grain of salt. The knowledge you have received consists of half-truths from the past and the present. And by the way, don't think the present is exclusive to human kind either. I'm sure that after our little encounter you can conclude that your kind is far from alone. Your historians have dominated for around 15,000 years at best but they've done an outstanding job of maintaining a firm grip on the control of history."

Nathaniel hunched in thought as his brain did its best to keep up. "So what else have I been lied about?"

The darkness seemed to smile at him. "Well for starters, let us say that my kind owes quite a bit to yours. After all, we are related. I'm sure you think the human race is incapable of producing a demon seed, but that's quite funny since werewolves are also direct descendants of your line. Genes work in mysterious ways and through some anomaly we and the other cubs were born."

The human's eyes dilated completely. Was all of this really true? "So now there are three great races?" he asked while thinking of what else this creature might have to offer him.

A short pause lingered in the air before the answer was given. "Try six. There's quite a lot that's been hidden from you, Mr. Runnels. In truth, we aren't the only descendants of humans, although being quite honest; there are certain anomalies that no one can explain."

The shadow offered another slice of silence so the human could compute, and continued only after Nathaniel had nodded that he had understood. "Apart from humans, you've met a vampire, moi, and I've told you about therians, what you know as werewolves, a term they rather dislike, I might add. Their true name comes from the Greek therion, meaning wild animal. So that gives you a perspective of how long they've been around. With therians, you have three races... but there are three others."

"I had mentioned that ages ago there was a Global War. What I didn't mention was that the geological repercussions of this conflict were massive. Rivers literally flowed with the blood of all world kind and that led to some odd events unfolding. It seems that when this blood collective combined with pollution and heavy amounts of magic, a new race was born, the photogeni. It is what your people would sophisticatedly call plant people. They are conscious and often assume human silhouettes but they are plants through and through."

Nathaniel looked skeptical but he had to take everything as true until he was able to prove otherwise. "All right," he said a little apprehensively, "so what else?"

The shadow moved a little closer to the gate and its silhouette became slightly more defined. "The next race is the root of the problem we now face and another of the reasons why you are here. During the Great World War, the vilest race we've ever known of was spawned by one of the most atrocious events to occur in this world, the Great Imposition. Thousands of elf, dwarf, and human females were ravaged until they died. Inside them a seed festered which fed on the womb until weeks later, the creatures inside tore free. The worst of it is that this race has continued to proliferate, even in modern times. Various societies have even protected them on several occasions."

Horror and disgust took over the human's face. "How could something like that possibly happen? How could they keep such a thing a secret?"

The shade gave a little indignant puff. "First off, being a reporter you should know how much truth is in the news. Secondly, the explanation can be summed up in two words: biological weapon. But let us finish the back-story first. Tell me; are you religious?"

The question took Nathaniel completely by surprise. "Well, I don't think so. What do you mean by religious though?"

"Hmmm... you seem confused. I may assume that your faith has been challenged. If that's the case, then that's quite normal, especially for someone like you. I meant to ask what your upbringing was like, if it did happen to be religious."

"Oh. Ummm... Roman Catholic. But what does that have to do with any of what we're talking about? If there's anything I don't trust it's organized religion as a whole."

The eyes flicked different colors until settling back into the cool controlled grey. "Right you are to do so, Mr. Runnels. Many wicked things have come from what many would describe as holy. As is often the case though, lies have roots inside the truth."

"I don't follow," Nathaniel said.

"Nor do I pretend you to be able to," the shadow responded. "What have you heard of angels? And what would you say if I told you that they exist?"

The young man's face contorted as he tried to not be skeptical. He'd seen enough movies and gone to his share of services, but his silence showed that this was hardly something he would believe in blindly.

"That's what I thought," said the shade after observing the human for a moment or two. "It might seem a bit much, I know, but they do exist. All of these beings exist. But unlike the other races, no one has any idea where angels came from except the scriptures your kind has efficiently edited countless times. What we do know is that angels are all around us and that they are quite different from what you might have seen or read of them."

"Let me guess, you'll go into detail later?" the human said.

"I apologize Nathaniel, you shall know in due time."

Before he could become irritated with another half answer, another empty pit appeared between the man's spine and his stomach. How did the vampire know his name?

The dark figure rose from the slumped position it had been in for so long. A lock clicked, the gate opened and a set of boots tapped against the stone floor as the vampire left the shelter of his shadow. A dark mane stretched down over pale olive skin. Deep red lips wetted themselves and the eyes that had been bodiless for so long, now took on a soft blue hue and showed that they were almond shaped. A faint scar traced the left cheek caressed by a small birthmark just to its left. The skin was tight. No wrinkles.

The blue eyes bore into Nathaniel and he could only wonder about what this vampire could do to him. The only thing he knew was that looking directly at the creature, there was only a slight resemblance to the demon that had promised him a painful death not too long ago. Having kept his hands in the pockets of his black pants, the vampire now pulled his right hand out and extended it to Nathaniel.

"Your wallet, good sir."

A nervous laugh slipped from the human as he gave thanks to the specter that now sat beside him on the small platform. The vampire examined him cautiously and after a detailed analysis and freeing the bonds on the young man's hands, he began to speak once again. "I thought it was about time I stopped being impersonal. After all, you've been through enough with what I've told you and your little ride on the subway. I still find it amusing that you question my sanity, my honesty and most understandably so, my intentions. That's quite all right, but in case there are any doubts still lingering, let me assure you that I am in fact a vampire."

Two sharp ivory fangs peeked from beneath his smile. It was not unlike a wild animal baring its fangs to intimidate an intruder or some prey. "Secondly, I am as sane as I could be, given that what you consider normal is quite foreign to me. I am logical, coherent and calculating, which brings us to my intentions. These depend largely on how you react to a proposal I am to offer you. So take heed of your answer. Absolution or damnation is completely in your hands."

The young man heard the words; he understood them, and he most definitely feared them, so he braced himself for his options.

"There is a seventh race," the vampire said. "Why not say anything sooner? Why is this race so important? Both very good questions. They are quite the mystery to be honest and their sole function seems to be the chronicling of what happens on Earth. You could consider them raconteurs, though I suspect they aren't exclusive to this planet. They also happen to be the key to the current situation. They are called the Uatu Kuriotes and are also the indirect reason why I chose you or more so, how I found you."

The vampire unbuttoned his shirt and drew out a thin long gold chain. Dangling at the end was a crystal disk that constantly changed colors. "This is an Eye of Cardino and there are only three more like it in the world. Its powers are yet to be fully understood, but one of its functions allowed me to find you. The rest of the information I know about you came from your wallet. But now I have to interrupt our conversation for this is your first moment of truth. You have three options for this particular moment. Either you don't go along for the next step and serve as livestock for my kind, feeding us with your blood until your body can take it no longer, you join me until next you get the opportunity to decide if you continue or you die... right now."

'Not many pleasant options,' Nathaniel thought. Especially since there was no mention about going free. Pausing briefly, he took a deep breath and answered: "Show me more."

The vampire nodded in approval. "Good. Now let us get you something to eat. You should still be pretty weak."

At the mention of the words, Nathaniel felt a sheet of fatigue fall over him like a lead curtain. As he stood up, the vampire waved his arm and the flames from the candles roared high to finally light the room. The ceiling was at least twenty-five feet high and the walls were all covered in symbols and etchings with dozens of angels drawn on the ceiling looking down on the platform he was sitting on. It was quite an intimidating scene, but there was one other small detail that stood out to Nathaniel: little engravings on the walls, which seemed to repeat one word over and over.... Dameos. The iron gate was then pushed open and a narrow corridor led to what Nathaniel hoped were answers or freedom.

Chapter 4: The not so primrose path

Nathaniel could barely see the torchlight's glow when he came to his senses and ran full speed to catch up to his makeshift guide. Up ahead he saw the vampire's black leather coat stretch down to his thighs. It perfectly matched the deep mane that seemed to float instead of laying there like any typical hair would.

"Where are we going?" Nathaniel asked.

"You'll see soon," the vampire replied still without looking back on his guest. "Hopefully now marks the moment when the scales of fate lean towards my side for a change."

As Nathaniel walked, he felt a growing need to get out of the corridor since claustrophobia and tension seemed to have been embedded into its design. Though preternaturally smooth to the touch, the wall somehow felt jagged and completely unnatural to him. 'Stone is not meant to feel this smooth he thought while caressing the corridor wall. Several steps ahead, he saw that the vampire seemed drawn by something intangible that had its hold on him and was pulling... hard. An awkward silence hung in the stale air and it intensified with every step they took until Nathaniel decided to cut through it. "So are you ever going to tell me your name?"

It seemed some strange force struck his guide across the chin, finally knocking some sense into him. He turned on his heels to face Nathaniel, torch in hand with eyes as black as the color would dare to be. The facial features seemed chiseled from marble rather than flesh, and a gentle strength that focused on his jaw made him look even more unearthly and surreal. While they gauged each other, only the torch crackle broke the silence as a strange cold wind slithered at their heels.

The vampire's face seemed vaguely familiar and even reminded Nathaniel of something he had seen in his life. A character from a movie, a person he had met or some work of art. Whatever it was, he could not put it down.

"My apologies, good sir," the vampire said with a light bow and a slightly embarrassed smile, "quite rude of me to say the least. Since I know your name you may have mine; I am Daniel of Montacre."

The vague halo of recollection sat just beyond reach of Nathaniel's memory. Daniel... the name sparked another connection but it was still a ways off. The light breeze at their feet slowly crept along and it actually changed direction while growing in intensity. It seemed to crawl up their bodies one millimeter at a time. The vampire sniffed at the air and seemed to sense something odd. He looked over his shoulder and scowled towards the darkness.

"We really should continue, Mr. Runnels," he said without a backwards glance. "There may be much to discuss, but for now, we don't have the luxury of standing by idly." No further explanation seemed to be necessary and he turned around to continue his march towards the unknown dark depths ahead.

The corridor seemed to lean up gently and Nathaniel hoped it led somewhere less constricted with something other than stale air to breathe. Although the path seemed to stretch into forever, every five yards or so he noticed that something seemed to be written low on the walls, a message seemingly chiseled into the stone and filled with some silvery substance.

$$\mathcal{D}ameos$$

The symbol puzzled him greatly. What it was or what it meant, he did not have a clue, but every five yards or so, there it was. Dameos.

It was the only thing breaking the seamless perfection of the corridor surface. Dameos. What language was it written in? Dameos.

Was it even a word? Dameos. Why did it keep repeating? Dameos. Dameos. Dameos. Dameos...

"Dameos," he said out loud.

The brisk pace jerked to a halt. Luckily, Nathaniel was able to stop before bumping into the back of the vampire. He did take a few steps back though. Body language can often let you in on someone's thoughts and the vampire's current corporeal expression was anything but normal.

"What was that?" he asked the human.

Nathaniel could tell the vampire knew the word he'd blurted out. The slightly jittery breathing made that clear even if his question feigned at innocence. It was obvious he'd touched a sensitive subject. He didn't know how to take the reaction and simply stared as the vampire once again turned to face him. This time the movement was more deliberate; although still of body, the vampire's face bordered on mad elation.

He whispered in a slightly maniacal tone. "What did you say? That... word. Say it again."

Rather than deny the request, Nathaniel opted to repeat what he had just uttered. "Dameos. It looks like it says Dameos on the walls and it was also written in the room we were just in."

The once black eyes were a distant memory as a kaleidoscope of colors flashed in the vampire's eyes. Blue, green, and red bled into each other until an intense cardinal orange specked the center of the cornea, spreading out until the entire iris burned with the color of a September sunset.

"Quite observant of you," the vampire said as he stroked his hands greedily and spoke with a calculating tone. "Let us save time by walking and talking, shall we?"

Nathaniel nodded and the vampire once again led the way. The path continued to climb endlessly and that odd breeze was starting up again. Though Daniel had said they would walk and talk, Nathaniel couldn't help but notice that one of those actions was not occurring after a couple of yards.

"So...umm... are you a count or a lord or something like that?" said Nathaniel. Silence may have been unbearable to him, but small talk had clearly never been his strong suit.

The vampire could only snicker at the pathetic attempt at conversation. "No, my dear Nathaniel," he said while clearing his throat of any latent laughter. "You should know that all vampires are not counts and I assure you, Dracula was not even half the vampire as your kind has made him out to be. Lord of the vampires? Please. If that idiot were ever to lead us, I'm sure he'd suggest some sun to get our daily required supplement of Vitamin D. Stoker did write a fantastic book, though."

Nathaniel's creased forehead meant he had no idea how to react to that comment. Was the vampire really serious about what he'd just said?

"Suddenly so quiet," Daniel said, clearly enjoying the young man's reaction. "Don't tell me you are that easily shocked. My Dear Mr. Runnels, do not worry. Closure and knowledge are two things I'm happy to say may be available to you soon, if things play out right. No doubt you still question the truths I've shared with you. But let us not forget, even the notion that the world was not flat took some time before humans accepted it. Your race clearly wins any time things come down to sheer creativity when justifying a lie."

Nathaniel glared at the vampire's back. He wished for some holy water or maybe a wooden stake. Then the vampire might be able to appreciate what he thought about all he had to say. Then he saw the word again. Dameos. What could it mean? They continued to walk and the word reminded him of emergency lights that lead the way to some safe exit.

"So how many tunnels are there in this place?" he blurted out without having a single moment to think twice. Again they stopped cold in their tracks.

That was the second time Nathaniel had said something to elicit such a reaction from the vampire. "How do you know that there are more?" the vampire asked, almost demanding an answer.

Since Nathaniel wasn't a fan of beating around the bush, hypocrisy or lying, he spoke his mind again. "Well something this well made is rarely if ever left as the single work of its creator. That word, Dameos? It seems like some kind of label. So naturally, if you need to label something, it's so you don't confuse it with something else that might be quite similar."

The vampire's smile refused to remain hidden and pure fascination bloomed on his face. "Good answer," he replied relishing the word good like some lush dessert. "Though I doubt any 'people' would be caught dead in these tunnels. Well... maybe dead. But you were not bothered by my potentially meaningless question and answered earnestly and to the point. You are quite the find. To humor you, I can share that this in fact is the Dameos passage within what is known as the Halo Maze. You're not supposed to be able to read the markings though. Well most humans are not able to read the markings anyways. They were written by the same people who made the maze; a bit obvious when you hear the name Halo Maze, I know. Feel free to admire and salute their work though. Angels do have a way of making magnificent things even for the most ordinary purposes."

Nathaniel took a moment to look at the tunnel in detail. "So are you allies with the angels?" he asked.

"Not quite," Daniel replied. "There's respect between both races and we do our best to avoid conflict; but at times, clashes are unavoidable. Paths cross, tempers flare and lives are sometimes lost. But for the most part, we steer clear of each other and mind our own business."

Nathaniel scratched his chin and debated whether or not he should continue to pry. Since he was a reporter though, he obeyed his nature. "So you took these tunnels by force... or were they given to you by the angels?"

The vampire sniggered with the raspy throat of a lifelong smoker. "You are quite the observant one, I must say. Fair enough. Here's what happened: In one of the conflicts between our kinds, we took possession of the maze after having slaughtered more than half the force stationed here. Lower echelon angels, I assure you. We sheathed our swords and offered a truce. Unwillingly, they folded their wings and acquiesced because they really did not have much of a choice. Their leader settled and accepted what was offered and that was that. To satisfy your unending curiosity, let me answer another question that might just be stirring in your head. The conflict began because the angel commander at that time interfered in an affair we had with a certain therian. We proceeded to send a clear message and acquired a new locale during the process. Although we do use this as one of our many posts, we do not stay for extended periods of time because the maze is far more intricate and well guarded than what we've been able to find out. So no matter how prepared we may be, an ambush is a constant possibility."

Nathaniel processed and filed the information while ignoring the cold that once again seemed to be climbing his limbs. "So needless to say, you don't trust angels."

Another flash of fangs showed on top of a smile. "Precisely my friend. Respect is one thing, trust is another. We trust no one."

The cold became more intense and Daniel looked over his shoulder yet again. "The gardens are not far off now and we really shouldn't linger in these passages. Shall we?"

They started walking again and a new sense of urgency became apparent to Nathaniel. While they walked, he got the sense that the compression of the tunnel was lightening slightly right before it opened up into a wide crossway where the ceilings stretched beyond the reach of his sight.

To Nathaniel, all directions looked equally uninviting. He only had time to notice that the hall was a cold gray and that light came from torches scattered in the distance. They then sped through the clearing to an entrance directly across from where they had come out, but even in the dim cavern, Nathaniel could make out a small speck in the darkness.

"Bisfernum," he said out loud after reading what was on the wall.

The vampire bent as he heard the word. "How...?" he started saying, but the words to finish the sentence escaped him. He paused briefly while looking around the vast expanse. "Let's keep going," he said, though there was really no need for it to be spoken.

They walked into the corridor Daniel had been aiming for and the strong breeze hushed down to a near halt. They pressed on and a few yards into the passage, Nathaniel saw the familiar scribble of Dameos once again. A few more yards and a set of thick iron bars appeared, blocking the path ahead.

A few steps from it, Daniel cleared his throat. "Open the gate," he called out in a serious voice. "We have a guest."

A deep hum hissed from behind the bars and after several loud mechanical noises, the bars began to rise.

Chapter 5: Eden? Not quite.

A loud crash clanged against the top of the tunnel. With it came the sweetest breath of air Nathaniel had ever tasted in his life. He breathed deeply and his lips let out a faint whisper: "Thank God." His eyes were closed and for some reason he thought he finally had an idea of what a near drowning victim feels when they finally breathe again.

After a few good draughts of clean air, he looked around and found himself in a wide terrace; a would-be stage for the next act. Thick foliage enveloped every wall and various shrubs and small trees laced the miniature veldt. The atmosphere was dark, but at least the air was clean.

The vampire marveled at Nathaniel and how he relished the act of breathing. He saw how the human scanned the area with a look in his eye that asked where are we now, so the vampire answered. "This, Mr. Runnels, is one of Eve's Gardens. There are quite a few strewn throughout the maze but you could consider this the centerpiece."

Four corridors lined the green walls on either side, two on the left and two on the right. It felt remote, unearthly and strangely beautiful. For the briefest moment, the young man even felt as if they were utterly alone; but all it took was one glance at the end of the miniature valley to realize how wrong he was.

Two figures lounged nonchalantly in garden chairs over at a little area that was quaintly perfect for a spot of tea. Their body language was casual and relaxed but their eyes burned jade green though not as bright as Daniel's. To the left of this scene Nathaniel saw a curious little tree, wide in span yet short in stature. Wood and foliage pretzeled over an area of about twenty yards. The bark itself might have been quite intriguing, but the human could not help but focus on an additional set of green eyes that peeked brightly from within the branches.

"Come Nathaniel," Daniel said, "I have a few friends I'd like you to meet." The emphasis on the word friends was a bit unsettling, but they made their way to the small table at the end of the grove, maintaining their course even when the vampire in the tree climbed down to cut ahead and be the first to introduce himself. He slithered his way to them, seeming to slide across the grass a lot more than firmly stepping on the ground. His green eyes met Nathaniel's and a fang bearing smile shone in the dim. His silver blonde hair, a pale white shirt and grey pants made him look eerily monochromatic, as if he were made of ash.

"Aren't you going to introduce your friend, Daniel?" the vampire hissed. Meanwhile he continued to meticulously scan Nathaniel like some authorized meat inspector.

"Hello to you as well Lucas, and to all of you," Daniel said as the other two vampires had already caught up. "This is Nathaniel Runnels, the human that, as you all know, is our guest for the time being... NOT our meal."

Nathaniel tried not to react to the vampires who didn't look much like hosts and rather more like beggars ogling over the day's lunch special. To say he was feeling a bit less than eager to make their acquaintance is an understatement that, for however true it might be, did not concern the vampires that stood before him in the least.

"Stout fellow we have here, eh?" said the vampire that Daniel had called Lucas. "Not too young, not too old and even though you are a bit taken aback from the situation, you don't stand down. Very good indeed."

Lucas walked around Nathaniel and continued to scrutinize every single inch of the young man. Though Daniel's face was stoic, Nathaniel had the sense that he would beat down anyone who tried to do anything to him... or at least that's what he told himself to stay calm. The inquisitive vampire then wafted the air as if sampling the bouquet of some delicate dish. With a satisfied voice and lightly glassy eyes, he looked deep into the human's gaze. "Been a while since your last good glass of wine, eh?"

Nathaniel held face while pondering if a vampire's sense of smell could be that well developed.

"You like Rioja but when you wind down, you'd much rather have a nice glass of aged Pinot Noir. Shiraz or Malbec if you want something with a bit more bite." He inhaled deeply tasting each breath he took while concentrating deeply. "But it's been months since you had any of those. If I may say so, gin is rather a poor substitute."

"My name is Lucas Mundiano," the vampire said as he mimicked tipping a hat to Nathaniel. "We should compare notes one day. I might just have a few selections you might be interested in." He finished this line by giving a wink and once again showing the glint of his pearly fangs.

Nathaniel nodded while ignoring the sweat that spidered down his back. Lucas nodded in return and stepped back as another vampire replaced him. This one had hair longer than Daniel's, refined cheekbones, a sharp nose, fine lips tinged dark burgundy and sad morose eyes, which made him look like a participant in a wake. He slightly bowed before the human and proceeded to speak in an even mannered tone, sprinkled with a hint of Scottish as he rolled his Rs. "Pleasure to finally meet you Mr. Runnels; I am Liam Dalry. I'm sure Daniel has told you nothing of why you're here, but you'll learn soon enough."

He winked at the human and took two steps forward right next to him, right at biting distance. Daniel didn't move, but Nathaniel sensed the vampire's muscles tense up. Was he ready to pounce? Liam didn't gnaw at his flesh though, he simply whispered into the human's ear. "Watch your thoughts, human. You may or may not be as welcome as you think. By the way, your mind speaks constantly so someone is bound to listen."

The vampire then gave Nathaniel a strong pat on the back and stepped away while puffing on a cigarette. Nathaniel couldn't help but let his thoughts wander. 'So they can read minds,' he thought.

"And how," Liam said while signaling Nathaniel to hush in a playful manner as he stood aside to allow the next in line to inspect the merchandise. This next vampire was a sultry vixen. She swayed catlike in front of Nathaniel and the human couldn't help but think they were taking turns analyzing him to obtain any and all information they wanted. Or maybe they just wanted to smell the living dessert that stood in front of them, even if they were forced to fast.

Dressed in black and grey, the seductress donned a blouse that did little to cover her supple flesh. Her tight navel was bare and Nathaniel guessed that her favorite victims were probably young virile men. Her olive skin might point to Arabic, Spanish, or maybe Italian descent but her eyes were definitely Persian. Looking innocent was not an option especially with a body that looked like it had come from Hell. Nathaniel found himself breathing her perfume deeply. Who knew what Liam or Lucas smelled like? Who cared? He could swim in this fragrance for hours, well if he lasted that long that is.

She stepped near him and let out a purr that made his skin ripple involuntarily, putting his hairs on end and dotting his entire body with goose bumps. "Are you sure we can't nibble just a bit Daniel?" the vampire said. "After all, it would be such a pity to let him go to waste."

"He is to remain unscathed Malia," Daniel said sternly, "by our hands at least." Nathaniel clearly did not enjoy the full implications of that comment but he was busy worrying about something else.

"You wouldn't mind if I nibbled on you just a tiny bit, would you?" cooed the lascivious vampire. "I'm so famished, and you seem to be just my type."

"Blood type you mean?" Nathaniel said. Though his nerves were a wreck, he had been able to respond, which took everyone by surprise, especially Malia who was clearly not used to being denied. "I-if you're h-hungry and w-want to smile, g-go buy yourself a happy meal... or something."

A chorus of muted chuckles broke the vixen's concentration and she hissed at him like an alley cat. In a weird kind of way though, Nathaniel could have sworn she had enjoyed the denial.

"We'll have a nice long chat later," she hummed in his ear. "Don't you worry."

Nathaniel swallowed deeply as lust and his survival instinct clashed in his insides.

"Don' put much 'tention to 'er Nat," said a grizzly voice from behind them. When Nathaniel turned around he saw two more vampires walking towards them from the opening on the wall now on their right. "Th' names Indigo," said the burly, broad-shouldered vampire with his long blonde hair divided into two long braids. His outfit consisted of a long black leather trench coat with matching leather pants and no shirt. It was pretty clear that his mission was to show off the finely chiseled body he had adorned with a series of tattoos that stretched along his chest, stomach and back.

"Pleasure to meet ye mate," the vampire said, while occasionally flexing his pecs. "Les see if ye'll be 'alf of wot's been sol' to us. Fings shod git purty' rough soon so I 'ope ye can hanle' sleepin' less, fightin' more an' runnin with th' pack. Thank God now isn' th' moment o' truth tho', eh? Wit' tha' hard'n Malia lef' you wit', ye'd be prime bait."

Nathaniel couldn't help but think to himself. 'Great; an asshole vampire. My luck has peaked.' A loud guffaw and a large puff of smoke came from the direction where Liam was standing.

"Wazup witchu?" Indigo asked. "It wan't tha' funny."

"Nothing, my dear Indigo," Liam said as he did his best to fight back the laughter, "just a thought that popped into mind."

The vampire towered over Nathaniel while glaring back and forth between him and Liam. "Welcome then," Indigo said while firmly gripping Nathaniel's hand. "'Ope ye n'joy yer stay."

No sooner had he said thank you to Indigo than the fifth vampire interrupted with a very loud Buona sera! His accent was obviously Italian and though Nathaniel had never seen him, something emanated that immediately had him looking as if he recognized him. "Good evening to you as well," Nathaniel said. His tone had switched from nervous to grave and serious in a heartbeat. "How do you do?"

"Very well," said the black haired vampire. "I am Vincenzo from Milano Italy."

"Wonderful city," Nathaniel answered dryly, "I've actually been there before, although I can't say I mind not having met you up until now. Something tells me I wouldn't have made it here tonight."

Liam's face turned grim and he shot a gaze at Daniel. Not a word was spoken between the vampires but thoughts seemed to fly between them like volleys of arrows between two warring armies. For his part, Vincenzo began anew and tried to overcome the awkward moment. He laughed and continued to speak, "Maybe it would have been like you say. Who knows? Besides, you are not my type as far as aroma goes; moltissimo musk. Add that you are male and it seems highly unlikely. I prefer the other human meat much more so."

"Oh?" Nathaniel said not about to change the mood. "So we have a regular Don Juan Count here? Or is it Count Don Juan? Doesn't matter, really. But tell me, didn't your mother ever tell you it's rude to play with your food. I can't imagine what she would say if she knew you actually screwed it."

The vampire stammered a bit but maintained his composure. Daniel's green eyes had made sure of that. "Well, is like steak, you see. Before eating, you must tenderize. After all, you're all just meat to me."

A long pause held the breath of all there. After all, Nathaniel seemed as if he had officially made his first enemy.

"But enough of that," Vincenzo interrupted, "welcome, Nathaniel."

Daniel and Liam continued to exchange glances as Vincenzo's reaction was nothing compared to Nathaniel's un-instigated outburst. The human himself looked quite baffled at his behavior, fully knowing that Vincenzo could have probably killed him on the spot if they were alone. But they hadn't been alone, and he was getting tired of these games.

Leaves reflected the moonlight while lightly dancing on a calm breeze that flowed through the grove. If anything though, the serene breeze actually made the moment that more tense. Trees and shrubbery remained indifferent yet Nathaniel now noticed that on the rim of the roof of the maze, countless statues looked down upon the garden.

Chiseled to perfection, one would be hard pressed to guess if they were flesh or stone. One did happen to stand out to Nathaniel. It wasn't because of the sheer beauty in its delicate outline, or the fact that it was quite perfect. It was the fact that it had glowing ice blue eyes and that it was breathing.

The eyes of the stoic goddess looked straight at Nathaniel. She was a hundred yards away, but her cold beauty could have been seen and felt for miles. Auburn hair, ivory skin, and a face Aphrodite would have coveted. After a thunderclap lit the sky, she was gone.

"That was Valencia," Daniel whispered in his ear. "You'll soon make her acquaintance." The vampire then stepped back from Nathaniel and cleared his throat to address his brethren. "I take it the others are out. Very well, for now I shall retire with our esteemed guest. Later on I will need the assistance of each of you. Until then, as you were and if you see any of the others, be sure to let me know."

A slight assenting murmur was heard and Daniel bid them off, not without exchanging one final glance with Liam.

"Come Nathaniel," the vampire said, "you and I have much to talk about."

They walked past the others making their way directly to the far wall. It was even more heavily covered in vines and leaves than the sidewalls. Daniel looked around as if searching and stretched his hand to knock upon the foliage. The green wall responded with a faint dull thud on solid rock.

Nathaniel didn't know what to do while waiting so he looked around only to see that they were completely alone again. For his part, the vampire seemed to be busy looking for something he'd apparently lost. When he looked a bit further to the left though, his eyes lit up blue and he seemed to float fifteen feet in the direction of a single, solitary red lotus.

The fact that he'd just seen a vampire levitate would have made other humans cower, but Nathaniel was through with being surprised if only for the moment. "What are you doing?" he asked.

Daniel smiled at Nathaniel and suddenly thrust his hand against the wall once again. Instead of the lackluster click of the last knock a deep hollow crash echoed deep within the wall. After about ten seconds, the sound finally ebbed away. A few seconds passed and nothing happened. Then a minute had elapsed and Nathaniel felt the urge to speak. "So now what are we supposed to do?"

"Human..." Daniel said without even looking at him, "does your kind know no patience?"

As if responding to both their questions, a single solitary leaf rustled high up on the wall, prying free and falling slowly until it landed at their feet. Then it sounded like a group of people was running through the deep brush of a wheat field. Up above, something was bustling in the vines although Nathaniel couldn't see what it was. The terrible rustling noise grew louder and inched its way lower and lower becoming more hectic the nearer it got. Then there was a snap in front of them; then a twitch, and suddenly all the vines in front of them exploded in movement like a pool of wild snakes coiling upon each other.

Although the young man jumped back, the vampire remained completely still in front of the vined frenzy unraveling before him. The wall seemed to crawl upon itself and slowly one could start making out what was behind the thick layer of branches and vines. After the sea of vines parted, a ten-foot wide column had cleared on the entire wall and a beautiful door the color of deep burgundy stood at the bottom.

Nathaniel first stared at the vampiric Moses and then at the bizarre door. Numerous symbols had been carved deep in the surface and instead of square edges, they were rounded. Daniel then drew a dagger from his coat and proceeded to stand directly in front of the door. As he neared it, one could swear that the surface rippled like oil in a vat while he grazed it with the dagger. Quite suddenly, he jammed the blade in the very center of the door up to the very hilt. A high-pitched grunt followed and then a series of mechanical noises and clangs chimed and clicked until the door skid back two inches and descended into the ground.

"Come, my friend," Daniel said. "It is time to learn."

Nathaniel was too dumbfounded to hesitate. After a few steps, he noticed that the same ethereal smoothness from the other corridors continued in this one. This time however, there was no torch leading the way. It was silent, damp and black. The kind of black that entertains the possibility that there is no God, and that there is nothing after one's final breath.

Four steps in and an icy cold grip clung firmly to his forearm. "Do not move," Daniel whispered. "Just a moment and we'll be on our way."

Nathaniel would have asked why, but the answer came quickly. As his eyes adapted, a faint distant light within the corridor came into view and next to that light, he could see that something was roaming; something that hardly seemed friendly. Loud stomps boomed and heavy breathing drummed along the corridor walls. Something blocked the distant torch for an instant and they heard as metal scraped on the floor. It was almost an instant and Nathaniel couldn't see it, but he knew it was massive and just as abruptly as it started, the noise faded away and the light came back into view along with two jade eyes within the darkness. "Pardon the lack of light," Daniel whispered, "didn't want to attract any unwanted attention."

A mute response from the young man was quite appropriate and a gentle tap on his back from Daniel prompted him to resume their trek, while the vampire lit a torch. The damp smell urged them to go faster than they would have normally done. When they reached the torch they turned right, much to Nathaniel's delight since it was the opposite direction of where whatever they had seen had gone. They walked on and Nathaniel found himself once again marveling at the sheer perfection of the paths. Every corner turned at a perfect 90-degree angle though the edges were perfectly smooth.

Left, right, right, left, and another left. The path was frantic and the still-fresh memory of whatever was roaming in the corridor was reason enough to walk at an equally frantic pace.

A faint glitter did catch Nathaniel's eye, and he could have sworn it read something like osdenti. 'So a different name for a different corridor,' he thought to himself.

"What do you see?" Daniel asked.

"What makes you think that I saw something?" Nathaniel replied.

"Mr. Runnels, not only does silence not suit you," the vampire said trying to keep his composure, "but I do not know what is more obvious, your breathing or your pulse."

Once again, Nathaniel chose to speak his mind instead of lying or misleading. After all, just four steps ahead of him walked what was probably the most effective lie detector he had ever seen. "I read something else on the walls," he said. "It looked something like osdenti."

Daniel maintained his pace, another left turn, a right one, and a straight line for thirty yards. "You keep surprising me Mr. Runnels; and for someone as old as me, that is quite something. But let's leave that for later. What did you think of your new acquaintances?"

"You mean your friends?" Nathaniel said, lightly mocking his host's tone in the garden. "Well I was able to notice that they seem to have some very interesting abilities."

"Oh really?" Daniel inquired as the corner of his eye shone bright orange. "Do tell."

Nathaniel swallowed deep and shared his thoughts. "Well, for starters, Lucas has an acute sense of smell. It seems that vampires develop their senses to a much higher degree; several levels more advanced than humans, that's for sure."

"Go on," Daniel urged.

"Liam is apparently able to read minds, although I'm not exactly sure as to what extent. And just from taking a look at his physique, Indigo seems to be a top level fighter."

"Interesting observations," Daniel said. He spun around abruptly to have his glaring eyes peering straight into Nathaniel's. The human took a step back, obviously startled by the sudden move and the vampire's fiery eyes, not to mention his sinister smile. The vampire seemed intent on prying more words directly from the source. "What else?"

"Well there isn't much to say about Valencia yet," Nathaniel said. "I've yet to truly meet her and though she's definitely enigmatic, there's a vicious cold to her essence. I don't think I've ever seen anything like her. Her eyes burn with a cruel silence that firmly establishes that the company of others is not something she truly cares for."

"Fair enough, Mr. Runnels," Daniel said, "but rest assured you'll be able to see firsthand just exactly what she is capable of doing. Anything else?"

"Ummm... Vincenzo is...well I can't really say what he is or isn't. Just meeting him was uncomfortable and you could say that my gut just didn't approve of him. The weird thing is that I don't really know why."

"Indeed," Daniel said while leaning against the corridor wall. "Tension and animosity were quite evident in that odd little exchange. Needless to say, this is a topic of great interest we should talk of later. But tell me, what did you think of our sweet little Malia?"

Daniel's smile lit mischievously as he looked at the human's reaction. Just her name was enough to remind him of the brief explosion that had rattled his brain. He kept silent which obviously invited the vampire to tease him. "Yes, yes man," Daniel began. "Apart from the raging from your loins she undoubtedly erected with her lustful ways, any other thoughts?"

Nathaniel looked at him resenting the topic at hand. "So you also read minds?"

"How coy," Daniel said. "Your pulse was loud and clear for all to hear and as if that weren't enough, the pheromones you burst forth were a sure giveaway for anyone in that garden. It was like being bombarded with pure essence of man. Take note, you could probably sell that to some perfume manufacturer."

The human did his best to shrug off the teasing, but Daniel's laughter boomed him right out of what little comfort zone he thought he could create for himself. "No worries, my boy," the vampire reassured. "You are definitely not the first to fall prey to the delicious musings of our dear Malia. Hell, I could easily be a fellow peer in that group. Luckily, I've been able to thwart any advance and have been victorious against desire and lust."

Nathaniel's face clearly indicated that any clarification would be most welcome. Daniel put his cold arm around the human's shoulder

43

and led the way down the corridor. "OK Runnels, I'll say this in plain English. Although we vampires need blood to survive, we also drink, and eat and most certainly have sex. It's just that vampires eat much less than what humans or a therian would eat."

"Interesting..." Nathaniel said. "So werewolves... um... therians eat as much as humans?"

"Oh heavens no," Daniel said. "Your average therian can at the very least eat eight times what a famished human can. They can start their day by devouring an entire human, eat a light lunch and of course, finish with a sensible dinner. Oh and a fun fact for you, neither vampires nor therians need to feed on blood on a daily basis to survive. Some sources might indicate that we need daily supplements while others insist that one or two humans a month is more than enough. The truth of the matter is that it all depends on the specific... individual? Although we thrive on humans, that does not mean that there aren't those of my kind that deplore the act of feeding on them. It is truly just a choice. What shall I have for dinner tonight? Fish, beef, some nice poultry or human. In a sense, you are the other, other, other white meat."

Nathaniel had a hard time digesting what Daniel was so calmly bombarding him with. Unfortunately for him, there was more to share from the vampire. "You should also know that human blood is one of our favorite seasonings for obvious reasons. Be it fresh or dried and in powder form, it always helps kick things up a notch or two."

'Human spice?' Nathaniel thought to himself, disgusted and offended. There he was, nothing more than a major food group for other species although he could also be ground up into spice. A bit of cardamom, basil and human. 'What else?' he asked himself.

"OH!" the vampire exclaimed. "We also adore blood wine. We actually have dedicated vampire wine makers that combine both elixirs most exquisitely."

'I just had to ask, didn't I?' the human thought, slightly annoyed.

"And don't go thinking we don't get drunk either," the vampire added. "We just need a little more than you." He suddenly twitched his nose and looked into the dark corridor behind them. "Let us pick up the pace though. You've heard some truths and although every word I say is suspect, I'm sure your gut feeling is ripping with tenacious curiosity."

A distant thudding sound had been closing in on them for some time, and now they rushed down the corridor while the noise kept getting louder and nearer. At the same time, Nathaniel perceived that the air was much less stuffy and almost pleasant. Actually, it was an old dusty and oddly comforting smell. He sniffed at the air and raised his eyebrows. "A library?" he asked.

"Quite correct, Mr. Runnels," Daniel replied. "There is still a ways to go, but your senses do not deceive you. Give me one moment; I must go ahead for just a second. Please, stay here and keep quiet for however long that second I am asking for takes. My apologies for keeping you in the dark."

As soon as Daniel finished his sentence, the torch went out. Nathaniel then felt as his guide leapt deep into a darkness that seemed to crawl with blind, hungry eyes. Apart from his breath, the only other sound was the ritualistic thumping that gradually got closer and closer. Then he heard metal scraping on the walls and ringing chains crawling along the floor. Nathaniel's eyes twitched in the gloom trying desperately to see anything while his lungs skipped a breath. As a perfect complement, a dry grunt began to heave grimly in the darkness. His heart beat out of control. Whatever was making all that noise was getting nearer.

The tunnel reverberated so much that whatever lurked in the dark could have been right next to him or in an adjacent passage and it would have made no difference sonically. He tumbled in the dark and wholeheartedly confessed his fear in hopes that some light might shine down. But nothing happened to clear up what was taking place. Only the darkness remained. Seconds peeled painfully slow as silence was the memory he most yearned for, but only scraping, thudding and grunting remained. Not even his thundering pulse could drum out the chaos in the tunnel.

It could have been seconds or minutes, but at last, his prayer was finally answered and some light literally shone on the situation. A faint torch glimmered in the distance. Daniel was holding it to light the way. The vampire's face looked severe and his whisper carried clear across the corridor. "Come Nathaniel. Come now!"

Just the excuse he had been begging for. At first, the young man took tentative steps, still shaken up by all the noise that had for some reason subsided, almost like it was fading into the distance. Daniel was fifty yards away but Nathaniel didn't want to rush since it was still rather dark and the last thing he wanted was to trip but the vampire urged him desperately. "Hurry Runnels! Trust me, you do NOT want to take your time."

"I can't see much here so give me a break," he said while bracing himself against the wall although he did pick up the pace some. The desperate look on Daniel's face made him wonder just what the hell was making that noise.

For an answer, he heard the chains much closer than a minute or two before. As is the case so often, Nathaniel followed his human impulse to be an idiot. He turned back to try and see what was there.

"You fool!!" Daniel yelled. "MOVE!"

Suddenly the scraping came from the floor right behind Nathaniel. A dark figure had emerged with too much speed and crashed into the wall. It gave a vile belch and roared hideously at the young man.

Daniel screamed at the top of his lungs. "RUN!"

Nathaniel forgot he was in the dark and ran as fast as his body would allow. The dry scrapes of hooves grinded against the floor behind him and only a large dark mass could be seen charging wildly in his direction. Daniel's jade eyes burned at the doorway, with a torch in one hand and a rapier in the other. He looked savage yet the sight of the vampire was endlessly more welcome to Nathaniel than whatever was behind him.

Thirty yards away. The breathing was louder meaning that whatever was tearing up the ground behind him was gaining ground. Twenty-five yards. Those were definitely hooves roaring mere feet behind him. Twenty yards from the door. Nathaniel could feel the warmth of the room reaching out to him. Fifteen yards. The snarls he heard from behind spat so close that he could feel the creature's breath. Ten yards away. Almost there, just a little more. At five yards Daniel yelled again. "Duck!!!"

A torch flew straight at Nathaniel's face and instinctively he tucked into a roll, tumbling through the doorway as the torch exploded against a wall of fur behind him. The wall had two black eyes of pure hatred and two massive horns that were still aiming for him before a heavy iron door crashed once as it slammed shut and a second time as whatever had been roaring down the tunnel had come to a sudden, thudding halt.

Chapter 6: Show and tell some more

"What was THAT??!" Nathaniel panted while rubbing the side of his head. He had just crashed into a wooden shelf just before hearing an explosion go off behind him. The frenzied dash had left him out of breath whereas the vampire was cool and collected as if he'd only dropped a magazine.

"Calm down, Runnels. He can't get in here." The vampire calmly adjusted his collar and straightened his shirt while Nathaniel did his best to regain his bearings. "It seems that yet again you've had the pleasure of having fiction become reality. I'd hinted before that many of your legends and myths are actually quite true. Consider this a fine Greek example of just that."

Nathaniel looked at the vampire dumbfounded. God knows what had almost run him down. Yet there was Daniel, seemingly immune to the fact that the only thing between them and whatever the hell had just chased them was an iron door with some funny drawings.

Daniel gave a sideways glance, chanced upon the hapless face of his human guest and gave him a smile. "I'm assuming meeting a minotaur was not in your plans for the day." He finished straightening his wardrobe and proceeded to walk towards Nathaniel to help him up from the floor. "Now why don't we fetch you some food and drink. You should be famished and plenty thirsty."

The vampire led the way from the entrance area into a large open room smelling of oak and cedar. Dark wood was the predominant material and one could almost taste the paint in the air from the various frescoes spread along the room in any free space not taken up by a bookshelf.

"Care for some wine?" the vampire inquired. "Blood wine, perhaps?"

The last phrase was added with the same wicked smile Nathaniel was getting used to seeing upon his host's face. "Water will do," he answered.

"The water I can get soon," Daniel said as he pulled out a bottle, "but some red wine can most certainly be arranged at the moment. Here you go; a fine cabernet... bloodless. Be sure to also help yourself to some fruit and bread. It may not be a real meal, but it's a start."

On the table there was a tray covered in berries, apples and some cantaloupe that seemed recently picked. The baguettes were laid side-by-side to the right and though not warm, they were still fresh. Nathaniel wasted no time and began gorging himself.

Daniel looked on, amazed at the rate in which food began to disappear. "Hearty appetite," he said. "You'd make a fine therian."

Nathaniel glared at the vampire with a mouthful of bread.

"Now, now," Daniel said in a calming tone. "Don't get all worked up because of that silly little comment, Mr. Runnels. I wouldn't want a guest to bother with such trifles."

"So I'm a guest now?" Nathaniel snapped when he was finally able to swallow the bread.

"Why of course!" Daniel exclaimed. "A forced guest, perhaps, but a guest nonetheless."

"Funny," the human said, washing down the food with some wine, "I once saw a movie where a kidnapper said something just like that."

The vampire lightly bit his lip and looked away for a moment. He then looked Nathaniel in the eye. "You might have a point," he said, "and I might even care. Regardless of that, let us talk a bit more of what you think reality is all about. Correct me if I take a misstep, but in a ways, you thought or still think that vampires don't feel or have many sensorial impulses. Well let me be the one to erase such notions from your mind."

"We do have impulses. Quite strong ones I might add. I'm sure you remember that sexy little nymph called Malia. Well she might be an extremely talented hunter, but that does not mean she did not fancy you. This is three centuries worth of experience talking, and I can guarantee that she was probably feasting on the pheromone dish you so coyly presented while denying her easy access."

Daniel then poured a glass of red wine for himself. "We lust and eat and drink and play and respond to our bodies' whims," he said. "If we do not eat, we might not die immediately, but we become rather sickly and grotesque. And if we fast too long, well we are very capable of dying. Your dear Dracula got to that point, hence us not having much of an opinion in regards to the infamous Count."

The vampire drank of his glass and gave some thought to what he was going to say next. "That does not mean that we are not bound by blood. We need the drink even if some of us don't want to accept it. But contrary to popular belief, we can drain the dead to feed, if need be. There are some rather unpleasant consequences though. We become rather weakened, and enter a zombie-like state. In essence, quality of life is wholly sacrificed in exchange for survival. Obviously, not many of us are willing to pay such a price. We feed on the living no matter the risk or cost for we prefer death rather than living a rotting damnation. And though this condition can actually be reversed, if prolonged, it becomes permanent."

The vampire shifted in his seat while draining what remained of his glass. "This is of much concern to my kind for if the human race suffers a devastating blow, then our supply would run short and pretty much doom all vampires. I'm sure you don't enjoy hearing such news or me mainly worrying about your kind because mine would be left without food, but I much rather honesty instead of comfort through misinformation."

Nathaniel had stopped eating altogether as he listened. His face was grim but he nodded for Daniel to continue. "Very well..." the vampire said, "what else are you interested in knowing? I must admit that it is quite entertaining to see your brain at work."

Breathing deeply, the young man chose his words carefully. He wasn't really in the talking mood, but since his captor could pretty much kill him at will, he humored him. "You spoke a bit about blood, human blood to be specific. You also said that you would go into detail later. I think we can call this later."

Daniel's eyes swirled from sky blue to that bright orange that had last come out in the tunnel. "Ah yes... blood," he said while serving himself another glass of wine. "We are not completely sure in regards to what it is that nurtures us, but from what I've lived, and that would be a couple of lifetimes, human blood is the richest in that unknown substance that helps us carry on. Call it our way of mocking Ponce de León's failed attempts in a similar venture. We have done extensive scientific studies and I assure you, it is not the plasma, nor white or red blood cells or any other tangible element that nurtures us. Actually, some of the more mystic of my kind suggest that the potency of human blood is due to a more hallowed basis, namely, the concentration of your souls."

Daniel sipped on his wine while Nathaniel pondered on what he'd just heard. He opened his mouth a couple of times, but words seemed unwilling to make their way out of him. After a fourth attempt, he was finally able to express himself. "So you're saying that vampires in actuality, might be... pretty much... feeding off our souls?"

"Possibly," Daniel said without the slightest trace of a flinch. "But let me pose one very important question to rustle that existential nature you so agnostically cling on to: what is a soul anyway? What is it made of? Does it even exist or are vampires simply echoing the worries of humanity? Sadly, no matter how long you have lived, there is no definite answer to this question and I, along with the rest of conscious kind, have only theories on which to mull over."

Nathaniel had pretty much forgotten the food. His mind was much more preoccupied with choosing his next question. "So just how long can a vampire live for?"

"Another interesting question, Mr. Runnels," Daniel said as he shifted upon the throne-like chair he had draped himself over. "My, my, how that curious little head works. Well to be quite honest with you, no one truly genuinely knows how long a vampire can live for because death rarely comes via 'natural' circumstances for us. Humans, however, have a myriad of theories in regards to us, which is wonderful since so many of you write us off as mere fiction. You could very much say we are god-like in that sense: revered, often spoken of, and yet supremely doubted. I can tell you a small tidbit, which is of much importance to this topic though. The oldest vampire whose acquaintance I've ever made was almost three thousand years old. For decades we all thought he was the oldest, but recent events have shed light on what that particular vampire had once said: There are tribes as old as and even older than him. The First Born, our originators... our genetic Genesis, if you will."

Nathaniel pondered a moment before his next question. "Do you think your kind and therians share the same origin?"

With a few glasses of wine in his system, Daniel gave the question some serious thought. "It is a theory I can see some sense to, so yes, you could say that I do think we share origins... to a certain degree."

"Then why should there be war and bloodshed between both kinds?" Nathaniel asked.

The vampire seemed to relish the moment before responding. "Fascinating," he said cynically. "I ask myself the very same thing of all human wars and conflicts. You'd think it ridiculous to have the color of skin, ethnic origins or religious beliefs be a motive for conflict. Now try to imagine being another species."

"Good point," the human replied. "How 'bout you though? Where are you from? What did you use to do? Are you a pure blood or were you bitten? You know so much about me; tell me about yourself for a change."

Daniel looked at the human with a suspecting stare. It was as if he wasn't sure if Nathaniel was asking sincerely or ingeniously disguising his sarcasm. "Fair enough, human; I do know quite a bit about you so it is only fair to make it mutual." He served himself yet another glass of wine and poured Nathaniel some as well. "Truth flows better with a bit of drink, don't you think?"

The vampire then stood up and gave a drunkenly courteous bow before falling over his chair once again. "I am a special case. I'm not a pure blood in the traditional sense of the term and I was not bitten. No; my story is much different and it goes as follows."

He tried to start twice before settling himself. "While I was just a wee little fetus in the womb; mother, my human mother, just happened to be attacked by a vampire. She was actually unaware of my existence at the time but the vampire was more than happy to let her know she was pregnant. He told her things like he had been in the mood for 'sweet and sour' for so long and she was just what he wanted, her blood having two distinct flavors to it and all. For a meaningless piece of trivia, the vampire's name was Roland."

He lost himself in his wineglass, licking his lips and filing his fangs with the tip of his tongue. It seemed his mind was reminiscing over something quite unpleasant. "When born, I already bore fangs as that of a pure blood, yet I was neither bitten nor born from two vampire parents. This should answer another query I suspect you might have floating in that overactive brain in regards to whether or not vampires can have offspring. We most certainly can. But when young we are quite weak and vulnerable because newborns need the richest of blood to thrive. One can survive with lesser quality blood, but to ensure proper development, only the purest will provide the required nutrients."

His breathing was drunk but he had definitely gotten into the chatty mood. "Luckily, my mother knew many people interested in the occult and they were the ones who put her in contact with some trustworthy vampires. I know it sounds borderline impossible, but I assure you; some of my kind are quite trustworthy. They took her in, showed her the ways of the night and helped her survive for the time being. So in reality, I have always been a vampire. I have never been or known anything else."

"So it can happen?" Nathaniel asked.

"Not often," Daniel replied. "Quite frankly, I am one of very few known vampires who survived into adulthood from being born in that fashion."

"So do tell," the human replied, "just how old does that make you?"

"Great question," Daniel said as he nodded sloppily. "Well, aging as a vampire has to be a fascinating topic for someone like you, who are so bound by your mortality and how short life can be. It's also an inconsistent development. We actually age as humans do until we fully mature. Once we reach that age, one year of aging for my case ceases to be equivalent to one human year. Think of it as in dog years and human years. Fifty of yours for one of mine. So pretty much I have a birthday every half century and you can see traces of aging in me. The bitten are different though. You can see some minor traces of aging, but for all effects, the body's development is completely stunted."

Nathaniel looked at Daniel and formulated a very important question. "So how old were you again?"

"Ah..." sighed the vampire. "My apologies, Mr. Runnels. I sometimes ramble off. Well if you were to lead yourself by what I said in regards to my aging process, then I would be... thirty-one years developed."

A quick mental note and Nathaniel had his next question. "Then tell me, when is it that vampires, or at least you, fully mature? How long in human years does it take?"

Daniel drained his glass and poured another. "That would be around the age of twenty-two."

Nathaniel sipped his glass, put it on the table, and looked down for a second. "So that would make you 472 years old?"

"Oho!!!" Daniel boomed. "Very good my dear friend. Quite quick as well. Have some more wine as a reward."

The young man responded by covering his glass. "Thanks, but I would much rather prefer some water right now."

"However, there's one thing you must take into account: I age faster than most other vampires. It's the human bonds in me, because of the method of my conception. Your average vampire would age about one year every full century in comparison to my meager fifty years."

The human looked him in the eye questioningly. "How can I be sure that you are telling the truth? Who's to say that you aren't merely toying with me to see how much I'll buy into this whole story without questioning one word of it?"

The now familiar smirk blossomed anew upon the vampire's face. "You have doubted me from the very moment we made each other's formal acquaintance. You thought me a lunatic and probably still maintain said theory even if you are clear that I am not someone who earns his keep playing music in the subway. The good part about your skepticism is that it is hardly focused or absolute. In a ways, there is a doubt within the doubt as to whether or not I should be doubted or not. That, ma' boy, is the reason why I've brought you to this dusty yet welcoming place. This is my archive, although this entire collection is only a fraction of what I've collected in my lifespan."

Nathaniel looked around now, finally taking in the countless rows of books, magazines, journals, and notebooks that lined the walls.

"Feel free to look over as much as you want," Daniel said while getting up to his feet. "After all, that's why I brought you here. Being a reporter slash writer slash whatever else you want to label yourself, I thought you might find this rather enlightening. So don't be shy, eat, drink and read to your heart's content. In the meantime, I shall fetch you some real food and water."

With that said, the vampire arched his back swigging the remains of the wine straight from the bottle. Nathaniel was still internalizing he'd be left alone when Daniel looked back from the doorframe. "Oh and please remember: our friend is still roaming outside. So unless you are preternaturally stupid, I wouldn't head out if I were you... Just a thought. Ta-ta."

Before Nathaniel was even able to react, the iron door boomed shut and he was alone... again. He turned around and stood in the entrance anew. This time he was able to truly take in the details of his present confines.

The narrow entrance area had a medium-sized wooden chair to the left of the door and next to it a tall wooden cabinet, the one he had crashed into when he'd come running in from the maze. After passing the small archway, he went into the wide room where he had been with Daniel not two minutes ago. This time he took close notice of the frescoes and saw how painting styles varied from portrait to portrait of the exquisitely detailed landscapes. They were a bit unnerving to look at because you'd expect that at any moment something would reach out from the canvas.

The first painting on the left side of the entrance showed a desolate desert whose heat you could almost feel. Another had a dark forest with trees that faded far off from where the painting ended. There was also one with a black ocean as ominous as it was beautiful, gently glimmering with moonlight and a lone island in the middle of the painting. Finally, there was a picture of a small village. Twinkling lights were scattered among the small houses and a grand castle lay just beyond it. Such beautiful paintings...

Looking back towards the table, he noticed something oddly offbeat. Something had changed, or shifted. He suddenly became aware of three large binders set upon the chair, but that wasn't it. A slight buzzing whizzed by his ear but he paid no attention to it. He'd just looked up and saw something that he couldn't grasp how he had not noticed before.

Made of ivory, gold and diamonds, a lone figure hung over the heavy table. Arms outstretched, hands bound to a cross, and the tragic look of dismay, pain and disappointment that had so often looked Nathaniel in the eye as a child now looked him in the eye as a man.

"I take it crucifixes don't hurt vampires," he said sitting back down at the table, separating the three thick binders. He looked them over and decided to start with the middle one. Its cover was quite worn from the passage of time and what had probably once been black had faded to ash gray. When he opened it, he saw a vast array of news clippings arranged by date.

There were literally hundreds of clippings and when he turned back to the beginning of the binder to truly read through it, he saw a stub from The Dallas Morning News showing a group of sheriffs surrounding two hooded men, bound and shot to the head. It was quite an unnerving visual since it was obviously an authentic news article: frail, yellow and cracked on all sides. But before he turned the page he noticed something peculiar in the photograph, a dark window in the background with its drapes pulled open and a face crystal clear in the photograph. Inside the room, cast in shadow, tacit yet present, an all too familiar smirk beamed at him from the dark.

Nathaniel clutched the binder only inches from his face to see if it showed any signs of being a forgery. It was as if he wanted to change what he saw on the page but to no avail. There was Daniel, peering through the glass into the camera. The date read: May 2nd, 1887. He turned the page and article after article, there he was, immersed in shadows, mocking time, history, even logic to those that would be so ungodly keen to notice the subtle nuance of the vampire version of Waldo.

Dallas, London, France, Hong Kong, Buenos Aires, Havana, New York, Rome... City after city, newspaper after newspaper, there was Daniel, casually appearing in each and every article. A good two hundred years worth of cameos and no forgery in sight. Each stub had decayed to a different degree, different papers and inks aged differently. Having actually studied forgeries for some time, Nathaniel could not find one single solitary trace, and no one can be that good.

He closed the binder, a few shades whiter than what he had been thirty minutes ago. The buzzing that had whizzed by a while ago was felt again and a small red speck he could hardly make out flew about the room. Nathaniel ignored it and then looked at the other two binders as he wondered what else Daniel had in store for him.

He was now looking through a massive photo album and there was Daniel, sipping tea high atop the mountains of Nepal, smiling below the Grand Sphinx that still had her nose, while he held a grenade. It became more surreal with each page he passed. A two-page spread had four big pictures on it of Daniel in front of Mount Rushmore during the different parts of the construction phases. Then he was next to the Hindenburg pointing his finger as if in a warning movement. But something grew alarmingly clear to Nathaniel. Something else was wrong in most of these pictures. In each photo, there was Daniel holding a wine glass, a lit cigarette or a cigar; at the Great Pyramids, on Easter Island, and there he was, coolly standing or sitting directly beneath one thing that just made no sense to Nathaniel.

"Daytime is always best for pictures," softly whispered a voice.

The young man vaulted from the chair and his throat choked on a yelp. It was as if seeing Daniel beside him had caused him to swallow a mighty scream. He stepped around his chair and sat back down, looking straight into the devil child smirk that was glaring at him from across the table.

"My apologies," Daniel said, obviously amused by the startle he'd offered the human. "I just couldn't help myself."

Nathaniel was four times as pale as he'd been when he woke up in the Dameos chamber, basically bordering on the translucent. "H-how long have you been there?"

"Oh not long," Daniel said pouring himself some more wine and sitting down. "You were so focused that I truly thought it would have been far too rude to interrupt."

Nathaniel replied desperately. "How can you be in daytime pictures? Aren't you a vampire?"

Daniel leaned back and put his boots on the table. "Ah yes. That. Well my dear friend, it so happens that one of the advantages of being half human, a dampyr as I think some of your kind would call it, is that I'm quite more resistant to sunlight than the vast majority of my peers. Think of me as a vampiric Hercules. One half human and the other, well you know..."

Nathaniel would have caught his breath but there were far too many things he needed to ask right now. "Majority? So there are more like you?"

The vampire's eyes glowed orange and the smile shone ivory at the question. "But of course, dear Runnels; it is not an easy thing to master nor is it automatically transmitted like some other powers are passed via bites. It is a rare advantage I possess and for that, many would have me slaughtered and torn limb from limb to find the missing link. The problem for them is that I'm not that easily bested, dissected or found for that matter and neither are any of the other day walkers."

As the human pondered all he heard, Daniel could not recall having met anyone who would internalize information so methodically. Nathaniel's head swam with all the images and news articles he'd read. Lord knows how long he had been reading when he was startled by Daniel's appearance. As usual, the vampire simply smiled on as the small buzzing noise that had been annoying Nathaniel for quite some time fluttered anew. "What the hell is that?"

"Never mind that now," Daniel said as he sipped on his wine. "You have not stopped reading for two hours. I'm sure you believe it was just a moment, but you've not let up thus making it appear as if you time traveled."

"And how do you know I've gone at it nonstop?" Nathaniel said clearly suspicious.

Daniel smiled even wider. "Let's just say something like a little bird told me."

Nathaniel didn't understand at all, but by now he was almost becoming used to that sensation where he was the only one to not grasp what was going on.

Daniel did his best to hold back the laughter. "Oh dear Runnels, I assure you, there is nothing and no one to worry about and there are no mechanical devices in these quarters with one wonderful exception." The vampire stood up and walked past Nathaniel. "Would you care for some music?" he asked as he stood next to a vintage record player.

"Fine," Nathaniel said. He played along because he did not have much of a choice. "What are you going to put on? Tchaikovsky? Beethoven? Chopin? Maybe a little Bach?"

The vampire gave him a curious smile. "Ummm... not quite." Flipping the switch of the record player, Daniel proceeded to put down the needle over a vintage vinyl. He stood upright, took a deep slow breath and closed his eyes as he savored the initial hiss of the LP.

Hiss turned to feedback and then a wailing guitar that had long been silenced in real life came forth through its recorded memory.

'Purple haze all in my brain.'

Open mouthed, dumbfounded, confused... Any of these words lack the necessary meaning to describe the exact face and state of confusion Nathaniel had just been hurtled into. "I rather think it fits your current state of mind," Daniel said in response to the human's face. "I was between that and the Floyd, but gut instinct prevailed and I just had to lean towards Jimmy. Not to say that your choices are not wonderful, but by now, if anything, I would have thought you'd be able to grasp that stereotypes can be quite mistaken."

The human responded by closing his eyes and gripping his falling head. "Man... my brain needs a vacation."

"Indeed," Daniel said, rubbing the human's shoulders in a mild attempt at solidarity. "It seems you made it through two of the binders, the third you can leave for later when you have more time, actually for when you have plenty of time. It is a comprehensive journal of my life on this Earth."

Nathaniel pried his face from his hands just enough to look at the tattered cover of the third binder – the title read Dawn of the Five Horizons. He sighed deeply as he fell upon his hands again, speaking between gritted teeth and tense fingers. "OK... I'm still trying to cope with understanding all I've seen... and lived... and read in the last couple of conscious hours. Not to mention all the crap you'd said before which is only now truly sinking in since none of this is fake. No matter how hard I've tried to find something that might lead me to believe that you're lying and completely full of it, I've failed. So if you don't mind, and it's not too much trouble; give me a second or two. My brain feels like it just got sat on by a big fat guy who loves cabbage and aged ham."

Daniel took an almost sympathetic tone. "I told you, lad... but it is quite understandable that you doubt any or all of which I tell you. Not even now do I expect you to believe me. That just doesn't seem like your style, does it? But your help? We could use it Nathaniel." He squatted to face level with the human. "We could really use it."

Nathaniel turned his face to look towards Daniel, weary and finally showing that fatigue had successfully caught up with him. "But why? What can I do that a vampire, an angel or a therian or whatever else exists in this world can't do better than me? If humans are so weak, what makes me any different? You have powers and... and abilities... and the chance to live several lifetimes. What does a schmuck like me have? Nothing!"

The incandescent orange of Daniel's eyes slowly swirled, gradually mixing with other tinges until a dull pale blue settled into the vampiric corneas that looked down upon the beaten human. "Again Mr. Runnels, your questions are impeccably stated even in your altered state and they most certainly need to be answered. You are very much correct to assume that my kind has powers and abilities but you also have to take into account one thing: abilities, skills, and talents differ from race to race not to mention from one being to another. Don't think your kind is helpless and cannot learn a vast array of abilities. That would be mistaken and quite untrue. The main problem humankind faces is not potential or the lack therein of it. Your problem lies solely on the limitations cast by a single nullifying factor: you haven't the time to discover and develop skills vampires and therians can take decades and even centuries to master."

Nathaniel breathed deep and sat up with his hands just touching while he looked in front of him as if pieces of a puzzle were on the table and he were mentally mapping out a solution. Although his mind and body had taken a fair amount of punishment, it was reassuring for Daniel that his guest was still quite able to sit back and think things through logically. After another deep breath, he looked at Daniel and was ready to continue asking questions. "So you're saying that humans can have abilities?"

"No, Nathaniel; humans do have abilities. Most times you just don't notice or aren't properly taught to develop them. Martial artists, boxers, painters, even renowned basketball and baseball stars have all honed some type of skill because they all have abilities that are inherent to them. You can work hard to develop a skill, yes; but sometimes you're just born with it."

Nathaniel nodded as he lightly tapped the end of his nose with his clasped fingertips. "OK... but how do you know which abilities you have or how many for that matter? Or is it that you have to stumble upon them?"

"Stumble?" Daniel asked. "Hardly. But that is the key to your entire ordeal. Ever since we began talking in the Dameos chamber, you've probably been asking yourself how I came upon you. Here is where you find out of some of the involvement of the Uatu. You remember that race I spoke to you about when telling you of all the races that currently reside on Earth?"

Nathaniel paused for a moment as he scanned his memory. "The Incandescent Ones you called them I think."

"The very same," replied the vampire. "Well, if one day you happen to look at someone through their visors, peer through an Eye of Cardino, observe someone in detail through a Lens of Jonah, or use a Salaman Pool, all of which are relics of the watchers, only then can you truly understand how I found you."

Nathaniel twitched at getting another half answer garnished with cryptic language. "OK, in plain English if you please and no trick answers; what do these relics do and what's their point?"

Daniel sipped the last remnants of his glass of wine. "Well, to be quite honest, the full range of what each of these things does is unknown to us. However, it is quite likely that there are uses we have not discovered yet. I told you a bit of the visors. They show the true form of the watchers and let you see and interact with the mid-dimension which they inhabit, the halfway point between this world and another. Basically anyone who wears the visor can see, feel and interact with those surroundings, even if those same things are inexistent on this plane."

Two big weary eyes dilated as much as possible in reaction to Daniel's explanation. The vampire noticed and opted to clarify. "Ok... Let's say there's an open space, an alley if you will, with a solid wall at its end. No doors, no trap doors, no tricks; nothing; just a solid wall. If you put on a visor and see that there is a stairway, then you can climb it. If you see a door, then you can open it and go through. It's complicated to explain. You really must see it, and you shall get to do so much sooner than you think."

The human simply groaned, "Ugh. My brain feels like it's going to explode."

"Let's hope not," Daniel replied. "There's much more to see and learn and I wouldn't want you to miss out. I mentioned the Salaman Pools, correct? Well these have been infused with mineral deposits unlike anything known to man. They're pale red and the water fizzes like seltzer. These pools can actually help restore vitality and even speed the healing process of wounds. But the purpose that most concerns us right now is that when someone bathes in those waters, all cardinal points are revealed and one's true potential is better understood. Not to mention that these same pools are at times used as oracles to help predict certain events."

The look of confusion on Nathaniel's face was worse than ever. "Oracles? Cardinal points??"

"Runnels, I'm referring to cardinal points quite different to those regarding North, South, East and West. Have you ever heard about pressure points?"

"Like in martial arts?"

"Exactly. Well you can compare cardinal points to them as if they were special pressure points that if pressed under the correct circumstances, dormant abilities are awoken and your true potential is unlocked. Don't think therians and vampires have all their abilities once they are transformed. We may have certain advantages, but most of our skills need to be unlocked, honed and perfected. Unlike humans though, we have the luxury of taking our time to learn each skill adequately."

"But where do I fit in all of this?" Nathaniel asked. "Mystic pools, visors, cardinal points, vampires, werewolves, a mid dimension? This is like an episode of the Twilight Zone, except weirder. I just can't see where I make a difference or what character I'm going to be except one of those extras with red shirts that vanish before the second commercial."

The vampire stood in front of the human and put his arm upon his right shoulder as a sign of solidarity. "Sorry to put you through this, lad. But quite honestly, it couldn't be helped and time forced my hand. There is still one relic I should talk to you a bit more about. Remember this?"

Nathaniel looked at Daniel as the vampire pulled a thin gold chain out from within his shirt in one fluid motion. At its end, an amethyst-like medallion seemed to beat like some kind of small crystal heart. Engravings surrounded the metalwork and they looked luminescent although Nathaniel could not make out what they said. The glass lens was almost like suspended water and in its center, there was a small red stone one could easily mistake for a petrified blood droplet.

"As I told you in the Dameos chamber, this is an Eye of Cardino," Daniel said. "This medallion will only react when someone with incredible internal strength and probably a dozen or so cardinal points passes nearby. I'm sure you don't remember, but we'd actually met before the night in the subway."

Nathaniel struggled for a moment before he was able to talk. "What do you mean we met? I'd never seen you before that night."

"Quite wrong; we'd bumped before in a train station while I asked for money. It was around half a year ago, the lens was going crazy so I decided to ask for money to see exactly who or what was making it react so violently. Six or seven people I'd asked for money when you bumped into me, hard. Lucky for you, you excused yourself splendidly and gave me a ten dollar bill. I spared slashing your throat because even though I was famished, courtesy, manners and generosity should be recognized and appreciated."

Nathaniel blew out his breath to gulp in another deep one while looking to the ceiling. "Thank you mom and grandma."

Daniel nodded. "Indeed. The peculiar thing is that I'd never seen the disc react that fiercely, and much to my surprise, the catalyst for such a reaction was none other than you."

A brief pause ensued. Both parties took a moment to gather their thoughts and each sized the other trying to gauge what the other was feeling or even thinking. Nathaniel went first. "So does that mean I'm the one?"

The trademark grin rose to Daniel's face as a familiar orange tinge also set into his eyes. "That's cute... no, dear Runnels. The situation at hand requires more than just a 'the one' to truly put things in order. The scope of this situation is global and either all who intervene succeed to some measure, or who knows what will happen. We most certainly need help for many have been lost on all sides still interested in the wellbeing of this world. Key figures whom you would hopefully be able to in a ways, fill in for."

This time Nathaniel pushed back on his chair and stood up. He let it all sink in while leaning back and bracing his head with both hands as he thought of what the next move or event would actually be. He wanted to take a minute to think things through, but even a vampire can be insistent when in a rush. "Would you care to share your thoughts?" said Daniel through slightly gritted teeth.

Nathaniel released his head and swung his arms as if warming up for exercise. "Well now you know how it feels sometimes. I just need a minute to gather my thoughts. Pardon my human shortcomings but I'm a bit tired to say the least."

He paused for another moment, which Daniel didn't necessarily approve of, but at least he continued the conversation. "Tell me one thing: why should I follow through with this? What does the human race get in return apart from a thank you note from our furry and fanged friends? How do I know that my actions won't bring on the end of the world or any other cataclysmic disaster?"

The vampire looked at the human. He breathed deeply while drowsily beating his eyelids as his hyperactive irises switched color yet again. Orange, red, black, jade... Nathaniel was already bracing himself for an attack when in a last swirl the eyes slid into the pleasant blue hue characteristic of this vampire when he was in control.

"I've said it already: one day yet you will learn to trust me blindly. For today though, I am humoring you. I'll answer your trite questions, even if to me the answers are so logical that you shouldn't even need to ask. Therians and vampires need humans to survive. We simply cannot afford to lose your kind."

Nathaniel took another pause and almost looked like he was feeling a bit good of himself and the stress he was causing the vampire.

Daniel suddenly felt the need to interrupt the smug look on the human's face. "Please remember one very important detail, Mr. Runnels. Don't go thinking you are the only one of your kind that can save the day. You most definitely are special and I won't pretend otherwise. But you are not the only "the one" we've found. So by all means, don't try my patience. Next time you feel the need to find out just exactly how much you can push me, realize that I'm under pressure to save the world and killing another human will not rob me of sleep."

A tinge of green flashed here and there but his eyes remained blue. In all honesty, Nathaniel could care less if they were blue, brown or yellow. He knew he could have his life ended in one or two movements and all done with that damned smile. Daniel then stood face to face with Nathaniel, inches away from each other where one could clearly feel the other's tension, scent, breath and disposition. It was pretty much too close for hypocrisy and definitely too close for comfort.

"There's another reason why you should go along," said Daniel in what appeared to be an even-toned manner.

"And that would be?" Nathaniel asked, resisting the urge to step back to create some space between them.

"I know you want to learn if what I say is the truth, the whole truth and nothing but the truth," Daniel said with bared fangs that pointed beyond his wicked smile. "I truly doubt you are satisfied with what you've seen and I still have quite a few things to share with you."

A physical standoff ensued and Nathaniel was not about to break face or back down. He had reached a point where he'd rather die than stand down. "So what's the next step?" he asked.

"Good attitude," Daniel said approvingly. "For now, it is time for you to eat. Later we shall continue your lessons regarding the real world."

Daniel swung his arm over the human's shoulder while he signaled to a covered tray that Nathaniel had not noticed upon the table. Pulling the cover from it, Nathaniel saw that beneath the cloth were two covered plates with filet mignons accompanied by sautéed potatoes. To the famished human, this was the edible equivalent of a stranded desert walker finding an oasis.

"Be sure to double check the meat," Daniel teased with his orange eyes alit. "One is a bit rarer than I think you'd care for."

Nathaniel hoped that this was not his last supper but with the unyielding hunger that continued to echo in his stomach, even with the bread and fruit he'd eaten, it hardly seemed as if he cared what happened. He pretty much assaulted his plate of food, slashing the meat and shoving generous amounts into his mouth as the still warm meal quenched the pain in his gut. The vampire looked on and seemed quite amused. "Don't rush too much now. We don't want you getting cramps or an upset stomach now, would we?"

Nathaniel gulped a mouthful of food before excusing himself. He paced himself and enjoyed the food, which he later learned his host had actually prepared for them. He was so excessively famished that he didn't even pay attention to the paranoid nature that would normally tell him that the food or water might be poisoned.

'There has to be a catch,' he thought. 'There's always a catch.' But nothing happened. He didn't keel over or lurch in poisoned anguish. He didn't faint, or pass out or even suffer the simple stupor of a food coma. He just ate.

Daniel then took the plates and put them on the tray and afterwards swished some brandy around which he'd just served himself in a beautiful wide glass colored light ochre. "And you thought I'd poison you," said the vampire with his usual smile. "How coy. And don't think I'm mind reading; I can see it in your face but still it's good that you ate and enjoyed. That way you are nourished and can appreciate the fact that I, regardless of my vampiric nature, can truly enjoy a pretty normal meal as well."

Nathaniel wiped his mouth clean as he leaned back in his tall chair, thankful to have satisfied his hunger. His face finally softened and relaxed a bit. "So now what?"

"Aha!" the vampire exclaimed as his eyes lit up in a bright orange flash. "Now we have dessert! Follow me."

And with a gallant swirl of his coat, he was already at the door, holding it open as he ushered the human to follow him to whatever it was that a vampire would call dessert.

Chapter 7: Enemies of a feather fight together

The darkness from the corridor pulsated as Daniel and Nathaniel left the iron door behind them. The vampire walked even faster than their original trek through these tunnels and spoke in rushed tones. "We mustn't be late, dear Runnels. Duty calls and there's not a second to lose."

The food and drink had pepped him up quite a bit while Nathaniel was still showing signs of lethargy and sluggishness. For his part, the human looked at the vampire and couldn't help but be reminded of a white rabbit looking at his pocket watch and remarking about how late he was.

"Now left here," the vampire instructed. "Our little friend is still making rounds somewhere and I doubt you want to meet up with him again."

"Nice understatement," Nathaniel said. He was more than happy to pick up the pace as long as he got to breathe fresh air and get out of those tunnels. They twisted and turned constantly in the winding maze, yet something intangible was in the air. Something Daniel smelled and Nathaniel sensed. Something was nearby.

Daniel slowed his pace and his body language suddenly seemed much less chivalrous and much more apprehensive of their progress. "Do you hear that?" he asked.

Utter - dismal - empty - silence

"I don't hear a thing," Nathaniel replied.

"Exactly," Daniel said. When Nathaniel turned to look at the vampire, he saw that his eyes were not orange or blue, or even jade. They had become a dark crimson red and his fangs had grown a full half-inch. "Do not stop," the vampire said. "Only a few more turns and we're out."

A verbal response was not needed. Yards flew by and the shining tunnel labels became a blur to Nathaniel. What bothered him most was that he could sense that his normally cool, collected guide was anything but cool and collected. Frightening a human was normal, but what the hell could frighten a vampire. After a sharp right turn, Daniel stopped in his tracks putting his hand on the chest of Nathaniel to also stop him. A long corridor was ahead with a fork at the end. "Here we are, Runnels. One more right turn and we're out of here. There's only one problem."

Daniel turned around and the human could see the face of his vampire guide as it twisted with signs of unease. "Do you get déjà-vu?" he asked the young man.

"All the time," responded the human, "Why?"

"Because I don't," the vampire said.

Daniel turned around and looked down the corridor. He was silent and still, two things that didn't promote spiritual ease in the human. The vampire then unsheathed his rapier and dagger and stormed down the tunnel. As Nathaniel followed him, he noticed that the same ethereal smooth perfection of the tunnel now looked perverted. Even if this tunnel was actually wider and more open than others he'd walked through, it seemed to press down on them, as if they were salmon fighting up a raging river. Their bodies felt something pushing them away. The air grew dense and suffocating, yet nothing was different. Three-fourths of the way there, they could see a wall and the fork in the road. Just one turn and they were out of there. Then a cold hard ball struck Nathaniel in the chest.

"Wait," Daniel said while pressing his palm against the human's chest once again; the metal in his voice was dull and heavy. He stood there, rapier in front. He'd sheathed the dagger so quickly Nathaniel hadn't even heard the noise a millisecond before the vampire had stopped him in his tracks. They were steps away from the fork yet they did not move. The vampire's head was bowed and Nathaniel noticed that he was looking at the floor. He tried seeing something, anything, but he couldn't find what would cause Daniel to stare at the floor as if a dead body was in their path.

"We are not alone."

Nathaniel almost swallowed the pounding heart that had made it halfway up his throat. His senses were scanning all around when he noticed something that almost made him panic, a slow, heaving dirge-like breathing. But Daniel did not move, regardless of how impatient his guest might have become.

"Let's make a run for it," Nathaniel suggested.

"I'd love to but it is not that simple," he replied. "Why don't you look over my shoulder about eight paces in front of us? Look closely."

Straining his eyes in the darkness, Nathaniel finally saw it. Not ten feet from them, drawn on the floor was a perfect heptagram. He didn't say a word since he didn't really understand the nature of the drawing or what it meant.

"From your silence, I can tell that you do not really know what it is you are looking at," Daniel said. "To offer an accurate metaphor, why don't you think of that cute little drawing as being the magical equivalent of a land mine. The problem is that if we step on it, I'm not really sure what will happen. If you wish to insist on going forth, by all means, go ahead. I'll be right behind you."

The human swallowed deep. He wasn't about to take Daniel up on that offer. "So let's turn around and leave."

The vampire laughed gently and Nathaniel could feel a hint of nervousness. "I would, it's just that the company I spoke of just happens to be behind you about twenty feet or so."

Nathaniel's eyes grew about four times their original size and his breathing seized momentarily. He turned around and life slipped into slow motion as the familiar black fur came into view. More unnerving though was what stood on the beast's left side: a female wearing a silver kilt and a semi-transparent veil depicting a moon, holding a long wooden staff in one hand and caressing the minotaur's mane with the other. Platinum hair, silver eyes that cut through the fabric and an ash grey shade spread from every inch of her supple skin to the last feather on each wing. The vampire from the courtyard had been a rainbow in comparison to the first angel Nathaniel had ever seen in his life.

"Hello, Sariel," Daniel said as he stepped around Nathaniel to be in between them and the human. "It's been a while."

"My dear Daniel," the angel gently rasped, "it has been some time, hasn't it? So nice to bump into you." Her tone was as monochromatic as her skin and she seemed lifeless yet oddly full of energy.

"What brings you to the neighborhood?" Daniel asked. "Perhaps just wanting to remember the good old days? Maybe dropping by for a spot of tea?"

The bile in the vampire's tone was more than enough to let Nathaniel know that trouble had arrived.

"Oh not much," the angel replied, "just visiting to check up on Asterion." She patted the beast and scratched the deep mane much to the approval of the minotaur. "After all, who knows what you've been feeding him if anything at all?"

Her dull tone was able to carry a sense of genuine cynicism while remaining completely detached. Any emotion was projected through her voice while her face was a blank canvas, unable to paint the slightest hint of feeling.

"Oh you know, we do what we can for the little guy," Daniel said, "his favorite has always been humans but they do run scarce these days, ever since you left. I wonder what daddy would think of all the things you did here before your departure."

She stepped forwards as she scanned both the human and vampire, disregarding the rapier that Daniel still held in his right hand as if it were a twig. "Ah Daniel," she said while attempting to sigh, "why do you insist on attributing gender to the Great One?"

"Well in all honesty, you definitely need a really big set of balls to let things get this out of hand without even considering to interfere."

Her platinum eyes flared yet no other muscle moved. "Hold your tongue, vermin. Thou shall not blaspheme his name."

"His name?" Daniel asked as his smirk finally made an appearance. "Dear Sariel, it never ceases to amaze me how easily, and quickly for that matter, you and your kind contradict yourselves. Let us put this debate aside and get to the matter at hand. What in Christ's name are you doing here?"

Although her expression remained essentially the same, her stone face became even grimmer. She then peeked over Daniel's shoulder to focus on something endlessly more interesting to her. "Who's your new friend?"

"Oh, this?" Daniel said as he pointed to Nathaniel. "This is a long lost cousin. I found him wandering about and recognized this birthmark on his cheek. Lo and behold, when I asked where he was from, he told me about his family and could you believe it, we're related."

"Hmmm," she sniffed the air deeply. Once. Twice. A third time. "Smells a bit young to be that close to you Daniel, don't you think?"

"Ah well Sariel, blood lines do have a way of branching off though I'm sure it's a concept you could never imagine since you don't do much of that procreating stuff. Oh and I think I missed your answer, why were you here again?"

The angel didn't shift position, smirk, scowl or physically do anything. She just answered the vampire. "Just dropping by, dear friend. Israfil was polishing his trumpet saying that soon it'd be time, but he didn't say for what it was time. Since I didn't know what he meant, I thought I might drop by to see how things were with you."

"Israfil, eh?" Daniel said, the sarcastic edge to his voice clearly gone. "Well, as you can see, we're just having a little family reunion here. Everything is pretty much in order."

"Is it?" she said with mock surprise. "Well, that's not what I heard. You'd do well to touch base with all your friends, I think. That way you can be sure that everything is as in order as you say."

Daniel's knuckles glowed like dots of white lightning from griping his rapier so hard; but he didn't dare raise it one millimeter. "And what does that mean... dear Sariel?"

"Oh, nothing," she toyed, "a little bird just told me that a thing or two were amiss. I also heard that Azrael has been mighty busy writing and erasing a particularly interesting batch of names."

As Daniel went rigid, the air went even icier. "Is that so?"

"That is very so," she replied. "And I also heard something fascinating through the grapevine, as humans say."

The vampire became even more rigid. "And that would be?"

The slightest trace of what could be a smile appeared on her lips. "And spoil you the surprise? You know me better than that. I would never do anything like that."

Daniel struggled to maintain his cool. "True, but you always tell me to keep the faith. Guess it was a bit foolish of me, but I said what the hell, let's give this bitch a chance."

Gray wings flared, startling the minotaur and prompting Daniel to finally raise his weapon. "Wrath is so becoming of you," he hissed at her. "I'm sure daddy would love to see one of his favorites reacting so humanly. Hell if we didn't know better, I'm sure my friend here wouldn't mind having a pass at you. What say you, cousin? Are you man enough to screw an angel?"

Her skin actually showed the slightest tinge of rouge in her cheeks, the perfect cue for Daniel to continue goading her. "I love it when you blush, baby."

"SILENCE!" she screamed. The pure disgust and contempt for the vampire finally showed on her face. "There's also one other small detail I think you should know, you bastard."

"Mmmmm... there was some fire with that," Daniel said as he savored the moment. "I could taste it. What other surprises do you have for me, doll? Mind the language though, there are young ones present."

Her scowl suddenly turned to a very evil smile. "Oh nothing, just that you would do well to make arrangements. You'll be visited soon."

The smug look that had beamed triumphantly on the vampire's face had suddenly been ripped off. "What do you mean?"

"Mmmm hhmmmm hmmmm hahahahahah." Her laugh was atypical and terrifying. There was no rhythm to it and Nathaniel realized why; she had never laughed before. This made her cackle as maniacal as it was loud. "You'll see," she said. "You'll see, very soon. For now, I must leave."

Daniel pointed his rapier to her face. "Tell me, Sariel, or get ready to go on an express train to visit daddy dearest."

She responded by turning her back on them. "I doubt that, Daniel. You might be able to handle me alone. But me, Asterion, and that cute little heptagram behind you, not to mention your dear cousin getting in your way, would make attacking me a rather foolish idea."

For however much he wanted to ram her through, he knew she was right and Daniel held his ground. "Fine then, off with you," he said dismissively as he lowered his blade.

"As if I needed your permission," she responded. "Asterion! Come!" And with that, she faded into the darkness of the corridor followed by the imposing minotaur. Daniel clenched his sword and sheathed it hard. He looked at the ground and grunted his disapproval. "Bitch. She left the heptagram."

"Ummm... what the hell was that all about?"

"Oh... you're still here," Daniel said to the frightened human. "I'd almost forgotten about you. Kind of kept to yourself there, eh? And that? That was an old... acquaintance of mine."

"But was that an..."

"An angel?" Daniel interrupted. "Yes. I thought the whole thing with the wings would have been sufficient for you, but I see you insist on reminding me just how human you are."

Nathaniel stood silent for a second. It was quite obvious that Daniel wasn't in one of his best moods, his eyes now burning jade green. But he did feel the need to ask a question. "Ok. So who is she?"

"First of all, let us go around the corner. That heptagram sure as hell won't let us pass. Lord knows what that thing will do to us. As for Sariel, well you could very well see she is an angel. One whom I don't see eye to eye with and haven't for quite some time."

"I noticed," Nathaniel said, "you almost looked like an ex-couple."

"Hardly," Daniel said with a look of disgust. "She is the angel of guidance and wisdom, or so they say. Supposedly she also represents self-control and tolerance, hence me having a grand old time at her expense. My main problem is that she never comes out to say anything straight. She just plants seeds so I can investigate and if I'm lucky enough I can find the answers I'm looking for."

"She also happens to be a Hashmallim, which is one of the Angel Assemblies. These assemblies are supposed to guard the balance of the cosmos and receive orders from archangels, seraphs or God himself if he even exists. They normally don't show themselves, but there can be exceptions..." His eyes swirled from jade to light blue as he held his silence.

"Which would be?" asked Nathaniel.

"Well she did mention three other things. Three details that will probably be important although they are quite disconcerting. For starters, she mentioned that Azrael was busy writing and erasing names. Azrael is another angel, actually an archangel, higher in rank than Sariel. He has under his power the Log of the Earth."

"So what does wood have to do with any of this?" Nathaniel asked.

Daniel rolled his eyes and lightly slapped his forehead. "Log as in Captain's log. You know, journal of events, a book with dates and entries? Twit. He's constantly adding and erasing names from that log because within it is a massive list of all the names of all the living beings of this world."

"So that's all he does?" Nathaniel said, a bit more careful to choose a smarter question this time around.

"Pretty much. That's his punishment for having disobeyed the Earth. To make a long story short, ancient lore states that the four closest angels to God were asked to bring back a piece of the Earth to the heavens. Three did not do so because the Earth declined itself saying that God did not need any of the Earth in the heavens. Azrael, however, like the good little soldier he's always been, disregarded the Earth and pried a handful of fresh soil to take back to his God. God didn't like that he didn't do as the Earth requested, and so, that's his punishment or the cheap excuse to stick him with such a bothersome chore."

"But he did as he was told," Nathaniel said as they rounded yet another corner.

"Exactly why I don't fancy trusting this God person all that much. He gave a clear order, it was followed, yet the soldier was damned. That's quite unjust if you ask me."

Nathaniel thought for a moment before his next question. "So do you think he can know something?"

"Well he knows a lot," said Daniel. "He'd pretty much put any living creature's memory to shame so maybe it'd be good if we could drop by and have a chat."

"And how do we do that?" Nathaniel asked.

"Good question," replied Daniel, "but there are other leads to follow as well."

They walked on and turned right yet again and finally Nathaniel could make out the door. But there was something else on his mind. "Do you mean the grapevine comment?"

"Very astute, my young friend," Daniel replied. "I have to figure that one out although I already have a hunch, which only leaves us with one loose clue."

They were finally in front of the door, Nathaniel a bit winded and Daniel deep in thought. "She mentioned Israfil," gasped the human as he caught up to the vampire who was already beside the door and unsheathing his dagger. "Who the hell is that?"

"Another angel who in fact has a very beautiful and intricate trumpet," the vampire replied.

"And what's so important about this trumpet?"

"Well dear Runnels, we wouldn't want him to blow on it because it'd be quite a significant and unpleasant signal. If Israfil blows his trumpet, it is the signal for the coming of Judgment day." Daniel looked at the gate and stabbed it once again with the dagger. It opened and they were both finally able to breathe fresh air, yet something was now wafting through it. Something neither could pinpoint, but when they looked each other in the eye, it was clear neither of them welcomed the new essence.

"Seems we don't have much time, so by all means, let us be off."

Chapter 8: So THAT'S the point

Daniel and Nathaniel ran across the garden to the first entrance on the right. It was a straight corridor lined with doors on either side. Once inside, the only sounds they could hear were the dull knock of their shoes on the floor and the rain outside. The young man toyed with various theories about what could be behind any of these doors, but he ended up assuming it was some sort of barracks where the tenants slept in.

Daniel realized the atypical silence and felt the need to offer some advice. "Runnels, before even considering doing something you'd later regret, please don't help yourself to open a door, any door, for that matter."

"I wasn't going to," Nathaniel replied as his hand returned to his side.

Daniel didn't even need to look back. "Right. Just a random word of caution so you don't find yourself face to face with an unpleasant surprise."

Nathaniel bit his lip and followed the vampire while thinking of all the unpleasant surprises he would like to give him. They sped down the corridor at a considerable pace passing door after door. No winding, no turning, just a straight never-ending queue of doors. Same frame, same knob, same wall, repeating endlessly.

The mundane silence pressed down on Nathaniel and in typical fashion, he broke it with a question. "Where are we going?"

Daniel didn't bother to turn around. "First off, we need to verify that you are not only in one piece but fully functional, barring human ignorance of course. Suffice to say that we need to see someone about something. Who and what you'll soon find out."

The pace continued to pick up the further they went. The corridor felt infinite since it was the same scenery recycling itself over and over like a cartoon from the 70's. They tread on and the same set of opposing doors seemed to regenerate every few feet. They'd passed what seemed like hundreds of doors. It was as if the damned trek down this damned corridor would never end.

"Here we are, Runnels," Daniel said, showing that there actually was an end.

The vampire did the honors of opening one of the hundreds of identical doors allowing the room to exhale a musky spice that laced the air. Although musty, it was oddly pleasant, like a room closed with your favorite incense burning a tad too long. The room opened up and chimes gently rang from somewhere within as an extremely bright and sterile white room beamed all around them. Nothing seemed to be moving within except an opening at the far right end of the room, from which a burgundy sheet swished gently. For a moment, nothing happened until a voice called out from the other room. "I swear, human! One could hear you thinking even without powers." It was a familiar voice that had flowed through the air from behind the cloth.

"Won't you make an effort to hush your thoughts just a smidge?" said the voice as one of the vampires from the garden walked out from the other room with a lit cigarette in his mouth. "Trust me, I have quite enough on my mind to have a human's incoherent banter interrupting my internal monologue."

"Hello, Liam," Daniel said as the other vampire turned to face one of the walls that had measuring equipment along with some vials and other medical paraphernalia. "Seems you are tinkering with a few things as per usual, so it should be no surprise if you have no idea as to who has dropped by to say hello."

"How is Sariel by the way?" Liam asked while still facing away from Daniel and Nathaniel. He then stretched his arm behind his back and pointed to the human while opening and closing his fingertips and thumb - the universal sign of chit chattering.

Daniel rolled his eyes. "Runnels, would you be so kind as to think of something else for a little while?"

Liam gave a puff of his cigarette smoke and turned to finally look in their direction. "Mind you, please don't think of something too distracting," he said. "I just had lunch and a vivid mental image of something like your naked grand mum relieving herself is the last thing I need at this precise moment."

Nathaniel did his best to keep quiet and think of something else, but he couldn't help but wonder just exactly what a vampire could have had for lunch.

"Tuna salad, mate," Liam answered. "But I'm due some human any day now, so please, do your best to not look appetizing."

A heavy gulp and deep breath later, Nathaniel found himself flooding his mind with bits of literature, song lyrics, philosophy and pictures. Liam continued to grin and presently directed his gaze to Daniel, yet didn't say an audible word.

'Don't let the human hear,' he thought to Daniel. 'So Sariel came by? What news did she bring and why did she come?'

Daniel scratched his head while he thought an answer. 'Clues and puzzles as per usual, old friend.'

'Damn her!' Liam thought. 'Although from the thoughts of the human, you pushed her quite hard Daniel: You love to see her blush? You really are a prick. Anyways, did she mention anything else that could be of real importance?'

Daniel leaned against the wall. 'She mentioned two names that prompted me to rush over.' He then paced along the room keeping an eye on Nathaniel. 'Her intent was as ambiguous as ever; you know how she is. She did say we should visit Azrael to check The Book and she added that Israfil is... tuning up.'

Liam's eyes gaped open in their pale blue splendor. Nathaniel continued thinking of random things and took no notice of the tension that now mounted between the two vampires. 'Israfil? Are you sure Daniel?'

'Why don't you ask for yourself?' Daniel thought as he nodded towards Nathaniel.

Liam took what was left of his cigarette, lit a new one before tossing the old one to the floor and cleared his throat. "Human!" he called. "I see you've had an encounter with an angel just a few minutes ago. What do you remember of it?"

"Not much really..." Nathaniel said half afraid to answer the vampire.

Liam responded by looking at him with a gaze so intense it could pierce metal and rock. Ever so subtly, Nathaniel's left eye began to twitch. An instant later, the vampire spoke calmly allowing his breath to empty his smoke filled lungs. "Plutarch once said: a pleasant and happy life does not come from external things. Man draws from within himself, as from a spring, pleasure and joy... and knowledge."

The effect was immediate. Nathaniel's brow bent and his mouth hung crooked. Liam took a good pull from his cigarette before elaborating. "My most estimably evolved primate of a friend, if your mind is a spring, I may drink from it when I choose. Don't lie to me or withhold information. Avoid me the trouble of looking around that muddled porridge you call a brain for the answers we need."

Daniel closed his eyes and smiled while shaking his head.

"Let us continue, Daniel," Liam said. "And you," he said while pointing to Nathaniel, with the cigarette in between his fingers, "sit tight... I'll be with you shortly and another note: Peter Paul Rubens was brilliant. I'd say he had the hands of an angel, but I'm not one for offending Rubens with such an insult. Regardless, good thought you chose there. Keep it up."

'Now, where were we?' Liam thought while facing Daniel and turning his back to the human. 'Ah yes, you do know what it means if our dear Israfil is meaning to play his most prized instrument, don't you?'

Daniel's smile evaporated instantly. 'I'm well aware Liam; hence my insistence on seeing you immediately.'

'You should be rushing to the Quagmire, that you should,' Liam thought as he returned to the wall to tinker with some vials.

'Oh? And why is that may I ask?' Daniel thought.

'Simple, mate; one must not tie a ship to a single anchor, nor life to a single hope.'

'Very true,' Daniel thought while returning his gaze to the young man. 'What of the human though? I feel I cannot leave him at the moment. It is quite hard to convince him of the truth for however obvious it may be.'

'I would imagine,' replied Liam in thought. 'We must make preparations to leave. Valencia also felt Sariel's presence and fears that her visit foreshadows something bigger that is on its way here.'

While the vampires continued to speak, Nathaniel was convinced they were too distracted to notice him palming a scalpel.

"Would you please put that down human?" Liam said out loud.

The corner of Liam's glowing eye faded when he turned back to Daniel. 'Go, Daniel. I'll look into the cardinal points but time is scant... even for us eternals. Lucky for you, I called ahead just in case. It comes in handy to have a Solomon Pool in a ship, wouldn't you agree?'

Daniel smiled and gave Liam a pat on the shoulder. "What would I do without you?" he said out loud. He then walked towards Nathaniel. "I have some business to attend to, Runnels. I shall leave you under the care of Liam for the time being. Pardon the sudden departure, but time is of the essence. There are people to get in touch with and actions to be set into motion if we are to have any sort of chance in this venture."

Nathaniel had a quizzical look not unlike that of a child who has just been given way too many instructions for him to fully internalize.

"I shall be in touch," added Daniel. "For now, I need you to cooperate with Liam. He's one of the few beings I'd trust with my life and you may do the same." He straightened his collar and walked towards the entrance. Before Nathaniel could react, the sash swished and a door slammed shut with the human barely getting half a syllable out of his mouth.

"He does that a lot, doesn't he?" Liam said.

Nathaniel rushed to the door. After stepping through, he realized that once again he was alone.

"You can come back in now," Liam called to remind him that he wasn't as alone as he thought.

Nathaniel walked back into the room slowly and reluctantly, like some first-grader who's just been abandoned at school or in a doctor's office.

Liam smiled with his cigarette still in his mouth, "Like I said human, I already had lunch so no need to worry."

This time, Nathaniel took the time to observe the vampire's features and how he moved; something he'd neglected doing until that very moment. Every single movement seemed to be half a step too fast.

"Pardon me if you mind my speed," Liam said while buzzing back and forth over the counter. "Unlike Daniel, I could care less if you're comfortable or not with my movements. I'm in a rush. By the way, come here, Nathaniel."

He hadn't turned around but he could feel the human's tense muscles and shortened breath while glasses clinked from his stirring. The vampire gritted his teeth and gave a deep breath. "If I meant to kill you, I would have done so by now. Don't think Daniel is the only reason you are still alive. We need you alive." "However, that does not mean you should give me any reason to hurt you because I can most certainly break you and put you back together, good as new. I'd also make sure the mending was done with a lot of pain because although I am normally the calm one of the group, I have reason enough to be on edge. And yes, vampires do get on edge, and no I'm not menstrual or mad and even less do I use drugs. So by all means, stop with the thinking. Now, please, come here and save me the trouble of having to wring your neck for you to do so."

The human's eyes remained blank as he walked towards the vampire. Liam then turned around in his grayish splendor with eyes ablaze and his cigarette half smoked. Gone was the dull pallor that tinged the iris in the garden replaced by an electric blue, clearly unsettling the human even more than he already was.

"The brightness is due to my level of concentration, Runnels," Liam said answering Nathaniel's question without having heard it. "Let's have a look at you." The piercing blue eyes were inches away as he inspected the human's eyes, open mouth, finger nails and other vitals, while never changing the focused doctor-like concentration.

"My apologies for my current mood, Runnels; but knowing of the angel's visit and what she said would put even the most cool-headed person in a state of flux. It's not a good omen and I fear plans shall need to be rushed more than would be ideal. And yes, as long as you don't know how to block your thoughts from me, I will know all you think. Follow me this way." Before Nathaniel could suggest his body to move as he had been told, Liam had gone through the fabric into the next room. Obviously he hesitated, especially being able to see the door to the passageway. But he knew better, it was obvious he didn't have a chance to escape, so he followed the vampire.

The room he entered was quite the paradox to the room they had just been in. The walls were stone and the only light available came from a dozen or so candles instead of fluorescent lights. Fine gold and bronze candelabra held each candle and the overall musk of the place had a certain essence to it not unlike a spice market at midday. It was pungent and smelled something on the lines of cinnamon, cedar, saffron, and freshly dug earth. It was oddly pleasant but unnervingly familiar. The contents of the room however, did not project any type of familiarity and in all honesty, the entire collection seemed alien to Nathaniel.

Various perches jutted out from the floor at regular intervals around the table. In other parts of the ample room, some even hung down from the ceiling. The ones on the floor were rudimentary yet solid bronze 'Ts' covered in odd etchings and symbols. At the end of the room awaited Liam, next to what appeared to be a perfect stone circle platform about two feet higher than the floor. To the right of Liam there was a gigantic lens about 5 feet in diameter held up vertically by another bronze stand and to the left of the circle, there was a metal table held up by only one leg on the back left side. Tears welled slightly in Nathaniel's eyes from the reddish mist floating through the entire room. The oval Dameos chamber had been bad in a way, but this room was so bizarre that it made the first one look quite hospitable in comparison.

Liam stood smiling beside the odd artifacts while lighting himself another cigarette. "Remember human, this used to be the home of angels; so please, don't blame the décor on us."

"Ok. So now what?" Nathaniel asked.

"Now you stand right... here." The vampire guided Nathaniel until he stood behind the giant lens. "Let's have a look now." Liam then pulled out a visor quite unlike anything the young man had seen. It had a smooth glass texture and the color of dark cherry wood. Liam breathed deeply and slowly raised the visor to his eyes. Two inches from his skin though, the object rushed out of his hand and clamped onto his face. He let out a little grunt and trickles of blood dripped down both sides of the gray face until he regained his composure.

"Pardon that," Liam said. "It's unpleasant but necessary. Now, where were we?" The vampire licked his lips and clicked his tongue as he concentrated on his human specimen. It was obvious that Nathaniel was uncomfortable, for it almost felt like that big lens and the visors left him naked to the vampire's eye.

"Don't worry, human; these aren't X-ray. But I must say; now I understand why Daniel has been fussing so much about you."

Yet again Nathaniel found himself dumbstruck and confused by something said to him. This was a trend he was easily getting to hate.

"Ok," Liam said peeking over the side of the lens with his visor. "Think back to when Daniel spoke of cardinal points. Your average vampire or therian has about six to ten cardinal points. Some have more, many have less, but that's a pretty fair ballpark. Daniel himself actually has thirteen and I have eleven. Do you follow?"

Silence.

"That would classify as a no," Liam said.

"All I know is that I know nothing," quoted Nathaniel.

"Ah..." Liam said taking the cigarette in his hand to smile freely. "Socrates."

"I noticed you enjoy Greek philosophy when you quoted Epictetus and Plutarch."

"Oh ho!!" Liam shouted. "That is a surprise. I'm glad you noticed. Daniel just nods and accepts what I say as wise most times without knowing what I'm even talking about."

In response, Nathaniel offered the closest thing to a smile one could manage if one were held captive and being stared at through a gigantic ochre tinged lens by a weird cannibalistic visor-wearing vampire.

"Thanks for the effort," Liam said reacting to the limp smile.

A vampire that also happened to be able to read minds.

"He is a man of sense who does not grieve for what he has not, but rejoices in what he has," Liam said.

Nathaniel scoffed. "And what might I have? I currently don't have freedom, don't have health, don't have..."

"A pair of fangs on your neck? A blade running you through the heart? Sunlight burning you alive? The need to drink blood? The realization that the world might truly end if you along with various already acquired and potential colleagues fail? Trust me, human, there is always something to give thanks for. You just have to want to see those things."

Liam stood aside from the lens and put his hands against the visor. He breathed deeply and tugged onto the latched visor prying at his flesh and after a short struggle showed two small gouges dripping dark blood on either side of his face. The pale blue had come back into his eyes but the iris of his eyes flashed with a variety of colors for a second or two, a reaction quite familiar given his previous captor.

"Don't think me like Daniel, human," said the vampire as he wiped the thin crimson streaks on his face as the small wounds mended. "His condition is far more advanced than mine."

"Condition?" Nathaniel asked confused by the word chosen by the vampire.

"His eyes are unlike anything I've ever seen," Liam said. "They react to each emotion he has. It used to be flashes of colors but now his eyes shift constantly and it has gotten to the point where he can at times control the particular shade of color, while other times he can't. It's because of the artifacts we've told you about and the amount of time he's used them. There isn't much we can do for him because we don't even know what the nature of his condition is. It could be an insignificant side effect, it could be something benign or it could be something malign. We really don't know. As for you though, I can remedy some of your complaints. Sit down on the table."

Nathaniel looked at the vampire cross-faced. Not only was he expected to lay down so a vampire could further examine him, but the table he was being invited to get up on had only one leg... a dainty looking leg at that.

"Trust me, it can more than hold your weight," Liam replied to Nathaniel's thoughts. He lit another cigarette and smiled at the hesitant human. "It's simple, mate: we can do this the easy way or the hard way. Vampires are a lot more practical than you would think, though I may just be speaking in regards to myself."

"Ok..." Nathaniel said as he neared the table.

"Remember, human, in the world of knowledge, the idea of good appears last of all, and is seen only with great effort. So please, make the effort."

Nathaniel took one last look at the table before responding. "All right, and that was Socrates again, right?"

The vampire smiled and nodded. "Now get on the damn table. You fuss more than a child trying to avoid a vaccine."

Nathaniel looked at the single-legged table once more. He pushed and pressed until finally deciding to ease onto it. The odd furniture did not tremble, creak, twist or fall; it did not even budge. It stood firm and held up his weight as if one had just placed a paperweight on top. The material was metallic but it wasn't cold like the tables in a doctor's office.

"Do your best to get comfortable," Liam said. "Actually, have you ever been to a chiropractor?"

Out of all the things Nathaniel might have been prepared to answer if asked, this was surely one of the most obscure queries that was not on any list of particular topics he'd think would be of interest to a vampire.

"So you know of it but have never been to one, that's fine," responded Liam without Nathaniel having uttered one word. "Well that random question I just asked you not forty seconds ago has everything to do with those precise points. If I lose you, feel free to ask away in your mind."

Nathaniel simply nodded and took a deep breath in response to yet another order.

"Cardinal points are like pressure points or chakras. They're spread throughout your body in a specific way to distribute and administer your energy. These can sometimes get blocked or obstructed and when cleared, abilities can blossom. Your senses are honed and what you normally wouldn't be able to hear or see is now your reality instead of a mere possibility."

The vampire waited a moment as he verified if the human understood. When he was satisfied with what he saw in his mind's eye, he continued. "To understand better, why don't we unblock some of your cardinal points?" Liam let his hands glide over Nathaniel and paused over his eyes. "First sight, then hearing," he said. "Then we'll see where we go from there."

With a sudden strike, Liam's nails sharply jabbed at Nathaniel's temples. Saying it felt like lighting shooting out of his eyes wouldn't be too far from what he actually felt. After the strike, Liam held a palm over the young man's chest pinning him down until the shockwaves of pain subsided. Nathaniel seemed dazed and his eyes were glassy with tears.

"What do you see?" the vampire asked.

It was quite a challenge to express the answer in words. Nathaniel gasped as every texture in the room jumped at him. Every contour was apparent and nothing seemed as dismally dark as had been the case less than a minute ago. If he focused enough, he could even see dust particles floating through the room. Liam then walked to a far wall and began to scratch tiny etchings as Nathaniel rose from the table. The vampire finished his work quickly and then looked at his human patient. "Can you see the writing on the wall?"

Nathaniel cleared his eyes and saw how the dark wall now seemed clear as day: He who submits to fate without complaint is wise. – Euripides. He turned and smiled to the doctor.

"Sit, Nathaniel," Liam said. "Let me now help your hard of hearing."

The human obliged by sitting down on the one legged table again. No hesitation, no fear, just as if there were three more legs to the thing. His newfound doctor continued to look over him. He was now at the end of the table where his head was, once again letting his hands flow over the patient's head and shoulders. His hands briefly glided over the neck as fangs got malicious ideas. Luckily temperance prevailed.

Both of Nathaniel's earlobes were now between Liam's thumbs and forefingers and after a twist and jab behind the ears, lighting struck again. Thunder now blasted through the man's eardrums. Again Liam pressed down hard on Nathaniel's chest to keep him from flying off the table.

"Let it settle down a bit," Liam whispered in what was the slightest, faintest murmur for any normal ear, yet a booming roar to Nathaniel.

The audio finally settled and Liam took out a small pin, which he showed to Nathaniel along with a tiny black pebble no larger than a kernel of black pepper.

"Oops," said the vampire as the small speck fell to his feet. "Could you get that for me?"

With one look, Nathaniel knelt down and found the pebble. While he was kneeling, Liam threw the pin clear across the room.

"Whoops again," he repeated with a cynical smile. "Could you get that too?"

Nathaniel didn't flinch. He knew exactly where the pin had landed. Upon handing the vampire his pin back, he did not need a map to understand what had been meant by blocked abilities.

"Exactly," replied the vampire as he puffed on a freshly lit cigarette. "Now you understand and now we're getting somewhere. How's your health been the last couple of years?"

The human didn't need additional instructions. He sat on the table again.

"Face down this time," the vampire ordered to which Nathaniel obeyed willingly. "Now about chiropractic; if you didn't know, the first thing to develop in your body when you're just a tiny bunch of cells still deciding to live is the nervous system along with your spinal cord. This organ pretty much defines your body. As your center of energy, it is best to keep it nice and healthy, straight enough to be considered optimal while still maintaining natural contours and having it be free from any type of blockage."

Nathaniel nodded as once again Liam began to scan up and down the human's body now indicating him to take his shirt off.

"Why do I have to take my shirt off for?" Nathaniel asked.

"I need to see as best as possible to unblock each and every subluxation in your vertebrae. Subluxations are deviations in your spinal cord. These are caused by piss-poor posture, injuries and other things. Now could you please take off your shirt?"

It took a moment but finally, Nathaniel sat up, undid his shirt and quickly lay down again.

"Relax human, I can control myself and then some," Liam said as he now coated his fingertips with reddish lacquer that smelled of earth and the slightest hint of cinnamon. "Breathe deeply, please."

After various slow deep breaths, Nathaniel's back was covered in dots and Liam now aligned his fingers with ten of the dots strewn across the man's back. There were a total of twenty. Inhale. Exhale. Inhale. Exhale. Inhale... Exhale... Inhale..... then another massive bolt of electricity shot through Nathaniel's body as sharp, rigid fingernails dug deep into the skin. Without giving time to let the pain subside, Liam shifted to the ten other dots and cracked the entire spinal column, bringing the pain to a crescendo three times as intense as it had been a second before. It didn't end there though. With a fluid motion, Liam took his index, middle and thumb fingers and burrowed at the base of Nathaniel's skull, causing the human to wail and roar uncontrollably. The flames of pain eventually died down and the trembling body slowly ebbed until it finally relaxed; renewed, rejuvenated and booming with energy.

Liam finally let go and walked towards the metal disc Nathaniel had initially been stepping on. He gave it a hard kick and the circle slid down with a heavy thud to show that beneath lay a fizzing reddish pool that glowed. The vampire then hobbled wearily to a corner and picked up a large dusty vase that had been on the floor. He slid tiredly towards a short pillar with a plate on top and after cleaning its surface, got some water from the pool and poured it onto the large plate.

He wasn't looking at Nathaniel but spoke loud enough so he could hear. "This, my sapien friend, is one of the Pools of Solomon." Liam's voice was an exhausted gasp. He was apparently quite spent after his exertion, but he continued with his explanation. "In large amounts it is a healing bath you may take advantage of right now and in small amounts, it functions as an oracle of sorts." When he turned, Liam saw the young man naked and stepping into the bubbling red pool.

"That's the spirit," said the weary vampire while taking another cigarette between his lips and lighting it. "Sit tight while we see if we can get a nice glimpse of the future."

Liam swirled the water and puffed smoke down onto the surface. Both hands trailed his nails on the surface, tracing intricate patterns. "Interesting..." he said as his eyes reflected in the red pool. "Just as I suspected. On their way and almost here. Damn it! Daniel thought it'd take longer but he was gravely mistaken. I've got to warn the others and we all need to get out of here right---"

The sentence was left unfinished and Liam's body lay unconscious beneath a bronze candlestick held by a dripping red stained body.

Chapter 9: The way out is in?

Nathaniel dressed quickly. It didn't matter if his entire body was still soaked in red water. It didn't matter if he was shaking with the burning flame of adrenaline coursing through his veins. This had been his opportunity and he was going to make the most of it. He had looked around for any weapon that didn't look like it came from a board game, but the candlestick appeared to be his only option.

On his way out, he passed the limp body of Liam and became aware of a swelling feeling tingling through all his muscles from whatever the vampire and the red water had done to him. He looked back at the pool thinking of how he had just submerged his entire body, head and all, going as far as to risk drinking the red liquid out of instinct in hopes of finding the way out he so desperately needed.

He rushed out of the room and started running down the corridor. The doors passed a lot quicker this time around and he didn't have to strain his eyes at all to see in the darkness. About halfway down the passage, he heard something that caught his attention. His eyes darted back and forth in quick bursts while his ears perked and caught sound of a gentle moan. Round and round he searched for the source of the noise until he caught hold of where it was coming from. Behind one of the clone doors a weak muffled whimper accompanied the rhythmic gnawing of flesh. On either side of the door, a familiar glow shone brightly.

"Aneil," he said out loud, as he read the label.

The moaning stopped as did the gnawing and Nathaniel did not wait around to see if the word had caught the attention of whatever was behind the door. He was actually a hundred feet away when

Valencia stepped into the dim light of the corridor with blood streaming from her mouth. She hissed and bared her teeth when she realized who had just interrupted her meal.

Aneil, aneil, aneil. The bright word had almost become a steady humming glow as Nathaniel streaked down the tunnel. He'd heard the rain crashing outside ever since he'd left the room where Liam still slept comfortably numb and had worried he might find his path blocked. He was quite happy to see that his luck had turned for the better and that the garden gate was open.

The rain beat down hard and it wasn't until Nathaniel was in the middle of the garden that he saw a white figure with dark, straight black hair standing in front of the only entrance he had not explored from the central garden. The figure wore a white tunic and held a brilliant white rose against his chest while smiling coldly, rain dripping from every faction. Seeing his choices rather slimmed down, Nathaniel ran across the center of the garden knowing his life pretty much depended on his speed at the moment.

The figure stood by and did nothing while Nathaniel reentered the Dameos corridor. His muscles tightened, tendons became taut, breathing flared and damp footsteps schlepped soggily down the narrow corridor that abruptly opened up in a wide crossing. He remembered it clearly and without much thought turned to his right storming down the dark path that was now impressively clear with his new sight.

"Bisfernum," he gasped as he could easily read the word even though the walls were several yards away and he was running at top speed. Actually, it was faster than he could have even thought he could run. "Another label, another tunnel," he told himself in between strides. "This must lead somewhere, damn it. Let's hope it's a way out."

He ran intensely but still didn't feel winded. He could easily see everything in the corridor and the smell and taste of the passage trickled with every detail. But two other senses had him at unease. For one, he could hear everything. His damp footsteps echoing down the corridor, the rain outside and a droning hum that was slowly increasing in intensity with every foot he gained in the corridor. To further promote his trajectorial dilemma, ahead there was a fork in the road. But that wasn't the problem.

He could feel something terribly wrong. Something was off-key and aggravatingly disconcerting. A moustache on the Mona Lisa, an extra chapter in a book, a discordant note within the symphony. Even as he slowed down, the hum continued to grow in intensity. Louder and louder until he could hear it all around, but he had reached the fork and a choice had to be made.

"Left or right? Heads or tails? Eenie, meenie, miny... oh for heaven's sake!!!" His scream of frustration bounced hard into the corridor. He knew that whatever the choice, now was the time to make it since he'd probably given up his location after his idiotic outburst. So he turned right and sped down the arching path of this section of the Bisfernum corridor.

Everything was crystal clear and it was still a little hard getting used to the clarity of his vision. It was like comparing the resolution of a thirteen-inch TV, circa 1973, and the precision of a high definition plasma screen kindly priced in the mid three-thousands at your local super store. The humming continued to get louder and he asked himself just how high the volume could go even though he still didn't have a clue as to what he was doing, where he was going or what was even making the sound. He just knew he had to go forwards. He continued to run until he was suddenly forced to skid to a halt.

It wasn't that he was winded (hardly as a matter of fact). He had stopped because before him knelt a dark figure veiled in a deep green tunic. It was facing the opposite direction and although he would have thought it was a statue chiseled in a position of a prayer, that idea lost all merit when the figure started getting up.

As the figure rose, it stretched its back and quite suddenly what Nathaniel had thought was a tunic split and spread into two large wings while the figure continued to hum its prayer. It turned around just as slow as it had risen and in its hand Nathaniel saw a long chain that looped around its neck shining bright green. It was actually a rosary, cross and everything, but the downcast eyes failed to make contact with Nathaniel as the prayer continued. Nathaniel still did not know what to do so he made an attempt at being logical and practical in a situation that truly did not call for either.

"What are you doing?" he asked the angel.

The downcast eyes opened wide and two green flames looked at Nathaniel, stoic, unmoving, unblinking. The angel then spoke in a gentle voice, "I'm praying for you to make the right decision."

As the figure spoke, a sudden shine came from the cross and caught Nathaniel's eye. It was quite atypical for a cross to give such a glow and the reason was simple. Most crosses weren't filed to have an edge that sharp. No thought went to his next move. He just turned around and sprinted as hard and fast as he could to leave the angel praying to whatever the hell he wanted to pray to.

He gasped and panted and really did not have the slightest interest to look back. Speeding like mad, the fork quickly came into view again and he just stormed by the entrance he'd come through and kept going forwards to the path he had originally overlooked. For a moment the passage leaned right and he just hoped the corridor was not a full circle.

The ethereal smoothness stretched on but Nathaniel noticed that the light got dimmer the further he went. He continued his run focusing on finding an exit when he suddenly found himself missing a step, and plummeting into a gigantic void. The blackness was absolute, the air was stale and he could have sworn that the icy cold grip of death had just clasped him by the throat.

The reality was much different. What felt like jagged crystal shards ripped into Nathaniel's throat while his feet dangled three feet above the ground, mere inches from the abyss he had been falling into. Any scream or plea he might have had failed to reach the air as he struggled to even breathe. That's because Daniel was making sure to tighten his vice-like grip more than enough to silence him while ignoring the rumble growing in the background.

"You idiotic, ungrateful, excuse for flesh!" spat the vampire menacingly, biting on every syllable. "How dare you defecate upon all I've done for you? Shelter you. Protect you from harm and heal you.

And these are the thanks the magnanimous Runnels offers? The others were right to want to feed on you and end your miserable existence."

The green eyes burned even more terribly than they had done so in the Dameos chamber. Daniel's tone rose and his grip squeezed further. "I show you the truth and such is your appreciation? I call off my brethren and here I witness your gratitude first hand; a dung pile for gold!"

A drop of blood specked on the ground from the wounds on Nathaniel's neck but the blood he smelled was from the vampire's breath. 'He's been feeding,' he thought.

"I tell you of the ancients, I've saved you twice from therians you didn't even know were after you and I was even willing to fight off that angel wench and her beast and this, THESE are the thanks I get? A buffoon primate pawn puppetted by the very society he despises yet when offered the truth and a way out of his fecally stained life, he runs away and takes those who want to help him and stabs them cohesively in their backs, twisting and grinding the knife of betrayal ever so gently with each step and each stride intended for escape. Why? Why? WHYYYYY? Why if I save you should you condemn the very hand that saves? Why is the peace we offer trampled on? Shelter, the truth you covet, aid, your wellbeing, nourishment... all these and in return what do I get? Protection and compassion for you, and what is there for me?"

Even on the verge of unconsciousness, Nathaniel could still hear beyond the verbal bombardment he was enduring, something more foul and frightening than the roar of a vampire that was seconds away from ending his life. Something more evil was just about to arrive. Daniel let go of Nathaniel's neck when he finally realized the answer to his question about what he would receive for all his trouble.

"Shit."

With a sudden crash, the hum Nathaniel had been hearing transformed into a roaring tidal wave of war cries reaching out from the abyss accompanied by a foul air that breathed rhythmically in and out of the void. Stench, plague and the echoes of a thousand leathery wings screeched from the darkness.

"Runnels," said Daniel without even looking at him, "do not look down or back, just run." The cries gave way to bodies that began flying up from the void and crashing against the ceiling. The situation completely twisted the concepts of time and space and the corridor suddenly seemed three times as long as Daniel pushed so they could keep ahead of the horde whose claws and talons tore behind them in pursuit.

The long curve eased now to the left and as the exit came into view, they realized loud grunting was about twenty yards behind them. Nathaniel kept focused on the exit and ran a straight line but that didn't mean he didn't notice the glint of metal as Daniel drew his sword. "Don't look back, human! Just go to the garden and take the first right; I'll catch up."

The vampire then disappeared from Nathaniel's side and stood to face the demonic landslide that roared from behind. Nathaniel followed the instructions impeccably, running full speed to get to the garden. No amount of shrieking, bone cracking or blood spatters would deter him from reaching the light. He smelled musky earth, and heard the rain still falling. He was nearing the exit fast and could see the dim light being split by thick sheets of downpour. Behind him, talons and claws slashed the corridor floor while heaving grunts prompted the young man to run faster still.

Jumping through the opening, Nathaniel broke through a sheet of water to reach the garden. He was already leaning to the right when he heard a terrible growl right above him, just before a cold slimy body slammed him against the floor with all of its weight. The smell was horrid, like burnt fur with sulfur and bile, but there was no movement. No claws tearing at his flesh, no teeth ripping his skin off or shearing his bones, just dead weight... literally.

He struggled and squirmed until he was finally able to shove the limp body off him and see what it was. His body shook involuntarily and Nathaniel's head didn't want to believe what his eyes were seeing. Its skin was leathery and black-brown; its yellow eyes were bloodshot.

There were scars throughout its entire torso and the long hairy arms had three sharp claws where fingers should be on a human hand. A look of confusion had been embedded on its face, an expression courtesy of an ivory rose that hung impaled from the side of the creature's head.

Looking around frantically, Nathaniel could not see anyone or anything except a trail of white petals leading to the gate on the right. He finally got to his feet and sped into the corridor he'd been sent to pinning his hopes on the new trail and totally oblivious to the wings flapping above near the rooftop.

Meanwhile, Daniel had been quite busy in the short time they'd been separated. He had become a one-man wall holding the demons at bay and obliterating most everything that came within his grasp or that of his starving rapier. Thick dollops of petrol seemed to splatter with every swipe he connected on the beasts and though he had been pressed and actually pushed back a few feet, the floor was covered in severed limbs while the jade fire continued to burn in his eyes. "Any limb you offer shall be mine!!!!" he screamed at them.

He swirled and kicked and roared like a maddened tornado. Horde after horde went to their doom as they faced the meat grinder. The blade was green black from all the blood from the several dozen that had fallen from his sword when he realized something. These weren't elite soldiers and upon slashing a demon arm clean off and seeing it fall to the floor, he saw that those claws weren't meant for combat. They were meant for digging.

"Runnels!!!" he screamed and cleaved a path towards the garden.

Nathaniel continued to run intensely. He ignored the stitch in his side and disregarded his flaming lungs. He just wanted to get out and catching eye of the glowing words, he realized he was in the Aneil corridor again.

He thought to himself, 'Isn't that the name of the other corridor? Did I get into the wrong tunnel? I'm sure I turned right and I had come from the left. I'm totally sure.' But before he could reach any type of conclusion, two wrecking balls crashed into his chest sending him tumbling like a pinball twenty feet backwards in the corridor.

He was just barely able to make out two yellow dots glowing in the dark. The paused and deliberate growling complemented the scraping talons while the predator gave all its attention to the scuffling man that had almost been broken in half by its fists. "Mmmm..... human," cracked a snarling growl. "I haven't had human in ages."

Nathaniel did not need a second invitation to ignore the pain, get up and run back to the garden.

***

Daniel vaulted out of the tunnel. The layer of demon blood that had covered him began to peel off his skin from the pouring rain. But even before he had gotten out of the tunnel he had heard a commotion outside. He had a few thoughts of what it could have been, but nothing like this. Part of the Magdalena brood was fighting against a hundred or so flying demons. Their black wings spread wide as many took turns swooping down while others surrounded them on the ground.

Daniel did not lose focus for a second. "Time to break the line," he said as he readied his blades.

All trees had been torn from the roots or chopped down and Malia, Vincenzo, and Lucas were on one side. Malia had run out of arrows, which would explain why she was ripping branches and using them as ammunition at the moment. Vincenzo swung a triple staff with blade tips at both ends and Lucas swiped at the demons with a long spear. The bodies that began falling behind them were the product of Daniel's ravenous rapier that continually freed the captive blood from the demons' bodies. When he was within earshot, he called out to Malia. "Where are the others?"

"I don't know!!" she replied as sycamore branches continued to fly and one even ripped into the eyes of one of the demons. At that moment, all vampires were able to hear a distinctly clear voice in their heads offering one perfectly simple suggestion.

'Hit the floor.'

All vampires obeyed and two mechanical banshees screamed with the arrival of Indigo and a pair of Gatling guns.

Black chunks of flesh flew all over as bones broke, wings were severed and the hundred goblins faced what seemed like a thousand times their number in bullets. After a full half minute's worth of ammunition, the garden had been wiped clean of anything that wasn't a vampire.

"Miss me?" asked Indigo. He dropped his guns and helped his comrades get up from the floor while Liam walked alongside puffing a cigarette.

"How could we ever survive without the sweetness that is Indigo?" replied Daniel. He then nodded to his friend and simply said his name. "Liam."

'Yes sir!' answered the telepath in his brain.

"Would you do me a favor and close up the gate I came through?" said Daniel out loud; "I'm truly not in the mood to entertain pests at the moment."

'Gladly,' the doctor replied in his mind. The ashen vampire walked a couple of steps and picked a grapefruit sized grenade from his vest to lob in the direction of the Dameos corridor entrance. A huge purple fireball spat from within the tunnel and the entrance crumbled upon itself, thus sealing it shut.

"Good, good," Daniel said. "And the others?"

Liam dispensed with the telepathy and answered out loud. "Mariana went to the tower to verify the arrival of our transportation. Claus and Efia went down the southern Aneil corridor to open a path for us."

Daniel nodded and then asked, "What of Valencia and Edward Louis?"

Liam looked rather somber, "No news... as for the human—"

He would have finished, but a heavy thud interrupted him to answer Daniel's question. Nathaniel had been thrown to the ground where he now lay gasping on the floor, badly battered and unconscious.

Daniel's eyes immediately flared into jade fire. "Liam, tend to him. Everyone else, kindly draw your weapons. This might get a bit rough."

Malia had already gotten two-dozen thick branches and had pulled various arrows from the dead bodies. Indigo drew two huge machetes from their sheaths. They then formed a line next to their leader. A huge roar erupted from the corridor Nathaniel had flown out of and the entrance belched grotesquely before something was sent soaring out of the opening. Something that hit the floor and rolled swiftly until stopping at Daniel's feet.

"Claus..." he said in barely a whisper.

A young boy's severed head held broken fangs and his lost eyes stared directly at his leader. Any final words had been lost, along with the rest of his body. Red tears fell upon the severed head before Daniel spoke through grit teeth, "Hello, Gressil."

"Daniel... you remember me," slithered a slimy crackle of a snarl. "It's been sooooo long."

Out of the gate emerged an abomination like some twisted gargoyle. It was brown-green in color, followed by a tail the size of a full-grown python.

"Somehow I don't think I can fathom it ever being long enough without seeing you, demon," Daniel said. "Would you care to tell me why you're here or should I simply run you through and get it over with?"

Before the beast could answer, the gate directly behind the group exploded and two pitch black bodies crashed to the floor and skidded to a stop some feet away. This time the eyes weren't of a friend but yellow and bloodshot, more goblins. Valencia and another vampire ran out of the corridor followed by a new horde of the digging beasts. Daniel looked on grimly as the scene unfolded.

"The human's patched up sir, I'm on the gate," Liam said as he ran forth to meet the oncoming wave.

Daniel casually flicked his sword and yelled in a deep voice, "Children! Let's play!!!"

The vampires obeyed their leader and shot out in different directions to break up the wall of bodies. Meanwhile, Daniel stood in front of the beast. "As for you and me, dear Gressil, may I have this dance?"

Behind them, Nathaniel was already fully recovered. Liam had made some adjustments on his battered body and given him more water infused with egnalem. As he felt his body heal, he looked upon the scene. Demons all around were falling dead on the floor while the ground further soaked in their foul blood. Malia continued to shoot down goblins with branches or arrows. Indigo sliced clear through the mid sections of some of the creatures and also beheaded two or three at a time with one strong swing. The others did their part to hold back the horde from Liam so he could get them another gift bomb.

Valencia and the new vampire fought bare handed, ripping through demon skin and twisting necks and limbs 'til they felt the welcome crack of bone.

"Behind you, Edward!!!" screamed the icy vampire as the vampire that had come with her ducked just in time to avoid a rudimentary axe that had been swung with vile intent. For its efforts, the vampire relieved the goblin of its eyes and ripped its jaw clean off.

Nathaniel continued to look on, almost catatonic while the ruthless fight raged on. Daniel struck at the demon but only managed to pounce on empty ground.

"Come on, Daniel!" Gressil snarled as pints of drool sloshed on the floor. "I'm starvinggg..."

Daniel attempted to offer his blade as a meal, but was parried by a giant razor sharp claw. Vincenzo on the other hand had been segregated and surrounded. He swung his triple staff slashing through dozens of the goblins but one was able to latch onto the staff that had actually run him through. He inverted the staff and cut the goblin's arms but not without getting tackled by twenty or more of the creatures.

"Let go of me!!!!" he wailed as he lost control but the only reply was getting pinned down and having the dying goblin he'd run through hoisted over his head. The beast ripped the massive wound in its stomach even wider to spill all its black blood down the helpless vampire's mouth. "Drink me up darling..." it hissed. It then laughed until it took its last breath looking straight into the eyes of the vampire it was drowning with its bile and blood.

Bodies began falling and a path towards the fallen Magdalenean was being forcibly forged by two sizeable blades.

"Get up!!!" roared Indigo as he saw Vincenzo free from the group of goblins but writhing on the floor and unable to get up.

Indigo swung at a few more creatures before hoisting his fallen comrade and tossing him fifteen yards over the crowd of goblins to land at the feet of the very vampire that was now tossing a grenade towards the sieged entrance. "Fire in the sky!!!" screamed Liam and then another huge fireball crashed against the goblins and brought down the entrance they were coming out from.

"Hear that?!" Daniel spat. "That means we're near closing time."

The beast replied by snapping at him with its massive jaws. Daniel easily avoided that strike but the massive tail slammed against his chest sending him reeling and falling backwards. He was just in time to look up at the demon that was now on its hind legs ready to crush the vampire when it suddenly buckled falling backwards to the ground and bellowing in pain. Its right leg lay five feet from the rest of the body. It had been cut off clean and now lay bleeding freely on the grass. The author of the cut stood behind the demon with a sword in hand and eyes glazed with hatred.

"Thank you, Runnels," Daniel said as he got up. Lucas, Indigo and Edward Louis took the opportunity and impaled the beast's three remaining limbs.

"As for you," continued Daniel to the fallen Gressil; "I believe you have something that belongs to us."

He walked to the demon and looked down in disgust. The rapier swung and the sound of flesh slicing was followed by cracking ribs. With three strokes, the demon's entire upper torso had been filleted opened. Daniel sheathed his sword and dug his arm deep into the bowels of the writhing demon. He was up to his shoulder when he came along what he was looking for and with a strong tug pulled out the beheaded body of a young boy.

"Claus will be buried with his brothers, dear Gressil. You'd be insane to think for one instant that I would allow you to desecrate his memory by literally defecating his remains."

No one dared speak and Daniel didn't mind the silence. The beast writhed even with all its insides spilled on the garden floor in a black pool beside him. Daniel meanwhile let the rain wash his filthy arm and then walked to Nathaniel. He turned to glance at the demon before looking the human straight in the eye. "The only way to return a Hound of Hell is with Heaven's Fire. Come with me. We need to get some things before we depart."

Nathaniel could only nod. Daniel looked onto the torn central garden and spoke to his comrades. "Say goodbye, children. It is time to leave Eden. Liam, please prepare the detonators, timer included and set them at both of the blocked entrances. I'd say eight minutes time would be ideal but feel free to adjust as you see necessary."

"Yes, my lord," Liam replied as he made his way to his bag.

Daniel turned to the others, "Indigo, Malia and Edward, double check the grounds and be sure to dispose of any wounded guest that might still be slithering about."

"Yes, my lord," they replied in tandem.

"Valencia and Lucas. Clean the body of our Claus and be sure to find a casket for him... a good one." Daniel looked at Vincenzo and after a brief pause said: "make sure to bind him and find a box for him as well. We'll see what can be done for him soon enough."

"Aye, m'lord," they said.

"Runnels, with me." With that, the vampire pulled Nathaniel by the shoulder and in little more than a second they were at the far wall and Daniel introduced the knife to open the door. Again Nathaniel was hauled by the shoulder and found himself flying down the tunnel until they reached Daniel's room. The vampire unlocked the door, disappeared into the dark and in an instant had the lights on. Nathaniel followed into the den where he was handed a very large duffle bag. "Take the books and all the journals in that row," Daniel ordered as he signaled to a specific set of books on the cabinet. "I'll be but a moment."

The vampire took a few steps towards one bookshelf and taking one step to the right seemed to vanish into the wall. Nathaniel didn't quite understand and then stepped towards the bookshelf himself. When he leaned against the wall and looked to the right he saw a small study hidden by the angle of the wall. In it was a desk with an array of keepsakes including a wind-up soldier toy, a series of Chinese ivory figures in different sexual positions, some pictures and a crucifix as Daniel finished putting a waxed seal on one of various envelopes.

"Done?" asked the vampire without looking.

"Ummm..." replied the confused human as the vampire tidied up his desk as if he were cleaning up at the office.

"Umm is not an answer, Runnels. Get the books so we can be off."

Nathaniel returned to the main room, piled the books in the bag and returned to the study in about a minute's time. "Done."

"Excellent. Let us be off then."

He took the stack of envelopes and put them in the pocket of a new coat he had put on while also taking a pistol, some swords, the crucifix and the wind-up toy. Outside, Daniel told Nathaniel to wait one moment as he walked towards the entrance of the corridor where they had met up with the angel Sariel. He wound up the toy some thirteen times while walking down the tunnel, set it on the ground lining it up perfectly with the other end of the corridor and let go. In an instant he rushed past Nathaniel, pulling him as they whooshed around corners. Nathaniel could just barely clutch to Daniel and found himself at the entrance in mere seconds. Out in the garden, Liam was the only one waiting.

"The others found Efia wounded but she will make it," Liam said. "Unfortunately, Vincenzo is already much worse my lord. Apart from that, all hands accounted for."

"Good," replied Daniel. "I take it the bombs are set so I think it's about time we were on our way."

They were walking towards the exit corridor when Daniel stopped.

"Almost forgot," he said as he dropped the bags and walked towards the still wailing Gressil. The demon tried to move but all of its limbs were firmly impaled by the three spears.

Daniel knelt and whispered into the foul thing's ear, "Listen here, you revolting congregation of waste. You are going to die real soon and do you know what else? You will get to see your little friends die as well. So if by any chance you happen to have any last words that include blaspheming any human God, this might help."

He opened his coat and took out the gold crucifix that had been on his desk. The vampire looked at the perfectly tailored figure, kissed it lovingly and drove it straight through the demon's larynx. He stood up, cleared his throat and walked to his companions. "Off we go," he said while wiping his hands clean on a handkerchief that lit on fire before he threw it on the floor.

Nathaniel was once again hoisted by the shoulder as they quickly flew right by the point he'd gotten to in the tunnel where he'd met Gressil. A left and a right and they were suddenly soaring upwards in a vent that seemed to be labeled...

"Necima," he said out loud.

"You see, Liam?" Daniel responded as they continued to soar upwards. "It might seem like something simple but this ability doesn't cease to amaze me, even if you did unblock his cardinals."

The ascent continued and a spot on the corridor had splashes of blood. Nathaniel thought that maybe that's where Claus had met his untimely end. Higher they climbed and he clutched to the bags because he knew his life depended on it. One final powerful leap and they landed in a small lush area full of trees, which was in essence a miniature version of the central Eden Garden that lay in ruins below.

The entire crew was there. Malia, Valencia, Edward, Lucas, Indigo, the rattling box containing Vincenzo, a quiet cedar coffin, and two beautiful women, one tending to the other.

"All heads counted for?" Daniel asked, ignoring the poor taste of the pun he'd inadvertently said.

"Yes, m'lord," Valencia answered.

Daniel looked at one of the beautiful vampires, "Mariana, any news of the transport?"

The female vampire tending to her wounded companion finished dressing the wound and rose. Tight black clothing clenched to her voluptuous yet solid body as she walked towards her leader. Her soft brown hair flowed over a gentle face, delicate eyes and features that hinted at Romanian or Italian descent. "At the docks already my lord."

"Good, it's been a while since I've seen your sisters. It'll be good to catch up. Anyways my friends, the clock is ticking so let's pick up the pace."

With orders stated, all gathered around a well that was at the far end of the small garden. Nathaniel was a bit confused but after all, when was the last time he'd been in any type of a situation that could be deemed normal?

Lucas and Indigo hoisted the coffin containing Vincenzo onto the edge of the well and dove in without a second thought. Next were Liam and Edward Louis who pushed the cedar coffin with Claus's remains into the well.

"Eight minutes, right?" Daniel asked as he pulled out an old pocket watch much like Nathaniel's, just a century or three older.

"Yes, sir," replied Liam. "We're right on schedule. Three minutes to go."

"Very good, old friend. I'll see you aboard."

"Aye," Liam said as now he and Edward followed down the well.

"Ladies, if you'd be so kind," Daniel said as one by one, each of the women vanished down the hole. First Malia, then Efia, then Mariana and lastly Valencia but not before giving Nathaniel her frigid stare.

"We'll be right after you, dear," Daniel said encouragingly. "Now go." And she went.

Daniel took the human's hand within his and gave it a firm shake. "Runnels, thank you for the assistance below. You might have just saved my life. I hope you continue to give reason for praise instead of punishment."

Nathaniel breathed deep but didn't cower, thus prompting a minor standoff between him and the vampire that ended only when jade fire ebbed to ice blue and a smile exposed two extremely long fangs.

"You truly never cease to amaze me," the vampire said. "Now down the chute. This isn't a well and you don't need to fly. Just jump off and we're on our way."

"On our way to where?" Nathaniel asked.

"Get up on this ledge," Daniel said.

"What for?" asked the human.

"So you can see where we're going," the vampire said.

He looked skeptical at first but quickly perched himself on the edge of the well.

"Can you see the ocean?" Daniel asked.

"Yes."

"Can you see the coast?" asked the vampire again.

"Yes."

"Can you see a black boat with black sails?"

"Yes."

"Then do the math." And with a firm push on Nathaniel's back, Daniel sent him crashing down the well while he snickered at the dirty trick before taking one last look at his watch. "Humans, you have to love them. Now off to my mistress the ocean." With that he jumped into the dark hole that led off to the coast.

Back in the central garden, a pair of yellow bloodshot eyes dilated as two massive explosions rocked with a huge blue flash that scorched into the sky. It took mere seconds for thousands of goblins to swarm onto the defiled garden where Gressil choked on his own blood and the lower half of a golden Christ. They were not the best conditions to explain what had happened, much less to try and warn them about the damage a little toy soldier could wreak on an army by just taking one more step over a curious star figure etched within a random corridor within a maze.

With its sails cast, the boat acquired speed quite rapidly, even though there was no perceivable wind. The deathly quiet of the ocean seemed like it could have swallowed a thunderstorm until back on the coast, a pillar of fire half a mile wide rose from what was once the Halo Maze.

Chapter 10: The Black Calico

Nathaniel's eyes glowed amber as they reflected the tower of flames. Without having to ask, he knew it had been the heptagram. On the sea, the entire ship meshed with the starless evening as the raging volcano that used to be the Halo Maze became a mere torchlight in the horizon they left behind. Small trickles of waves danced against the wooden hull and the sails ruffled soothingly. All of the Magdalena Brood stood top deck waiting to greet their saviors. Shadows seemed to twist and stretch until one after another, vampire women emerged from the thin veil of darkness they so deftly traversed in. Mariana for her part tied a delicate black ribbon to her right arm and saluted towards the helm.

"Report!" called out a strong female voice. Nathaniel could not see who spoke, but the voice came from the helm with purpose behind every syllable.

Mariana gave a small bow before addressing the helm. "M'lady, the Magdalena request your assistance and safe voyage across the Atlantic. We were ambushed in the maze by an enormous horde and it's truly the work of Lady Luck that most of us were fortunate enough to come away relatively unharmed."

"Most?" questioned the steel voice from the helm's shade.

"Yes, m'lady," Mariana answered. "We have one casualty, one wounded and one who was forcibly fed dark blood."

"I see," said the voice pausing momentarily. "Grace! Louise! Tend to the wounded. Give her fresh clothes and dress her wounds."

Two female vampires flowed out from the shadows. One had a long black mane tied in a lengthy braid and olive skin. The other had rosy white skin and reddish brown curls that hung lushly beyond the midpoint of her slender back. They made way towards the sleek and still elegant figure of Efia and helped her below deck.

Once again, the voice called out from the helm. "Cheng! Nelly!"

"Yes, m'lady," sang two more women emerging from the shadows. One looked of Asian descent while the other evoked Nordic traits, most probably Swedish or Norwegian.

"Take the cedar box and clean the body. It has a destination, a family and we must prepare it flawlessly. Treat the boy as one of ours."

Their orders given, the vampires obeyed, picking the coffin up effortlessly and disappearing below.

"My thanks, m'lady," Daniel said, feeling the need to say something at the moment.

"Silence, Montacre!" boomed the cold steel voice. "You have no place speaking at this moment."

Thick knocks banged on the deck of the helm as two light bright purple eyes broke through the haze followed by an elegant woman whose mere presence demanded attention. Soft porcelain skin and gentle factions did nothing to conceal her power and grace.

"I've lost count of how many times I've saved your ass," she spat towards the vampire. "Tell me, what can I do for the magnanimous Daniel of Montacre this time around? And please, save the pleasantries for someone who actually gives a damn."

"All right," said the vampire composing himself. "First and even if it is a pleasantry, my thanks to you for coming to our aid, for caring for our fallen and tending to the wounded. Now for our other needs: Passage to Spain and later through the Mediterranean and any other necessary destination we might need to go to."

"Would you like your potato baked, fried or mashed along with that order?" she scoffed. "Or perhaps this ship looks like a taxi to you, Daniel? At the very least humor me with a motive."

Daniel fought the urge to raise his voice. "Fine; you saw that wonderful light show we left near shore? That was a keepsake from Sariel."

Any trace of a smirk left the pirate captain's face. "What did she want?"

"I don't know. She simply pointed to Azrael's book and mentioned that Israfil seems to be tuning up."

The purple in her eyes wavered for a moment. "This is no joke," she said. Her lost eyes showed she understood perfectly.

"Jane," Daniel said, "I don't toy with matters like these."

She looked down at the deck for a second as her thoughts collided on each level of consciousness. "Meet me in my quarters."

"There are some other things, m'lady," Daniel said. "One of our men was forced to drink demon blood, goblin to be precise. He's in the other coffin and to be honest, we don't know what he'll look like since he was already changing in the gardens. I'm sorry but I'm not one to leave a man behind."

"But a woman has never been a problem," she said with ice in her voice that could freeze hell.

"Jane, that was—"

The fourth word in that sentence was left on the cold hand that raked across his face. She hadn't even seemed to move, because she was that fast. "That's the second time you use my name without permission! I suggest you take heed and show the respect you owe!"

Daniel took two steps back, still in shock. "M-my a-p-pologies, m'lady," he said with a slight bow. "It shall not happen again."

"Good."

"Although there is one more thing," he added.

"You're quite right about that, Daniel," she said stepping towards the group and pointing to Nathaniel. "I'd like to know exactly why a human is aboard this ship and why I shouldn't simply rip his throat out."

Nathaniel who had been happy to be a part of the sidelines had suddenly been thrust into the limelight, and he wasn't too elated about that happening.

"Please ensure that no harm comes to him," Daniel said.

"Any reason why I shouldn't just have a bite?" she said while sizing the human up.

"Actually, there are a few things," Daniel said, bending to the ear of the vampire to whisper something. After a few words, a look of comprehension seemed to dawn on her face.

"I see," she said as she walked towards the human. Much like the other vampires who'd so generously analyzed Nathaniel before, she scanned him entirely going around and coming back to face him only to extend a lazy hand in front of the young man. Instinct took over and Nathaniel took the chilly hand and gently kissed the back of it. "A pleasure, Mr. Runnels," she said smiling. "I am Captain Jane Rivers and the Corsaires welcome you aboard the Black Calico."

"Th-thank you, m-m'lady," Nathaniel stuttered.

She continued to smile mischievously. "You should take some pointers from this one, Daniel. He might be able to show you a thing or two about manners. Mary, Anne, Wendy!"

"Yes, m'lady!" choired three astonishingly beautiful vampires.

"Be sure to show Mr. Runnels to his quarters," she said with a wide smile. "Give him a few scrubs and make sure to give him something of Jack's so he can wear fresh clothes. Also, be sure to not bite him, my dears. He might be a tempting morsel, but he is a guest and as such should remain unscathed. As for the rest of you, Devi will show you to your rooms and make sure you have everything you need. Daniel, come with me to the helm, and Mr. Runnels? I'll be expecting you for dinner."

That last bit of information came with a wink of a purple eye and a sly smile. Captain Jane then turned to the helm followed closely by her obedient lapdog, who had just a few hours ago been Nathaniel's captor.

"What about me, m'lady?" rang a dimwitted voice from the throng beyond the discussion.

"Oh..." she exclaimed distastefully. "Well I wouldn't worry too much, Indigo; you'll be in good hands and shall find rooms with accommodations that are more than adequate."

"But..."

"But that is the treatment you shall receive," she said with the steel in her voice growing cold and ruthless. "Abstain from biting the hand that feeds, or you might find yourself surrounded by indigo amidst the waves. I take it you still don't know how to swim. Am I right?"

The massive brute could only mumble in response. "Uh-uh... much obliged, m'lady. Ummm... sorry."

"Eloquent as ever," she said dismissively. "Now that that's taken care of, Daniel, make sure to bring your coffined friend with you."

They all parted ways as the majestic black galleon soared across the smallish waves fiddling on the ocean's surface. Six black sails strained and pulled the craft speedily across the water on a night where not much wind was actually blowing about.

- Below deck -

The ship was even longer and larger than it seemed from the outside. The interior of the ship was crafted intricately and with awe-inspiring precision. Nathaniel walked flanked by three vampires and if he had to be honest with himself, it was the first time he didn't mind vampiric company or the fact that he was still not cleared of his position as human hostage or potential meal.

The vampire to his rear right was the one called Mary. She had auburn hair, light brown eyes and milky white skin. Anne had short crop blonde hair fashioned in a Caesar look with matching thin bangs. Her firm steps rang from behind and to the left of Nathaniel. Leading the way, Wendy waved her streamlined body like a flowing flag that danced on a gentle morning breeze. Her feline eyes had caught his attention upon their first meeting regardless of the peeking fangs that showed with the gentle curve of her smile, which was either genuinely kind or simply eager to feast on him.

"Where are we going?" he asked.

"We are to take extra special care of you, Mr. Runnels," Wendy said through her slim smile. "You are our guest and those are the orders."

"Yes but this ship..."

"This ship is the Black Calico, sir," interrupted Anne. "It used to belong to the great Calico Jack and m'lady happened to come by it one day and claim it as hers. Little by little she's assembled the crew and we've been roaming all seas ever since."

"Oh. Ok. So where..."

"Across the Atlantic, Mr. Runnels," Mary said. "That is what your leader requested and what m'lady consented to."

"Ok but can I finish my sentences once in a while?" he said quickly before any of the vampires interrupted him again.

"Our apologies," he heard in surround stereo.

"Thank you. Now how about in this ship? Where are we going to now?"

"Well..." Wendy paused as her eyes squinted malevolently as she looked behind her shoulder. "We're to care for all of your needs."

She opened a door to her left and gave him a wry smile while looking at him from top to bottom.

"Don't worry, Mr. Runnels," Mary said, joining Wendy and Anne. "We won't harm you. Remember, direct orders from the Captain. So by all means... relax and step inside."

- Back topside -

"Put the box there, Daniel," Captain Jane said. Daniel obeyed and did his best to hold his tongue. Meanwhile, he hauled the vibrating coffin to where she had told him.

"Thank you for everything," he said when he'd finished lugging the coffin to the place indicated. "Sorry I've been lost for a while but Jane-"

Another slap cut his sentence off, shutting his mouth with a rigid thud.

"But nothing, Daniel," she said coolly as if she hadn't just slapped the taste out of his mouth. "There have been quite enough excuses by now. Eight years and I only know of you when I happen to be passing by and you just happen to need my help... again. This has been the pattern for over a century and I'm an idiot for responding to Liam's message."

"Well... that's not exactly true..." he said, wavering in a futile attempt at self defense.

"Not true?!" she berated. "January 13, 1915. Earthquake in Italy, you are stuck under the rubble, I arrive to rescue you. September 9, 1924; the Hanapepe Massacre? Yeah, that time you and your drunk friends decided to munch on those poor sugar cane workers saying they had to be the sweetest drink in the world. March 2nd 1944, a train stalls in Italy and over four hundred perfectly healthy people "choke" to death... Yet another convenient cover up.

"Those were my drunk years..." he said trying to justify his actions and failing miserably.

"Of course," she said while almost declaring that last part with open arms to the Atlantic. "I forget that there is a conscience within the creature. You laid low until you simply decided to tell Van Allen of the radiation belt so he could have some recognition. Mid February, you meet up with that team crossing the Antarctic, as if we hadn't done that countless times, and help them in 'the first-ever' crossing of that continent. Then you told me about Lituya Bay and said we'd get to see one of the most incredible things in history, and you were right and we saw the mega tsunami in all its glory after that massive landslide. That was nice. Actually, that entire year was nice. But it couldn't last and you had to disappear again."

"Yes," said Daniel. "The next time we saw each other was five years later with that Jesus Cloud thing in Arizona."

After he spoke she actually smiled. "You always have been an asshole."

"But it was funny... wasn't it?" he said allowing himself the smallest of smiles while speaking.

"Yes, but saving you in Bali wasn't," she replied soberly. "We really were ridiculously lucky that time Daniel. I saw you a few times here and there, but if there was any place I was sure to see you it was in '77 for the last guillotine show."

"The good old days," he reminisced fondly.

"Quite..." was her dry response, "which is why you later beheaded those hijackers in Somalia."

"Couldn't let that happen twice in a month," he said defensively.

"And the German Autumn, Daniel?" she said without missing a beat. "What you did in Stammheim?"

"That was... pleasure."

"Just like September 17th, was it?" she asked, maintaining her attack. "Yes. On that day you killed Somoza in Paraguay and then Richard Chase 'died of an overdose', how convenient."

"The bastard was being called the Vampire of Sacramento," he said while holding his hands over his head as if trying to establish it had been the most natural thing in the world. "He had it coming and David Chapman was lucky I didn't get a hold of him. Humans keep killing the nicer ones of their race, don't they?"

"I'm sure they all had it coming, Daniel," Jane said crossing her arms. "But as per usual, afterwards, poof, you're gone. I see you next time in 1994 for a day and nothing until today. I see you and you insist on acting like nothing's wrong."

"Jane I—"

His sentence was cut off once again by the knife hand that slashed the vampire's already sore face.

"Just tell me where we are going, Daniel," she said coldly while turning her back on him again. "You can keep your apologies and explanations."

"Fair enough... m'lady," he said while still rubbing his sore cheek. "I told you of the news from Sariel."

"Yes, about Israfil as well," she added.

"Correct. First we must go to Spain. I need to take Claus to his brothers and he must be laid to rest as should be."

"And you have to ask for their help as well... I'm not stupid, Daniel. Then what?"

"Well... there's France, Crete, and Alexandria for starters."

"What have you gotten me into, Daniel?" she replied, trying to summon patience from where there was none. "Never mind. What about this?" she added while pointing to the ever-shaking coffin. It rattled violently and the rough scraping grunts coming from within carried with them the scent of death. "Seems the cat is not exactly out of the bag, Daniel."

"As I mentioned earlier, m'lady, Vincenzo was forced to drink goblin blood. I'm not sure he can be saved but I wasn't going to leave him there and... and.... and I thought you could help."

Her eyes could have burned a hole in his head. She then undid one of her scarves and pulled out a dagger. Before Daniel could even ask what she was doing, she had already slashed her hand and pressed the scarf against her wound. It took about three seconds for the cut to heal and another second for her to throw the scarf overboard.

"I'll explain what we'll do," she said. "In about two hour's time, you'll fetch your friends. If we're in luck, you'll thank me and so will Vincenzo."

- Sometime later below deck -

"That lucky dog," Indigo said while putting his ear against one of the support columns. "They've been at it for an hour."

"Jealous, Indigo?" Liam said as he leaned against the cabin's windowsill.

"'Course I am!!!" barked the braided giant. "We ge's th' normal treatment while that monkey gets all the luxury."

"And by luxury you mean sex?" Liam ribbed while puffing on his cigarette.

"Hush Liam," Edward Louis said while holding back a chuckle. "And hold your tongue, dear Indigo. The Captain is not your biggest fan and she already offered to give you to the sea once."

"Hold me tongue? Hell! I'd ra'er em hold it fer me!" lamented the brute.

"And of course YOU are the most deserving of the lot?" Malia spat as she tended to Efia.

Indigo stepped away from the wall and looked at the vampire seductress. "You know you can't resist me, baby."

"You're exactly right," she responded with a whiff. "I can't resist you and I can barely stand you either so keep your sausage to yourself."

"Quiet down..." said a cold voice that silenced the entire group without having to go to great lengths to raise its volume. In a dark corner sat Valencia. "Focus on getting rest. That includes resting your mouths and any other body part, Indigo."

"Hear, hear," Lucas said in a much more than half asleep voice.

At that moment, Daniel barged into the room, his face looked grave and the tone of his voice matched it perfectly. "Indigo, Liam, Valencia,

Edward and Lucas, follow me topside. You are needed and staying here is not an option." He turned and left the group as abruptly as he had arrived and now headed down the corridor towards Nathaniel's room.

"Charming as always, isn't he?" Liam said half smiling as he made his way out of the room.

Daniel gave a solid thud to the wooden door and called out, "Casanova! Feel free to pull up your trousers. You're needed topside, NOW. You can continue your frolicking later."

With another about-face, the vampire stormed down the hall and jumped up the entire flight of stairs in one leap. Scrambling topside, they could see that dawn was only about an hour away. This was something to worry about since everyone was not as fortunate as Daniel, to be able to tolerate or even survive sunlight.

Each was given a length of rope as they stepped on the deck and each length had a perfect noose at the end that tightened at the slightest tug. Before they could ask what they were there for, the rumbling wood could be heard from the left side. Next to the main mast, two corsaires fought to control the possessed box and Captain Jane stood by polishing a foot long blade that cut through the blurry pre-dawn haze with its ethereal purple glow.

"Attention, all of you!" she yelled commandingly. "Seems the theme of this evening is choice. You have a comrade who drank demon blood. From each of your faces and the things you've done to this point, this means that you have no idea what this implies."

The box continued to growl and the wood seemed set to give at any moment.

"Unfortunately now is not a time for many questions and I shall pose one question and one question only; do you wish Vincenzo to live?"

Everyone was too shocked to reply and it did not take long for the beautiful sea mistress to grow impatient with her audience. "Yes or no?" she yelled and after a moment's silence, she added. "Or shall I decide for you?!!" She now drew the long sword and put it against the box next to where the neckline should be.

"Yes..." called out a lone voice... a lone human voice. "Please save him. I'd misjudged Vin..."

"Touching story!" Jane said cutting him off. "Maybe you can tell me later over tea. For now, do you others agree or does the human stand alone?"

Daniel quickly stepped beside Nathaniel, soon followed by the rest of the group. Meanwhile the box rattled and roared about to burst into pieces.

"Good!" the captain said while nodding approvingly. "Finally a consensus. Now, follow my orders and don't ask questions unless you feel like losing your head to my blade." The wood splintered as the struggle within continued. "Four limbs, one head. These ropes? Two on each limb, you for the head." She addressed the last order to Nathaniel.

"But..."

"You spoke first so you get the head," she stated matter-of-factly. "Simple as that. Now get ready!"

Everyone spread out on the deck as the captain stood next to the coffin, which she held down with one leg casually pressing down on the cracked surface. After surveying the crew's position, she took ten paces away from the rattling box and shouted. "Ready?!"

Everyone seemed ready, standing by and in an instant Jane turned around, drew two vintage pistols and fired six perfect shots, two for each of the three locks on the cover of the box. After a small explosion of dust and wood, an acrid smell wafted into the air as a rotted mound of a creature crouched ready to strike. It looked like a beast pulled from the sixth circle of hell. Vincenzo's eyes were pitch black and a small yellow iris gleamed in the haze.

"Now!!!!" screamed the captain and nine ropes sprung towards the monster but the beast's movements allowed him to escape six of the loops. Daniel and one of the Corsaires had the left arm and Valencia had the right leg, all others missed but they were quick to reel in the rope for another shot.

Jane then jumped the ten paces she'd taken from Vincenzo and buried her palm deep in the chest of the mutated vampire knocking him backward. "Again!!!" she roared as she narrowly avoided jagged claws of what was once a vampire hand. Again flew the loops and now the right and left legs were totally secure. The right arm however still clawed at anything it could reach.

"Pull the rug from under him!" she commanded. With a strong pull from all sides, the vampire flew into the air. After Nathaniel had snagged his head in the noose, the monster had finally been secured.

Jane walked beside the tied beast and still looking at him ordered in a clear loud voice: "Twist the newborn. His head must point to the deep and his legs towards the night."

They all pulled and split in groups to best hoist the vampire in the position the captain wished him to be. The ones with the legs bound darted towards the higher deck while the others stood firm on the main deck until Vincenzo looked like a blackened upside down version of Da Vinci's scale of man. Jane then came towards his face, peering into the black eye, completely unbothered, although many of the others could hardly bare to watch.

She spoke to him casually, "So Vin, you still in there?"

The thing merely growled and bared teeth that were only too willing to bite her throat out.

"Now, now, Vin... if there's nothing left of you then I'm afraid you have to go. But... if there's still anything left to save then you shall be saved."

She peeled the long thin purple blade out of its sheath and the creature that used to be Vincenzo shuddered at the sight. It was an odd blade that stretched a foot in length, hooked, then curved down to have the hard edge protect the knife hand. Its material was a dark almost black purple and in the hands of the captain, it almost seemed to beam and beat with a pulse.

"I....hrrrr..." cracked a voice of bubbling asphalt.

"Speak up dear," she replied consolingly, "I didn't catch that."

"I....i....it... hrrr... hurts," rasped the inverted vampire.

She smiled and then spoke in an almost motherly tone, "Good enough for me. Wendy, Mary! Get the bowl."

"Yes, mistress," the Corsaires replied and in an instant came back with a large bowl about a foot deep and wide and long enough to hold a body.

Jane continued to look lovingly on the twisted beast. Her eyes twinkled and she smiled gently before slitting Vincenzo's throat. A strong stream of black oil poured out of the wound, splashing on the basin below as most of the others looked upon the scene in horror.

"Hold tight, you scum!!!" the captain roared when the ropes slackened. "This is the only way to save him! If you entrusted me with your lives, don't start doubting me now!"

The hold on the vampire returned and tightened though many had to look away. Nathaniel was not one of these. He watched unblinking as the bowl filled with the blood, which seemed more like crude oil. Drowned screams from the wounded vampire slowly became softer until his eyes slowly lost their blackness.

Minutes felt like days and each drop seemed like a gallon had just spewed forth. The scene was curiously juxtaposed by the constant caressing of Jane as she nursed the drained being. She looked over her shoulder and called out to the helm, "Any luck up there?"

"Three large tuna and working on what seems to be a hefty marlin."

"Good," she said in a whisper, before calling out. "Someone bring those three down while they continue working on the other."

Grace lobbed herself to the helm and leapt back in an instant bringing the hefty load. "It's almost time," she said as she observed how the blood now dripped weakly from the wound on the throat.

"Yes, Grace," the captain said without looking away from Vincenzo. "Now ask our dear friends to loosen the slack and have someone assist you in removing the arm and leg bonds."

Following the captain's orders, the slack was loosened and the vampire crumbled to the floor. His eyes were glazed and brown, their normal color although they still bore a light tinge of gray. The captain knelt down beside him not caring about the mess and putting her hand gently upon the vampire's forehead. With her eyes closed, she began to murmur what seemed like a prayer. Daniel had walked next to Nathaniel's side and looked on.

"What is she doing?" the human whispered.

"Blessing him," the vampire replied.

Nathaniel suddenly realized how dramatically things had changed from something utterly atrocious to a beautiful rebirth, whose prayer said:

> *"From death to life*
> *and earth to water;*
> *he shall be delivered.*
> *A kiss of knife,*
> *embrace of mother,*
> *I join his water to my river.*
> *Salt shall cleanse his wounds;*
> *waves shall cleanse his soul*
> *our lives are now in tune,*
> *behold we become whole."*

Finishing the sentence, Jane drew the blade out again and delicately sliced two slits on the jawline of either side of Vincenzo's head and commanded, "Cast him to the deep!"

Three Corsaires took the weakened vampire and lobbed him into the sea with the noose still around his neck. Jane stood up and headed to the top most deck. There another pirate vampire stood battling with a rugged fishing line.

"How are we doing, Anne?" Jane asked.

"Almost there, m'lady," the vampire said. "It's a strong one but it shouldn't be more than a minute or two."

"Good. We shall need it soon," she said as she lunged back towards the main deck and stood right next to the mainmast.

Wendy, Mary and Grace were holding three large buckets with the huge fish inside to keep them alive for a few more instants as another Corsaire brought with her a huge conch shell that she put in the hand of her captain. Jane looked upon the large shell, dusted it a bit even though it sparkled and with a deep breath blew a heavy sounding note that drummed in the air and deep into the ocean. She blew three more times and handed the instrument back to her crewmember. Looking towards the lighting horizon, she knew she didn't have much time. The captain then walked towards Nathaniel and held out her hand for him to follow and led him to the rope now being secured by three Corsaires and said:

> *"Saved from life*
> *And brought from death.*
> *First of word and now of hand.*
> *The willing fate doth now command."*

She put the rope in Nathaniel's hand and he had no need for any instructions. He knew what he had to do and began pulling on the rope. He took his time first and then started to get into a faster rhythm. His arms burned with the burden of every inch he gained. All stood by and none helped him because he knew that they couldn't.

He forced himself into a sort of trance and although an inferno burned in his arms, his eyes were cold as ice as he replayed everything that had happened; re-assessing each word; analyzing each event. Recent happenings seemed eons ago and the vampire who he had despised in life now came to actually be a fraction of his being.

The fire continued to tear his limbs but there was no give in the human. A mixture of an apparent awakening and the red waters he'd drunk and bathed in. He could hear everything but listened to nothing; see everything but observed only himself from a detached perspective, pulling and pulling. Hauling one back from death as the body slowly crept over the rail to finally slump on the deck.

Nathaniel fell back and his chest heaved. Vincenzo lay there, a pale blue gray, almost faded completely from existence. Jane stepped forth and once again knelt beside him.

She put her hand over his forehead and gently whispered, "Let my dreams be thy thoughts."

She moved her hand down over his eyes. "May the sea be your home."

She slashed her finger and squeezed some drops into his cracked open mouth. "Let my water end your drought."

She moved her hand on his breast. "And never again be alone."

Vincenzo's eyes blinked wearily and after having seemed quite dead, everyone witnessed the exact opposite. Mary handed her captain the fish.

"Three times life lesser than thee," the captain said while Vincenzo fed on all three tuna, sucking them dry, gasping and moaning at the pleasant feeling of the cold blood actually warming him.

He was actually able to sit up by his own accord and after finishing the third large fish, Jane helped him up and led him to the high deck. Each step was a tremendous effort but they reached the top and Anne had just about finished pulling the gigantic marlin from the sea. The captain knelt down and invited Vincenzo to do the same as the fish kicked and fought against the rigid hold of the mistress.

"The sea gives life and I shall take it," she said.

Vincenzo repeated the words and heaved on the line to finally pull the fish onboard. Taking a moment, he looked down at the creature and then fell on the majestic fish breaking through the tough scales and outer skin with his fangs to drink the sweetness beneath. He pulled with all his might and his mouth gladly drank the blood as the large gash Jane had made on his throat sealed shut. The smaller slits remained open however. Jane held him in her arms as he fed and with her eyes closed, and etched a long curved C, much like a wave on the vampire's forehead.

When he had finished drinking the last life of the magical beast, Vincenzo stood up, breathed deeply and said:

> *"Life has given life.*
> *And in debt from death, I owe mine.*
> *The sea is my father*
> *And you the mother of me,*
> *For now, forever."*

She smiled and caressed the vampire like a newborn cub. "Go my child. The deep awaits. Tell of the challenge nigh and I shall call you when the time comes."

He replied by embracing her like a mother he had been separated from at birth until he caught eye of Nathaniel and walked over to him. "My thanks, little brother. May I be able to return the favor and to my captain, Daniel, if you need me, just ask mother to call."

Daniel and Vincenzo exchanged looks, fraternal smiles and a firm handshake until the reborn vampire jumped into a run and dove to the sea that now glimmered like bubbling fire. A brief pause was then broken by the ship's captain. "Day is upon us. Light bearers please stay top deck. All others may fall below."

There was a great stir as orders were followed though Daniel and Nathaniel remained on the flight deck. "You did well, Runnels," Daniel said. "Go get some sleep." Nathaniel nodded limply and bowed towards Jane with a hoarse m'lady until he was out of sight.

Jane smiled as she turned towards the vampire. "See, Daniel? Manners."

Chapter 11: The First Vision

Nathaniel had barely been able to bathe before passing out. He'd been escorted by Wendy to his room and had plopped down on the bed while still wet. He'd fallen in such a deep sleep that he was surprised he could even dream, much less think clearly while dreaming.

'I see static...' he thought to himself. 'I hear buzzing... This is a dream... I know I'm not here, yet here I am... I feel my body sitting in a chair but in reality, I'm aware that I'm asleep on a large bed below the deck of a galleon called the Black Calico. I know the waves are crashing outside the walls of where my body is. I can actually hear and feel them... but that's far away from where my mind is; where I am, yet I am not. Here, there is no water.'

In real life, Nathaniel barely moved an inch, but in his mind's eye, he floated in perpetual darkness while thinking to himself. 'A TV set startles me when it suddenly buzzes and whirrs in front of me. It came out of nowhere; then again, I am nowhere. It's as if the set is trying to regain reception to continue with its regularly scheduled program but all I see is digital rain. Layers of static slosh against each other within the confines of a wooden box and a screen.'

'I'm dreaming... but I'm aware, in control... lucid. My duality is now threatened by a trinity of consciousness. Consciousness, unconsciousness and that state we call soul.'

He asked himself deep within his mind, 'How can everything feel so real if this is a dream. I know it's a dream. But this chair is real. I am real. That television monitor is real and that door behind the TV is also real.'

Within the perceived darkness, Nathaniel sees a floating door and the floating TV. He barely notices when a patterned carpet floor appears to give context to the object. The door opens by itself into pure darkness. Nathaniel almost feels fear, but he's actually able to deny that feeling entry into his mind. He sees as an even darker piece of shade seems to slip into the room, gliding and sliding rather than walking. It seems to be an acre away, and slowly it takes on the silhouette of a man. Each of its steps fails to fit perfectly with the distance the shadow travels. It was the physical equivalent of a poorly dubbed kung-fu film. Sounds end seconds before the entire movement has completed.

Nathaniel continues to observe the shade's movement and the figure pulls a chair whose sound is also completely out of sync with its movement. It puts the chair next to the television set and glides to the wall on the young man's left side. After a moment, light suddenly slashes Nathaniel's corneas.

'It... hurts... but I'm... dreaming,' he thinks to himself before fully observing the figure that had walked in through the door; 'Black trench coat? Black hair? A stubby beard? Who is this guy? Well at least his steps are finally synched to sound and movement. He sits, crosses his legs, lights a cigarette and begins to talk to me.'

"Care for a smoke?" the man asks in a southern accent as he swats dust off his trench coat.

"No thanks, trying to quit," Nathaniel replied.

"Man oh man," said the figure while giving a hearty chuckle, "when you can't even enjoy a smoke in the privacy of your own dreams you have to be really messed up. Besides, nobody likes a quitter, but you can suit yourself. More for me, he he."

'His black cowboy hat and slight southern twang would normally annoy me,' Nathaniel thought to himself, 'but it's a dream so he's excused since it's my fault he has that accent.'

"What's your name?" Nathaniel asked.

"Me?" said the man in the trench coat in mock surprise. "Aw hell mister, you dreamt me, you might as well name me since I can technically call you daddy."

'He toys with me,' Nathaniel thinks to himself. 'Fair enough. If I've dreamt him up, it wouldn't be any different since I know he's pulling my leg. He's obviously exaggerating his accent just to see if he can piss me off.'

Nathaniel decided to patronize as his response. "Well I thought of Billy-Bob, or Sammy-Joe or some other hick two-part single name, but since I dreamt you and we could be friends, I'll leave it at Bill for short."

'He's not the only one that can try to piss the other off,' Nathaniel thought smugly, childlike in his satisfaction of having spoken back to the man in the chair.

"That's a fine name you gave me there, Nat," the man said while taking a drag from his cigarette, "but make sure you pronounce it very Hispanic like. You know, Beel or sumthin' like that. Makes me feel like I'm a sexy villain in one of those Mexican novellas. You know the type, nice and fabricated, like your reality."

Nathaniel hadn't expected the figment of his imagination to be so condescending, and he paused briefly before replying. "Whatever you want... Beel... now that we're properly acquainted though, care to tell me why I'm dreaming of a sun deprived hick instead of some eighteen-year-old brunette who's requesting the very things I'd pay a hooker to let me do to her."

"Well for starters, I'm sexier," said the man in black.

'He smiles like an asshole,' Nathaniel thought. 'I like this guy, even if he is a dream.'

The stranger continued, "Second off, banging three hot blood suckers in one night does seem like more than enough to quell the desires of a human libido, don't you think?"

'How does he know?!' Nathaniel thought.

Bill gave a wry smile as he puffed out the smoke of his cigarette. "Hey numbnuts!" he said in mock whisper before cupping his hands to shout at the young man. "I'm in your mind. Of course I know what you've been doing. I may be backed up enough to generate wax darts for semen, but your pipes are most definitely clean. Oh and by the way, there's no need for that internal monologue crap. I can hear everything you think in surround sound but if you talk to me, I'll be spared the massive echo effect which I'm sure reflects the hollowness of your head. I'm here to talk."

Nathaniel scowled at how his dream was progressing. "Just to talk?"

"Well of course not, you jack hole," Bill said. "Don't you think it alarmingly random to have me here with a high quality television set such as this? What is this, circa 1983, or some other year from that dusty memory of yours? Anyways, having this set here, I think that at the very least, I should have something to show you."

The man opened his trench coat and pulled out an archaic piece of rectangular plastic with spindles. The young man's face was the very picture of confusion.

"A VHS tape?" Nathaniel asked.

"Hey, you dreamt it," Bill said redirecting the blame to the dreamer. "If it's too obsolete for your taste, feel free to update your inner child."

Bill then stood up and put the tape into a VCR that had appeared beneath the television set. He then dragged his chair next to Nathaniel's, sat down, pulled two beer bottles from his trench coat, cracked them open and put one in the young man's hand. He also pulled out a remote control from another pocket in his coat and clicked play. A moment's silence passed until cheesy guitars, a lame drum beat and a funk bass began to play as the title screen faded in. – Girls and Boys Interrupted-.

"You have got to be kidding me," Nathaniel said fully aware of the type of movie he was watching.

"Shhh... concentrate," Bill said. His eyes might have dried up but his mouth watered at the cavorting bodies that began undulating on screen.

Nathaniel sipped at his beer as the show continued and held the bottle up to the light. India Pale Ale, his favorite. At least that part of the dream was spot on.

Bill cackled. "Women on women and women on men, just as nature intended."

"Is there any point to this?" said Nathaniel uncomfortably even though he continued to watch.

Bill scoffed. "What do you think son? Do you need a point when it comes to a good skin flick? Geez!!! Kids these days. But correct me if I'm wrong, but it seems Melissa has a hold of your attention."

"Huh! What? Melissa?" Nathaniel stammered as his attention was brought back into the room in his dreams.

Bill had to hold himself from laughing. "Yeah, Runnels. The buxom brunette with great lips and an Italian voluptuousness not easily ignored."

"Ah... well."

"Focus, man," Bill said turning back to the screen. "The interesting part should be coming up right about... now."

At that moment, a hideous growl roared from the speakers, breaking the rhythmic melodies of moaning, flesh slapping and wah-wah guitars. The screen suddenly stained with blood but the people could still be seen trying to defend themselves from hideous brown-grey demons with razor sharp teeth, hollow black eyes and armor fashioned from bone instead of steel. The beer had long ago fallen from his hands, but Nathaniel could not stop looking.

Fifteen bodies now lay torn apart onscreen. The killers slowly walked away dragging a few corpses and leaving a blood soaked rubble of the once pleasure bound oasis. A few bodies still twitched, taking their last breaths until the screen cut to static.

Bill turned off the TV and was no longer in his smug and smiling mode. His beard, though quite unkempt, gave him an air of wisdom. "I could lie and say that this is just a dream, but I think you know better than that. The people you saw on the screen were a vampire brood that went by the name of the Lygophilials."

"........The... what?"

"Ly-go-phi-lials, Runnels," said the man in black snapping his fingers to bring Nathaniel out of his stupor. "What would be best known as the 'Lovers of the Dark' although as you saw, they took that name a bit beyond just a cool moniker."

"What were those things?" the human asked, still staring blankly into the ocean of static.

"Wraiths," Bill said shortly. "I'm pretty sure you heard about them but had no idea of what they actually looked like and though you didn't get a full blown shot, you get the picture."

"They're... horrible..."

"Well that falls a little short," said Bill. "By the way their names were Melissa, Aria, Cytherea, Linda, Tara, Alicia, Jessica, Alden, Eva, Jeremy, David, Ronald, Elliot and Yulia. Fifteen vampires decimated in seconds because they were caught off guard. Tell your friends back at the ship that you should have welcome and unwelcome visit soon, though I don't know in which order they'll arrive."

He tucked his hat back on and gave Nathaniel a pat on the shoulder before picking up spilt beer. "Damn, son... even in a dream, it's a shame to spill good beer. See you soon."

Jimmy Hendrix's Voodoo Child then began to fade in as background music while Bill walked towards the entrance. The man tipped his black hat to Nathaniel and opened the door to what was supposed to be darkness. Instead, a massive ball of fire swept past the cloaked figure filling the entire room with flames and as his flesh bubbled and charred, Nathaniel could see the standing skeleton that was once Bill holding up a peace sign before crumbling outside the door.

"AHHHHHHHHHHHHHHHHHHHHHHHHHHHHHH!!!!!!"

Quite suddenly, Nathaniel's flesh no longer burned. His eyes weren't bitter with smoke and there was no fire, only the faint taste of hops on his lips and the smell of nicotine and flint in his nostrils.

"What a messed up dream," he said to himself as he got up from the sweat-drenched bed. He turned to the side and sat up, half bent towards the ground as he felt the cold floor against his feet. "Tiles?!" he asked out loud realizing he had not woken up in the Black Calico.

'It had all been a dream,' he thought to himself. He was really in his apartment, he had his favorite t-shirt on, the bed still held the contour of his body and a stack of overdue bills teetered to the right upon a table in a most Pisa like fashion. He stood and walked to the bathroom and took a leak worthy of an over-hydrated camel with a severe addiction to diuretics. Hell, he even farted a couple of times just to see how his 'water pressure' would be affected.

He could still taste beer on his lips though... and he hadn't been able to enjoy a nice brew in ages. "Weird how the mind can play tricks on you," he said to himself. "A few synapses, taste triggers, memories and voilà, you'd swear you just had a beer."

A minute and forty seconds later, the final drops signaled the end of the camel's reign. "Geez I'm thirsty," he said to himself.

He took a glass, held it under the tap but no amount of twirling could remedy the absence of water thanks to the untamed bill that had subsequently become a toddler of debt after months of not being paid.

"Good thing there's a bottle in the fridge," he said as he remembered. He then looked to his left at the ¾'s filled toilet bowl. "If it's yellow, let it mellow," he said and closed the lid without flushing.

Nathaniel then opened the door to the family room. It was dark as hell and he tried screwing his eyes to get some magic owl sight or something. It didn't work. He edged along the flat trying to reach for some type of furniture to guide him towards the fridge but he couldn't find the small round table, the desk or the lazy boy he'd fetched from a yard sale. He did manage to stumble against something cold and soft on the floor, twisting his ankle in the process.

"What the hell was that?" he said as he tried to get his balance back. Another stumble and two steps later, Nathaniel slipped and fell in what felt like paint. "What the...? A leak? And what the hell was that back there?" he said as he sat in the dark and looked towards where it was even darker.

After a moment, he got up and was able to finally get to the refrigerator door half afraid of what he was going to find inside as he gripped the cold metal handle. He breathed in, centered himself, concentrated and gave the door a solid pull almost yanking it off its hinges to find... a half eaten loaf of bread growing a bevy of fungi worthy of the most prized Petri dishes, four bags of leftovers he should have probably disposed of the preceding month and a jug of water. He could have sworn it was a bottle, but it's been a crazy few weeks, so it's ok to confuse something that trivial.

He sighed in relief and laughed at himself while reaching forth with his left hand. Fully extended and grabbing the jug, he suddenly found himself unable to move. His hand was gripping the handle of the jug that had the water he so dearly needed but small droplets fell within the once white refrigerator. First the lower tray started to look like a freshly painted Japanese flag but soon it looked more like an inkblot test... a red inkblot test. His stomach seemed to linger between dimensions as he continued to stare onto his blood drenched arm. Finally, he willed himself to look back to the living room.

The naked bodies were familiar, as he had seen them just a few minutes ago even if it had been on a VCR tape within a dream. The entrance to his apartment had been ripped wide open and the trail of dragged blood stained bodies had caked dry. But everything was only half clear. He only had the light from the refrigerator and the entrance light to see by. He took three steps, felt as he stained the wall and hesitated to flip the switch. Who would want to clearly see the massacre he was standing in? He closed his eyes and finally flipped the switch upwards. His eyes wanted to stray from any thought of opening but he had to. He had to see the carnage left in his apartment and see if he could understand why such a tragedy had happened there.

When he did so, Nathaniel gave a cry and jumped back slamming into a hollow wall. His eyes had opened to the cold distorted reflection of his face on a steel elevator door.

"What the hell?!!!" he said quite startled.

The elevator bell chimed before a loud obnoxious voice rang inside his ear. "Sixth floor; linens, leather cabinets, dead bodies, Viagra induced rigor mortis and dental floss."

To Nathaniel's left stood a man dressed in a bellboy outfit. He wore a black cowboy hat and said howdy with a slight southern twang. He also happened to be holding a lit cigarette in one hand and a megaphone in the other.

"What is–?"

"You're dreaming, kid," said Bill looking almost bored of the situation. "Simple as that. But never take a dream for granted. So how 'bout now? Care for a smoke?"

Nathaniel didn't know where this was going but felt obliged to accept those three inches of carcinogenic relief rather than think this one through.

"Thatta boy!!" Bill said grabbing Nathaniel by the shoulder and urging him on. "Suck on that puppy!!"

After a moment's settling down and three drags from the cigarette, Nathaniel was finally able to talk. "What the hell is this Bill?"

"I told you grasshopper, it's 'Beel,'" said the man in his bellboy outfit. "You should know the answer better than anybody but since you apparently need me to spell it out for you, it's a D-R-E-E-M."

"Yeah but why the hell can't I wake up?" Nathaniel asked, clearly affected by his current circumstances.

"Nat, seriously, did you NOT have a childhood? Did you never sing kids songs? Mary had a little lamb? A pile of spaghetti? Row, row, row your boat?"

If possible, Nathaniel became even more confused.

"Life is but a dream, genius," Bill said, apparently pointing to the obvious. "Why can't it be? Why not treat it as such? Why can't you dare to dream a little dream? What's keeping you from living that fantasy?"

"Because I'm human and for starters, I can't fly," the young man said.

"Oh can't you?" Bill responded with an evil smile. "What about airplanes, rocket packs, hang gliders and stuff of the sort?"

"Those are mechanical solutions," Nathaniel said practically.

"Exactly," Bill said with an air of satisfaction on his face. "I couldn't have said it better myself."

"Said what?" asked Nathaniel.

"What you just said," Bill replied.

"What? The mechanical part?" Nathaniel said, still trying to make sense of the situation.

"Bingo," Bill said as he winked at him.

"And what's that have to do with anything?" asked the young man, desperate to understand.

"Yeesh. You guys really don't get it sometimes. Humans I mean. If mankind has only developed mechanical solutions for a variety of problems, it is merely because they are content with developing such type of solutions. You're all conformists and you really don't have to be that way. Remember that, Nat. Oh and this is your stop by the way."

DING

With a heaving gasp Nathaniel sat up on his bed. He looked around and recognized the wooden furnishings, the ample bed, the heavily spiced aroma from the waters of the bath and the familiar rumbling of the waves. He was awake, or so he thought. He pinched himself and it hurt, as in REAL pain. After a few seconds, he breathed deep knowing he was in fact awake and on a boat in the middle of the ocean. However, when he exhaled a heaving breath, smoke spread forth and everything he'd dreamt came back to him in a sudden surge not unlike the throwup he spat onto the floor. All the images and words swam around in his head but he finally felt awake and aware. One of the Corsaires shot into his room.

"Are you all right sir?" asked Wendy with her gown half open inviting him to remember the glorious body that had danced with his only a few hours ago, or had it been longer?

"How long have I been in bed?" he asked, quite pale and trying to regain his composure.

A bit stupefied by the question, she gave him a look as if she were talking to some insane vagabond. "Ummm... you've come to your room not four minutes ago. I'd just seen you off to bed and was beginning to change. Don't worry though, I'll get a mop and bucket for that. Try to go topside and get some fresh air, sir."

Nathaniel nodded and stumbled across towards the door. He stopped next to her, looked straight into her eyes and smiled while apologizing for the mess. She smiled back and insisted that he needn't worry and they both carried themselves endlessly different than their previous encounter would lead one to think they would.

'So this is how Adam and Eve must have felt like after realizing that they had been naked in front of each other,' he thought to himself.

Out in the hall everything was quiet and still except for the creaking of a sturdy door with a crest insignia that had just shut when he stepped into the hall. He shrugged it off, ignoring the fact that it was Captain Jane's cabin and hauled himself topside to a supremely calm and cloudless morning. Nathaniel swallowed the fresh salt air and immediately felt better as the dim twilight screwed with his vision. It was light yet dark and his eyes were still groggy even if in reality he hadn't slept at all.

A small glow came into view at the front of the boat and a figure sat lying sideways atop the rail. The speck of light suddenly pulsed brighter and a moment later a cloud of smoke rose from the source.

"Bill? Not another dream," Nathaniel said as he surged straight towards the figure obviously angered at his continued failed attempts to wake up. "What the hell do you want, Bill? I mean 'Beel'! There, I said it the way you like it."

"Well some peace and quiet would be nice," said a familiar voice that was not Bill's. "As for this bill, well I may be a doctor but every treatment you have received is free of charge."

Nathaniel felt like a jackass as he came into view of the smiling vampire. "Oh... sorry Liam."

"For the bill thing or for having given your best effort to smash my head in with a brass candelabrum?" Liam asked, making Nathaniel feel like even more of a jackass. In the shade, the vampire smiled as smoke slipped through the crevices of his teeth. "Don't worry, human. I'm smart enough to understand and apply the concept of empathy. In fact, I would have done the same in your shoes. Now for the other thing, who is this Bill character?"

Nathaniel shrugged because he felt so embarrassed at that moment. "Ermmm... it... it was just a dream. Sorry. It was just real vivid and... it was just horrible."

"Hmmm. So you say you had a complex dream where you retained the name of a central figure, whose name is most likely Bill and was such an immersive experience that you thought you were still dreaming even though it's obvious you're awake. Seems to me like you had much more than just a dream, Runnels."

"Maybe..." the human said, "...but it was so weird. Something about Lygophilials or something like that and death and..."

"What did you say?" Liam interrupted allowing his cigarette to dive off into the water. Quite suddenly he looked a lot less cool than he had two seconds before. "How do you know that name?"

"Well, Bill showed me a video where they were having this huge... ummm... encounter. That is until wraiths came and battled them. Well it wasn't really a battle, it was a pretty one sided massacre."

"Describe these wraiths," Liam asked, completely focused on what the human could share. "Tell me the whole dream."

Nathaniel proceeded to tell him every detail of the dream he could remember. How they were killed, how he saw them dead twice over, first on the tape then in his apartment which transformed into the room he saw on the video and how Bill had said something of welcome and unwelcome visitors.

Liam thought for a few moments before he was able to talk to Nathaniel again. "I'll speak to Daniel of this, Runnels. Thank you for sharing. Now do try and get some rest. Something tells me that these visitors are a lot closer than we'd like them to be."

He looked upon the waves and lit another cigarette. Nathaniel understood and as soon as he'd gone below deck, Liam's breath heaved deeply as blood tears welled in his eyes. "Bear patiently, my heart. For you have suffered heavier things."

"Homer," said a voice from behind as a hand clasped his shoulder and Daniel stood beside his friend. "Don't think I don't pay attention, old friend. Now how about you tell me what the human told you?"

Liam smiled and patted the hand on his shoulder as his tears finally broke away from his eyes.

Chapter 12: An evil wind

Faint scratching on sea-hardened wood nudges Nathaniel awake. To him it sounds like the hands of a thousand lost children reaching out to him from the murky depths of the ocean. As his eyes try to rip away from his attempt at sleep, he notices that the volume neither increases nor decreases, but remains constant. He sits up suddenly, confused at the source of the noise and allows his eyes to roam around the room. In the cabin, shade mingles with light and columns of liquid blackness seem to surround him.

In his exhaustion, he wasn't sure if this was yet another of a long line of dreams. However, unlike the lucid reality he had roamed freely in the confines of his mind, some nearby presence seemed to echo distant memories of the empty space beneath his bed as a child. In contrast to those childhood memories, this time he was pretty certain that the floor beneath his bed wasn't empty and that he was far from alone. Claws whispered invisibly inches from his face and little pops and hisses creaked beside his earlobes.

Within the darkness, a slithering sound began molding itself into words until a revolting voice spoke out. "Hello, Massssster Runnelsss. Sssso good to sssee you. How isss all?"

The human's pupils dilated to their maximum but still Nathaniel could not see a thing. The voice seemed to hiss a chuckle and continued to spittle from the dark. "Oh my powerful massster, don't try and sssolve thisss and every dilemma. After all, you're only human, and you already do much more than you should. By all meansss, be at eassse, forget your worriesss and letsss talk."

A greenish glow slowly outlined a silhouette on a large chair ten feet from the bed. After looking at it for a moment, Nathaniel realized that it wasn't that someone or something was immersed in shade... it was that whatever was sitting in the chair was the shade.

"Don't worry," hissed the voice, "no need to pinch yourssself. Thisss isss jussst another dream."

Cold droplets bled from the granite tense face of Nathaniel. Even if this was a dream, recent events prompted him to worry for his safety... especially in the confines of his own mind.

- Topside -

Tension was far from exclusive to Nathaniel's quarters. Nighttime was nearing and an auburn sunset was in the process of extinguishing on the horizon. Daniel, Jane, Liam and another corsaire were the only ones on watch since they were the only vampires unaffected by sunlight, with the exception of Lucas who was roaming somewhere below deck. Daniel looked tired, weary, yet supremely focused. His eyes bore onto the edge of the sea as Jane stole a look every once in a while to keep watch on him. "You seem tired, Daniel, go get some rest."

Daniel huffed a stubborn smile, "Much obliged, m'lady, but no need. I'm fine as is."

"You don't look fine, Daniel," she said, clearly showing she wasn't convinced. "When was the last time you got some sleep?"

"Sleep?" he said with a tragic smile, "wow... I think it was 1984, but I can't say for sure."

"I'm serious, Daniel."

He looked deep into her eyes when he replied. "So am I. I haven't been able to sleep in over two decades. It's taken me over twenty years to find the solution to this catastrophe we're about to face and it so happens to have come by way of a human, of all the things."

The Black Calico swayed gently to the rhythm of the breeze, but her captain's eyes were not lost in the cerulean horizon. They bore into Daniel as words wanted to climb up from her lungs. She knew him... better than most anybody in this entire world... and she knew that for however casual he had said it, he had spoken the truth.

Daniel's face suddenly became even more rigid. The crevasses in his forehead cracked seismically as he caught sight of a raging storm starboard side. Jane looked in the same direction but didn't seem too concerned.

"Nothing to worry about, Montacre; it's just a storm. They tend to happen."

Silence drummed on the scene as a familiar set of jade eyes faded into view. "It's not the storm that worries me, captain. It's what's riding inside. Listen closely."

Dumbfounded, Jane did as Daniel suggested. She heard the rhythmic splashing of the waves and the wind strumming its chiming strings, yet there was something else. There might have been the creaking of the sturdy galleon but also... far within... distantly, yet clearly... there was laughter. The faintest trace of a tyrannical guffaw that slowly grew louder. She also noticed how the coal stained cloud continued to disobey trade winds which blew in a different direction, instead insisting on crawling towards their ship.

At that moment, Liam jumped on the top deck with a look as grim as Daniel's. "Sir, there is something you must be informed of."

"Actually old friend, we're quite preoccupied at the moment. Haven't you seen what's making its way towards us?"

"You know me better than that, sir. But it is not the only thing of importance at the moment."

"Then spit it out, man."

"I'm well aware of what's happening starboard side, sir, but a ship has three more sides to it and although fore and aft sides may be clear, port side is not."

The concerned look in Liam's eyes chilled Daniel. "What did you see?"

"Friend or foe, I know not which it is, my lord, but on a horse he rides upon the water."

"How long to full sunset, m'lady?" asked Daniel looking towards the captain.

"Fifteen minutes," she answered coldly, still looking at the storm.

"And how long do you think before that thing lands here?" he asked looking at the storm clouds.

"Half that. Maybe a bit more if we turn port and sail full speed."

Daniel's eyes switched from one color to another as his mind raced. Finally they settled into deep crimson like a slot machine showing its winning colors. "Wake the others, Liam. Have them prepare for when the sun has completely set. It's going to get mighty bumpy soon."

"Aye, sir," Liam said.

"What course should we take?" Jane asked.

"......... Maintain course, full speed ahead."

"Aye," Jane said as she held the wheel firmly.

"What of the human sir?" asked Liam.

"Leave him below; it's the safest place to be right now."

- Below deck -

Nathaniel continued to struggle and the shade continued taunting him.

"Sssooooo... tell me... what doesss your majesssty want now?"

"M-m-majesty?" stuttered Nathaniel.

"Of courssse... Here in the dream world, you are king. Here... you even have a crown and ssscepter. Behold."

The shade then stretched out holding something in its clutches. Every time Nathaniel thought he'd be able to see an arm or other clearly visible body part, the shade would stretch to veil the carrier. A golden crown and scepter were placed on the bed and Nathaniel couldn't help but marvel at their beautiful craftsmanship.

"Th-thank you, b-b-but I'm n-no king to b-be c-c-crowned," he said with teeth chattering. A deathly cold had taken hold of him.

A slithery gasp was released and two swampy green grey eyes came into view.

"My king, how can you sssay that? Many weeksss were ssspent forging sssomething worthy of thy nobility. It containsss jewelsss with all the colorsss of your majesssty, the only true great man. The one who rejected hisss primate ancessstry and walked hisss own path."

"P-primate ancestry?" Nathaniel asked. He had continued to struggle and after some effort he almost felt as if he could move again.

"Well, my liege, ssscientific findingsss ssshow and defend the theory of evolution. Being that you are man, it isss only natural to asssume you are the greatessst of them all, therefore, the king."

An oily fragrance started to circulate throughout the room. Musky and old, it smelled of rotted thyme with moldy wood. The resolute sternness that had attempted to burn through the shade melted away from Nathaniel's eyes. They now grew foggy and complacent and he giggled drunkenly.

The shade shifted slightly and the slithery voice coiled out to the young man. "What isss ssso funny, my king?"

"Hee-hee... dude... you actually sound like Mrs. Blaline from the fifth grade...hee-hee. She always went on these stupid rants about evolution. Bla, bla, blaaaaaaa... hee-hee."

The slithery voice coughed and scratched its throat. For a moment it sounded as if it was choking, but in reality it was morphing. After a moment, instead of the sinisterly slithering voice echoing from the dark, out boomed a husky woman's soprano that now rolled its Rs rather than slither its Ss. "Now, now Rrrunnels. Evolution is a rrremarrrkable thing and you must embrrrace it with prrride."

Nathaniel found it hard to speak but he was able to at least slur dumbly. "He-he-he... he, he, he, he. That's funny, Mrs. Blaileen. The funniest part is that you're dead. He, he, he..."

"Oh?!" boomed the green grey eyes, "but have you forrrgotten that this herrre is a drrream you arrre having?"

"True..." Nathaniel replied, getting drunker by the second. "He...he, he.... he......Drrream a little drrream forrr meeeee," he sang.

"I'll do anything you want, my king. But firrrst trrry yourrr crrrown on and see how it fits."

Nathaniel looked at the heavy crown at the foot of his bed. He still smiled a dumb smile, but his eyes frowned upon the crown. For some reason he hated it and for some other reason, it seemed to move of its own accord.

"Ummm..... how about no? He, he, he... Crowns are for princes and kings or even a knight, and I've never even jousted."

After speaking these words, Nathaniel leapt from the bed and started galloping along the room, as a child would while mimicking riding a horse. He went in circles and slapped his thigh hard as if pushing his horse to go faster until he darted for the door. In a blink of an eye however, he found himself flung back onto the bed by a piece of the shade.

He moaned a bit as he tried to get his breath back and looked into the green grey eyes that now breathed the musk directly into his face. His mind took a wrong turn and he forgot the why, where, what and how of his immediate existence.

"Wouldn't want you running around and making a big fusss of thisss, now would we?" said the slither as it returned to voice the shade.

The silhouette shifted in its veiled throne but remained seated even with the ruckus that could be heard topside. Unfortunately for Nathaniel, none of those noises were remotely near his cabin door.

"Now... where were we?" asked the filthy voice.

- Topside -

Daniel sets a series of arrow quivers along the rail of the ship. No less than three dozen packs of twenty arrows each were set up along the starboard side while Nelly, one of the corsaires, loaded a series of pistols she later put up on racks. After she set them, the guns would be ready to fire with a simple grab and twist.

"Nelly!" Jane screamed as she tied the rudder to secure the current course. "Get the flares, all of them! We'll need them to see anything in that damned slosh!"

Jane looked starboard and stared into the storm. It was seconds away. The sun teased at fully setting while winds howled and spat on the hard working sailors. The hideous yelping laughter reminded everyone that this was no ordinary storm, this wasn't anything natural or made by the graces of God or nature. This was hell in a cloud and it burned across the Atlantic with them in its path.

"Liam!" the captain yelled. "Spears, javelins and nets to port side! I know of nothing else we can throw and kill with but if you see something, bring it as well."

"Yes, m'lady!!"

"Nelly!!! Where the hell are those flares!! Also get arrows and anything else you might need."

"Everything is ready on deck, m'lady! Fifty loaded single round pistols, twenty loaded double shot Winchesters, fifteen flares and a partridge in a pear tree."

The vampire smiled before handing her captain the flares. Jane couldn't help but give a rain soaked smile. "Thanks dear, I needed that. Now off to the crow's nest. Take what you need, hold off as much as possible but be careful. I don't know what I'd do without you."

"Let's hope I don't let you find out, captain," she answered.

Jane embraced the young vampire's face and traced the shape of a wave on her forehead but without digging and cutting skin as she had done with Vincenzo.

"Is everyone on alert, Liam?" Daniel asked.

"Aye, sir. Everyone is armed and ready at the first glimpse of nightshade. I left Nathaniel alone. Let us hope he doesn't get chivalrous when all hell breaks loose upon us."

"Good, I'll check on him later, but for the moment, wear your best poker face, my friend; we're on."

Clouds swirled directly overhead but the setting sun still allowed faint glimpses of the Black Calico's deck. Wind veins streaked and at a distance, a dark ball of utter blackness crept slowly towards the deck.

Nelly called from the crow's nest. "Impact in thirty seconds!!"

The silence was as if God himself held his breath in anticipation. The calm before the storm. The deafening silence.

"Twenty seconds!!!" she yelled again.

As the great unknown wrapped itself and spread to all directions, Liam couldn't help but speak his mind. "The beginning is the half of every action."

Daniel smiled and while holding the tight bowstring offered his own words. "As God disposes, man laughs or weeps. Let us laugh old friend, for death comes to dance and we are not to deny the wench our charity..."

Silence breathed upon them. All hands pulled tightly on their bows and eight shimmering eyes did their best to cut through the grey gloom they wished was already pitch black. A small splash finally quibbled on the side of the boat closely followed by a bigger one. The waves continued to grow in intensity until they desisted from merely slapping the hull and began raising the galleon with large swells. First it was five feet that the boat rose and fell; soon it was ten and soon it didn't matter because they were constantly falling or rising.

A light fizzing noise gave way to a small glowing dot that soared into the sky. It exploded into a red afternoon that blossomed over the ocean and beneath its red glow, hundreds of figures could be seen swimming towards the Black Calico.

"Fire!!" Jane roared and twelve arrows flew from four bows killing at least ten of the water demons. In an instant, thirty scaly creatures flew from the water and boarded the mighty black ship. "Aqueors!!! Fire at will!!" She fell back from the steering wheel, barely ducking beneath a heavily rusted axe that nearly cleaved her in two. She returned the favor with a blow of her blade, which struck in the exact middle of the furry scaly brow of the water demon.

Fifteen of the thirty creatures had already died when two massive green fireballs crashed against the hull. A third even larger fireball soared through the sky and crushed through one of the windows, effectively lighting the ship on fire, inside and out.

"Tend to the flames!" the captain roared. She then tore straight through the midsection of a demon while plucking her bow to force feed an arrow to another foul beast.

Net in hand, Liam enveloped a group of five demons while running towards one of the roaring fires. A full quiver from the crow's nest courtesy of Nelly took care of that group while the vampire doctor pried the lit planks from the boat and cast them into the ocean. But another wave had risen and the laughter that had momentarily faded came screaming back towards him. He cradled against the port side nets looking for cover and was just able to see a large tentacle receding into the ocean. It had left even more demons.

Another flare flew into the sky while the ship's lower deck belched huge rolling smoke clouds. Suddenly, the floorboards broke out and the lower deck doors flew open. Arrows flew in every direction and shots cracked loud from the darkness below.

Leading the cavalry up from the inferno below, Lucas walked determinedly to the gun rack and started taking a series of pistols. Two he slipped into the front of his trousers, followed by two for each front pocket and two for the back pockets. For good measure he took two more for each hand.

With a flick of his thumb, he let off one shot that killed a flanking aqueaor. He took the opportunity to be efficient and stabbed another water demon in the eye with the empty gun's barrel. He then took his other gun and shot another monster in the head, quickly discarding the empty barrel to take the two front pocket guns. Two more demons fell quickly but he suddenly found himself wrapped from behind by two slimy arms. Without losing his nerve, he greeted the sneaky bastard with the two rounds from the guns in his back pockets, picked up a spear and continued to rage his rampage on the enemy.

Indigo was set to continue the warpath he'd begun back at the Halo Maze plowing through almost a dozen aqueaors with a hefty battle-axe. His face clearly showed he still remembered there was a debt for his fallen comrade and he was going to collect his payment in demon blood. Countless limbs fell on the deck as swarms of the beasts continued to flood the Black Calico.

Then the laughter began again. It came from all directions. It circled around the boat and as they fought, no one could help but concentrate on that instead of the demons that kept falling to the blades, arrows and gunshots of the vampire battalion. The entire deck was covered in the black oily blood of demons and it finally seemed like the battle was tilting to their side.

A piercing shriek signaled the death of the last aqueaor on deck and the laughter vanished suddenly. Daniel was covered in black blood as was his sword though his eyes burned severely in their jade glow. "On your toes, people..." he called out to his comrades, "this isn't over by a long shot."

He looked around and to his relief and satisfaction saw allies standing over fallen enemies. Malia, Mary and Wendy had been knocked around pretty badly, but they were ok. Luckily the other fire on the top deck had been put out. Unfortunately, the one in the lower decks still raged on.

Quite suddenly, a thought struck Daniel. 'Nathaniel's in danger.' He also realized that the danger was far from exclusive to the human by looking at the crew. Liam still looked winded from a blow from the tentacle and although Lucas was reloading several of his guns, he had also taken a couple of hits.

Daniel looked all around and called out to the captain. "Are you all right, Jane?!"

"Yes, Daniel."

He called out again. "Liam, Lucas?"

"Fine, sir."

Seeing his intentions, Jane now called to her crew, "Corsaires, sound off."

One by one the vampire pirates began sounding off until an awkward silence lingered long enough to prompt the captain to call out. "Nelly! Sound off!!"

No answer. Smoke gelled with darkness and visibility was piss-poor even for a vampire.

"Nelly?!" the captain said, her voice beginning to quiver.

No answer.

"How 'bout Indigo?" Daniel cried.

"I'm still here bu— YEORGHHHH!!!"

When Daniel looked towards the direction of that gurgling scream, he saw his friend stabbed through the chest by a large rock spire which proceeded to lift him several feet up in the air before pulling him off into the dark waters.

"NOOOO," Daniel roared. He ran to the rail but only had enough time to see the eyes of his friend as the shadow of death eclipsed them.

He shook with uncontrollable anger while stepping backwards slowly. All the others followed his lead, but Daniel's grief was itself interrupted by a broken voice swollen with sorrow.

"N-N-Nelly?"

Daniel immediately regained composure. "M'lady, we need to focus. It is Belial who is upon us."

Every muscle within her small but powerful body became tense and alert. She knew that name.

The largest wave they had yet seen crashed against the Black Calico and everyone on deck stumbled and fell awkwardly. When they were able to regain their bearings, they quickly realized that instead of another battalion of aqueaors, twelve enormous tentacles slivered across most of the deck. Instead of an octopus or a squid, the tentacles held up a large torso whose skin faded from charcoal black at the tentacles to fire red at the neck. Daniel looked the creature known as Belial in the eye and pointed his still hungry sword at the beast.

"Well isn't this lovely?" crawled the maggoty voice followed by a slurp and wheeze. "A big blood-sucking family."

The monster slithered easily on the blood sloshing on deck and for however grotesque it looked, it moved with the grace of a demonic swan.

"My dear Captain – slurp wheeze – It's been quite a while. How are those adorable aqua bats of yours doing these days? – slurp wheeze – Fine I hope but uncalled which is odd coming from you. But don't worry, I have some –slurp wheeze – soldiers on their way to give them a message from me."

The vampire captain clamped her teeth with rage and her expression made her seem ten feet tall rather than her vertical reality, which was barely more than half that.

As Belial's black button eyes scanned the entire deck to see where everyone was standing, a smile lurched on its face. "Dear Daniel, I'd almost overlooked you – slurp wheeze – You I haven't seen in centuries. So nice of you to be here. – slurp wheeze – Come to think of it, your braided haired friend seemed to have a message for you.

Unfortunately I couldn't understand one word as he drowned, so I'm afraid I'll owe you that one."

The huge rock spire danced behind the wobbling creature like a drunken cobra. It bent to the front to graze the noseless nostrils on the beast's face. "Mmmm... I can still smell him, Daniel. The bite I had was delicious and though I can't wait to finish that plate, you know I'm a fan of variety and I must thank you for this divine selection. Oh, Captain Jane? That lovely girl that was in the crow's nest? Absolutely delicious."

Trickles of blood streamed down both Daniel and Jane's chins as their fangs dug deep into their lips. Everyone had a weapon in hand and they all aimed towards the demon. Then the red light that had been shining above flickered. When it faded, all went completely black and this time there was no one to fire another flare.

Laughter began. Wicked laughter and nothing else. No waves, no wind, nothing except laughter... and the faint clatter of hooves.

- Below deck -

Nathaniel continued his own struggle.

"Don't fight the missst, my king. The more you ssstruggle the worsse it will be for you."

As the voice continued to coax him, Nathaniel struggled in his bed but couldn't move. He felt his arms firmly pinned to the mattress even though nothing held him down. His legs were bound apart but again, nothing seemed to be holding down any of his limbs. Sweat rolled down his face and his eyes splintered red from the exertion.

The reality was that through those very same bloodshot eyes, he saw his hands tied by dark strands of shadow. His feet were clamped down by mighty claws of shade and in front of him, he only saw a bending wall of blackness that flowed and ebbed like satin sheets, floating by themselves.

No matter how he tried, he couldn't see that his hands and feet were free and he was certainly not able to see what lay beyond the dull green-grey eyes. On the chair sat a massive serpent whose crown was like a cobra's and its body that of a full grown python.

The power of the mist was such that where Nathaniel saw a heavy crown and scepter, in reality there was only a large sacrificial dagger set beside the body of a dead and dried snake which was coiled to make a thin circlet. Where the young man saw a shining sapphire, a piece of rotten flesh was lodged into the snake crown. In the place of the bright yellow sunstone on the right, there was really oxidized fool's gold and for the large red ruby apple in the front of the crown, there was a large plump spider. Its venom sack was the size of a golf ball and the fiery amber color signaled the presence of deadly poison.

The voice slithered all over the young man's body. "Come now, King Runnelsss. Put on thy crown!"

Nathaniel's body arched and struggled but it would not obey; his will to scream was drugged by deception.

"Just a glimpssse of thee wearing thy crown, sssire; nothing more doth your ssservant asssk before I go on my way and let you wake up. I ssswear."

The human continued to struggle and contort in resistance but to no avail. The snake became frustrated at his willpower and began to raise its voice. "Don't you want to be more than human?! Don't you want to finally conquer the next step of evolution?!! DON'T YOU WANT TO BE A GOD??!!!!"

A reservoir of tears banked in Nathaniel's eyes. His muscles ripped at themselves and the agony he was experiencing tore at the very core of his soul. His eyes darted back and forth but all he saw was shade... except for the window. So that was where he focused. He knew he couldn't let go of anything that remained free of the shade because he felt like that was his last chance at any type of salvation.

Waves danced on the boundless ocean outside and his mind tiptoed on the distant crests, attempting to escape via disembodiment. He'd seen dark figures leaping out of the water as the smell of burning wood spread about while smoke rose to the sky. He was filled with fear until all of a sudden snow began to fall inexplicably in the middle of the ocean while thunderous gallops bent his pulse and a grayish white shadow passed in front of his eyes.

The serpent hissed desperately. "Put the crown on, you fool!!! Do it NOW!!!! DO IT!!! DO IT!!!!"

A large crash then battered the cabin door and a flash of green ripped clear through the shade. The weight suddenly came off Nathaniel's body and he sat up on the bed to see Daniel standing over the headless serpent grabbing what had once been a crown and scepter to his eyes.

The vampire stood at the side of the bed. "Are you all right, Nathaniel?"

The only response was confusion distilled through terrified eyes. Liam then came into the room, sat on the bed and pulled out a pouch that smelled like freshly sawed sandalwood and cinnamon. He took a pinch of whatever was in it and held it under the human's nose, instructing him to breathe. Nathaniel flinched and fidgeted like a boxer after being given smelling salts.

"You made the acquaintance of an old foe," Liam said, "a foe that used to go by the name of Iblis." He consoled the human by rubbing his left shoulder. "It seems we've all been under attack during the last hour. But ignorantly, we all thought you'd be safe below deck."

Daniel then stood beside the young man. "Actually Runnels, you may be familiar with this demon. He had actually been sentenced to hell when he vowed to bring down humankind. Legend holds that the first time he attempted, he succeeded by prying humankind from its original grace through an original sin. It's a good thing that history will tell of his fall here."

Nathaniel seemed shaken but his face showed that he understood. "This was —"

"The Bible might not all be true," interrupted the vampire, "but it's not all fiction either, human. Consider most books, especially Genesis as works of fiction based on truth."

"But the shade... the crown."

"All part of its talents, Nathaniel," Liam said. "This snake crown was what he wanted you to put on but he couldn't force it upon you. Free will need not only apply to righteous acts. You had to choose to put it on for yourself even if he was more than willing to coerce you into doing so."

"What happened above deck?" the human asked.

Daniel's face grew severe. "If you can walk, you may come and see."

After some effort, they exited the room and emerged from the deck stairs. The air was still blistering below deck from the fires, but luckily they had been controlled. Outside however, it was snowing. Nathaniel looked around and saw various corsaires scrubbing the black blood to channels running along the sides of the ship, something he hadn't noticed before. His puzzled stare prompted Daniel to answer his silent query.

"We were attacked by water demons called aqueors and a creature known as Belial, a very powerful ocean demon. The blood from all of the creatures slain is swept to those channels which themselves feed the ship. In short, where you would use coal, crude oil or petrol for fuel on other ships, the Calico uses demon blood; and trust me, after tonight, it's pretty much a given that there won't be a shortage of fuel for quite some time. Although the Calico will also need plenty of blood to heal its wounds. I could explain in detail, but suffice to say that this ship is more than she seems."

Nathaniel seemed too exhausted to complain at the cryptic explanation and continued to look around at the carnage on deck. He saw deep scratches on the floor, broken masts, missing planks and torn sails. "Is everyone ok?" he asked.

Daniel looked down grimly, having come upon the topic he'd most like to avoid. "No... Nelly, Anne, Devi and Indigo are lost."

Nathaniel could actually feel the pain in Daniel's voice even if the vampire's tone and body remained stoic, but that didn't keep him from inquiring further. "And this... Belial?"

"Well to be quite honest, we weren't doing that well. Sure we killed every aqueor that came on deck, but Belial was the real source of danger and the one who caused most of the damage. He probably would have finished us off if not for him."

Daniel then pointed to the pilot's deck. There stood Jane beside a frozen abomination and in front of them stood a large majestic white figure which looked like an animated ice sculpture. The angel's large wings were tucked behind him, and he looked like he was made of frost which glistened with the torch lights. It spoke to the beast but remained emotionless until its gaze flowed over in the direction of the human. He stopped talking and exchanged a deep gaze with Nathaniel. After saying something to Jane, she walked towards the group.

"Raguel will see you now," she said with an eerie sense of calm in her voice.

After Liam took his leave to help on deck, Daniel and Nathaniel walked towards the glacial angel.

"Runnels," Daniel whispered, "this is Raguel, his name means Friend of God. He is second in command of what you'd call archangels though their real name is the Amesha Spentas, otherwise known as the Holy Immortals. This particular Amesha Spenta is the archangel of justice, fairness and harmony. His mission is to maintain balance always. Basically he watches over all other angels and makes sure everyone works well with mortals in the moments angels have to intervene in the doings of mankind. This means that he issues punishment for angels who have broken angelic law."

After a few more steps, the white grey eyes of Raguel met with Nathaniel's simple brown irises. Beside the angel, the beast Belial stood frozen up to its neck. Its breathing came and went in spurts of frozen chatter. "D-d-da... mn.... Iblis f-f-failed."

"Silence!" Raguel roared as he struck the demon's face splattering frozen black blood on the deck. The angel then turned to the vampire and human and spoke calmly as if nothing had happened. "Hello, Daniel," he now said in a deep chilly whisper. "Seems you've been busy lately. So this is the human?"

"Yes, Amesha Raguel," replied Daniel in a very formal tone demonstrating the respect for the angel's rank.

"Thank you for the decorum, but there will be no need for formalities. I've been speaking with our little friend here and it seems your intentions are known. As you are aware, I am not allowed to show you the safest path but it is not against celestial law to warn you that it is a long and harsh road that awaits you. If you are to have any chance in this venture, you will require much more help than you'd wish you had to ask for."

"For now, you have my word that the rest of your ocean voyage shall remain uninterrupted; a small token afforded due to this demon's interference. I suggest you heal your wounded, mourn your fallen and continue to assist this young oneironaut. He needs guidance and protection. If killed, all won't be lost but I assure you that alive he will prove rather useful."

"Yes, Raguel," Daniel replied.

A low rumbling laughter broke out causing all eyes to turn to Belial. "You... will NEVER survive," said the frozen demon. "ANY of you. Th-th-the end is n-n-nigh. Dark ar...mies are unit-t-ting. We sh-sh-shall be vic...torious and your w-w-world will c-c-ome to an end."

"Is that a fact?" the icy figure asked. "That's good to know because it means that they won't miss a general."

The angel then picked an ice shard from his wings, stabbed the beast in the eye and followed that move with a heaving blow that crushed its frozen body. A light shone brightly amidst the rubble of frozen flesh and seven large balls of black fire hovered momentarily before shooting off in different directions.

"Damn," the angel said as he followed the lights with his gaze. "I guess that's a task we'll have to pursue at a later time. Now I must depart. May God be with you."

"Yeah... If his schedule isn't too busy," Daniel said scowling.

The faintest of smiles came to Raguel's face as he whispered one word. "Incorrigible."

"Captain!" called out the ice angel in salute to Jane.

"My lord," she replied.

"Send message to your Daubentons. They are to go to the Indian Ocean and await further instructions."

"Yes, my lord."

"Be well, my child," he told her, "dangerous events have a way of finding your beloved Daniel. And you Runnels, a pleasure."

Sheer instinct dictated Nathaniel's reaction and yet another small smile came to Raguel's face as he looked down to the outstretched human hand. "He could teach you some things, Daniel," the angel said as his icy hand embraced the warmth of Nathaniel's. He then jumped over the side rail and floated down to a mighty steed that like its master seemed made of ice. It stood on a frozen platform and every step it took immediately froze the water that lay beneath.

Raguel kicked the horse and it reared its legs up high in the middle of the ocean. "God's will be done!" he said in a booming voice and the horse stormed off forging a frozen path across the Atlantic.

In the opposite direction of the angel, something finally showed to soothe some of the woes of the crew. Something simple, permanent and firm.

Land.

Chapter 13: The Street With No Name

Morning nears at the Bay of Cadiz in Spain. Its waters wash over the sands of Playa la Victoria, which look out towards the sea as a beautiful black galleon passes near the beach. The irony of the name of the beach does not escape Nathaniel... Victory Beach. While he ponders on all that's occurred in the last few hours, the vessel slows to a halt several hundred yards from the shore and he listens as a small raft drops into the water. He turns around and is greeted by various figures converging on the main deck while he feels others rustling below. When he looked toward the helm something else caught his eye. It wasn't another attack or some supernatural creature. It was one hand holding another. He couldn't help but smile as Daniel and Jane stood in front of each other.

Though she tried to hide it, Jane's eyes glistened with concern. "Be careful, Daniel."

"Careful is my middle name," replied the vampire with his trademark smile.

For once, she humored him and smiled back. "Actually, you don't have a middle name."

Daniel continued to grin. "Ah yes, but if I did, it might as well be Careful. Good solid name, Careful."

She sighed and smiled. "You'll never change."

"Not if you enjoy me this way I won't," he said. "But seriously, thank you for..."

"For the trip, for the effort, for the rescue, and the food, you're welcome. Anything else was not a favor, so no thanks needed."

Daniel looked to his feet smiling. "You'll never change either."

Jane actually blushed. "Good of you to notice," she said after regaining her composure. "Now get going. Remember to look for Tobias and show him the medallion I gave you. You still have it don't you?"

The vampire's response consisted of opening his shirt and showing the chain that led to the Eye of Cardino and next to it a copper medallion with the inscription - No 8 do -.

Jane focused on the lens and caressed his right cheek. "Be careful, Daniel... please."

"Yes... m'lady," he answered with another smile before setting off to meet with the crew on the main deck.

All members were there hovering in the predawn gloom, including Nathaniel. Daniel turned to speak to them. "I know it is not in our nature to separate at times like these, but it must be done. I must go alone with Runnels to gain passage to Claus's brothers. Make your way up the Guadalquivir River when I send word. May fate be kind to you and may the woes on the sand wash away with the tide."

"Sir..." Liam called, "remember that you are an actor in a play which a manager directs."

Daniel smiled. "Epictetus. In other times, such a statement might apply but this time there is no script and we improvise." He shook the hands of all and called to Nathaniel. The human looked around and met various kind smiles, pats on the back and firm handshakes. One by one they gave their best until it came to Malia... beautiful Malia.

"You and I have unfinished business," she whispered in his ear. "I'll be thinking about you... and from the looks of things, it seems hard to fathom that you won't think about me."

Daniel gave a loud snort. "Even after facing death God knows how many times, a man is still but a man. Off we go."

They climbed down to the raft and after reeling in the rope, they shoved off to shore. Five minutes later, Nathaniel looked as the same raft that had just brought them ashore gurgled and sunk. Daniel had unplugged the drain hole.

"You never know when you might need it," Daniel said noticing the look on Nathaniel's face. "Now... we need to do something about our attire."

"Wendy gave me a satchel with some clothes for us. They're simple, plain and modern so we shouldn't have any trouble."

The vampire actually chortled. "Casanova's being taken care of eh???"

Nathaniel ignored the comment and set off to search for a place to change doing his best attempt to hide his red cheeks. After they managed to dump the old set of clothes, they started walking up the streets that twisted and bent into each other from beyond the sands.

For some time, Nathaniel seemed to mull over something until he finally looked to the vampire. "Daniel, what did the angel call me last night?"

"Oneironaut?" Daniel asked quite clear as to what the human was referring to. "Took you long enough to ask."

"Yeah; what is that?"

"Well you had a vision, correct? A type of dream sequence where you were completely conscious and aware? Well traveling through dreamscapes and seeing the things you saw means that your mind can travel in dream state and still live and learn. Without knowing it, you extended yourself beyond the confines of your body and tapped into something much like a collective consciousness. Though it is still not confirmed that the Lygophilials are in fact dead, me and Liam are quite convinced that they are. Exactly what happened, I cannot predict or deduce, hence us being here to find out. The Lygophilials had their quarters here in Cádiz."

"Yeah, but where in Cádiz?" asked Nathaniel as he followed Daniel into a very narrow street.

"Funny you should ask Runnels, we're already there."

The entire block was devoid of a single door or window. It was just a long flat and smooth wall that reached the next corner. Nathaniel looked up and down the small side street with a quizzical look on his face, half dumbfounded by that whole thing about oneironauts and half perplexed at his current position in the middle of a shrivel of a passageway. "What do you mean we're here? This side street doesn't even have a name."

"Well, remember what I mentioned of special visors of the watchers. This was way back in the Halo Maze. I think Liam put one on to observe your cardinal points. It's time for you to see if more of what I say is dung or fact. Put these on."

Daniel handed Nathaniel an exact replica of the visors he'd seen the vampire doctor use in the maze and a vague recollection of how the visor clamped to Liam's skin squirmed in his stomach.

He groaned as he handled the visor and the vampire smirked at him. "It'll hurt, Runnels, but trust in that I won't leave you out here alone."

The visors looked harmless enough, but Nathaniel knew what they did, or at least what they did to stay firmly in place. The rest was taking Daniel's word for it although he'd soon know exactly what it was like. He hesitated nearing them to his face in expectance of pain. He tried once... twice... a third attempt failed.

"Oh come on, you big baby!" said Daniel who already had his visor on.

It was clear Nathaniel would gladly offer a slap to take the visor off the vampire's face but instead he slammed his own into his visor feeling the steel clamps bite hard into his face as everything around him melted into a shower of falling light. Everything shone and only a set of cold vampire hands helped him regain control.

"Easy, boy. Easy," Daniel said consolingly. "Give it a second, breathe normally and try to let your eyes adjust."

Slowly, Nathaniel's breathing went from heaving gulps of air to deep controlled and measured breaths. His eyes burned much like happens when you've been in salt water too long.

The vampire continued to coach him through the process. "Come on, open them slowly."

The bright light had faded and now everything looked tinged in some red color like that of the Eyes of Cardino, the healing water he'd bathed in the Halo Maze or the red spice powder known as egnalem. Everything seemed to be bubbling and if one could ever survive submerged in cola; this is what it would probably look like from below the surface.

He looked at Daniel and saw him without a visor on and before he could ask, the vampire answered. "The mid dimension shows things differently, Runnels. In our dimension we are wearing visors, it is five AM and we are standing in a doorless, windowless alley whereas here, the second sun has risen and it would be more like afternoon. Oh and there are these steps and door to take into account."

When Nathaniel looked to his left, there they were - a set of stone steps and a half open door. "What about the wall in our world?" he asked.

"We'll pass through it like you would water. Now follow me."

Before doing so, Nathaniel looked at the wall and saw two inscriptions in silver letters lit like the ones back in the Halo Maze. One inscription was embedded on a crest that read 'Lygophilials' and the other was a square block that read emanon.

Daniel noticed the young man had seen the plaque and smirked. "The street with no name seems to have a name after all, doesn't it?"

"No name backwards, hardy-har."

"Gooood," said Daniel still smiling. "Now let us go up then, there reeks the smell of many deaths and one has already arrived and left."

They went up the steps, pushed the door open and walked into the invisible mansion. Everything was deathly silent and beneath their feet streaked a trail of blood that stretched up a white marble staircase that they followed.

Everything seemed broken or smashed and the smell of death was quite fresh in the air. It didn't take them long to find where the carnage had taken place. A door lay ripped from its hinges and blood splatter painted the floor. In through the door they went and Nathaniel was struck by a horrible sense of déjà vu since he'd seen this exact same scene before in his dream. But now it was in full color and included surround sound and scent. Bodies lay literally ripped apart on the floor with body parts jumbled to such an extent that you didn't know who the owner of which limb was.

"It's only the men," Nathaniel said as he remembered the dream and compared. "In my dream no women were left behind, they were taken away by those... those... things."

"You're not completely correct, Runnels," Daniel said as he rushed to a corner where a once beautiful woman was on the floor. The same woman Nathaniel had seen in his video and that had captivated him before she had been butchered.

Daniel knelt down and spoke gently. "Melissa, don't move."

"There...was...no... war...n..ing," whispered her broken voice. "They... k...killed.... everyone." She fell on her side and hunched her deathly pale body. "They... would have ... taken me... but... I was t-too... damaged."

Daniel took her arm and as he pulled it back, saw a massive wound on her stomach that was still pouring her life on the floor.

"Lord..."

"Daniel... They are too... s...strong... we need... EVERY one... e-even... th-th-therians."

"Melissa... we can't it's too..."

"Don't be ...STUPID... Daniel. Uhhnnnn.... We ... need ... everyone..."

Nathaniel could only look at the once divine beauty now dying in Daniel's arms. Her deep curls were drenched in blood, her full lips cracked and dry and the beautiful eyes reflecting death.

"Is ... this... the one, Daniel?" she asked.

"Yes, Meli."

"Then get him... out of... here and s-s-safe."

"Don't worry, once we get you—"

"Leave... me... be... Daniel," she interrupted.

"But-"

"But nothing," she said summoning all her strength. "It is ... my time... Give this... to ... Liam... and tell him... I loved him..." She wept. "I... always... loved him... but... I have... to ... go... now...."

Her eyes then lost what little light had been flickering a second before and remained looking at Nathaniel with a gentle smile frozen on her face. Daniel looked at his hand and saw she had placed two vials in it. After closing her eyes, he stood to face Nathaniel. One vial he placed in his coat pocket while the other remained in his hand.

"Had you ever met her Runnels?" asked the vampire.

The young man was still at a loss for words from the scene that had just unfolded before him. "Umm – no. I've never met her before."

"Then why do you look at her as if you know her?" the vampire interrogated. "Have you ever seen her?"

Nathaniel's eyes swam in the memory of the recent dream. He remembered her undulating body and the sheer sensuousness and fire with which she made love. "She was in the dream I told Liam about."

Daniel looked at him sideways and clenched his jaw, clearly suspicious. "This is for you," he said as he handed Nathaniel the second vial of blood. "What you do with it is your concern. Now off we go. Friends will come soon to care for the bodies and we do not have time to spare."

Down the winding stairs they descended. They then walked through the bloodied hall and out the door. Once outside on the small street, Daniel pried the visor off his face, leaving two gashes on his temples, which quickly began to heal. Nathaniel was a bit more hesitant. He remembered what Liam had gone through to take off the visor and had just seen Daniel's wounds. He wasn't too thrilled to share in the pain.

"We don't have all day, Runnels. Whenever you're ready."

Nathaniel gave the vampire a spiteful look then gripped the visor with both hands firmly and yanked with all his might only to feel... nothing.

Daniel gave a little snigger at the young man's reaction before clarifying. "It only becomes resistant after repeated usage, Runnels. Let us be off."

The human rubbed the weariness from his eyes and followed Daniel who was already quite ahead.

"There should be taxis driving up ahead," the vampire said. "We'll need to take one to our next destination but one second, I will also need to send word to Liam of what has happened."

Daniel then pulled out a wooden box from his coat which had a bunch of holes in it and the letters RM engraved on the cover in golden letters. When he opened it, a flashing red blur buzzed out from the box. It flew to and fro over Nathaniel and even danced in and out of the human's open mouth while he stood lulled by the crimson dervish.

It finally stopped on Daniel's neck and after a second, Nathaniel could finally see it. It was a large red mosquito that now proceeded to pierce Daniel's flesh to feed.

Instinctively, Nathaniel reached out for the bug and swept full force before a frigid vice clamped on his forearm. "Would you mind?" Daniel said bearing his teeth. "I'm trying to send a message."

A second later the mosquito disengaged and flew off while Daniel released his firm grip on Nathaniel's arm.

"Pavlov would have loved you, Runnels. A couple of bells chime and you slobber. A bug flies nearby and you swipe at it. Please feel free to go to your nearest Buddhist to learn the value of all life instead of obeying your every impulse. Now let's go."

"Wait a minute," Nathaniel said, "that's what was in your room in the maze."

"I don't deny it," the vampire said with his scheming smile. "I had to keep an eye on you to make sure you behaved while I was away. Lucky for me, it's also a handy way of communicating sensitive messages to others like me. So please, mind the merchandise and let's go."

Nathaniel followed Daniel down the narrow street and rubbed at the tingling spots where the visor had clung to. As their steps echoed down the alley, the sight of them slowly faded in the dark reflection of two crimson eyes. This gaze now turned to the wall they had just come through and gave a low rumbling growl. The hulking figure cracked all its bones and seemed to swell as a low hum seeped from its body. The corridor started to crackle with electricity and the figure walked to the wall and passed through it, without the need of a visor. Upon entering, a yellow toothed smile shone in the limelight as the creature relished in the smell of death and decay.

Its steps were heavy as they scraped the marble floors. After surveying the entrance, the thing spoke in a deadly snarl. "Now... how about we find out who's been talking to their friends?" The awful voice would have been bad enough, but to make it worse, the pale grey mouth where the sound came from failed to fully articulate all the words that slithered out.

The coat that covered the figure was suddenly flung to the floor revealing a black leathery creature covered in hair. The grey skinned face that warbled with attempts at speech clung to the body because of three copper clamps that bore grotesquely into the black flesh, which would definitely explain the ventriloquist enunciation from seconds before.

The thing sniffed heavily and worked on gaining a trail. Sniff... sniffffffff... "Who told those two little birds about what happened here?"

Dead bodies were flung left and right as the creature's red eyes scanned every corpse within range, but it still didn't find what it was looking for. "No. No. Noooo.... Not this one either.... Ah-hah... here we are." As it said these words, it stood over the dead body of Melissa.

Kneeling down beside the still beautiful woman, it sniffed heavily, relishing the freshness of her death. The mask did its best to smile but the loose skin turned awkwardly and screwed up more so than smile.

"So you're the one who has been talking," it gargled, allowing a piece of slobber to fall on the floor. "How about you tell me all that you told them."

It then cackled maniacally while hovering over the lifeless body. From its mane, the demon took out a long needle, two coins and ripped some hair off its massive forearm. Melissa's naked body was then dragged unceremoniously to an open area and stretched out. The monster then crossed her legs at the ankles and placed her arms by her side pointing downwards to form a type of human arrow with her head pointing south. The two coins were placed over her eyes, the hairs were spread on her lips and the needle was stuck through her larynx. The beast then pulled out a crimson colored tuning fork and while standing over her, took one of its long claw nails and snapped it against the metal. Instead of a ping or a clang, a slow buzzing hum resonated across the death ridden hall. Then the monster breathed deeply and spoke over the deep vibration.

"Soul of dead, return from ascension.
Severed lifeline be restored,
Free thy secrets from skin deep bondage.

163

I reward revelations with silver soiled.
Murmur commands, now answer my questions.
Return from heaven and obey me."

When the demon had finished its prayer, it looked down on the beautiful woman's corpse, as if looking for any sign of movement... a breath, a twitch, anything... until there it was... the slow ticking of lips. "Hello, Ms. Bardizbanian," it said as it saw her mouth quiver. "A pleasure to make your acquaintance."

Her lips trembled but the rest of her body could not move. "B-b-but... I'm d-d-d-dead."

The flaccid mask looked down on her. "Not quite my dear, but very good to see that you still have your wits about you. Let me make this clear, this won't take long unless you do not cooperate. My time is short since friends of yours are on their way to clean up this delicious mess. But I require some answers you have. If there is any doubt within you, please let me assure you that non-compliance will only cause me to prolong your agony even further. After all, just because you're dead doesn't mean you can't feel an entire legion of my demons befouling your body. Tell me, can you even imagine what it would be like, if every single cell of your being could feel the pain of being chewed and digested."

"Go to hell!!!!!" Melissa screamed in horror.

"Only on the holidays, wench," said the creature as it gave her a wretched attempt at a smile. "Why don't we see how this feels?"

The demon then stomped on both legs of the corpse and Melissa screamed in agony as bones crushed in her lifeless legs. "Now I think I have your attention."

Chapter 14: La Corrida

Seville at night is a no man's land. The sheer beauty of the city and its gardens is enough to mesmerize you into not noticing the different dangers that lurk in the shadows once the sun sets.

Nathaniel was already weary of a full day's worth of not finding their contacts. "We've been searching all day, Daniel, and still no sign of Tobias."

"And we shall keep looking human," Daniel said. "No one said it'd be easy." A moment later, the vampire's focus centered somewhere in the bushes and he seemed to see something of importance. "Wait one minute, Runnels. I must check something. Don't talk to anyone and do not move."

Without another word, the vampire walked into the shadows, where it appeared he was not alone. For his part, Nathaniel wasn't in the mood to pay attention. As happens with groups after being stuck together too long, the young man was even thankful to finally have some peace and quiet from the constant banter of the vampire. Disregarding the orders given, he proceeded to walk around the central gardens of the Alcazar of Seville.

There were still quite a few people up and about. On more than one occasion, Nathaniel noticed how a local gypsy offered to read tourists their fortune with rosemary leaves. That was actually the tactic they used to hypnotize people to such a degree that they focused on all the fortunes they were told without noticing those which were stolen.

Luckily, Nathaniel didn't have anything valuable on him except his father's pocket watch, which he clutched in his fist. He simply admired the lush scenery while looking at the picturesque scene as it bathed in the warm light that glowed from the light posts.

He walked aimlessly and pretty soon the spot where Daniel had faded into the shadows was completely out of sight. He didn't care. He simply focused on the warm night air, and the strong scents of grass, earth and dirt mingling with dampened steeds that were led around the gardens near the Alcazar. Birds chirped, random whispers chattered and a clicking of hooves neared from behind.

A black carriage had parked nearby and a slender figure in a mustard yellow tunic jumped off and walked in Nathaniel's direction. An odd gut feeling prompted Nathaniel to pick up the pace. The figure lined up behind him and actually called out to him in Spanish. "Permiso, señor."

Nathaniel responded by accelerating more than moderately but the figure still kept calling. "Permiso, señor. Permiso."

The young man didn't even think about looking back. It'd be too obvious that he knew some Spanish. If instead he played the role of ignorant foreigner, then his rudeness wouldn't even be questioned. But no matter how much he sped up, the voice called from the same exact distance; never more, never less. "Permiso, señor. Permiso." It finally became too much to ignore and he looked behind to see how much distance they had between each other.

No sooner had he turned around that Nathaniel gave a scream and stumbled to the ground. He had met the face of the man in the yellow tunic only a foot and a half away from his own.

"Perdóneme, señor," said the man in the yellow tunic as he helped Nathaniel up.

After swatting the dust off his clothes, Nathaniel cleared his throat in preparation for the fake broken Spanish he was going to use. "N-no entiendo... perdone."

"My apologies, sir," responded the man in yellow. He had a sweet Spaniard tone with a slight overemphasis when he pronounced each syllable and a slight hiss any time an S was used. "It is just that you dropped this back there." That's when he handed Nathaniel the watch the young man swore he still had clutched in his fist.

Confusion mixed with embarrassment, apparently his favorite cocktail as of late. "Uh... th-thank you. Sorry, I don't have any money so my thanks are pretty much all I can offer."

The man in the tunic smiled. "Do not worry, sir. God does not intend ever to charge for any favor, big or small."

Nathaniel smiled back. "True, but if there's anything I can do, please let me know."

"Actually... my master is in the carriage I was in and he asked if anyone outside needed help when he heard the watch fall. Maybe you could step inside and say hello. He's quite old and it might cheer him up to know he helped someone." As the man finished this sentence, the carriage which he spoke of seemed to materialize at a distance. It stopped beneath a lamp post, seeming to be led by the wind, since no one was steering the horse.

The young man in the tunic saw the look on Nathaniel's face. "You'd be surprised how smart an animal can be if you cease treating it like just an animal."

Nathaniel couldn't disagree though when he looked again at the odd carriage, he could have sworn the horse gave a small bow when they made eye contact.

"This way, please," said the man in the tunic as he opened the door for Nathaniel.

It's not often Nathaniel saw someone in a tunic and though he was sure the young man was some type of monk, there was something still quite odd about him.

"My apologies, I have not introduced myself. I am Azarius and within is my master. Please." The young monk signaled for Nathaniel to get in the carriage and suddenly he felt like he did not have much of a choice, but he didn't feel threatened either, so he went along and stepped inside.

The carriage was actually very comfortable and the rich smell of leather had been apparent to Nathaniel long before he even heard the door click open, or even looked at the old blind man that sat inside. When he got a good look, Nathaniel could have sworn the old man was actually sitting on air, centimeters above the seat he was supposed to be occupying.

"Hello, Nathaniel," rasped the old man in an old hearty voice, tinged by Andalucian decent and a propensity to roll r's and over-pronounce each s. "You do not know me. I had not met you. But I do know who you are and you were sent to look for me. I am Tobias and this is The Carroza del Destino or Destiny's Chariot. Now let me ask you, do you know why you are here?"

Nathaniel's pulse was having a hard time getting past his current situation. This old man knew who he was and though Nathaniel wanted to reply right away, Tobias's voice had almost slipped him into some kind of enchantment. Through sheer willpower he forced himself to answer. "I am here because I can help. I'm not sure how, but that's the best answer I can give you."

The old man gave a sage-like smile. "You answer with honesty. Something tells me this is not the first occasion in recent memory where you have had this type of encounter. But to help you on your journey let me read your cards. Who knows? It may make things a bit clearer for you."

Nathaniel looked at the old man as he pulled a beautiful deck of cards from his sleeves. "Tarot cards?" he asked.

The old man shuffled the cards intricately. "Not quite. This is a very old deck and although there are a few typical cards of the tarot, there are quite a few that cannot be found anywhere else. Now please, cut the deck, shuffle it and take eight cards."

"Why eight?" Nathaniel asked.

The old man gave a small indignant puff. "Because I said so should be enough of a reason, but you desire an explanation, so be it. Eight, though itself a good number is written in the same manner as the symbol for infinity. Because energy is not created nor destroyed, it is itself infinite. Therefore, 8 cards are able to define your place within infinity."

Nathaniel didn't necessarily understand, but he didn't want to push for a more detailed explanation. He shuffled the deck as instructed, drew the eight cards and placed them next to the old man. He also could not help himself and waved his hand in front of the old man's face.

"Mr. Runnels, I am blind, but very perceptive," he said with another puff. "I am also easily annoyed; so kindly stop waving your hand in front of my face. Now please, take the cards you just placed beside me, shuffle them face down and pull out one card. Order is of the most importance in these things."

Now that he was completely embarrassed, Nathaniel followed the instructions obediently, drew one card face down and held it in the palm of his right hand.

The old man nodded in approval. "Muy bien, now put your left hand over the card and flip it so the left hand now has the card, face up." Nathaniel obeyed the instructions and the old man nodded again. "Good, now put your right hand where I can feel it and look at your card."

Nathaniel looked down and saw a great bunch of grey clouds depicted on the card with a bunch of dots embossed on the surface. "Braille?" he asked.

"Well I am blind," said the old man, "but that does not mean I cannot see. You are disheveled, unshaven, and weary. Oh and those clothes you are wearing? They are not yours."

Nathaniel's mouth hung in confusion. "How....?"

"Easy," said the old man interrupting him. "The strange clothes I perceive because of the sound of the fabric. When you wear your own clothes, you are one with them. The complete opposite applies to strange clothes. The fabric is still not used to you and it makes sounds as it tries to adjust to you. As for the part of being unshaven, I can smell the additional oils on your skin. And the part about being weary is easy; I can hear it in your voice."

Nathaniel's mouth gaped in awe. "That's incredible."

"To me it is second nature," the old man said. "From the shiver in your hands because of the coldness of mine, I can also tell that you suspect that I'm older than what you originally thought. You are correct in your assumption. Shall we continue with the reading?"

"Umm, yes please," the young man replied.

"All right," the old man said as he touched Nathaniel's right hand while leaving the left alone. "I see clouds in your beginning. You were immersed in the deepest of fogs. Metáfora of course, but a good one. Beginnings are typically very hazy."

Nathaniel tried to sound confident when he spoke. "Simple enough."

"As are most beginnings," the old man answered, "but your right hand shows something else." Tobias felt the lines and contours on Nathaniel's right hand and started to caress the card on the young man's left. "The clouds may symbolize smoke which might mean that you were blind. Does that mean anything to you?"

"Maybe," Nathaniel said. He had been to enough tarot readers to not want to give too much information since they should be the ones doing all the work.

"Hmmm... Get the next card and put this one next to me, por favor."

The second card showed a gigantic lightning bolt and the old man started off with the dual reading this time, Nathaniel's right hand in the old man's left and his right on the card. "A lightning bolt. Light, danger, energy. This might represent the light that guides your way but there's one thing you need to remember about lightning."

"And that is?" asked Nathaniel feeling a bit skeptical.

"It never strikes in the same place twice," the old man said as his blind eyes and broken corneas looked deep into Nathaniel's young functional retinas. "You are special and I understand the situation better."

Nathaniel wasn't sure how to react. "What situation? What do you know?"

The old man looked back down to Nathaniel's hands. "I can only speak of the cards my son. Either I continue or I do not."

Nathaniel wasn't sure he liked where this was going, but nature does tend to prevail. "Please continue."

The old man smiled gently. "Don't bite your lip too hard. I might be old but if you bleed, I might not be able to deny my nature. Next card, please."

The next image was beautiful but macabre. A prisoner is bleeding and weeping uncontrollably. Meanwhile, the devil holds him against his chest and next to them there is a bloody whip on the floor.

"Ah yes," hummed the old man, "el diablo que consuela – The Devil that Comforts. You'd be surprised how often the devil is misinterpreted and how hard it is for people to see him. It seems most people see black and white, white and black, and in reality, life is a lot more about the grey. Captors often resent their roles and even come to love their prisoners. But don't close yourself to only one interpretation. That's something very important because every single thing in life can have a different meaning and significance depending on how you look at it."

"If you say so," Nathaniel said. "Next card?"

"Yes please... y gracias," the old man said.

Again Nathaniel took the card and placed it next to the old man and pulled a new one from the deck. A very stormy day, grey and opulent. There were two flagpoles in the picture. One with a red flag, the other with a white one. The red flag seemed to be blowing madly while the white flag and everything else in the picture for that matter, seemed utterly still. "This is your present, Nathaniel. There was recently turmoil and even grief, but that is nothing. The red flag of war dances wildly while everything else is at peace."

"A calm before the storm?" the young man asked.

"Something like that. A word of advice: be sure to let this be the only time you wander off so irresponsibly. Azarius could have killed you. It was lucky he was not a foe. Actually, you could even call him my guardian angel. But you will have to be more careful, my friend. Next card, please. This will be your immediate future overlapping your present."

Draw, flip, show. Nathaniel looked down and saw a man tied to a post shot to death with arrows. The old man grew quite stern. "Dios lo ampare," he said gravely. "This is Saint Sebastian. A great man and a saint of various noble things, though his death was one of the most painful. He was shot with arrow after arrow after arrow after arrow until finally his will could not keep his body alive any longer. You will be tested very soon and it will be up to you to not fail... and to not die. Next card."

Nathaniel wanted to ask the old man what he meant. He wanted answers. He wanted more information. He was tired of confusion. Of deciphering riddles. The old man sat in his side of the carriage and again looked at him deeply with his blind eyes. "Next card, Nathaniel. Do not make me ask for it again."

Nathaniel shivered a little at the tone of the old man. The carriage was comfortable but still small enough for a deathly blow to be hard to miss. Draw, flip, show. He had lost count of how many cards had been flipped and how many times he'd felt forced to acquiesce to the orders of a vampire. He hoped that one day he would be the one doing the ordering.

The old man interrupted his thoughts. "The voice that binds."

Nathaniel wasn't sure of what the old man had meant until he finally saw the card, he understood better. A crowd of people, hands interlocked as one person among the group spoke... or was he singing?

The old man looked especially stern this time around. "Remember this card. This is you. Next card, please. Time forces me to hasten."

Nathaniel stared at the old man as he drew the next card. A field with tall grass and nothing else.

"Grass?" asked the human.

"Yes, grass. But look closely. To the left side."

Nathaniel did as instructed and saw that while most of the blades of the grass leaned right, there were six or seven blades on the left side of the card that leaned to the left. "A snake in the grass," he asked.

"Hah," laughed the old man. "Ya entiendo a Daniel. You are quick of wit, my young friend. This card insists that you be wary of those near you. Your final card, if you please."

For one last time, Nathaniel did as asked and took a card from the deck. He feared what was on it as he pressed his palms together, flipped the card and drew away his hand. "Blank?"

"As are you, my friend. Keep that one, it might help you later."

"But it's blank," the young man said.

"It is simple," started the old man, "one can only see that much into the future. There is a line, a path and when you follow it, your future becomes clearer. But we have arrived at your stop. Be on your way and may we meet each other again."

"But..."

"But nothing, child," the old man interrupted. "What was mine to show you have seen. When the time is right, we shall meet again. Until then, keep the card safe. Nos vemos." The carriage door then opened.

Nathaniel stepped out into the warm Seville air. He looked back into the carriage and felt the need to at least ask one question. "What about the other cards?"

The old man responded by giving him a smug smile. "What? You mean these cards?" He then showed the young man the deck.

"Maybe I'll need them for guidance," Nathaniel said.

The old man smiled wider. "Oh really? What good are these cards if they're all blank?" He handed Nathaniel the deck and card after card, they were all blank.

"But..."

"Nathaniel, what you drew, no one else can draw. Such are these cards and such is their vision. Use your head, remember, internalize and be on your way. You should be thankful you have one card to keep, even if it is blank. Now we must be off. Andemos, Azarius."

"But now what?" asked the young man.

The carriage did not stop but Nathaniel could clearly hear the voice of the old man. "Now you go face your test, San Sebastián."

As the cart moved away, an old building appeared behind it. It smelled of earth, blood and battle. An entrance was directly in front of him and to the left side of the white wall with brick orange detailing, a small sign read Plaza de Toros Maestranza... a bull ring.

Doors stood open but the black void within was anything but inviting. Nathaniel forced himself into the passage because somehow... even if it was one step at a time... he knew he had to.

Darkness completely enveloped him and he felt for the cold wall to guide his path. A few yards into the dark, a faint glow seemed to light within and call him forth. Twenty wide paces later, he was at least at ease that he could see his own hands. Nathaniel looked around absentmindedly until he decided to stand with his face near the candle before going forth.

"Hello, Nathaniel," said a voice that startled him terribly. A head had materialized from the darkness, seemingly floating in the air. Sharp cheek bones, a thin chin and lush brown curls ebbed with the flicker of the candle wick. Black on white eyes stared down at the young man until the head floated down and warm hands met his to help him up. The odd thing was that the light only glowed on the sharp face, though none of the other features.

Nathaniel shrugged off the cobwebs from the fall and suddenly saw that the face he had seen a moment ago was now bearded, droopy, wore tinted glasses and smiled like a child who's just about to deliver a punch line.

"Bill," Nathaniel said.

"Not so loud and dang it, Nat, you keep forgetting that Latino accent I'm so fond of. Oh well, if you insist on Bill, then Bill it is, though I'll always prefer the sound of that Beel.

"But you're a dream," Nathaniel said. "How the hell can I even see you?"

"Two words: day dream. With enough endorphins and total darkness, you can get there, ma boy. Call me crazy, or more so, call you crazy, but I just thought I'd pop on by and check up on you. Seems you had a pretty rough time the other night, huh?"

"Rough? Hell this has been insane."

"And it's going to get crazier. Trust in that, but you'll have to keep it together. Although we still have a lot to talk about, it's your turn to pay your dues. Keep walking down the tunnel and you'll find your test."

Nathaniel looked to the opening and then back into the darkness. "What test? Bill... Bill?"

And as if made of smoke, the face disappeared and the cold blackness was there again, reaching out from all sides. He started walking again. Step, step, breath. Step, step, breath. Pacing in such a manner kept his attention on the rhythm rather than the black absence that closed from all sides until... light. Dirt. A large ring with the heavy musk of bull and steed mixed with dusty earth and the heavy essence of blood in the air.

He emerged out from the tunnel only to face hundreds of black caped figures in the stands staring back in silence. Nathaniel would have thought them statues, but occasional movements put an end to those thoughts. These weren't statues. They weren't people either. He was in a proverbial vampiric lion's den and three vampires glided in his direction to greet him. One had a long beard, beady eyes and ruffled curls that jutted from under the cone cap he wore. The middle one was a woman with a thin hard body, pronounced cheekbones and full lips like slices of pomegranate stained wedges. The one on the right was an old male with trembling lips but precise eyes.

When they stopped in front of the human, they spoke in unison: "Long have you traveled friend and already you've survived great feats. News travels fast and it does seem as if you might be the hand we have been looking for." Upon finishing their discourse, all three pulled out colored glass discs much like Daniel's. But unlike the ones Nathaniel had seen, these discs did not cling to their faces, much less dig into the flesh.

"Ah, yes," they all said in tandem, while looking over the human. "The news is true. The news is good. Now let us see how he fairs in the test." With that they floated backwards towards the sidelines, jumping up and over a ten-foot barricade without taking their eyes off Nathaniel. Hundreds of jade luminescent eyes suddenly seemed to switch on and beam upon Nathaniel where he stood proud for them to see, much prouder than he would have ever thought he was capable of.

A muted trumpet sounded, loud, clear and distinct but without the reverberation typical of the instrument. Something made Nathaniel think that the sound would not escape the ring. At the other end of where he stood, four people came out of the opposing entrance. The three in front held two barbed sticks in either hand, which were decorated with little flags of different colors. There were two men on either side and a woman in the middle. A second woman stood behind them with a simple Andalucian outfit and a long thin saber in her left hand. Two horses suddenly ran out of the tunnel and mirrored each other's run. As they crossed paths behind the group, they galloped fiercely towards Nathaniel only to cross paths again, not five feet away from the human.

The echoless trumpet sounded again and a slender yet robust figure walked out dressed in a beautiful black outfit, lined with gold thread and exquisite detailing, a small bullfighter hat, a cape and a longer and thinner sword than the one being held by the second woman of the group.

A soft fabric suddenly caressed Nathaniel's shoulders. "That's Carlo in front. The rest of the cuadrilla includes Serj and Guilherme as picadors, or lancers. Kahn, Osman and Lydia are the banderilleros and Diana is the sword servant."

Nathaniel hadn't even turned around to see who had put a cape on his shoulders. He knew it was Daniel. "I was wondering when you'd turn up," he said with an oddly calm voice. "So glad you could make it to my execution."

"Ah Runnels, optimistic as ever, I see."

"But of course," Nathaniel replied. "I can't help but smile at the fact that I'm going to be slaughtered like a bull except I don't even have horns to defend myself."

"Dear Nathaniel," said Daniel in mock indignation, "you'd think I'd forget about you? I'm hurt." Without another word, the vampire handed Nathaniel two machetes which had been painted bone white. Then he began wrapping the young man's hands so that the blades became an extension of his body.

Nathaniel let out a small snigger. "Nice; you gotta love the metaphor."

Daniel finished fastening the blades to the man's hands and looked him in the eyes seriously. "Come with me, Runnels; we must show your colors to the crowd."

The vampire led the human in front of the crowd of jade eyes for everyone to see the blue, cream, and crimson mantilla draped over him. The trumpet sounded again. Daniel gave the human a pat on the back and leapt up to the box seat where the three elders that had welcomed the young man were sitting, along with a strong chinned vampire with a silver mane and hawk eyes.

As if by instinct, Nathaniel threw off the fabric and sized up the cuadrilla. He then looked at his hands. The white color of the blades made them look more menacing than he would have thought. It was a blank canvas and he needed something to paint with. He looked at the vampires a few yards away and knew that red dye was only a slash or two away.

He took another deep breath and said "Tercio de Varas". He knew the first stage of a bullfight was to taunt him to see how he would react and observe. What blocks he would use to defend from a strike. "Thank God for those sleepless nights with cable TV. Good to know being a couch potato can actually come in handy sometimes."

All three banderilleros came forward and Nathaniel swung the new extensions to his arms to get a feel for them. The banderilleros wore light coffee colored clothes with black sashes. The vampire Daniel had told him was called Kahn had long blonde hair bound in a ponytail and he was moving towards Nathaniel's right. The one with the crazy black mane was Osman. Pretty soon they were both positioned on either side of Nathaniel, flanking him. Meanwhile, the scarlet haired Lydia stood directly in front of him.

For his part, Nathaniel was actually more scared than anyone could tell, but because he was convinced he was going to die, his main concern at the moment was to put a good show and maybe get a partner or two to carpool on his way to hell.

His heart slammed out from his chest and his eyes were sharper than a blade. A sudden thrust from Kahn had the vampire tasting dirt after Nathaniel sidestepped and tripped his assailant. It had all been footwork and where Nathaniel had remained solid and holding firm, the other party had lost their footing and been left a dusty mess on the ground.

"Just the trick to make you make a dumb move," he whispered to himself. A thought quickly silenced by the tearing of his flesh. A banderilla from Lydia. The hooks on the stick had buried themselves on his back and a warm wetness began to trickle down his spine before the sting set in.

The muffled cries of the vampires thumped all around, much like muted piano strings playing a melody. Incredibly, Nathaniel remained unfazed, even when Osman and Kahn doubled on him to give the solitary banderilla some company. Weapons clanged and Nathaniel moved like a possessed beast whose mind was turned off while the killing instinct was set to high.

Kahn and Osman continued their assault but every strike they tried was parried. At the other end stood the servant in front of the master and a mounted horse on either side.

On the balcony, more eyes keenly watched the battle. While all in attendance were impressed, one pair of bright multi colored eyes focused so much that they could have taken the young man's pulse without touching him. It was not perfect but what Nathaniel was doing was anything but passive. Daniel wanted to scream and cheer but his agreement with the elders and the silver-haired vampire impeded him from making any verbal connection to his fighter.

"I thought you said he was passive," spoke a reedy whisper of a voice.

Daniel shrugged back to the vampire. It was obvious that the one who had spoken was the leader because of the chair he was sitting in. In it, the vampire sat a bit restless while petting a second smile that adorned his adam's apple.

Daniel wasn't in the mood to make a tribute to Marceau Marceau just because he couldn't speak. Besides, he was too busy seeing Osman get swept just like Kahn had, but this time Nathaniel had followed the move with a kick to the head, disregarding the additional banderilla that stuck into his flesh. Kahn struck with both his sticks but found only air for a moment, and then the heel of a boot broke his jaw, leaving him as useless as Osman. However Lydia connected her second lance on Nathaniel's left shoulder. She dragged and swirled her feet in a salute to the crowd and left the ring while being showered with crimson lilies.

No sooner had her shadow disappeared and the unconscious banderilleros been taken away than the two picaderos bolted out in Nathaniel's direction on their horses.

They flew tandem and mirrored each other's movement. One went left, the other went right and they both swooped into Nathaniel as a symphony of sounds all crashed into each other. On the human's left, metal clashed from his machete against Guilherme's lance. On his right, padding tore and a slashing sound gave passage to a splatter due to Serj's connecting blow. Now another warm stream flowed from Nathaniel, this time from his chest.

The air swam with blood and hunger flared around the entire ring. More than one mouth could be felt salivating but Nathaniel kept his eyes on his attackers. He didn't care about the blood loss or the pain. He just cared about the torero he was about to kill.

Another swooping of the horses and the grit teeth of the human threatened to explode under the strain of his focus. As all the figures converged again, metal clashed against metal and two hard thuds thundered leaving the two picaderos fallen on the ground. One with a slash on his stomach and the other one with the other's lance impaled in his left lung. Nathaniel had blocked one blow and parried the other before returning with the slash that had downed one of his opponents.

He tasted his own blood and smelled it as well. He now pointed to the thin nose of Carlo before clanging his blades and charging madly towards the matador. His wild eyes would have scared even the reaper away. He slashed and thrust and met air, the swish of a cape and the sting of a thin blade piercing his left arm twice. Clearly Carlo was not about to lose face in front of his master or his peers.

But that didn't mean the human was going to stop trying. In his second attack, Nathaniel screamed before attacking, banking on the adrenaline spike to counter the massive loss of blood. He managed to nick the cheek and chin of the champion while sustaining no less than thirteen blows across his chest, back and legs. He fell to one knee momentarily but his eyes never left the prize. He roared like a mad bear and lunged repeatedly, striking, swiping and stabbing while disregarding each and every blow he received until a second finally stood still for Nathaniel.

He saw an opening, an instant to slash and claim the head of Carlo. His left hand swung lazily to draw the parry while his strong arm swung with everything he had left. Carlo couldn't see the blade because his head was turned.

'Let death take us both,' thought Nathaniel. 'Let my first kill be my last and let this blade strike true.'

A thunderous clang suddenly interrupted the man's reverie. The sound reverberated in the entire arena and Carlo stood holding the white metal blade, stained blood red. The maddened eyes of Nathaniel looked at a thin blade held by two small arms which had successfully blocked his death blow. Carlo withdrew his blade from the man's midsection because even if Nathaniel's blow had been blocked, his had connected and had run the human through.

Nathaniel took two steps backwards and fell on the ground with his arms to his sides. It didn't take long for the blood to start dripping on the ground but he wasn't about to go beyond the threshold of his knees.

"Do it," he told the vampire as he coughed up blood. He closed his eyes and waited for sweet release, but after a few seconds he was starting to lose focus. He had lost too much blood. But he forced himself to stay on his knees. He was just waiting for that sweet blow to dislodge his head from his body... but all he heard was one word. One word spoken by a thousand voices which filled the arena in a chorus of three syllables.

"Indulto."

The formal pardon asked by the public to spare the beast. Nathaniel's eyes rolled and he swore he even saw the orange handkerchief fall from the balcony, followed by Carlo thrusting towards Nathaniel's heart, but without a sword to give him sweet death.

Nathaniel's eyes rolled blank and all turned to black. He heard faint distant voices, metal clicks and clangs, the sound of children talking, singing and praying and lord knows what else. Then silence. Utter silence for what could have been an eternity or an instant until a clear voice offered him two words.

"Wake up."

Chapter 15: A meeting with the Laius

Nathaniel opened his eyes. The light was dim so he was spared the usual sting when waking up to brightness.

"Good to see you awake," said the soft, gentle voice of a boy.

"Where... am I?" shrugged Nathaniel as he bent up clutching his midsection. It stung terribly and upon looking down, he saw that he was covered in bandages.

"You are safe and in the recovery room of my home," said the gentle voice.

All around him in the gloom, Nathaniel saw happy paintings, the alphabet, and other small cots which were empty. This would explain why his feet were supported by a perpendicular bed that needed to be placed there so his legs didn't dangle off the end.

"You've been unconscious some time now, Nathaniel," said the voice. "You took quite the beating at Maestranza and if it weren't for Liam, you would probably be dead."

"Who are you? Where are you?" said the human as he coughed and did his best to clear his throat.

"Have some water," said the sweet voice as a twelve-year-old boy stepped into the gentle light.

Nathaniel was perplexed but thanked the boy for the water he now gulped wearily. "Thanks," he repeated while giving back the empty glass. The boy wisely refilled and returned it, still smiling at him.

"Now that you have one less worry, I am pleased to make your acquaintance. My name is Jeremy and you are within the walls of the St. George orphanage in Segovia. The name is really Orfanato San Jorge but trust in that no one pays much attention either way, so we can be at peace."

"So you're a child vampire," Nathaniel asked.

"Depends on your definition of that term. If you refer to a pure blooded vampire born vampiri, then no." The young boy showed the scars on his neck. "I along with my brethren were turned at very early ages and although some of our features show signs of age, like minor wrinkles or a stray grey hair, we are bound to live our lives in the bodies of children. It has its advantages and its drawbacks but for the most part, we can manage."

"I would imagine," Nathaniel groaned as he held on to his wounds.

"You put up quite the fight, Nathaniel. Word has it that if not for Diana, you would have taken off Carlo's head."

The human sulked. "Yeah..."

"Don't be too upset, my friend. The others you wounded would have also died if not for their doctors and the fact that they are vampires."

"Good; there's no use killing pawns if the king lives."

The boy couldn't help but chuckle. "I'd swear you were Daniel's son. I can see why he likes you. How do your wounds feel?"

"My whole body feels as if it's been passed through a meat grinder."

"I'm not surprised. You've had a few rough days not to mention about three hundred wounds courtesy of Carlo. But with the balms and oils made with egnalem, you should recover soon. That and the unblocked cardinals, again, courtesy of Liam."

Nathaniel's face grew a bit solemn as he thought of how he'd knocked Liam unconscious at the Halo Maze and how the vampire continually managed to save his life or heal him. Luckily, a warm scent broke his trance and he saw the boy with his legs crossed drinking some tea. Nathaniel gave a peculiar smile at the sight of the boy. One thing is to see a child wear their parents' clothes clumsily; another thing is to see a four-year-old walking elegantly in high heels or tying a Windsor. "How old are you?" he asked.

Jeremy set his teacup down on the saucer before replying. "Me? Oh very old. Trust me, I've seen my fair share of days... well nights in my case. I am not as fortunate as Daniel and some of the others. I am leader of the Laius so you can trust that at the very least, I am older than you."

"Laius? That name is Greek right?"

"Correct, it is..."

"It comes from Oedipus King," Nathaniel interrupted. "The father of Oedipus was Laius and the term Crime of Laius came about because of how he raped the child Chrysippus."

"Thus tainting his entire childhood," completed the child vampire with more than a hint of amazement in his voice. "Since we were children when our youth and innocence were taken from us, we adopted the name to go with our tainted childhood eternity. I further grasp Daniel's insistence on you."

The child stared solemnly at the floor while perusing over the saucer and teacup before downing the remaining tea. A knock at the door broke the momentary trance and after inviting whoever knocked to come inside, a small girl entered and gave a piece of paper to Jeremy. While he read, her small green lit eyes stared at Nathaniel in amazement, or was it hunger?

"Thank you, Nico. Tell the others to continue with the preparations. Also, please have María and Iphigenia tend to Nathaniel's wounds and tell Zaid to please find some decent clothes for him."

Nathaniel still had trouble seeing a twelve-year-old express himself in such a manner and be such a convincing leader, even in trivial dealings. But as he thought this, the odd image of the child drinking his tea was slowly being stripped bare in his mind's eye. It was as if he could see past the boyish features and small body. The hands suddenly looked rigid and adult while his eyes showed signs of fatigue and weariness inappropriate for someone younger than fifty. The boy's body had a slight slouch, his jaw line seemed unnaturally rigid and his nose languished far too long on the warm aroma of the black tea.

"Have you been a father long?" Nathaniel asked, interrupting the conversation. Both child vampires stopped cold in their conversation.

"That'll be all, Nico," Jeremy said as he led the girlish vampire out the door. "We'll talk later."

Nathaniel continued to look over the room until Jeremy returned, still shocked at the young man's sudden comment. The human could only smile at the reversed roles. "It took me a while but I recognized the signs even hidden below that wonderful façade."

"But... how?" asked the child vampire.

"It's a combination of things. You remind me of my brother Charles and when he had his first baby. He was happy, enthused, obnoxiously proud and supernaturally exhausted. I somehow forgot you looked like a child and saw my brother in you. I've been seeing lots of things clearer lately."

"I heard your eyes were like that of a wild beast at Maestranza."

"We each have our modes for specific moments. That moment called for me to be a beast and to trust my instincts. It could have gotten me killed, but not caring actually helped me in the end." Nathaniel's eyes glassed over and he almost seemed medicated. He didn't care and wasn't worried, a combination that suited him just fine at the moment.

"I have some errands to run, but my assistants will tend to you shortly, Mr. Runnels."

"I'm Mr. Runnels now? That's a shame; being called by my first name was quite refreshing."

The boy smiled and seemed to finally take in more than a fraction of a breath. "My apologies, Nathaniel," he said smiling while he put emphasis on the human's name. "You will be tended to shortly. After you have finished, you may come to my office down the hall."

Jeremy then stepped out and after only a few seconds, two nurses came to clean and dress Nathaniel's wounds, which were healing quite rapidly. They were young but not much for talk. It was quite possible they had been given specific orders to carry on in such a fashion, so Nathaniel didn't insist too much. Apart from brief kind hellos, they limited themselves to look at each other occasionally to exchange huge monologues in brief glances. Wounds tended to, the young ladies bid him farewell not before having one last look at him for whatever gossip they would share beyond the confines of the room.

Next came another gentle knock, this time the visitor was a young olive skinned boy with sandy hair. He possessed the same kind but silent disposition of the girls and he helped Nathaniel change attire to a maroon colored long sleeve sweater, black trousers, and rugged boots which were a bit too tight, but would have to do for now.

Nathaniel gave him many pats on the back but their communication was limited to a dozen or so exchanged smiles, nothing more. After the boy had left, he took a few moments to breathe. The empty infirmary echoed with his breathing. The ointment that had been put on his wounds had been infused with egnalem. Its aroma lingered in the air, simultaneously soothing and invigorating him.

He stood up and looked behind the curtain. Through the window, he could see a beautiful cloudless afternoon happily flowing in the picturesque town and a beautiful aqueduct in the distance. "Segovia... what a great place to die in."

Having had his share of in-room sightseeing, Nathaniel stepped out into the hall and found a swarm of children running all over the place. The racket was dreadful but it showed how airtight the rooms were, because from inside, he hadn't been able to hear a thing. It looked normal enough, but as he walked along the corridor, something seemed a bit odd, although he couldn't put his finger on what it was.

This thought was quickly taken from his attention as he saw the familiar face of Wendy kneeling down and talking to someone who was just covered by the edge of the wall. She seemed to be trying to console that person although she managed to see Nathaniel and wave hello. Nathaniel came nearer and newly found his throat dry as happened so often when he looked into her feline eyes.

In front of her sat a boy some eleven years old. He appeared to be trying to dehydrate himself through his eye sockets as torrents of sobs threatened to flood the entire wing.

"What seems to be the problem here?" he asked the beautiful vampire and the child.

"Hello, Nathaniel. This is a very special friend of mine named Peter," she said while gesturing to the weepy faced boy.

"How do you do?" chimed the human in his most charming attempt at sounding friendly. He suspected the boy was years older than what he seemed, but he was behaving childishly enough, so he tried to humor him. "Why so glum chum?"

Wendy looked at Nathaniel and smiled shyly. "It seems he has a problem with my chosen trade of plundering."

The boy proceeded to wail in protest. "You promised!! And you broke your promise! Never a pirate!!! ANYTHING BUT A PIRATE!!!"

Nathaniel was clearly not used to dealing with children when they were having a fit, but that wasn't about to dissuade him from trying to calm the child down. "Come on Pete; she's a good pirate. She's not like one of those Black Beard or One Eyed Willie types. She just loves the freedom of the sea."

It took about half a second for him to realize just how ill equipped he was in regards to consoling a child. Peter cried even louder and lunged at his darling Wendy, clutching at her shirt and bumbling in between moans in a language that Nathaniel clearly did not understand. He might have had some dense moments in his life, but at least for this occasion, he took the cue, whispered to Wendy that he was sorry and left to give them their space.

He stepped back into the hall and turned and walked towards Jeremy's office. Giving a knock, he opened the door but found that the office was empty. Regardless, he stepped in if only to escape the ruckus from the halls. When he closed the door and really took in the surroundings, he couldn't help but marvel at how soundproof the room was. He also realized that although it was empty in regards to other people, it was far from empty regarding content.

A massive bookshelf stood behind a deep burgundy desk that was better fit for a Fortune 500 company CEO than a twelve year old. There was a beautiful globe next to it, with Old English writing on it. It looked at least two and a half centuries old. The windows were frosted, the desk lamp was green and the leaning pile of papers on the desk looked like the recycling pastime of an obsessive compulsive stenographer. To the left was a beautiful oil canvas in which a small figure had been drawn on top of a mountain as he clamored towards the heavens while a lemon yellow sun hung on top of it. The arms were like a V reaching for the sky and in the foreground were no less than thirty bodies strewn across the basin in a sea of maroon below.

"That was a gift from Edward Louis," said the voice of the boy from behind Nathaniel. The young man hadn't been frightened; he was more impressed that the child vampire had slipped in without allowing any noise from the hall to enter with him. "There was a time when he called me King Jeremy the Wicked. Mostly it was an endless jab since I wasn't much for battles or slaughter. I might add that like many of you humans, I'd rather not know where my food comes from."

Nathaniel smiled as the young boy vampire stood beside him to look at the painting.

"Ed also thinks quite highly of you. Told me all about how you chopped a demon's leg clean off at the maze. So tell me, how are you feeling and please don't toy around with how your body feels. I've seen you heal and I spoke to your doctor."

"Well I'm not wonderful," Nathaniel said as he turned to face the boy vampire. "I'm still trying to make sense out of all of this and the conflicting emotions of every event. I'm told I'm special but expendable. I feel invincible one second and utterly defeated the next and I don't know where all of this is heading. Apart from that, everything is Kosher."

Jeremy kept looking at the painting. "I could say that what you're experiencing is completely natural for a human. I could even try and lull you to sleep with a thousand human physiological reasons for this, but there's something more important still."

"And that would be?" Nathaniel asked impressed with this line of thought.

"That anyone from any species would be just as likely to feel that way. There is no human psychology or even human feelings. There is psyche and feelings. If you can understand that, you'll understand your purpose here."

Another silence lagooned between moments as they continued to look at the painting. "It's a nice painting," Nathaniel said.

"Yes it is," Jeremy replied.

"So did you get that bit from a fortune cookie or did you read Chicken Soup for the soul?"

"Neither," the child vampire answered. "It was today's horoscope." They both smiled while still looking at the painting.

They liked each other and it had everything to do with Nathaniel finding someone who shared his sense of humor.

"You a Leo?" Nathaniel asked.

"No, Cancer actually," Jeremy replied.

"Damn it. I knew you'd be the end of me."

Jeremy smiled again. The same could be said about him liking Nathaniel.

"There's actually something I wanted to ask you," the young man said.

The boy vampire finally looked at him directly. "Do tell."

"Well, is it just me or are there human children in this orphanage?"

A wide smile bloomed on Jeremy's face. "Well, if there's any lesson I've been able to take from some of your most notable figures, it is that equality should know no religion, no gender, no race and in this case, no species. Some of my kind don't necessarily approve but this is not an experiment and it's not being carried out to win anyone over. It's my way of showing that humans and vampires can coexist. In case you're wondering, I am happy to report that there has never been an attack between races and that the children get along very well. It all goes quite under the radar but it is definitely a necessary step, or at least I think so."

"That's very impressive. If there's anything I can do to help, please let me know."

Jeremy smiled again. "You already are doing something Nathaniel, but if there's anything else, I'll be sure to let you know. I promise."

"Thanks," the young man said. "So is there going to be a ceremony for Claus?"

"Yes; during the night we shall prepare him and send him off as is our custom."

"Which would be?"

"You'll see, Nathaniel," replied Jeremy pensively.

"All right. I'll leave for now so you can get back to whatever you need to get done."

"My thanks," the vampire said.

Nathaniel gave Jeremy one final pat on the back and exited the office only to bump into Wendy.

"Hello again to you and your breast," he said. "Sorry for the bump."

"Don't worry," she said while noticing the look on his face. "You're in a rather pleasant mood. Everything all right?"

"Yeah, I was just chatting a bit with Jeremy. We talked a bit about a few things about the orphanage and he told me about Claus's ceremony tonight.

"It should be around four in the morning."

"Good to know. But we were able to have a nice normal chat, something I haven't had much of lately. I'm actually feeling much better. It's like he knew exactly what to say."

"Probably why he was called the wicked once," she said with a little snort. "But he really is a good psychologist."

Nathaniel smiled as it all made sense now. He then caught sight of something Wendy was holding in her hand. "What's that?"

In the vampire's hand, a little thimble rode on one of her fingers like a little toy helmet. "Oh this? It's just a kiss goodbye from Peter."

Chapter 16: A farewell to Claus

It was near dawn. High atop the Orfanato San Jorge, forty-four people stood on the rooftop while a beautifully decorated body faced towards the East. All but three figures were covered entirely with gold mesh tunics. Jeremy had explained to Nathaniel that it was their way of keeping the sunlight at bay.

Liam, Daniel and Nathaniel stood by the lush bed of dandelions, orchids and yellow roses as they bid farewell to the young boy lying atop the heavenly bed of flowers.

Claus had been cleaned and dressed immaculately. He seemed like a full grown cherub taking a sweet nap in a celestial garden. His strawberry blonde locks draped gently around his face, disregarding gravity just as they might have done when life had coursed through him. He wore a silk tunic that had three crests. One was for Saint George, in honor of the patron saint of the orphanage. The second was a cryptic insignia of a broken heart; something the visitors had found out was the symbol for the Laius. The third was the form of a flower made up of interlocking hands, the Magdalena crest. Across his neck was a gentle chain of heather that covered the scar of the blow that took his life.

Despite the sad event, Nathaniel couldn't help but appreciate the beauty of the scene. Not even a murder of crows in the distance could distract him from the peaceful setting.

While Nathaniel continued to survey the scene, he noticed when a figure stepped up next to Claus looking like a small golden druid because of the gold hooded tunic. "It is time to welcome our brother into the new life," said the gentle voice of Jeremy. "He has been liberated from the eternal prison and is finally free to roam to where and when his essence wishes. Let us escort him to the light and bid our silent farewells."

After speaking those words, Jeremy stepped forth and placed a dried yellow rose on the bosom of the child. One by one, every figure stepped up, said a few quiet words and put the flower next to the body. Last in line was Daniel. He had a hard time holding back his tears but managed to kneel down next to the boy, kiss his cold hand and whisper, "Sleep well, little brother." He then kissed the forehead of the boy and placed something beneath the child's hands.

The dark began to turn to gloom and the gloom woke into morning. The golden figures stood by and once a pure ray of light touched the boy's skin, a fire awoke and began to grow around the delicate body. The sight was hauntingly beautiful but amidst the crowd of golden cloth, a human hand held on to a vampire's shoulder in a silent display of kinship. On the ground, red stains became clearer as human and vampire tears combined in their sorrow.

Chapter 17: A visit to the Valley of the Fallen

Escorial in Spain is beautiful in ways only a master painter could grasp. Every stone, every shrub, and every occasional patch of snow seems to have been deliberately placed to create scenic perfection. Many a person with wavering faith has come here if only to rekindle the extinguished flames of belief.

At night though, it is the polar opposite. The lush countryside is replaced by a cold and brooding monolith of a mountain bordered by the black pool of the valley below. On this night there is a new moon and the word darkness takes a whole new meaning. Torches on the walkway cast jittery shadows all around, but four of those shadows moved with a purpose all their own.

The front hall facing the valley looks like the perfect marriage between religious faith and any hell of your preference. Regardless of it being an abbey on one side of the mountain, a basilica on the other and having a gargantuan cross atop the heap of ancient granite, few things seemed remotely saint-like in this setting. It didn't help that it was half past ten and that the basilica was still open. They weren't supposed to be expected.

With barely a pat on the stone steps, the group let themselves into the deep tunnel where tourists mingled during the day, the devout congregated at all times and demons could very well have received their blessings, for all they knew. Their steps tread lightly but the echo could not be ignored. The click of their steps whispered lightly until a tap-tapping began to sound in reply.

Each of the four figures stopped instantly and began ripping away at the darkness with their eyes attempting to find the source of the rap-rapping on the chamber floor.

In response a sliver of a voice crept through the cracks in the darkness. "Mighty late for a prayer, doth thou not think?"

A moment of their silence showed their surprise at their non-tangible welcoming committee. Unfortunately for their peace of mind, the voice wasn't about to accept their silence and just leave. "I agree that faith, prayer nor communion should ever require a schedule or appointment, but an explanation would be nice. Come forth friends and let us not keep hold of secrets before the presence of the lord."

A bright pillar of light shone in the center of the main basilica and the group walked towards it since the tap tapping was also making its way towards the light. They stood in front of the pillar until finally the source of the rapping came into view, a friar dressed in black who walked on crutches. One of his eyes was covered with a burgundy bandage with a golden cross etched on it. He stepped from the shadows and gave a peculiar smile, genuine but at times crooked from the exertion of walking on the crutches or maintaining his balance. "Welcome, brothers," he said in a friendly voice. "I am William, the night warden for this temple and secretary to the Gerald order or brood, as I suspect you call your congregation."

Jeremy stepped forward to respond. "Thank you, brother William, for seeing us at this hour."

"No need, young brother," William responded, "we have heard news from the Rooks that you might be visiting and left the lights on. We also found out about the Lygophilials. It is sad."

Liam's jaw clenched at the mention of the group. He had not been able to go with Nathaniel and Daniel to the mansion at Cádiz, because he could not bear to see the ravaged body of his beloved Melissa.

"We've had scouts looking over most of the recent proceedings," William said. "It seems as if time has finally become a luxury we do not possess. We are aware that you require assistance but before involving ourselves, there is something we must verify."

"And that would be?" Daniel asked.

William gave a simple smile. "Why your faith of course."

The placid handicap that had been standing in front of them suddenly leapt in attack swinging his crutches. At the same time a barrage of taps, clicks, whirrs and raps began to pop to life from the shadows around them. From their left an armless man sprang and kicked Liam clear across the hall. He had a solid wrap on his upper torso, a burgundy sash with the same golden cross as William's eye patch and loose black pants that ruffled with his remarkable speed.

From their right side, a woman with no lower torso clawed with her heaving arms, caught hold of Jeremy and threw him back about thirty feet. From behind Daniel, a silent arm pulled his head back and down, slamming his skull against a floor. The author of his fall had been a beautiful woman with closed eyes and a deep maroon cloak and hood.

For his part, Nathaniel had successfully blocked William's crutches but had struck towards the left a full foot above a head that crashed into his ribs throwing him against the wall. Incredibly, he still managed to land on his feet. Regrouped, the fallen comrades looked at who had actually just toyed with them, five seemingly helpless cripples.

"Funny that the only one aware was the human," boomed the deep voice of the green eyed hulk who was bound to a wheelchair.

"Hello, Christopher," Daniel said while still holding onto his ringing head. "So nice to see you."

"Hello, Daniel," responded the vampire in the wheelchair. "Before you ask why we attacked, you should know that you and your band have been followed for some time by something that has all the tools and intentions of obtaining the information its master requires."

Daniel immediately gave his full attention to the regal speaker bound to his throne.

"Seconds after you left the lair of the Lygophilials, something arrived. Something that brought back the soul of Melissa to her ravaged and lifeless body and forced her to speak. He used the soul pitch, a hexagram and demonic resources we dare not mention within these walls... He also took the body."

The only sound in the hall came from Liam as his throat caught. "Meli..."

Daniel looked at his friend but quickly returned to the conversation. "Murmur; it has to be."

Christopher nodded. "You know your enemies well, as far as information goes that is. He also managed to see your human's meeting with the seer and the outcome of what happened at Maestranza. He'd lost you for some time but was able to catch up in time to see Claus's ceremony thanks to more unholy help in the form of a crow."

"Barbatos," Jeremy said, soaking the name in hatred.

Christopher looked towards the child vampire. "Correct, my young looking friend. So as you can see, great many forces are working against you and these are merely the ones we know about. Remember that in war, no tactic is too bizarre, extreme or evil when victory is the only issue at hand. Morality is not for the warrior who chooses to fight, it is only for the soldier who blindly obeys yet still has a conscience."

"We need your help," Daniel said.

"Quite," responded Christopher, "but you need the help of many others as well."

Daniel looked suspiciously towards the crippled vampire. "What do you suggest?"

Christopher answered curtly. "We fly to France, mend ways with the therians and unite forces. Other things must follow but we need the hordes, for starters."

"Consort with the enemy?" Daniel asked. "Are you mad?"

"And are you stupid?" snapped Christopher as he raised his brow. "Alma took you down without you knowing it. Heather almost threw Jeremy off the cliff, Liam is lucky Franz pulled his kick or else his head would still be rolling and William and I incapacitated your quite able human. Actually, allow me to introduce myself, young man."

The vampire gave one push of his wheels and held out an open hand towards Nathaniel. "I am Christopher, leader of the Order of Gerald."

Nathaniel took his hand and shook firmly. "Patron saint of the disabled."

"Very good," Christopher said as he nodded. "Do you know why you fared better than your companions?"

"Luck?" the human said.

"Hardly," responded the vampire sternly. "It is because you trust no one here. Not a single soul and you fend for your life because you think anyone, anywhere, at any time could very well kill you. Your friends however have been spoiled by eternal life and still think themselves immortal, even if they just held a ceremony for one who passed on. A lovely myth they enjoy, but if it drinks, eats, breathes and fornicates, trust me that it can die quite well. The only reason you got hit was that you did not expect a blow from so low. The only reason they are alive is because our intention was not to kill."

All remained silent looking at each other. They knew full well that any distaste for blunt honesty didn't matter when they were being told the truth.

"Where are the therians and when can we see them?" Nathaniel said.

From the shadows, the vampire in crutches spoke. "Their faith may waver father, but they've instilled it correctly."

"Aye, William," Christopher said while smiling broadly to Nathaniel. "Aye, indeed. My dear human, that's the spirit we need. One thing though; William, would you and Alma mind taking care of the unwanted company?"

Without a word the two crippled vampires sped off down the long hall snapping and clapping in the darkness.

"What's wrong?" Daniel asked.

Christopher's hawk eyes followed his companions. "Murmur also has messengers. We're merely neutralizing his surveillance."

The two vampires returned and threw a pile of small bodies into a heap. Christopher looked over the carcasses and counted. "A serpent, a spider, a rat, and a cockroach. Four is not six and he always sends six." Christopher's eyes looked quickly around the room and suddenly clapped his hands. "Aha!" Down fell a small green fly onto the heap. "That's five, we're still short one."

Nathaniel's eyes had long been searching in the darkness to his left. He gave three slow steps and then pounced towards the vampire Alma. After snatching at her neck, he stood holding a black scorpion by the tail. "Six," he said calmly as everyone gave a small shiver.

"My thanks, young brother," Christopher said. "Her life is mine and we are in debt. Murmur is a master of many poisons, remember this... you too Alma."

Nathaniel nodded as did Alma, clearly affected by her close encounter to death. The human then crushed the scorpion beneath his boot.

"Please rest for tonight and tomorrow until beyond dusk," Christopher said. "Then we may go to Castle Margeride."

Jeremy stepped forward with concern on his face. "Do you have couriers, father?"

"We shall get you in touch with your brothers and sisters soon. But do not worry; they are being watched and guarded as we speak. Trust that your unconditional kindness and the food my brothers receive do not go unnoticed."

Jeremy looked confused so Christopher clarified. "Don't you think it curious that so many vagabonds frequent the surroundings of your orphanage? Handicapped vagabonds? It's the least we can do. Your work is too important to allow it to be destroyed by anyone. But now it's time to go to your rooms. We must clear our minds to focus on what lays beyond."

Jeremy was still a bit shocked from the confession, but managed to respond. "Yes, father. Thank you."

"No, my child," Christopher said. "Thank you. It is quite possible that humans and vampires will one day coexist thanks to your efforts. Now off to bed... except you Daniel. You can come with me for a moment."

"Yes, father," Daniel said. The wheelchaired vampire then gestured the others towards the tunnels that led to the abbey behind the mountain.

Nathaniel looked back and puzzled over the thousands of questions he had regarding the religious inclinations of vampires, the Orfanato San Jorge and the temple. How many more vampires were there and where did they live? Also, how could something as closely related to demons as vampires have such religious fervor? How long had Jeremy been trying to unite races? These were questions that roared in his mind.

"Faith turns its back on no one, Nathaniel," said Liam. "Heathens, witches and the impure are seldom named as such by a higher power. Prejudice and bigotry is more than likely the exclusive work of fanatics."

Nathaniel's eyes stood open in shock. "You can read my mind again?"

"Yes, but only me. Think of it as an exclusive frequency so I can avoid any other heavy object you want to throw at me. But no worries mate. It's not open all the time, although something tells me we might need this. We'll only be able to communicate telepathically when we are paying attention to each other. A clear connection and we're good to go."

Nathaniel didn't know what to say and simply let his shoulders sag. "If you say so." Towards the entrance he saw Daniel and Christopher making their way outside and suddenly, he noticed everything wasn't as dark as it had been a few minutes before.

Outside in the cold fall air, Christopher spoke to Daniel. "You must be more careful, my friend. Things are bound to get complicated and we need to make sure all forces are accounted for."

"I know," Daniel said. "I'm just a bit tired."

"Still haven't slept?" asked Christopher.

"Nope," Daniel responded.

"Strange really. How long has it been now? Twenty years?"

"And counting. Maybe it's been longer. It's been a while since I kept real track of the days. There hasn't been a treatment, drug or anything that has helped. Even when I've been weakened to the verge of death, nothing."

"It seems you can't give your soul some peace, my son," Christopher said. "It must come naturally."

"I know... but either we win this battle, or everything dies."

Christopher puffed a small laugh. "That's your problem, child. Always negative, always expecting the worst outcome. It's good to be grounded Daniel, but being a pessimist is as illogical as being an optimist."

"But if all comes out all right, then it's a surprise. If all comes out wrong, you expected it. It's win-win always."

The wheelchair bound vampire scoffed. "Idiotic justifications aside, it still keeps you from sleeping, Daniel. Try and enjoy life a little more. Who knows? It might actually be pleasant for a change."

"Right... so how are your forces? We're quite shorthanded even with the Rooks, the Corsaires, the Laius and what's left of the Magdalena."

Christopher actually gave a cheerful little hum. "Well.... I think we might be able to give you a hand."

The handicapped vampire then took a torch from a column, lit it and held it high in front of the ledge overlooking the Valley of the Fallen. Daniel could only gasp at the sight below. "Christopher... you know of course that to me you will always be a superman."

The vampire looked a bit confused. "But I'm not human."

"Don't worry," Daniel said as his eyes began to glow orange, "neither was he."

Beneath them, flames started to appear like stars in the coming night, until a thousand flames seemed to dance in the valley below.

Chapter 18: Business is on fire

While shadows danced to the rhythm of torchlights at the bottom of the Valley of the Fallen, far away from the Spanish night other bits of shade traversed within the dark. Whereas the shadows outside of the basilica had been cast by Nathaniel and company, these bits of shade had no owner and crawled on their own like sentient globs of oil.

There are literally thousands of ways to communicate known to mankind. What humans fail to recognize is that there are just as many ways to communicate not known to mankind. These drops of darkness jumped from one shadow to another, disobeying light sources and disregarding the normal conventions of light physics. What in essence should be mere projected silhouettes careened to their own rhythm until reaching a gigantic crack in the ground that exhaled sulfur and ash. Through the fissure they slipped and fell into a dark void that seemed to drop into oblivion.

Seconds turned into minutes, feet turned into miles and the shade droplets pulsed lightly until they splattered on an iron oxide floor several kilometers beneath the surface of the Earth. Slowly, the shade matter tingled and vibrated until congealing back into their shapeless forms. Magnesia and silica protruded from the solid walls and the drops started sliding in the direction of a light at the end of the tunnel.

Further down the path, a veil of flames covered a space where two figures stood near vials and flasks, which were actually on a bar counter. All of the walls were flame, but inside, the temperature though far from cool, was not boiling. On the bar, different bottles held rum, whiskey, gin, vodka and various other typical spirits. Apart from those bottles, there were other flasks which held other types of spirits including bile, mashed organs and sautéed eyeballs.

Inside the space, two figures stood on a rug made of human skin which was stretched on the floor. It seemed like the devil's office if ever a demon had need of an office in the first place. The apparent host remained unfazed by the heat. It was a gruesome creature that sat behind an onyx desk on a large black mahogany throne-like chair. In its right claw rested a glass filled with green liquid and an eyeball floating phlegmatically to cap off the revolting cocktail.

The other party sat shy and uncomfortable. The Shirley Temple in his hand did little to dissuade anyone from thinking he was a moronic would-be pedophile missing a backbone. Probably something the hulking figure in front of him wouldn't mind having a taste of.

Outside the area, the drops of shade bounced and divided like black mercury and the large beast noticed the presence. The black leathery brute snapped its fingers so the curtains of flame opened to give them access. "Pardon me governor, or would you prefer me to call you pastor?"

"Either will do," said the small man. He may have responded in a squib of a voice, but the matter of factly tone demonstrated that he was neither impressed, nor intimidated.

"Ahh..." the demon sighed. "Church and state, together again." he said while eying the liquid discs that slipped past the flames into the makeshift chamber. "My apologies though, but I must take this message."

"Not at all," responded the pudgy little man.

The drops of shade bounced into the hellish office, pooling into larger globs on the floor. The mass coagulated and curdled as it climbed the desk. Then it spread like pancake mixture the color of oil on the desktop and in a moment began to fizz and bubble, without the need of a flame. Little black wisps of smoke that came from the broiling concoction seeped up each of the beast's nostrils. As this happened, ripples of energy seemed to eddy up its face and body. Somehow the small man knew those were currents of information that slipped within the creature on the other side of the desk although there also seemed to be something else moving beneath its skin.

The circle of liquid shade continued to boil, quickly reducing its circumference until the only thing that remained was a small black wafer. The creature made gestures unknown to any religion known to man. He then put the disc in his hand and took it to its pink mouth where it fizzled and evaporated with a puff of smoke.

The scrawny man shrugged slightly at the sight. "Trouble?" he asked upon seeing the beast's leathery brow crack with concern.

"Nothing of concern," the beast replied. "Mind it not for it has nothing to do with you."

"Ah..." remarked the governor skeptically. He suspected something was amiss and wasn't about to be hypocritical.

The demon saw the face of cynicism. "I assure you governor—"

"Elliot," interrupted the flaccid man.

"Elliot..." the demon said through his teeth. "I assure you that there is nothing occurring which we cannot handle.

"I'm sure," responded the man unconvinced. "By the way, this wouldn't have anything to do with Montacre and some human he's found?"

The demon looked surprised. "My compliments on your informants. They must be a clever bunch of children desperate to serve their master."

The man replied in a condescending tone. "Trust me, dear Samyazza, I know of things and have seen events that would have your teeth chattering and your nails more than half eaten, regardless of your prestigious title of heaven seizer."

"Fair enough," said the demon in a businesslike tone. "As far as our arrangement, there seems to be no..."

"When will I get the wings?" the human interrupted, once again.

"... problem with having them for you soon," the demon finished, clearly controlling the annoyance of being interrupted, yet again... by a human.

Elliot gave no importance to the irritation he caused. "How soon?"

"I couldn't say, really," the demon responded. "It's not like we can go to one of your department stores and pick a pair up."

"What about one of your own kind? Wouldn't those work just as well?"

"Only to a certain degree, Mr. Elliot. Apart from needing every available hand at the moment, such a variation may prove problematic for you and your... intentions."

"I see," the human said as his eyes narrowed maliciously. "So in essence, you still don't have my wings, don't know when you'll get them and can't spare one of your own."

The demon ground its teeth in anger, but kept control. "That about sums it up... sir."

But Elliot hadn't finished. "All this while I continue funding you and recruiting and submitting hosts. Hmmm... and where is your master? Though I appreciate this wonderful attempt at making me feel comfortable in an office-like setting, Hell is Hell, and it just amazes me that with all of the aid I've given you to remain relevant and grow in strength the last decade or so, I have not yet made the acquaintance of your master."

"Father has been busy and indisposed as of late. He would apologize in person if he could."

"I'm sure he would," Elliot said. "But I swear, it's almost as if he were not even here."

At hearing this, the demon became slightly uneasy. "Then where would he be?"

"You tell me, heaven seizer. It's just an observation. I must admit, the human skin rug was a nice touch, but don't think for one second that I take kindly to delays on receiving my part of the bargain or having some lower caste demon waste my time."

The repugnant face of the demon became even more hideous from grinding its horrible teeth. He spoke as if on the verge of losing his patience. "We are aware of our arrangement and of our debt."

"I'm sure you are," the human said. "That is why your delay seems to be so convenient. Listen Samyazza: demon, goblin, wraith or whatever else your band is made up of are hardly reason enough to get me remotely rattled. But by me being late for a scheduled rendezvous, you can be sure someone will come directly here because they'll know where I'll be. Hell may be quite the terrible place, but I'm sure you wouldn't appreciate sharing your secrets with hordes of fanatics that are itching for judgment day, not to mention angels gaining access to the fiery pits."

"Point taken, governor," the demon replied.

The human smiled as patronizingly as his face would allow. "Please, call me Elliot."

The demon swallowed more of his pride. "Pardon."

Elliot got up from his chair and put on the coat he had draped over the wooden chair he had been sitting on. "Make sure to tell your father I came to visit... again."

The demon also got to his feet. "I'll be sure to relay the message."

With a tip of the bowler hat he put on, the small man turned around facing the wall of flames and walked directly towards the fire. Like a theater curtain, the flames lifted allowing him to pass and closed once he was gone.

The beast sat back down in his chair to brood. He hated the sight of humans, but having to be courteous to one exercised demands on him that he wasn't comfortable with, even if he was a demon. "Damned monkey. Who does he think he is?"

Outside the veils of flame, the small insignificant man walked in between two lines of demons. He hardly seemed to notice, mind or even care about their presence. He took small steps and moved like an elder but something clearly clawed beneath the surface of his skin. His entire countenance was frail but his eyes burned fierce enough to cause some of the demons to pull away from his gaze. The humongous stone cavern trailed off into the darkness and he walked as nonchalantly as a babe crawling through the living room of a house in the suburbs.

A black wall came into view and his dainty figure made its way towards it. A single iron door stood in front of him with a button to the left of it. Elliot pressed the button with the bottom of an umbrella he'd been carrying. The button sizzled as it lit up. Some seconds later, the door opened and inside was a small elevator with three buttons. They were all written elaborately, the bottom one reading 'H', the one slightly above was a 'P' and the top one was 'L'.

The governor pressed the top 'L' button and as suddenly as the door closed, it opened up into the backroom of a pantry. He stepped out of the elevator, walked out into a kitchen and passed two double doors into a big mess hall where countless people were eating at tables. It was a kitchen for the homeless and the hall was packed with people eating. As soon as Elliot stepped into the hall, dozens of gazes turned towards him while dirty smiles shone in the path of the pastor. Thank yous rained on him in countless languages. A few young ones even ran up to hug the frail old man.

"There, there my child," he said sweetly. "I hope you've been eating well. After all, we need you strong, healthy and plump."

One of the small children looked up with a toothless smile. "I ate all my lima beans, Father Elliot."

The pudgy man smiled sweetly although his eyes narrowed oddly. "Aren't you the sweetest thing? Why I could just eat you up."

Of course the child giggled and another teen came near the rosy cheeked man. "Father, you should really quit smoking. You know it's real bad for you."

"But my child, I don't smoke," he responded a bit confused.

"Really? Then how come you always smell like an ash tray?"

The man suddenly became aware of the scent the young boy spoke of, forgiving his blunt honesty. "Ah... that. Well he who consorts with demons and devils has to put up with the stench of their sins."

The youth opened his eyes in awe. "Whoa... that's deep."

"You have no idea, my child," responded the old man. "But unfortunately I must be on my way."

The disapproval was unanimous. "So soon?" said a young woman that had recently joined the throng around the man. "Won't you eat with us?"

His eyes met hers directly. "I promise I'll have you for lunch soon sweet one. But I really must go. I have a flight to catch."

A trucker stood up when he heard this. "JFK?" he asked.

"As always," responded Elliot.

"I can give you a lift," said the large man.

"Thank you, dear friend. You are too kind."

"Don't mention it, padre. It's the least I can do and as long as there's fuel in my tank, you can count on me."

"I'll keep that in mind. Now all of you, back to your meals please. And don't worry about me; I'll be back before you know it."

"All right" – "OK" – "Come back soon"

"Most certainly, my children," said the pudgy man.

With that, the pastor patted another little child on his head and made his way out to the street passing below a crest that hung above the entrance, which read:

> *Let us take from the weak the burden of work,*
> *the burden of hunger and the burden of life.*

Chapter 19: Rue Garoux

France has a countryside that seems taken out of some esoteric poem proclaiming the beauty of life enjoyed at half speed. The grass seems unnaturally green, the light shines coyly off every surface and even cows seem to replace a typical moo with a more sophisticated meh. In short, everything seems to become quaintly French... everything except a caravan of black cars with black tinted windows making its way through the black asphalt scars of the countryside.

The convoy maintained a level pace obeying speed limits imposed by law, regularly overlooked by authorities and quite ignored by local motorists. The three vehicles moved at exactly the same speed and maintained precise distance from one Citroën to the other. Apart from the make, color, model and speed of the vehicles, they shared one other detail that was of the utmost significance: Spanish license plates.

"Are we there yet?" Daniel asked from the back seat.

Christopher turned around in the front passenger seat and looked the vampire in the eye. "I swear Montacre; you're as bad as a child on a road trip with the persistent desire to urinate."

"It's been twelve hours. An ETA shouldn't be too much to ask for."

The leader of the Order of Gerald rubbed his eyes wearily. "No it isn't, unless it's the twenty-second time you've asked, which it is. So feel free to relax, we also need to arrive at night and if you hadn't noticed dusk is still over two hours away."

"Fine," Daniel said as he slumped back into his seat.

William was driving and Nathaniel was in the back right passenger seat with his head against the window, his eyes lost deep in the beautiful countryside and his mind miles away.

"Can't we go any..."

"No we cannot go any faster, Daniel," Christopher snapped. "We have three vehicles transporting vampires across international borders and not all of them are as lucky as you to be able to tolerate sunlight, hence the wonderful tinted windows on the cars. We need to time tolls, pit stops and our arrival with the night. Besides, we are nearly there."

Daniel continued to protest in whispers, "For freaking fromage's sake."

William's good eye looked through the mirror and caught sight of Nathaniel. "Ho, Runnels. Are you all right back there?"

"I'm... fine," the young man replied in a dull voice.

"You don't look fine," the vampire responded. "Can't sleep?"

"And you're not helping, but thanks for asking."

The one eyed vampire smiled. "Not to worry, young friend. There's a simple solution. Father?"

Before Nathaniel could even ask what the solution could be, Christopher put the seat all the way back, pinning Nathaniel to his chair. In one fluid motion he jabbed his fingers against the human's temples and right behind his jaw, instantly rendering the young man unconscious. Christopher then returned his seat to the original upright position as if nothing had happened. Daniel didn't even flinch; he almost envied the sleep the human had been given. Unfortunately, it wasn't like he had not attempted that move before and all he'd received was a huge headache.

For Nathaniel however, after what seemed like an instant, he felt himself being gently pushed awake. When his eyes were able to focus, he could see that the cheery green countryside had been replaced by a thick shroud of black and that the cars were in fact slowing down.

"I trust you slept well," Christopher asked.

Nathaniel felt his body rested and the hum in his head had vanished. "That felt like a second."

Christopher adjusted the mirror in the visor to look directly at his guest. "More like four hours. It's eight o'clock"

The more Nathaniel looked out the window, the more he felt like he'd slipped into some sort of parallel dimension. He could scarcely see into the darkness even with his improved eyesight. "Why is it so dark?"

The cold eyes of the Gerald leader once again looked at the human through the mirror. "Because that's the way they like it."

Nathaniel still didn't seem to get it, so Daniel added the obvious. "Therians," he said in a cold voice.

"We're here," William said.

The cars stopped and everyone got out of their vehicles. It seemed they had arrived in a cozy little town which had been drenched in silence. Because of the preternatural darkness, buildings looked like halfway houses to stay in during your descent into madness. Worse still, the only noises they could hear were the ones they were making, even if their movements were nearly silent.

Daniel made some hand gestures over his head so everyone could see. All eyes focused on the non-verbal communication, nodded and split into three groups of three. "With me," he whispered to the human.

A thick haze rolled in and it became harder to even keep track of the others. Visibility was limited to only a few paces ahead. Along with him, Nathaniel walked with Daniel and Christopher. Jeremy had gone with Heather and Alma, while Liam was with William and Franz. However, before long, each group had lost track of the other.

The musky scent of dew suddenly grew much stronger and it had nothing to do with the grass that might have been cuddling droplets. The air became thicker and everyone's eyes started to burn lightly, welling with tears. Nathaniel suddenly smelled something else in the air. He sniffed deeply and his face had a mix of realization and confusion. "Is that..?"

"Garlic," finished Daniel. "These town folk are overly superstitious which is both good and bad."

"How so?" Nathaniel asked as he watched his step.

Daniel remained walking forwards. "Well for starters, they think we can be hurt by garlic, some old folk legend that also seems to have reached human ears. Quite funny actually; you'd be surprised at how good garlic can be for the body, human or otherwise."

Nathaniel started to screw up his nose from the powerful smell in the air. "Where are we going?" he asked.

"Le fin du monde," replied the vampire as if it were the most natural response in the world.

Nathaniel couldn't help but feel a little despair. Daniel noticed and after a low chuckle clarified. "That's the name of the inn we're going to. Rather odd I agree, but it's where the Rooks told us to arrive. But this blasted fog has made it just a little hard to find the inn, which is on Rue Garoux."

Daniel suddenly saw the human's arm dart past his face pointing firmly. "You mean that street there," Nathaniel said.

Through the thick mist, a corner appeared with an old gas lamp burning brightly. Christopher looked at the human a bit amazed that he'd been able to see anything in the haze, a look Nathaniel was able to see for himself. "Wow. So that's how I look most of the time I'm with you guys?"

The vampire in the wheelchair could only chuckle in his seat.

"He does that," Daniel added, proud of his find.

"Zee inn iz zis way," said an old woman's voice, causing all three to jump back. When she finally came into view, they saw it was a small woman. She was old yet extremely elegant, almost regal. Her clothes might have been from the country, but her posture, her composed expression and the sheer air about her commanded respect. She spoke with a very thick French accent. "Alzou ze cuztom iz to allow you to azk my nem, your zilenze forzez me to introduze myzelf. I am Mizz Fawn and I am ze keeper of le Fin du Monde Inn."

"So the inn is nearby?" Daniel blurted.

The old woman raised her nose and narrowed her eyes while her nostrils flared slightly.

"Pardon him madam," interrupted Nathaniel, "he is barely trained." The old woman allowed herself the smallest of smiles before Nathaniel continued. "We were wondering if you could be so kind as to show us the way to the inn."

"Zeemz time 'az a way of doing away with your mannerz, Daniel. Your young friend 'owever, 'e knowz 'iz plaze or at leezt 'az ze cortezy of showing reezpect towards 'iz elderz."

Christopher wheeled up to the old woman. "My lady," he said with a light bow, "he meant nothing by it. He is merely under great duress and his mind is merely tense."

The old woman looked warmly at Nathaniel and Christopher before turning back to Daniel. "You do well to come with zuch lovely company, Montacre. Eef not, your little oddyzzey would be cut rather short."

The vampire could merely respond by biting the inside of his cheek.

"Ah... you zee?" she said. "At lazt it knowz when to 'old itz tongue. Come along now, zupper iz nearly ready and I'm zertain you all 'ave 'arty appetites."

"Quite, madam," Christopher said, "but we have some companions with us."

"Worry not, young friend," she told him, "zey are already at ze inn. You were ze onez that ztrayed ze farzezt."

Christopher seemed confused. "But we were all walking in a straight line until we came to this corner. How might it have been possible to go the wrong way or split up?"

She smiled warmly. "You did not arrive on ziz corner of your own accord. Now keep cloze. Ze inn iz juzt ahead, but zat doez not mean you cannot get lozt."

They all decided to just follow the old lady to wherever she led them. As the fog continued to roll and the damp air clung to their clothes, Nathaniel looked back and saw how the lamp stopped shining and disappeared altogether. Before he could ask anything, Mrs. Fawn spoke. "We're here," said the old woman and out of the fog came the side of a building with a sign reading Fin du Monde and another saying No Vacancy in French.

"We were that near?" Daniel asked incredulously.

The wise eyes of the old woman met his. "Perzeption iz evryzing, dear Daniel. 'Ou zez we only took twenty pazez? You of all should know better zan to let your zenzez dezieve you. Now in you go."

"Yes, madam and thank you," he said to Mrs. Fawn.

"Zee?" she exclaimed. "You can ztill learn new zingz yet."

The fog almost seemed to be trying to get indoors but it pooled up at the entrance without so much as peeking in. Inside, the air swam warm thanks to two fireplaces in the cozy lobby of the inn.

"Where have you guys been?" asked Liam looking a bit concerned.

"What do you mean?" Daniel asked in return. "We just split up not fifteen minutes ago."

"Are you mad?" responded the doctor vampire. "It's been four hours Daniel. We had supper and tea and everything. And if it hadn't been for Mrs. Fawn, we would have never found this place."

Christopher had a quizzical look in his eye as if he thought his leg was being pulled. He looked towards his faithful friend. "Is this true, William?"

"Yes, father," answered William. "A few times we were about to go out to look for you, but Mrs. Fawn insisted we keep indoors and wait it out."

"Yeah," added Jeremy, "and then she pops out of the inn for ten seconds and finds you lugging around."

Daniel seemed a bit confused by it all. "Well we did speak for a bit, but we got here rather quickly."

"Talked for a bit?" said Liam incredulously. "I literally mean it took her ten seconds to find you."

Everyone in the lobby looked baffled and they turned to the sweet old lady that stood in the foyer. "It's simple really," she said now in fluid English, "in the river of time, this inn has no master, and since this inn is inside this town, the same applies for the village itself, for the moment. You are all correct and incorrect in what you see and say. It's all relative really, but it's just my way of showing you that in life, absolutes are definitely not as common or easy to come by as you think. Now let us feed our recently arrived guests. No buts. The rest of you, feel free to have more cake, some tea, a nightcap, a bath or simply tuck in."

Liam looked directly at Daniel. 'Be careful of this woman,' he said through his thoughts.

The old lady looked at the vampire like a mother who smiles while she's being lied to. "Really, Liam, it is rather rude to whisper secrets in front of others."

"But I didn't..."

"Off to bed, my child," interrupted the old lady, "your friends need to supper."

Like a small boy who'd just been chastised in public, Liam tucked his chin down and made his way up the stairs.

Mrs. Fawn then turned to the rest of the group. "The rest of you, choose what you may, but leave something for your friends."

While the others served themselves, Nathaniel, Daniel and William sat down in a small table for four that already had the plates served. "Pardon the lack of space," said Mrs. Fawn, "but I'm sure the lodging offered shall more than meet your needs."

Each place at the table had a metal dome plate cover, except Mrs. Fawn's. They all sat down and when they uncovered their meals, their mouths could only water at the singular delight of every dish. Nathaniel had a lush steak with béchamel sauce, sautéed potatoes and a deep red glass of cabernet, Daniel's dish was steak tartar and white asparagus, and Christopher could only smile at the Andalusian dish of slow cooked meat with bread known as Pringá. "This reminds me of home," he said, "thank you, madam."

Mrs. Fawn smiled at him, moved by the tears the vampire held back. At her side, Daniel inhaled the delicious aroma of his plate but before taking another bite, he realized something. "I do not mean to be rude, madam, but we are rather pressed for time at the moment."

"Actually, you are not," she said while looking at him from above the rim of her glasses. "It's remarkable that none of you have asked about the time. Not one comment in regards to what your companions said earlier, not even you Christopher."

"Truth be told, madam, I was rather pressed to first ask where you got this lovely reserve. Like the dish, it stirs memories that are quite priceless."

She smiled at the charming vampire. "It is rather nice, isn't it?"

"To be honest," Christopher said, "it's perfect. But I was wondering how a charming woman such as yourself got hold of this particular bottle of blood wine."

Nathaniel paused mid chew, terrified of the glass in front of him and how he had been enjoying it so much. Thoughts of how he was losing his humanity flicked through his brain.

"Relax, Runnels," Daniel said, having realized the signs of panic. "You are drinking a bloodless vintage. I however am also enjoying blood wine, though not the same year or from the same vineyard as Christopher."

Mrs. Fawn just smiled and gave a small bah, as she waved off the inquiry. "Eat your food before it gets cold. Theories should really be left to scientists."

"But how did you know this was my favorite wine?" asked Christopher.

"And mine," added Daniel.

"...and mine," Nathaniel said.

"Ah, my poor little fools," said the old lady while she took turns looking at them. "If I tell you, will you promise to finish your meal?"

They all looked at each other and nodded in agreement. Mrs. Fawn then hunched forward ever so slightly and spoke in the faintest of whispers. "Time holds all the answers."

A moment or two of perplexed silence followed. Before any of the vampires or the human could say anything, Alma came in guided by Heather who was walking on her arms. "Mrs. Fawn, we'll be turning in now."

"All right, sweet children," said the old woman as if they were her own offspring. "Off to bed then, although I must ask, did you have some lemon cake?"

"Yes, Mrs. Fawn," they both said, "it was wonderful. Did you need help with the dishes?"

"No my dears, but thank you for asking," the kind woman said.

"All right, good night then."

"Goodnight, children." After the old lady had spoken those words, the vampires left.

"We really must be off," Daniel said. "There is little time to spare, much less to sleep or have tea or any of this."

Mrs. Fawn gave Daniel her full attention. "My dear child, you truly have no concept of time. You specifically, the dreamless one."

"And what's that supposed to mean?" asked Daniel.

"You know what it means," she said giving him that warm smile. "How long has it been?"

Daniel's eyes threatened to jump out of his skull and his tongue had abandoned him when he would have wanted to reply. Christopher just smiled as he took his final bite and downed the last of his drink. He then turned to Mrs. Fawn. "People always wonder of heaven and hell, of their particular deity of choice but I must admit, I never thought I'd have the privilege to meet you, madam."

Mrs. Fawn gave a radiant blush and smiled coyly. Christopher wheeled next to her, looked upon the gentle wrinkles and smiled tenderly. "Thank you for the meal, mother. I'll be off to bed now."

She gently pressed her hand against his cheek. "There's a room for you on the ground floor. I know you can manage upstairs, but look at it this way, you'll be the first one to know when breakfast is done."

He caressed her hand as a son does to a mother. "How could I say no to that? After all, mother knows best, especially this one." He moved slightly forward and gave a kiss to her cheek. He gave the others a nod goodnight and left the table to Daniel and Nathaniel to mull over what had just been said. The next four minutes were spent in silence as they finished their meals and the warm lemon cake that had appeared to just come out of the oven.

"Timing is everything," said Mrs. Fawn as she put down the dessert dishes, "don't you think children?"

"With all due respect madam," started Daniel, "do you know how old I am? I think it interesting that you would call me a child is all."

She looked at him as one does a hopelessly naïve pup. "Sweet Daniel, you are not as advanced in age as you think and in comparison to me, you have barely lived, no offense. Let's just say that counting in centuries does not make you older than moi. Now off to bed."

She took the plate from in front of him, but he was still on the defensive. "I don't sleep much."

"I know you don't, child. But I'll bring you some tea and at least you can rest."

For once, Daniel seemed to resign to his conflictive nature. "Fair enough, Mrs. Fawn. Thank you for the lovely meal."

She smiled at him. "My pleasure, Daniel, but I hope your young friend can find it in his heart to help an old woman with the dishes."

"Of course, ma'am," said Nathaniel as he wiped his mouth and picked up the remaining dishes.

"Then I bid you both a good night," Daniel said.

Mrs. Fawn looked at him sweetly, "I'll be there shortly dear. Up the stairs, third room on the right."

"Thank you," he replied.

As Daniel left, the woman and Nathaniel both looked at the mountain of dirty dishes. "Get the tea for Daniel, Mrs. Fawn; I'll get started."

She gave a grandmotherly smile. "Proactive and eager to help. Montacre has no idea how fine a choice he made."

"So I keep being told," Nathaniel responded.

Mrs. Fawn continued preparing the tea while Nathaniel made his way through the dishes, the smell of lavender in the soap water soothed his senses and he remembered good times helping his mother at home.

"I'll be right back," said the sweet old lady as she held the tray with the piping hot kettle, two cups and a clear glass container filled with a rich amber colored syrup.

Nathaniel looked at the bottle curiously. "Blood honey?" he asked.

Mrs. Fawn smiled. "Vampires will be vampires. I won't be but a minute."

Nathaniel nodded for her to go and scrubbed and rinsed the kitchenware with great care. He could hear the tinkling of the tea set rattling on the tray as she went up the stairs, followed by a click of a door as it opened and closed. He hadn't gotten through two dishes when he heard the click of the door once again and now the sound of descending steps.

"Sorry I took so long," the old lady said cheerily when she came back into the kitchen.

Nathaniel looked at her with narrowed eyes and a curious smile. "Something tells me that no matter how I reply to your comment, there will be a retort that will just confuse me further. So I'll just say don't worry, I know you're rather busy."

She responded by putting her hands on her hips. "Now how come you can understand better than that silly lummox, Montacre. It took me ten minutes just to calm him down."

"Ten minutes?" he asked, obviously trying to not get confused. "If you say so. Oh and I had forgotten to mention that I noticed you lost your accent ever since you stepped into the inn."

Her smile did not waver a millimeter. "The saying does state that when in Rome, do as Romans do. So call me a Roman... or in this instance, a French Roman."

They washed the dishes quietly for a couple of minutes before he spoke again. "Mom always said that doing the dishes was everyone's task."

"Wise woman," Mrs. Fawn replied. "Maybe a little more of that going around would help people get along better. It might even be possible for people to stop calling me Father."

Nathaniel stopped washing the dishes for a moment and looked at her quizzically. "Who are you ma'am? Seriously. Are you death?"

The cackle that woman let out would have woken up everyone in the house, but oddly no one seemed to stir. "Heavens no child!" she said while catching her breath. "Death is far younger than I and she was born out of spite, originally. Actually, she's changed a lot throughout the years and has become rather pleasant company as of late. As for me, you needn't worry who I am, just know I'm here to help, just like you. This forthcoming battle wasn't yours but you are needed and I truly think that's what your life needed."

"What? A little action and adventure? Maybe a kill or two?" asked Nathaniel as sarcastically as his voice would allow.

"No child," said Mrs. Fawn quite sternly, "a purpose."

He became silent but instead of confusion, it was the unflinching hand of truth that had silenced him.

"You do not need to give me an explanation of why you are here," said the old woman. "Trust me I know a lot more than you think."

"Then tell me what's going on here? What's wrong with this place?"

"Wrong?" she replied. "Nothing's wrong with anything here child. Right and wrong are just as relative as all other concepts in this reality. That you do not understand something does not mean it is wrong."

"Ok. Then why is this inn called The End of the World?" he asked.

"Oh that... well it used to be called the Begin-Inn of Time, but no one got the pun and business was awful. A simple name change later and all the pessimists of the world started looking me up. Silly how you all sometimes behave but between the good bed and board, the trendy name and the best lemon cake in existence, people tend to come back more often now."

"I don't understand," Nathaniel said in complete honesty.

"Well you haven't had a slice of my cake, have you?" she said with that beautiful smile she had.

"No, but that's not what I meant," he replied.

"I know child, but I don't think you're supposed to understand just yet," she said. "Come here to the entrance one moment."

She then led him to the threshold of the entrance door. "Can you see this change?" she said while pulling out some loose coins from her apron.

"Of course," he replied.

"Can you feel the change?" she asked while putting the coins in his hands.

"Yes."

"Can you hear it?" she asked after taking them back into her hand and giving them a shake.

"Yes, what's the point?"

Mrs. Fawn then opened the door and threw the change out into the fog swamped street. A moment or two passed until Nathaniel became utterly mystified. "Why... why didn't it make a sound?"

"Why indeed?" she replied sagely. "Can you see the change now?"

"No," he replied.

"Can you hear the change?" she asked again.

"No."

"Can you feel the change?"

"No."

"Exactly. So what makes you think there is or isn't change happening out there or anywhere?"

"I don't know," he replied.

"Which is exactly why you should have a piece of my lemon cake, because that you can understand."

Nathaniel smiled in his confusion. "You're a wonderfully odd woman, but I like you."

"And that is more than enough for me," she replied. "You'll be leaving soon and I want you to feel as if time here has been good to you."

"It has," said Nathaniel. "Now where's that cake? If anything can be a slice of home, it's lemon cake."

The old woman turned around to look him in the eyes. "My dear, you are wiser than you know."

Chapter 20: Castle Margeride

Everyone was awake, fed and felt strangely replenished. Breakfast had been delicious and Mrs. Fawn was taking the last of the dishes to Nathaniel, who was already finishing the morning batch of cleaning. Everyone else helped clean up and after getting their belongings, the group of nine stood by the open door with the odd mist still reluctant of entering the inn.

"Why doesn't it seep in?" asked Nathaniel as he looked down at the wet fog pooling on the threshold.

"What is not welcome here cannot enter," Mrs. Fawn said, handing him a towel to dry his hands.

Afterwards came warm hugs from everyone as they said goodbye and clung on to the old lady as if trying to get her sweet smell to rub off on them. Liam had still been a bit embarrassed by what had happened the previous night but after a brief chat with Mrs. Fawn and a firm pat on the back, he had calmed down and looked quite relieved.

One by one they kissed her and held her tightly. When it came to Nathaniel, she smiled as broad as she could and almost crushed the breath out of him. She gave him a piece of cake covered in foil and he gave her one last kiss before she came face to face with Daniel.

The vampire looked at her as if he wanted to say a thousand things. "Mrs. Fawn, is there any way I can show my thanks?"

"You just did, my son. I know you are thankful and besides I couldn't allow you to keep believing that time is not on your side."

The vampire blushed half embarrassed, half genuinely chuckling. "I promise not to say that again."

She raised an eyebrow and smiled cleverly. "At least you didn't say ever. Be good, dear boy; I hope you're able to sleep soon."

With one last pat on the back, they all left in unison. After a few steps, Nathaniel couldn't help but look back longingly only to see the warm lights of the inn dim slowly to dark. When he looked at the sign, he noticed that it no longer read "Le Fin Du Monde". In the place of the name of the inn there was a weather beaten sign that read Boulangerie... a bakery...

"Let us be off, Runnels," Daniel said from behind him. "Time has been most kind and we must make the most out of the untaxed rest we were able to enjoy."

"Un-taxed?" the human asked.

Daniel smiled. "Look at your watch. Maybe it'll help you understand a bit better about what just happened."

Nathaniel did as the vampire suggested and slipped out his watch. It was renewed, polished and read the time quite clearly through the glass, although he had to tap it and verify that it was working properly. It read eight sixteen and the young man clearly remembered that they had arrived at eight. "But..."

Daniel didn't let him finish. "A small gift from our dear friend, Mrs. Fawn. You may also care to notice that the lamp we'd seen is no longer there and that the fog around us is now lighter, though it is still unnaturally dark."

Still dumbstruck, Nathaniel followed Daniel turning Northward up the street, followed by the other seven. They walked through the still thick mist where shadows began to lurk within the confines of the earthbound clouds, accompanied by the occasional click in the darkness.

Everyone was anxious but no one drew a single weapon. The low clicks and scratches from a moment before had vanished and shadows now began to line either side of the road; large seven foot pillars, which stood three feet apart. Tension increased fourfold when a rhythmic choir of breathing started to weigh upon them. To add to the anxiety, up in front, a small shadow came bounding along the road. It bounced and weaved making the fog swirl. Daniel signaled to the group to hold their current position.

He looked to his right. "Liam, do not draw your weapon."

"But lord-"

Daniel interrupted, "Mate... trust me on this one."

Daniel took a few steps forward and waited for the twirling bit of night to stop dancing. He then spoke in French, "Bonsoir. Je veux alles aux le castille."

"Mon Dieu!" said a small girl's voice in a thick French accent. "Your French iz terrible."

"And you don't sound like Shakespeare either," Liam snapped, which prompted Daniel to look him sternly and exchange a few inaudible words so that Liam stayed quiet.

"Aha!" said the voice. "Ze flying rat 'az a flying tongue." As soon as the sentence had been spoken a small girl no older than twelve bounced to a halt two feet from Daniel. "Alo!" she said in a bubbly squeak of a voice.

Daniel stayed calm and serious, though somewhat friendly. "How do you do, miss?"

"Non, non messieurs. I am soon to wed Prince Gevaudan. I am 'is nouvelle."

"My mistake, madam," Daniel said, "and my regards to the prince for his fine taste in royalty but I must ask you to accept my apology."

"An' why iz zat?" asked the little girl.

"Well me and my companions have rather lost our way. We were looking for Castle Margeride and were wondering if you wouldn't mind us troubling you so that you may show us the way."

"Ah! The cassel is this way," she said and began strolling off with the company doing its best to follow behind. After a couple of hops from the girl, she called out loudly. "Eet iz them! Eet iz them! They wish to go to the castle!" After she yelled, the fog slowly faded allowing the peaks of the castle towers to come into view.

"They're going to ambush us Daniel," Liam said.

Daniel smiled calmly. "Old friend, if they were going to do that, we'd be dead already. Those aren't pillars on either side of us."

As the veil of fog finally vanished, the castle came into clear view, as did the road and the hundreds of therian soldiers flanking them on both sides. Daniel seemed unbothered by the appearance of the therians, although his company was less confident. All eyes stared at the group of vampires and the solitary human in their midst.

An old lady came running from the castle calling out what appeared to be the girl's name. "Angelique!! Angelique!!"

The little girl continued to skip along until the old woman was able to catch up and have her in her arms, quickly verifying that no harm had come to her.

"Lovely girl you have there, madam," Daniel said to the old lady as he approached. Her response was a quick look that turned her eyes blood red and a roar that rose from her diaphragm like a horrendous earthquake. Daniel didn't move an inch.

"Who are you?" growled the old lady in a voice more apt for someone who has been possessed.

"We came to see the Furies. You may say it is Daniel of Montacre who has come to see them."

Her response was another inhuman growl. Daniel had expected it but Nathaniel felt a familiar tingle in his stomach, letting him know that he's far from being in control. A fact made all that much clearer thanks to the old woman wafting the air with her nose, like a predator catching the scent of unwelcome company.

"What is that piece of meat doing here?" she grunted while hiding the girl behind her large grey skirt and pointing to Nathaniel.

"He is part of my company and we all mean to visit the castle, if Aureus would agree to a temporary truce."

The old hag snorted loudly and looked him sideways. She showed her teeth through a fiendish smile but Daniel little more and would have yawned in her face. "Listen here, dear lady; I'm sure you'd love for me to explain all of this in detail while I scratch your belly and feed you biscuits, but we really do not have the time. So either fetch me your master, let us in or show me if your bite is as mean as your bark."

Before a hair covered claw could strike down on Daniel, it had been caught by a long slender arm. The old woman had vanished. In her place stood a demented version of the grandmother of that girl with the little red hood. Her arm was being held firmly back by a young man.

"Calm down, Lara," said the fair haired young man, "he is just a stupid rat." He caressed the mane of the heaving therian that now slowly reverted to human form. "I cannot say how much I've missed you Daniel, for I haven't."

"Nor I you, Aureus. But desperate times do call for desperate measures such as these, n'est pas?"

"Oui, Daniel. I see you've not come alone. Curious company to be certain, though an honor to have the presence of Gerald members here. I bid thee welcome though neither scent, nor taste, nor sound, nor sight deceive me, you have a human amongst you."

"Yes. I did mention about desperate times, did I not?"

"I see. Lara, take Angelique back to the castle. I will have a word with our visitors so you may notify that we'll be having guests over."

The old woman nodded and gave a sigh but not before saying some curses in an ancient tongue, spitting at Daniel's feet and pelting him with three cloves of garlic.

"Charming," the vampire said as the old lady stormed off with the young girl bouncing along just ahead of her.

"I'd apologize for my aunt, but she'd have me neutered before the sun came up," Aureus said.

"So it does come up?" Daniel asked.

"Yes, when we want it to. More importantly though, might I inquire as to why I'm having preparations to receive vampires in a therian household? Not to mention the fact that you brought a human. Pardon my insistence, but the other elders are far less keen to give a damn about why you're here and would rather just have the villagers do away with the lot of you while we dine sapien prime rib."

"Before you continue to slobber," said Daniel, "please be aware that I've had some visits from our unmutual friends."

Aureus became quite serious. "What do angels have to do with this?"

"Quick for a mutt," said Daniel as the knuckles of the therian thumped tellingly. "Sariel passed by and gave me the news that Israfil will be, oh how did she put it, tuning up soon."

Immediately the tense jaw line of the therian smoothened loose and the iron fist which was clenched fainted with the realization of what Daniel had just said.

"Now that I have your attention, care to invite us in?"

Aureus looked from side to side, nodded tersely and waved them onto the castle road rather insistently. "Daniel, walk ahead with me, please."

The therian led the way along with Daniel and the group followed. They had walked a few paces without saying anything until Nathaniel could no longer hold his questions and looked towards Christopher. "Why did no one else speak? Daniel could have gotten us killed!"

Christopher took a deep breath before speaking. "Child, if more than one person talks to a therian, they accuse of trickery and of trying to drown our message in words. They don't tolerate more than one person talking at one time. The arrogance and pompous attitude was more than just Daniel being Daniel. It was his way of demonstrating he has no fear and that he is who he claims to be. Trust me, there is no lack of dislike between us, as you can tell from Liam's behavior, but that doesn't mean that some of us can't try and coexist."

Nathaniel continued to walk as the castle drew closer and grew larger. It was as if it sprouted from the countryside itself, and its size seemed to spawn extra levels with every step they took. The massive wooden doors in the entrance opened outwards, and eight massive wolves stood on all four paws, four on each side with huge red eyes looking at the group as they entered. Although the smell of food and shelter attempted to welcome them, this couldn't help but feel as if they were literally walking into the mouth of the wolf.

The castle opened to a courtyard filled with wolves of all colors and all sizes. "These are the gathering grounds," whispered Christopher to Nathaniel. "It's where wolves congregate and where younglings find their mates in spring time."

Right after the meeting grounds, a stone wall stood before them where engraved it read, All who enter, shall enter as equals. Everyone started kneeling and bowing to the wall before crawling through a small slit in the stone about four feet high. The crawlspace was just over five yards long, with an exceptionally clean marble floor that made it easy to slide on. It opened into a great hall lined with various chairs and sofas. A huge green flag flowed over the largest wall depicting various animals looking at each other within a circle. Among the animals were a fox, a bear, a hyena, a panther, a lion and a wolf.

"What's with the zoo on the flag?" Nathaniel said. For a response a massive hand clasped him on the shoulder.

"Those would be therian ancestors," said a voice so low it made James Earl Jones sound like a soprano.

"Hello, Beorn," Christopher said as he wheeled to the aid of Nathaniel. "Good to see you."

"Likewise, Christopher, although your snack of a friend tempts me to say otherwise." The man towered over seven feet tall and was just as massive horizontally. His chin seemed made of granite and his mane looked like a bound constrictor hanging from his head. "But you know I have a big heart. So don't worry young one. You are forgiven, but just this once."

He then laughed like a God of Thunder and Nathaniel could only nod apologetically since he couldn't even hear himself think.

"What brings you all the way from Canada?" spoke Alma, the blind Gerald vampire, stepping towards the large man.

"Alma..." he sung sweetly. "Now you I do enjoy seeing."

"Pity I cannot say the same because of my condition," she giggled.

"My apologies, my dear; I meant nothing by that."

"I know you did not, but come; lead me some place where you might tell me of your recent adventures and what brings you all the way across the Atlantic." The giant offered his arm and gently led her to a couch some ways away so they could talk.

"You are lucky Beorn is a rather nice fellow, Runnels," Christopher said. "That comment might have cost us."

"I'm sorry, I didn't think..."

"Exactly. We are guests in a therian house and Daniel must speak with the elders."

Jeremy and Liam now neared them. They had been talking to some other therians while Heather, William and Franz talked to another group. "It's kind of hard to believe you are all enemies," Nathaniel said.

"Well from your country there was a bitter Civil War," Liam said. "The same could be said for our species. Just because we are at war doesn't mean some of us cannot be civilized and get along. Pardon earlier, but with few exceptions, I'm not a big therian fan."

"Besides, it's always good to have some diplomatic relations," added Jeremy.

"If you say so," the young man replied. "Where's Daniel?"

"He's already off meeting with the Furies trying to explain the situation. We won't see him for some time," Liam said.

"Wow, I didn't even notice when he left."

"They can do that," Liam said. "They often only let you see what they want you to see."

Just then the little girl from the entrance came pulling on the sleeve of a young man with light brown hair who in turn was followed by an older looking man, generously scarred throughout his entire face with hair as red as a ripe apple.

"Gevaudan! Gevaudan! Theez are the strangerz I zpoke of to you, my love."

"Aye, Angelique... I can see," the younger man laughed as the small child continued to tug on his shirt. "Greetings, kind friends and welcome."

"We will care for your needs," added the stout red headed man. "This is Prince Gevaudan, and I am Rufus."

"So what brings the Wendigo tribe to this estate?" asked Liam. "Beorn, Gevaudan, and Rufus? This doesn't seem like a typical field trip, much less a coincidence."

"I have to agree Liam," Rufus said. "We have also had some bad tidings and news to worry about."

"I'm sure you have, but pardon my bluntness, have you been attacked, or any therian horde that you know of?" added the doctor vampire.

Rufus replied uncomfortably. "No. Of course not."

"That'll change soon," Nathaniel said.

The therian looked at the young man with murder in his eyes. "Is that a threat?"

"No... just a gut feeling. Notify your friends to be on the lookout."

"Humans are so paranoid," Rufus said.

"And every other species is so cocksure. Maybe that coupled with our mating habits might explain why we outnumber all of you a thousand to one."

"Watch your tongue, boy," Gevaudan said. "If you're not careful, I might just allow myself my favorite dish."

"And if you are not careful, I might just get a new fur coat out of this."

Gevaudan stood dumbstruck as did Rufus until both of them laughed so hard, everyone's eardrums were left ringing.

"This pup has quite the bite I bet," Gevaudan said. "Might I have the pleasure of some conversation while we down some beer and mead?"

"Remember Gevaudan," Rufus said, "we must tend to all of them."

"Oh... true, true. Then let us share a pint later on. By the way, I seem to have missed your name."

"Nathaniel Runnels. A pleasure to meet you both."

"Aye, lad," Gevaudan said. "Good to meet you even if the situation hardly calls for celebration."

"And why should it not?" rang a velvety but very powerful voice from the back left staircase. "We congregate with our enemy's enemy who in turn is our enemy as well."

Down the flight of stairs walked a blindingly beautiful woman with bright ruby eyes and hair that glowed like strands of white moon. She wore a long white fur gown fastened in the middle by two large opal buttons. Though the gown was firmly set on her waist, it clearly showed silky white skin taut and tight with vitality. She spoke while stepping delicately towards them in her bare feet. "If you ask me, it's a most wonderful date to celebrate."

Nathaniel could barely whisper. "Who...?"

"Luna," replied Liam in hushed tones. "One of the eight Furies."

"I take it you've had a long journey. Rufus, Gevaudan, please show our guests to their quarters."

"Yes, madam," Rufus said. "Some are entertaining a bit of talk though."

"Very good of you to consider our guests. Take those speaking later, but the rest, be sure to take them as soon as possible."

"Yes, m'lady."

"From the Eight Furies to you, welcome to Castle Margeride. I am Luna. Is there anything I could help you with before you are shown to your rooms?"

"Y-yes, madam," William said barely holding his balance on his crutches at the sight of the ivory beauty. "Do you happen to have messengers? A group of comrades waits downriver for confirmation to approach."

"Of course, William. I'll call for couriers immediately."

"Thank you, madam."

"Anything else?" she said as she surveyed the guests until meeting eyes with Nathaniel, who had not been able to stop staring at her.

She smiled slyly surveying him as had happened to him so often lately. "Just to make sure, I'll see you all in your rooms soon."

Upon uttering that final statement, she waved her long gown around and showed that beneath it, she wore only a thin chain on her waist with a sliver of silver slipping down the small of her naked back.

Nathaniel heaved a deep breath and did his best to not make any noise as he saw the powerful woman head off up the stairs she'd come from. "Rufus?" called Nathaniel with his dry mouth. "Any chance of getting some wine and a hot bath prepared?"

"I'd think you need a cold one after that," said the red headed therian with a laugh. "I'll arrange it. Follow us unless you wish to speak more. Might I carry your chair for you Christopher?"

"I'll heave my way around, if you don't mind."

"Not at all. If you wish, your room is on the first floor. Third door to the right."

"My thanks again," Christopher replied. Afterwards he fastened a sort of seatbelt on his chair and pushed off with extreme speed, braking and lunging up the stairs like the most natural thing in the world.

Rufus looked on, suppressing the fact that he was quite impressed with the Gerald leader. "The rest of you may follow me," he said and started walking towards the stairs. The therian went at a fast pace and before long, they had cleared three flights of winding stairs, taken two left turns, a right one, and another set of stairs. Occasionally Rufus stopped to sniff at the air and after a few more turns, the group arrived at a door with a white rose hanging from a ribbon next to a lamp.

"This double suite is for the ladies."

Heather passed forward on her two arms, gave thanks to the large therian and went into the room.

"Further down to the right are two doors for William and Mr. Franz."

"Thanks," Franz said.

"You're a quiet one, aren't you?" Rufus said.

The vampire nodded as if it didn't matter and went into his room.

Meanwhile, William balanced on one crutch long enough to shake Rufus' hand. The therian gave a curt nod and faced the remaining people. "You three, follow me."

They went down a long winding set of stairs then up a very steep one into a hall with an additional row of rooms.

"Pick the rooms you wish, all are fully accommodated and quite comfortable."

"I'll take this one if neither of you mind," Jeremy said as he slipped into the first room on the left.

"I'll take the one on the right then," Liam said. "I'll see you later, Nathaniel?"

"Sure," answered the young man as Liam gave one last look before slipping in the room.

"And you Runnels?" asked Rufus.

"Where's the largest bath?"

The therian smiled. "That would be the room at the end."

"Then that'll be my choice."

"You also asked for some wine?"

"Oh yeah, that would be great. Feel free to bring the one you think suits me best since I can tell you've gotten a fair whiff of me."

"A nice light cabernet I think," said the therian after a quick sniff to verify. "Two bottles will be brought soon along with fruit and cheese."

"I can't thank you enough."

"Don't mention it, but please, do me the favor of not wandering through the castle. It's not the place for a human to be walking about alone, especially since you would probably get lost."

"I noticed your sense of smell is what guides you. Follow the nose wherever it goes, right?"

Again Rufus smiled at the human. "Precisely, so please humor us. Stay in your room."

"Don't worry," replied Nathaniel, "I have no need to meander and if I have an emergency, the last thing I'd do would be to make it hard for any of you to find me."

"Good to know you're a sensible one."

Rufus nodded to the human then disappeared down the stairs they'd come through. Looking around the hall, Nathaniel noticed orchid blossoms spread throughout the hall as he walked towards his room, their aroma lingering sweetly in the air. He passed the rooms where Jeremy and Liam were, plus three additional sets of doors until reaching the end of the hall. The door opened into a vast open room with a large unlit fireplace to the left, a vast rug with a sofa facing a table in between it and the fireplace, and a large plush chair and pillows.

Next to a windowsill on the right was a large bathtub with a fluffy white robe already set out on a small table next to the bath. Between the sitting area and the bath, there was an enormous bed with white sheets and large red round pillows. Above it there was another large window where Nathaniel could see that he was either in a corner room or at the edge of a tower. He really had no idea where in the castle he was, but it wasn't as if he minded.

"This I could get used to," he told himself, focusing on the amenities.

He started getting ready for his bath when a gentle knock sounded from the door. "Come in," he said, not even looking at the entrance. The door clicked as he slightly stumbled while taking his boots off. "Please put the wine over there by the fireplace. Thank you."

He heard the tray set down with the light chink of a few bottles and more than one glass. He thought that was a bit weird and spun only to fall hard on his backside since his boot had decided not to cooperate with him. Although quite embarrassed, he did not proceed to take the boot off at the moment. His jaw had turned to jelly and his eyes opened wide as caves as he stared into a lush white coat, two shining opals, milky white skin like the moon's surface, platinum silver hair and two intense ruby eyes.

"So should I take this as a sign that you won't share a glass with me?" Luna said.

"Uh... um...."

"Actually I was expecting a - yes m'lady I'd love to share a glass of your fine cabernet with you - so I'll just ignore the lack of reaction and go ahead and pour two glasses for us, all right?"

Nathaniel merely nodded as he sat there staring at the therian goddess while she poured the wine for him. The way she stood had one powerful leg in view and his eyes feasted like a cannibal's. She then walked towards him, set the glasses of wine on the bath table and knelt before him. "Let me help you with these boots first, before you hurt yourself."

"Th-thank you, m'lady."

"Your most very welcome," she teased as one boot and then the other came off. "Now up we go," she said while hoisting him to his feet as if he wasn't a full grown man. "Cheers, Runnels," she said while handing him his glass.

"What should we toast to?" he asked.

She pondered for a second before replying. "How about to peace, love, prosperity and great sex?"

Nathaniel's heart gave a jolt and the Lady Luna chinked her glass playfully against his. She caressed his cheek with her right hand and he saw how the finger nail from her index finger grew longer and longer. He finally came back to his senses with the sound of his shirt buttons falling to the floor.

"Don't worry, Runnels... I may bite, but you won't mind."

Before he could reply, a loud knock boomed on the door and a deep voice called from the other side. "Lady Luna?!"

She gave out a sigh. "Yes, Bisclaveret?"

"You are needed downstairs, m'lady."

Nathaniel could have sworn that her grit teeth increased in size. "Can't it wait? I have urgent matters at hand."

"Nice way of putting it," whispered the human as he trembled in her grasp.

"No, m'lady," insisted the voice outside the door.

"Fine; I'll be right down."

"Yes, m'lady."

Luna still held Nathaniel firmly. "Call this a to-be-continued, sweet boy. Have your fill of wine and fruit for I expect you to give me the type of fill I yearn for."

"Yes, m'lady."

"Such a sweet thing and nice manners. I hope you forget them by the time I return. Enjoy your bath." She gave another turn that flared her gown again, flashing her naked body as it had happened on the ground floor. "Oh, and Nathaniel..."

"Yes, m'lady?" he asked, struggling to sound calmer than what he was.

"Something to keep your mind busy," Two clicks of her opal buttons later, Nathaniel's jaw drooped towards the floor weaker than ever.

"Cheers," she said. After buttoning herself, she left the room.

Chapter 21: The Second Vision

The bath was completely full. The first bottle of wine was completely empty, the second bottle of wine was either half full or half empty, depending on your point of view in life, and Nathaniel was either more than half drunk or less than half sober. He put a warm wet towel over his eyes and combined with the bath water and the wine, he was borderline blissful. An empty glass dangled in his hand and he found himself halfway between sleeping and dreaming.

Clearly the bottle of wine was too far to refill his glass so he lay in wait for the wine to somehow come to him. For now at least he was content to allow the warm towel to cradle his eyelids and woo him to sleep.

Warm currents of water began to swirl around him like an underwater massage. For some reason, it didn't strike him as too odd. He noticed however that with each serpent-like caress of the currents, the water level decreased until he felt his naked body curled up in the empty tub. From the bliss he had been in, he was cold and naked and then quite suddenly found himself wearing pants and a long sleeve shirt.

His heavy body suddenly felt as light as his wine laden head and from floating in water, he was now floating in the air. He peeled off the moist towel off his eyes only to see a white blur of space as his clothed body lifted several feet while rotating slowly. The blur undulated and came into focus and white space spread out in every direction as far as he could see.

"What the hell is this?" he asked himself.

"Whatever you want it to be," replied a distant voice.

"Who's that?"

"Who do you want it to be?"

"Is this real or am I dreaming?"

"If you dream it, is that not real enough?"

"I want to land."

"Then land."

Though still surrounded by white emptiness, a feeling of something surging towards him came over Nathaniel until he saw that the vast expanse was really the inside of a giant cube. It was contracting rapidly until he saw a floor rushing up towards him at a highly accelerated rate.

"Not so fast," he said in a calm voice.

"As you wish," the distant voice replied. The walls slowed down until it seemed like his descent was in slow motion allowing him to tiptoe onto the white floor beneath him.

"Why's everything empty?" Nathaniel asked.

"Because you wanted it so," replied the voice.

"Ok, then what if I want to be back in the castle room."

As soon as he had said it, he found himself in his room but instead of being on the floor, he was standing on the wall next to his bathtub, which was still full of steaming warm water.

"Ummm... why am I on the wall and why doesn't the water fall?"

"Simple," said a voice from behind the sofa, "gravity doesn't necessarily apply in a dream and regarding the water, even if you ask for that, you don't really want it to happen, so it won't move."

"And you would be?" Nathaniel asked. He had turned while standing on the wall to face the sofa, but he suspected whom it could be. After all, it wasn't like he hadn't been dreaming like this as of late.

"Call me a fellow oneironaut," the voice replied. "A traveler of dreams though much more experienced than you. Feel free to hop down and also get yourself some wine if you want."

Nathaniel looked down into the tub of warm water. From his perspective, the bottle was standing above and to the right of him, next to an empty glass. "Won't that spill?" he asked.

"Remember, Nathaniel, you make the rules here. This is your dream."

Nathaniel clicked his tongue and took the glass from the table. Rather than pick up the bottle he simply flicked his fingers and wine poured out in a perfect arc. When enough wine had been served, he did another motion with his hand and the pouring stopped. He looked at the floor in front of him and tried putting his foot up but found that gravity did not want to cooperate for him to get off the wall and onto the floor.

"Hesitation? Fear? These are not things for the lucid, Nathaniel. Simply do it."

With a shrug and a deep breath, Nathaniel looked at the floor once again, focused on it and willed himself to jump from the wall only to land on the floor in time to catch the different splashes of wine that still floated in the air as if the liquid floated in zero gravity.

"Nicely done. Now sit. We have much to talk about."

"Who are you?" Nathaniel asked only to reach the chair, look at the sofa and see... himself. "What the?"

"You said you needed to sort some stuff out internally," said the second Nathaniel, "so here I am."

"But...."

"It's a dream, deal with it."

"Ok... why am I, why are you... ummm...."

"Why are I here?"

"Uhh... that."

"Well it seems you are getting the knack of travelling through the Lucid."

"The Lucid?"

"Yeah. You can call it that, or the Dreaming but I prefer the Lucid since we're conscious travelers and we don't merely traverse through the surreal imagery of dreams. We create; we mold; we harvest. Care for a grape?"

"No thanks."

The other Nathaniel ate a couple of grapes and shifted on the sofa. "Ok, so here's the deal. You're still adapting and odd as this all may be, you're not even kind of freaking out. That's a great start."

"Well I figured there's not much sense to that, so why bother?"

"True, that and being exposed to the egnalem has made you a lot more receptive."

"Ok, so why are you...? Um....."

"Why are I here?"

"Exactly."

"Great question, but I think it's rather simple," the other Nathaniel said.

"How so?" asked the original Nathaniel.

"Care to venture a guess?"

"We wanted to take a good look at ourself?"

The other Nathaniel opened his eyes amazed. "Wow... on the first try."

"Ok, this is totally weird."

"You think? Shucks, I'm the lucid manifestation of a conscious reflection and I'm weirded out. But I have to jet now. We have more stuff to talk about but you have an appointment."

"Oh? With whom?"

"Dunno, but you left a message on my phone that you had a meeting at eight and although watches don't work in the Lucid, it feels like eight, so I'll just leave. Take care."

"Ok.... We'll do so, I guess."

The Nathaniel on the sofa got up, walked to the window, opened it, grabbed the rail and pulled himself sideways up and out of the room.

The Nathaniel on the chair slouched back feeling completely drained mentally even if he was dreaming. His reverie was cut short thanks to a large grappling hook crashing against the ceiling. It had come flying from beneath the water's surface in the tub. The line was pulled taut and the rope tensed as something pulled from within the water until a hand reached up, pulled and deep dark glasses, white skin and a stubbly beard peeked from the edge of the tub.

"Bill?"

"Hey, you," said the man as he pulled himself up from the water. "Feel free to give me a hand here. I really should quit smoking because there's being out of shape, then there's me."

Nathaniel ran over and hauled Bill out from the tub. He wore black pants, a black leather jacket, a red undershirt and clearly showed signs of ungroomage. For his part, Bill pulled out a pack of cigarettes and started packing it.

"Aren't those soaked?"

"If this were real life, of course they'd be wet. But as you've found out, the Lucid is quite cooperative with what you want to do when you want to do it."

He struck a match, lit a cigarette, pulled out a comb and with two strokes had his hair dry. "Basically, my little furry friend, here you can potentially do whatever you want to do, and you can also see a great many things."

"I noticed last time. Isn't there anything I could have done to help the Lygophilials?"

"From within the Lucid? Only to help yourself. There is nothing you could do for someone else from your dream except communicate, but most times people write these off as simple hallucinations, instead of real messages. Funny huh?"

He looked around at the room he now stood in and pulled a beer from his jacket pocket. "Nice room. A bit old school but very nice, my friend. I'd use some other adjective, but none comes to mind at the moment."

"Why are you here?"

"That's why I didn't use more adjectives. Hold this a second," he said while giving his beer to Nathaniel.

He walked back to the tub and reached into the water, dipping his arm up to the shoulder. He seemed to be scrounging about, shuffling different things underneath the surface. "No, no. That's not it. What's THAT doing here? Nope. Not that either... Aha! There it is." He pulled a large sledgehammer out of the tub, held it in his right hand and took the beer from the human's hand.

"This setting you put up? It's nice... but I have to show you something."

Bill then wound up the large hammer and wailed against the floor. After the massive hit, there was a crack and splinter before both fell through into darkness.

Nathaniel had clearly been startled but he didn't yell or scream. He was amused but unfazed by the current situation. He knew it was all a dream, so there was nothing to fear. Bill looked at him and nodded approvingly. "I'm impressed. You've matured a whole lot for just a few days."

"Thanks, I guess. But how about we stop for a drink somewhere, Bill?"

"Sounds like a plan. But actually, I'm going by the name of Lou now. No Hispanic accent for the name, no special intonation, just plain ole Lou. It's my middle name and I was told my mom was fond of it."

"Then Lou it is. Though next time I hope you won't change the name again. Kind of confusing if you ask me."

"You never know with me kid. I got a bunch of names I like. As for stopping for a drink, I have the perfect place."

The blackness they were falling through began to take color. Blues and reds mingled with the black, a yellow here, an orange there, neon green came as the perfect touch and slowly, the welcome nudge of a bar stool nestled beneath them both. A stage appeared, along with a fully stocked bar and when a shiny column came into view, the strip bar music began.

"You have a one track mind, Billy Lou," Nathaniel said.

"And you act too old for what you really are, Nat. Bartender!! Two tequila shots, a pint of dark stout and whatever my friend's having."

"Make mine a Guinness."

"Well met and one of the shots is for him."

"No thanks, Lou; that's the devil's juice."

"That's why I like it so much, ma' boy! And I in-sist." he placed the shot in front of Nathaniel when he put the emphasis on the last word. "Tequila shots need company be it a friend or a beckoning navel. And for the record, even though I'm sure it'd be lovely, I'm not particularly in the mood to have my tongue near any part of your body. Now drink up, don't be a puss."

Nathaniel looked at him and gave half a smile while mouthing the word bastard to him.

"Uno, dos y tres. Slam it down your gullet, slam it on the table! Uno dos y tres!"

They drained their shot and slammed the glass hard on the table.

Lou rippled with aftershocks of delight. "There it is... Brrrrrrrrr! Now for bidniss, my friend." He swirled in his chair and faced the empty stage while inviting Nathaniel to do the same.

"Waitress!!" Lou called while sitting next to the stage and a very familiar face came to their seats.

"Valencia?" Nathaniel said.

"Do I know you?" replied the icy vampire.

"Don't mind him, darlin'. He can't even seem to enjoy his own dreams. However, me you could really help if you broke these bills for me."

Lou handed Valencia ten hundred dollar bills. "Break 'em in tens, would you, darlin'? Thanks."

The vampire took the bills, handed back the change and didn't even spare a look to Nathaniel. "Why didn't she recognize me, Lou?"

"You know the real thing, Nat, not the person in your dreams. The only reason for that happening is that right now you either don't want to know her, there are other matters at hand or that her function here is to facilitate, nothing more."

"You think?"

"I dunno. I'm just offerin' some options so you can shut up and enjoy the titties."

With a snap of his fingers, the music started to boom in the otherwise empty bar. Lou danced in his seat and cheered in the direction of the stage. The clicks of high heels and the tinkle of beads on the doorway gave way to five beautiful women who took the stage. Lou whooped and blew wolf whistles while Nathaniel stood with his mouth gaping. Mary, Anne, Wendy, Malia and Luna each stood on the stage staring down at him, each with an outfit that would make a preacher beat himself mercilessly and repeatedly.

"Fine selection, ma boy!"

"But Bill, I didn't do anything..."

"First off, it's Lou now. Secondly, I'm not one to keep score, Nat, but last I checked, three down and two to go from that lineup."

The girls posed and danced all looking at Nathaniel. Wendy walked over in a tartan skirt, did a split, grabbed him by the neck and buried his face in her breast. She pulled him away and said: "I came first because I'm your favorite." She kissed him gently on the cheek, stood up and left.

Mary and Anne came forwards. Mary was dressed in black and knelt facing away and in white was Anne, who slid down face up and held her legs up in a tight line. They spoke in tandem: "We came second and third because you came last and we want another round. Call us." They both gave him twin kisses on each cheek and went away, leaving Luna and Malia on the stage, still dancing, still staring.

Luna was the first to move getting on hands and knees until reaching Nathaniel and flicking her tongue lightly on his nose. She was dressed in silver and spoke just inches from his lips. "I came on all fours because not only do I travel that way, that's the way I like it the most." She grabbed him by the collar and kissed him passionately. "I'll see you soon?" And as suddenly as she'd sprung forth, she left the stage.

Malia was the only one left. Dressed in red, she danced a little longer than the others turning around and pulling her hair up to reveal a scorpion tattoo on her neck and two snakes coiling on her lower back. She finally came to Nathaniel, jumped off the stage and straddled him on the chair. "I think it's about time we got a little more personal."

"So why are you last?" he asked between nervous breaths.

"Easy," she said, "because you're afraid of me." She nibbled his neck and ear and he moaned in approval.

"Is that right?" he said while he inhaled her intoxicating fragrance.

"Oh yes," she said. "But do you want to know what the best part is?"

"I'm dying to know," he said.

"Perfect answer," she said while kissing him deeply.

"Really?" he asked as he kissed her back.

"Completely... because...." She moaned and kissed him deeper.

"Because....????" He rolled his eyes and drank her kisses.

She kept feeding him her lips. "Because...." And then she tightened her thighs.

"Yes....?" he asked once more.

She pulled back and looked him straight in the eye and a split tongue like a snake's flicked him in the eye. Before he knew what was going on, he found himself smothered by pythons and suffocating in their mortal coil. He yelled but no sound came out of his mouth. A vice like hand suddenly grabbed hold of his and pulled him up for what seemed like hundreds of feet until he stopped ascending and fell three feet back onto a bed.

Looking for Lou, or Bill or whatever he wanted to call himself this time, Nathaniel suddenly found he was looking into his own face once again.

"Nice scene. I was especially fond of that outfit on Luna though I think the snakes in the end were in bad taste."

"Whh... hnn.. how...?"

"Rest," the other Nathaniel said calmly. "That was a hell of a ride you just had."

"B... bu... but this is a dream..." stammered Nathaniel still shaking.

"So? A dream can be very real. Remember the ship. Remember the first video Bill showed you."

"You mean Lou."

"No. I mean Bill. Lou you just met. Bill was the one with the video."

"But it's the same guy."

"Yes and no. It's like saying you and me are the same person. It's kind of relative, really."

"Damnit... my head."

"You think that's bad, wait 'til you wake up for real. Then you'll really know what a headache is."

"Why do I keep dreaming of sex?"

The other Nathaniel laughed. "It's in our nature. Fight as we want, it'll always be there. Remember that. Nothing and no one can easily deny their nature. Last I checked, we'd slept with three of the girls. But don't focus on the breast; that was eye candy. The rest is what you should focus on."

"But what does it mean?"

"Dude... that's for us to figure out later. Right now, it would be best if you just..."

"Wake up," said a sweet sultry voice.

Nathaniel woke up with a start expecting to find himself licked once again by a long snake tongue. But that wasn't the case. He was alone. Completely alone. He looked only into his reflection in the mirror that followed his every movement. As he looked into the mirror, a suspicious thought crept into his mind. Was this his reflection he was looking into, or a highly choreographed version of himself?

Chapter 22: Check Mate

A pair of jade green eyes stare at a roaring fire in a large castle suite. Two bottles of blood wine lay dry on the floor and the flames bounce off an Ivory and Onyx chess set on a table near the stoic figure of Daniel.

His stare was cold and lost but his bent brow creased with worry. The meeting with the Seven Furies had been tense. At least the memory had faded enough to leave him be, even if his mind was drained. Some of the Therian elders were on his side: Luna, Aureus, and even Corsac, once a nemesis and now a powerful ally. But Madonna, Phoebe, Vilkacis and least of all Gilles Garniere would have nothing to do with their union.

Those were the names of all the Furies, but one hope remained. The oldest and most powerful Fury, Uroc. Some of the other therian elders were just as old as some vampire elders, but Uroc's age seemed to dwarf them all. Among therians he was revered as the Ancient and among all therian hordes, much more order prevailed thanks to his actions. Even if he'd lost in votes, Daniel could still appeal to Uroc.

The last swig of blood wine remained in Daniel's glass but he almost seemed reluctant to finish it. He swirled the last of the deliciously viscous liquid, while his eyes remained on the fire. What would he do? What would happen? These answers eluded the leader of the Magdalena as two brown eyes burned savagely in another room for different reasons.

Nathaniel breathed wearily as he swam in the visions of his trek through the Lucid. His reflection stared back but it still seemed a perfect pantomime rather than a reflection looking at him through the mirror. It was him... but it really wasn't.

The bath had long gone dry, the wine still flowed through his veins and his thoughts rattled mercilessly between his temples. Bill and Lou... one and not the same. What the hell was going on in his head? He had just gotten used to the level of oddity that had permeated his reality and now this. The egnalem's slightly sedating effect had worn off and he was assaulted by visions, truths, lies and possibilities.

"You're good," he said to the mirror. "I know you won't thank me for the compliment, but I know you can hear me. I'm not sure why you're here right now, but I'm pretty sure you're on my side."

He stopped talking and smelled the air. His eyes narrowed and his focus became razor sharp. Something was nearby. He knew it, but he didn't care. He just got up and opened the faucets to fill the tub again.

Back in the other room, Daniel's glass was empty. He hadn't moved one inch, but the glass was vacant. His breathing had picked up slightly but he did not move. His eyes bore into the fire and his glassy skin danced with the shadows of flame. "You're as fast as ever," he said while his eyes stayed on the fire.

A low dark voice heaved from the shadows, "You young ones can't have all the fun."

"I take it you've spoken with your comrades," answered the vampire, finally calming down.

"Naturally or else I would not be here. It's been some time, Daniel. Last I heard of your whereabouts, you were being yourself while Saint Jane continued to be your own personal savior."

"Things don't change," he said with a small smile. "If not for her, I'd have died more times than I care to admit."

"She's a fine choice for you, son," said the dark voice.

"She's the only choice... and I'm not your son, Uroc. Have you come to hear my request or to play games?"

"How about both? Chess?"

Daniel rolled his eyes, "Whatever gets you to offer a sympathetic ear. I'm white though."

"Racist," said the voice with the low grunt of a laugh.

"Not at all," the vampire replied. "I'm more a species-ist and I know I'm not the only one."

"Justifying yourself, Daniel?"

"Not really," the vampire replied. "Just making a point since some of your furry Furies reminded me why hating your kind is so easy."

The voice shifted to another part of the room. "And those that stood by you?"

"They I would die for," said Daniel without blinking.

"Careful what you promise, vampire. You have the first move. Feel free to stay in your chair."

A grayish figure could be seen walking in the shadows and only two strong hands shone in the firelight as they pulled the table closer to the darkness.

"Pawn to E4," the vampire said without looking to the table. "So should you ask or should I make my case?"

"Pawn to E6," said the faceless voice. "Why is the human here?"

"Pawn to D4," Daniel said as he continued to stare into the fire. "You know, for a wise ancient, you don't seem to know much. That human has a plethora of cardinal points and ten of them have already been released. He'll now heal faster, see in the darkness, be supremely stronger and more agile, his sense of smell is heightened, his sense of taste as well. He can have any woman he wants, or at least be quite more persuasive and his reflexes have been filed to deadly sharpness."

The hidden figure hummed as he thought of his next move. "Pawn to D5. And the others unlocked so far?"

"Oh those? Well it seems he can walk through the Lucid and has glimpses of the future. Knight to C3."

"An oneironaut?" asked the deep voice.

"And potentially a seer," Daniel added stoically. "Hell of a weapon, don't you think? Your move."

"What's going on, Daniel? I've seen reports of angels assisting you, not to mention that you and your band of misfits have escaped death at least two times recently, well most of you. I am sorry for Indigo and the other Corsaires that fell... but now you come here... why?"

"Did your reports tell you of my encounter with Sariel?"

"I might have read something related to her," Uroc said as if not wishing to reveal all he knew. "She's the closest an angel could ever be to a wench."

"Maybe... but she did help us escape. Your move."

"Bishop to B4. So what did that winged harlot have to share? More of her cryptic joy I'm sure."

Daniel nodded but still sat without looking at the shadow. "Yes, but she made it quite clear that Israfil was tuning up. Bishop to D3."

"Israfil?" asked the therian Elder.

"The one and the same," Daniel responded as if it were the most natural thing in the world.

"The day of judgment?" Uroc asked, his deep voice slightly cracking.

"Well that is his purpose but good to see that even in your wisdom and greatness you can still get rattled. Your move."

"This is no joke," replied the therian.

"I know," Daniel said his eyes still lost in some distant plane. "That is why I'm glad I have your attention. We need to all join forces. Vampire, therian, angel and the photogeni. Your move."

"Are you insane?" called out the voice, clearly altered by the suggestion. "All of us?"

"Anyone willing to risk everything for life on this planet is invited. Your move, therian."

"And the humans? Will they help?"

"We have Runnels. Sorry, it's the best I can do in such short notice and something tells me that if humans haven't taken a side, it won't be ours when they do. Your move."

"They can't be that insane or stupid."

"No? If not for one human being, the Cuban Missile Crisis would have been the beginning of the destruction of the Earth. One Russian made the call not to launch... quite a few other people were more than content to go to war. Oh, and it is still your move."

"Well since you insist on being in such a hurry, I'll just have to eat your knight so you can eat my bishop. Bishop to C3."

"Pawn to C3. Funny how a little pawn can do away with your rook while it took all that to take my small pawn."

"You act too swiftly, Daniel."

"And you fail to begin to act, Uroc. Though I hate the adage, in this case it applies. The means justify the end and time is finally not a luxury neither of us can squander. Your move again."

In another room, Nathaniel was in deep thought inside the bath. He was completely submerged in warm water with the exception of his nose and eyes. His stare possessed a deep seeded focus and he breathed deliberately rather than allowing instinct to dictate his need for air.

In deeply. Out slowly. In as he savored every last drop of air, out until his lungs could exhale no more. His eyes remained on one spot on the ceiling. Two inches of pattern that became a universe which he swam through with every breath. Meanwhile a vision kept flashing before his static eyes.

"Scorpion... scorpion... scorpion..." He repeated the word and twitched every single time he said it, at times even splashing water on the floor.

The dancers in his dream came forth in his mind's eye but he pushed them out of his head. He tensed and grimaced as words tried to break free from within. "Br... bur... buh... buh... breh... break.... Break ... break...f....f..free Br.... Break... fuh... furh frrrr... free... Break free. Break freeeeeeee."

The room's lights flickered once... then again... and again as he continued. "Buhrr brrrr...break furrreee.. break freeeee." His deep brown eyes swam in a reddish hue and bubbles began to fizzle everywhere in his sight. He sat up and saw a large swarm of black wasps fizzling and fidgeting in the air like some bad computer animation. His expression didn't change and it was almost as if he were in a trance, but he wasn't. He looked at the wasps as they pointed at something behind the wall. The wasps neared the door as one by one, little red scorpions lined in front of the doorframe, forming a living crawling red carpet. A glowing red shadow suddenly appeared steps away from the door.

He laid back down to lose himself within the two inch universe on the ceiling. Nathaniel breathed deeply and licked the egnalem spice off his lips. Earthy and robust, he tasted egnalem though he knew he hadn't ingested any for a time now, but in the reddish brown hue of the mid dimension, it was all around him and the water he now bathed in was the color of vibrant rust and tasted of the purest spice.

A hissing grew in his ear. "Drink, drown. Drink and drown. Drink and drown. Drink and drown. Drink and drown. What's up is now down. Drink and drown."

"Can I drown in the mid dimension?" Nathaniel asked out loud.

The hissing continued. "Drink and drown. Up and down. Hurt and fear. For the seer. Drown in spice. Warm and nice. Drink and drown. Drink and drown."

His eyes narrowed. He breathed deliberately. In and out. In and out.

"Up and down," he whispered and sunk his face deep in the bath tub. Bubbles tickled his face but his eyes remained strangely calm.

Half a minute. A full minute. A minute and a half. Time trickled by and Nathaniel's face did not move. His pulse did not falter and his lungs did not cough out the warm liquid that flooded them. In essence, he was calmly drowning himself. His body should be fighting this but instead, it absorbed the crimson liquid that had replaced the water.

His mind roamed within the two inch universe of pattern that stared back from beyond the surface of the spice water. He soared through the subatomic beauty of fabric and waves of particles danced with him every step of the way. A single dust cloud fogged his view from above the bathtub and he saw himself submerged and naked in the large bath.

"I look in peace," said the mirage that floated above his drowning body.

"Yes you do," said a familiar voice with its Texan accent, "but you still need to unlock a cardinal point."

"Good to see you back Bill or Lou," answered the projection of Nathaniel.

"I thought you might need some help with this one," said the bodiless voice.

"What should I do?" Nathaniel asked.

"Simple. Continue to breathe deep. Focus on yourself. Focus on the very center of your forehead and breathe towards it. Now make a prayer and with your middle and index fingers, bring the focus to your third eye."

"But..."

"No buts, Nathaniel. Focus. Ignore the protons and electrons. Feel with your mind's eye. Breathe deeply and full. Float through the skies above Castle Margeride and take the eternal fall. Plummet like a fallen angel."

Clouds now floated all around Nathaniel and his image looked down the hole of a nimbus well that looked over the castle.

"Drink or drown," said Bill or Lou.

"Up..." replied Nathaniel while basking in the red sun shining high above the clouds in the mid dimension. He pressed his fingers to his forehead, then the tip of his nose before touching his lips and allowing gravity to claim him. He plunged through the passage through the clouds. The air frothed and the smell of egnalem was everywhere.

His pulse did not quicken, his eyes did not tear and hundreds of feet passed like an afterthought. Down he fell and the castle finally came into clear view. He was God's Arrow and nothing would stand in his way. He pierced floor after floor until once again he found himself in the two inch universe of fabric on the ceiling of the room. He soared through space and matter and all the while, there was only one reaction that came from his body... a complacent smile.

He finally floated back into the room and fell like a timid feather that wanted to keep away from the floor. His body lay still in a trance beneath the water and he reached out to touch the middle of his forehead. His specter and his body were perpendicular and at the slightest contact a bright red light exploded in the room.

His only self was the one submerged. He had drowned without drowning and rose from the water like a spire from Poseidon's trident. He didn't breathe out hard. He didn't sneeze or cough. He simply allowed the water to exit his body. Eyes unblinking, the only remainder of his experience was the half smile that curled on his lips.

He gave a stretch and looked around the room. All was eerily quiet and when he looked at the door, his eyes dilated and his breathing picked up ever so slightly. "Come in, Malia," he called out.

A short click and the creaking of the door gave way to the confused expression of the vampire. Nathaniel ignored the fact that he was naked and looked at her with a calm focus that rattled her every nerve. "I've been expecting you," he said... still smiling, still unblinking.

Elsewhere, jade green eyes still looked upon a fire.

"So are you going to make your move or shall I make it for you?" Daniel said, finally looking in the direction of the figure veiled in shadow.

"I'm merely assimilating what you've said, Montacre," the therian replied.

"And I simply look to spur you to react and fight," Daniel said, banging on the armrest. "This is no time for paused decisions! We have not the luxury of living as we have for so long. Now move, or does the great Ancient not work well under pressure."

A sound like buckling metal came from the shadow. "Pawn to H6," said the raspy voice.

Daniel didn't offer him a chance to think. "Bishop to A3. Your move again. I know that's not how you play, Uroc, but you are not owner of all rules and the game that has claimed lives the last few days is not one to be taken lightly... or slowly. Move."

"I take orders from no one, whelp," snarled the shadow.

"I am no whelp, and I'm not giving orders," Daniel replied. "I'm making a point."

"Oh really? And what would this point be?"

Daniel did not hesitate to respond. "Act now or forfeit the game. Act now or forever hold your peace."

The shadow seemed to pulse. "And you suggest?"

"My kind is gathering forces. The angels seem reluctant yet willing, I've met with the Watchers and after here we mean to see the photogeni."

"You're crazy, you know that?"

Daniel stood and faced the darkness. "I am maniacal. I am psychotic. Call me what you will but I am acting and mobilizing to do what I can to avoid the annihilation of all life, though I'm sure the demons will find a way to make us useful rather than simply obliterate us. Oh, and it's still your move."

"Knight to D7," said the raspy voice.

"Queen to E2," Daniel spat back.

"Aggressive move, vampire."

"Desperate times, my friend. Desperate times."

"And what guarantee do we have that your plan will work?"

"Whoever said anything of a guarantee? Master Uroc, you seem to overlook the fact that there is no insurance coverage for this type of scenario. The only guarantee I can offer is that for the duration of this conflict, therians will not be attacked from our side."

"Can you guarantee that?" said the dark voice calculatingly.

"Could you guarantee the same from your kind? They've behaved rather well up to now, but like any relationship, beginnings tend to be rosy while subsequent encounters grow tainted."

"Pawn to E4," Uroc said. "Shall I move your bishop there as well?"

"I'll take your suggestion. A pawn for a pawn while doomsday is upon. A pawn upon a pawn for up on here doth time run up and away. Your move, kind sir."

Back in the other room, Nathaniel spoke to his visitor. "I had a dream about you."

"Oh did you?" answered Malia as she looked over the naked glistening body of Nathaniel. She found new muscles and tighter crevasses to hang her eyes on and she lavishly drunk the sight.

"Yes," he said calmly. "It was you and me, here... now."

"So you're a psychic now, Nathaniel? I find that even more appealing because now I don't have to tell you how to satisfy me."

"Indeed," he said, standing before her and reaching for a robe to put over his body. "I think I can give you what you need." He then stepped out of the tub, walked up to her, drank her essence and held her tight by her arms.

Her breathing quickly became broken and rigid just before she dove head first into a passionate, forceful kiss. He responded in kind but unlike the unbridled passion of the vampire, his breathing was even, his heart did not pound and his approach was completely deliberate.

"Take me now," rang the clichéd line from her mouth. Nathaniel stopped kissing her and led her to the bed. He ripped her shirt and exposed her left breast at the same time he tore the skirt she wore. He devoured her while her moans of ecstasy sang to the rhythm of his strumming fingers. He knitted wave after wave of pleasure.

She screamed like a woman possessed. "Take me!! Don't make me wait any longer!!! Don't make me beg. Take me!!!!"

He proceeded to throw her on the bed and slide in between her legs.

Malia could only reply with strangled moans of pleasure. She pulled his hair, he fed deeper and before she could finish, he stopped kissing and took the vampire. Her eyes transported into some other nebula but his face remained rigid. Unflinching, unaffected, unmoved. His eyes looked into the mirror and saw winks he didn't give. She arched her back and he now saw a smile he didn't smile. She reached beneath the bed and he saw eyes staring to where he wasn't looking and a second later a cracking thump brought silence.

In Malia's hand was a silver dagger clenched tightly and hungry for blood. But the dagger that had quenched its thirst was in Nathaniel's hand, buried to the hilt into Malia's chest.

"Wh... h... how...?" she struggled to whisper.

"I told you, I had a dream of you and me... here and now. You chose to follow the script, I had other ideas."

Blood flowed from her mouth as she struggled to speak. "I... I... loved you."

His eyes were cold and devoid of emotion. "I've had better." After two swipes of his blade, her body lay motionless beneath him.

Back in the other room, the game continued.

Uroc's shadow sat low thinking the next move. "Knight to F6. And the human?"

"Runnels is a bottomless well of potential. He's only beginning to awaken to what he can truly be."

"And that is?" asked the therian.

"The Deus Machina," Daniel said piercing the darkness where Uroc sat.

"God within the Machine?"

"No, Master Uroc. Not Deus ex Machina, but Deus Machina: the Machine of God. Most people are familiar with the other term but please do not misunderstand. The Machine of God is in reality a human whose complete potential is harnessed, or so say some ancient lore. Unfortunately, no human has survived long enough to get to that point. You should have seen him at Maestranza. And that was just the beginning."

"Did he really do all of what I've read?" asked the shadow.

"To put it simply, those vampires are lucky to be alive," said Daniel. "His eyes are what bothered me the most though. And pardon my delay. Bishop to D3."

"I'd almost thought you'd forgotten about the game, Daniel. Pawn to B6."

Daniel sat back down and lounged in the chair. "Not at all. But you really shouldn't try to play other people's games you know."

"And why would that be?" the therian asked.

"Because you're bound to make a stupid move," Daniel said, turning back to the grey hands. "Queen to E6. I'll have that pawn thank you very much."

"My move a stupid one? You've just lost your queen and eaten by nothing more than a pawn. Pawn to E6, your move."

Daniel looked once again into the fire. His eyes glazed over and a sort of odd half smile broke upon his lips. He smelled the air and pondered on what his nostrils told him.

"Your move, Daniel," insisted the elder.

Daniel paused for a moment, and his eyes looked towards the ceiling as if he'd sensed something. "Do you feel that?"

"Feel what?" asked Uroc impatiently. "I only feel the need to finish this game. Your move."

Daniel listened hard. He could hear tainted fabric whispering crimson memories in the hall.

"Your move, Daniel," the therian insisted.

"Is there really need for another move?" Daniel asked. "Can't you feel what's coming?"

"The only thing I feel is the satisfaction that comes from bringing the great Montacre out of his comfort zone."

The vampire turned to the shade again. "Have you now? Or is it that your sense of smell is not what it used to be? Or worse yet, have you spilled so much blood you don't even know if there's a fresh batch in the air? Smell."

"More tricks to keep from playing," said the shadow. "Make your move, vampire. I'll finish you in less than five moves after yours."

"And still you insist on talking based on race? You haven't the foresight to see that this is endlessly larger than any species."

Naked feet on cold stone drew nearer to where the two continued their verbal jousting.

"You claim the power of your pawn and you probably think it is the weakest piece of all," Daniel said.

"I've taken your queen," said the therian. "That's evidence of what I think of the power of a pawn. Now make your move, Montacre."

"The trick of chess, just as in war is misdirection."

The door crashed open and there stood Nathaniel, drenched in blood and wearing what used to be a white robe. His eyes bore through the shadow and from it to the terrified face of Daniel.

"A game of chess?" the young man calmly remarked. "Seems someone risked a queen to take a pawn." In his hand was the severed head of Malia. "Too bad pawns can also prove lethal. Sorry Daniel, but she tried to kill me."

Daniel's mouth hung limply. "How did you know we were here?"

"I just did," replied the human. "Fine game you've been playing. I'm guessing he still hasn't noticed."

Daniel shook his head and even chanced a smile. Nathaniel looked into the shadow again. "Funny. I'm the weak ignorant human and you can't even realize when you're beat. Powerful you may be, but if anything, I've noticed this vampire is smarter than what you give him credit for."

From the shadows came a deep dark breath and a large grey mane. The eyes were fierce and teeth were bared as a seismic growl hovered towards the blood soaked human.

"You can have this," Nathaniel said as he handed the head over to the powerful old therian. "That means we're not safe in your precious castle and this would explain the information the enemy has obtained. By the way, you've lost the game. With one move Daniel will checkmate you, but he wants to see if you'll accept defeat and join us. I don't like vampires either but either of your kind is a hell of a lot better to live with than a demon. Now swallow your pride and see that Daniel is not the only one who has sacrificed his queen to try to get the upper hand."

Uroc faced the chessboard. "But how do you..."

"Bishop to G6, correct Daniel?" The vampire smiled confused but nodded marveling at what was unfolding in front of him.

"Then checkmate, Master Uroc. Now that that's over, I will bathe but I suggest mobilizing everyone to get the hell out of here."

The therian was still trying to process his defeat. "But..."

"Look at the board and move on," Nathaniel said to the therian just before glaring into Daniel's eyes. "I'll be in my room."

With that single look a world of understanding crashed into the vampire's eye. "How..."

"You said it best," Nathaniel said. "There is no piece more lethal than a pawn if moved correctly. I'll see you later. Tell the others of Malia and plan our next move."

Nathaniel then exited the room leaving Daniel looking at the bloody wake the human left. The vampire then looked at the old therian who just stared at the chessboard while holding onto the severed head. A wounded look washed over him and the wolf faded, leaving an old man looking pensively at the chess pieces until he knocked his king over.

"What do you need of us, Montacre?"

Chapter 23: Just inn time

Six pairs of wings float over Rue Garoux. Six figures circling overhead before descending slowly in a wide cyclone towards the ground.

The first one to touch down hovers lightly and transitions from flight to walk in one fluid movement. His wings are a dark grey sprinkled with occasional white spots and his robes are pitch black. His face is stern but his eyes are gentle and they follow the crimson wings of the second angel who swoops down aggressively only to turn up at the last second and hop to a landing next to him.

The first angel stretches his wings and sings:

> *"Now that we have landed gently,*
> *Something comes before my eyes.*
> *Here this town its roads lay empty,*
> *Long before we've flown its skies."*

Silently nodding, the second angel looks around. His eyes are solid white but his hair and robes are just as red as his crimson wings. He picks at the air with his nose and a troubled look veils his face. The first angel looks at him queerly and decides to sing some more:

> *"Tell me now o brother mine,*
> *What's for us to do?*
> *Look around, read all the signs,*
> *These cubs have flown this coop.*
> *Nothing scented, seen or heard,*
> *Changes what is true.*

> *'Tis an outcome most absurd,*
> *What are we to do?"*

The second angel's face showed no emotion but his voice showed annoyance and scorn. "I really do wish you'd shut up, Nelchael. Let us wait for the others before we decide our next action."

A third angel now tumbled recklessly through the sky. He swooped left, banked clumsily to the right and instead of the grace of both other landings, this one had the intentions of imitating a skipping stone with a crash and two twists, ending with legs and wings flapping like some bad ski accident.

The red angel rubbed his eyes and sighed. "Asael...."

"Nice, nice landing hee-hee," the third angel said in a child's voice. "I tumble-tumbled like dirty laundry." The third angel looked at himself, all bruised, covered in dirt and sprawled with joy screaming. "I AM dirty laundry, I am. I needs a washing and scrubbing cuz I'm dirty, dirty, dirty."

"Sit down and shut up, Asael," said the second angel. "Something's wrong and I don't need your idiotic rambling distracting me."

"S.. sorry, Rosier... I... I.."

"Please, just shut up," said the crimson angel. "My head needs to think and you are like sand grating my gears."

A fourth angel floated down slowly, gliding like a tossed silk sheet, until tiptoeing smoothly onto the ground. The first angel obviously felt the need to sing.

> *"Brother here these two now bicker,*
> *But more pressing matters wait.*
> *Seems in haste we still did linger,*
> *Nothing, no one now remains.*
> *Crimson brother's now a smelling,*
> *Something that's gone quite amiss.*
> *Seems the lady traitor's missing,*
> *Touched now by death's sudden kiss.*
> *Brother silly has been scolded,*

Please be gentle, I insist.
Now's the time to change what's planned,
Tell us what steps to take next."

The deep brown wings tucked tight behind the green robed angel. He looked at his surroundings and his yellow eyes streaked through the dark. He sniffed deeply and never blinked, taking and drinking every cell of information that surrounded him. He stared around like a hungry tiger almost ignoring the three other angels.

"It seems something foul is up, Turiel," said the red angel Rosier. "What are we to do?"

"I'm quite aware of that, brother," said the new angel severely. "Nelchael might annoy you, but he always offers the information I need."

The dark winged angel smiled in satisfaction at being defended while Turiel continued to stare around. Asael sat on the ground scratching himself and picking at his wings.

"Stop that," Rosier scolded.

Turiel's yellow eyes continued to look around as the remaining two figures still floated overhead. "There's no one left here," said the angel now frowning at the nearby inn. "Buildings are empty, the cars we saw from above were abandoned and no one is left in the castle. Only that little hotel remains inhabited but I can't put a smell to the place."

He continued to sniff and stare while Nelchael stepped to and fro like some carefree soldier patrolling his post. Rosier stared with his white eyes towards Turiel and Asael once again got to picking at his feathers.

"She loves me; she me loves not," Asael said as he picked at the feathers from his wings.

"Stop that," Rosier said though no one paid attention.

"She loves me; she loves me not," continued Asael.

"I said stop that," Rosier repeated but everyone continued to ignore him.

Above them one of the angels broke from the formation and flew off. Turiel's yellow eyes followed him. "Ananiel goes East," he said pensively. Let's wait for what brother Armaros has to say."

The angel that still floated now swooped aggressively towards the ground.

Asael continued picking his feathers. "She loves me; she loves me..."

"SHUT UP!!!!" Rosier screamed.

The childish angel cowered behind Turiel but above, the angel still in flight pointed his wings straight to the heavens and fell eighty feet landing with a thunderous crash on the floor next to the throng of angels. He dissected his surroundings with his pure amber eyes, no whites to them at all. His chin was wide and seemed chiseled from granite plated with iron.

Rosier approached the angel. "Big brother, there seems to be a problem."

The massive angel stared his white eyed brother sternly. "A problem? One problem? Seems like more than that to mine eyes. First, where is the whore you mated with? Second, where is everyone else? Third, who's in that inn? Fourth, what must be done to stop you from besmirching your younger brother?"

"I'm sorry brother Armaros, I am..."

"A poor excuse for a Nephilim and getting on my nerves," said the large angel harshly. "Leave your brother alone or answer to me. Now apologize."

"Sorry Asael..."

"No harm no foul, bigger bro," said Asael cheerily. "But biggest bro, don't kill 'im, he didn't mean it, right Rosier?"

The large angel looked down on Rosier, while still talking to Asael. "All right. I won't kill him. But only because you asked, me little one. As for the other matters at hand. I sent Ananiel East to scout for any sign of our beloved pack. Your wench is dead though. I smell her blood in the air, though only traces of it. Seems the body was taken away... and I also heard her whispers of laments as she descended to hell.

Seems mother still doesn't take kind to traitors. Which only leaves the matter of this inn to clear up."

Armaros started to walk towards the little inn, but he hadn't taken ten steps when he stopped. It wasn't that he had sensed something else in the vicinity; it was that he had distinctly heard three sets of feet following him instead of four. When he turned around, he saw that Asael sat cross legged and quite reluctant to even stand up. "Little brother, why don't you follow?"

Asael crossed his arms tighter but spoke gently to Armaros. "Time's on their side, Big Brother. We shouldn't go in there."

"We're all here little brother," said the large angel reassuringly. "There's nothing to worry about. Nothing's going to happen."

"Exactly," replied Asael.

"Exactly what?" Armaros asked confused.

"Nothing," said the angel from his seat on the ground.

The leader of the fallen angels seemed even more confused. "What?"

"That's what's gonna happen, Big Brother. I'm tellin' you, time is on their side."

"Come, Asael," snapped Rosier. "We waste time with this childish behavior."

"Rosier..." Turiel said warningly.

"I'm not saying something out of place," he told his stoic brother. "He's behaving like a cherub."

"Your mother's a cherub, beet face!!!" Asael screamed.

Armaros settled the argument by slamming his fist on the ground. "Silence! Both of you. To the inn now. Do not make me repeat myself."

They all followed Armaros this time and knocked on the quaint little door of the inn. They waited a moment as little footsteps made their way to the door. Three clicks and a turn of a door knob and before the five angels stood a sweet old lady that was barely five feet tall.

"Good evening, gentlemen," Mrs. Fawn said. "May I help you?"

Armaros stepped up, towering over the old woman. "Where is everyone and why are you the only one still here?"

The old lady responded by raising her eyebrows and taking her time to give a reply. "A good evening, hello or excuse me would be nice. How very rude. First there's an earthquake like a stampede came through the main road, followed by barking and even howling... howling I tell you. Or was it howling first and then the stampede. Well I just went to the cellar and stayed there 'til all of those things went away. I was so frightened, like one time Bertha heard the winds picking up and insisted a wild pack of baboons had flown off to..."

"Madam..." Armaros said interrupting her, "excuse me and pardon the interruption and the rudeness, but when was this?"

The old lady began to sniff at the air and look all around. "Is something burning in the kitchen?" she asked.

"What?" replied the fallen angel.

She sniffed again. "Oh no... the lemon cake. Come in dears, I'll be with you in a second." She scuttled into the kitchen and the five angels stood at the doorway looking baffled and confused. They heard her voice coming from the kitchen: "Come in boys, you can take off your coats and I'll be with you in a second."

They heard an oven opening and various plates and dishes being tossed in the wash bin. One by one they walked into the inn passing the threshold as an odd blanket of fog came out of nowhere to flood the street, though it did not seep into the inn. When they were inside, the voice of the sweet old lady called: "Shut the door, please. Don't want any of that fog seeping inside."

Rosier walked towards the door while Asael checked him to make sure the crimson angel didn't see him as he picked at his feathers. The hulking Armaros stood a bit dumbfounded near the opening of the kitchen twitching as the clanging of pots and pans continued. Turiel took a seat on the headrest of one of the couches and Nelchael looked at his nails in a rather bored fashion. Rosier closed the door half looking his older brother with a gaze that asked why they didn't just wring the old woman's neck to get the information they needed. Asael was now entertaining himself by flapping his wings to turn the pages of a large book that stood in the hall.

The old lady suddenly rushed out, saw the angel and gave him a look like a grandmother who has just found a baby with his hands full of ketchup practicing finger painting all over a white blanket. "Please leave that alone, dear," she said gently. "That book is very important and mustn't be damaged. I'll bring you something you'll love soon enough."

"Something for me?" asked the childlike angel. "All righttttttttt!!!! Thank you missus. Hee hee hee!!!"

"Don't mention it darling," she said sweetly. "Now, would anyone like some tea?" She looked around as if the creatures in her inn were the most normal thing in the world and not five fallen angels with bad intentions.

Armaros insisted on returning to the conversation they were having. "Actually madam, we were wondering about the noise you heard before. The howls and the stampede? Do you have any other information regarding that?"

"Heavens me," said the old lady, "now that was a ruckus. I haven't even gone outside since that racket begun. I wonder if Bertha is all right. I've called her a couple of times, but no answer."

"The town is completely deserted, Mrs..."

"Fawn, dear; call me Mrs. Fawn. Pardon me, but at my age, things get a little foggy in the brain, not to mention my eyes and ears."

Armaros continued. "So Mrs. Fawn, you don't know anything about anyone ever since the loud noise passed?"

"Not a peep," she said resolutely. "It's funny though, people say they can't find time to visit or that there's never time to come and see me and I'm right here. You just need to look for me to find me. But no, there's never time they say. Poppycock and hogwash, I say to that."

"Very well said, Madam," replied the large angel. "But we really should be off. There are pressing matters to be dealt with. Thank you for your time and have a good day." Armaros then looked outside and saw that the thick fog had settled on Rue Garoux.

Mrs. Fawn looked past the hulk and noticed the same thing. "If you need to see a bit better, head left on this road and walk towards the bright lamp on the corner of Garoux and Ronian."

"My thanks, m'lady, and good day," said the large angel as he opened the door and with a final nod walked out of the inn into the thick fog. The remaining angels bowed and were on their way although Asael got a hug and a kiss on the cheek.

"You're a very smart one," she told him and with one last warm smile, she gave him something covered in foil and closed the door.

The other angels saw the bright lamp they had been given as direction and walked directly to it. With every step, the bright grey fog thawed until a much darker scenery faded into view. When they reached the corner, the fog had lifted completely, leaving them beneath the blanket of a dark starry night.

Armaros blinked in confusion. "What just happened?"

Asael walked up to his brother and patted him on the shoulder, "I told you time was on their side." He then held out the foil Mrs. Fawn had given him to offer his brother. "Lemon cake?"

Chapter 24: A little Cretian jazz

The trip from Castle Margeride to Pont D'Auvignon had been a long one but luckily there had been no problems during the trek. Finally the vampires had rendezvoused with the Black Calico and it was now time to part with the therians.

Daniel looked at the horizon as he remembered the words of the Ancient Uroc. "We reconvene in four week's time at Sri Lanka." That had been the date set for the meeting of whoever was to take part in the battle. Uroc had given his word that the participation of various hordes would be a given and that no harm would come to vampires from their hands. This included the Wendigo horde from Canada, the Kitsune werefoxes from Japan, the Bouda hyena men from Africa, the Nahuales shape shifters and the Runnas tribe from Argentina. Not the entire therian population; then again, the same had happened with the vampires since all broods had not responded. In the end, the ancient therian had wished them well and hoped that more hands would join the cause.

They now headed down the beautiful Rhone River at a speed far greater than what any ordinary galleon should have been capable of handling. The large ship sliced through the water like fresh sharpened shears through paper.

Jane had offered a dry welcome though her eyes lingered slightly on Daniel's stern face. "All's well?" she asked.

"End's well," responded the vampire. "My apologies, m'lady, but the cogs are in motion, the plans have been set forth and whatever is to happen, will happen... soon."

"And now where to?" she asked him.

"We must set sail to Crete, m'lady. There's someone there we must have a word with." When he finished his sentence, his eyes roamed the countryside deep in thought.

Jane looked at him and when she spoke, she finally softened her tone. "Daniel, what is it?"

He took a long breath before voicing his thoughts. "How I wish I could be on this river with you and no other care in the world. Instead, I have to worry about war. They say all is fair in love and war, but I can attest to war never being fair and love never more fair than what I have for you. I need to rest, m'lady. Please, care for Runnels and if it's not too much trouble, fetch me when we arrive."

A blush had blossomed on her face that would have been visible in the darkest most moonless night and she was barely able to reply. "As you wish, Daniel."

"My thanks, m'lady," he said while turning to leave.

"Daniel?"

"Yes, m'lady?" he answered turning to face her.

"You don't have to keep calling me m'lady," she said softly.

He gave her his typical smile. "Yes I do. You are my queen after all." He stepped to her and held her in his arms for a brief moment, speaking through an embrace as only lovers can before he left below deck.

Stern side near the front of the boat, Nathaniel stood looking at the water as eddies echoed off the edges to meet those that slipped off the beautiful vessel. Up ahead he saw the split where the river broke into the Grand Rhone and the Petit Rhone. A warm glow followed by a faint hint of tobacco came to rest beside him. Even though he didn't turn his head to look, Nathaniel knew it was Liam. Now two people looked upon the fugue of eddies resonating long after the powerful galleon had passed.

"He who submits to fate without complaint is wise," Liam said while puffing tobacco smoke.

Nathaniel didn't stop looking at the water. "Maybe for Euripides, but whoever said I wanted to be wise?"

The vampire gave a little laugh. "Just my way of saying one must be content even in times of trouble, young friend."

Nathaniel took a moment to gather his thoughts. "If man is moderated and contented, then even age is no burden. If he is not however, then even youth is full of cares."

Liam nodded in approval as he sipped on his cigarette. "Plato did say it best."

"Maybe, but I don't think I was designed to be content," Nathaniel said.

Liam pondered over his cigarette before replying. "So in your case, you wish to avoid the sins you never commit, for those are the ones you most regret."

"Precisely," Nathaniel replied. "Though I am in luck."

"Oh?!" exclaimed Liam, "and why is that?"

"Because no human condition is ever permanent," Nathaniel said. "That way I will not be overjoyed in good fortune nor too sorrowful in misfortune."

"You are a special one, Runnels," said Liam smiling broadly before returning the cigarette to his mouth.

Nathaniel answered the vampire's smile with his own and now turned to look forward to the front of the boat. As the sunset approached, the Camargue Delta took on an ethereal glow which the human couldn't help but marvel at.

The vampire used his dying cigarette to birth a new one. After one long pull deep into his lungs, he spoke so wisps of smoke would tickle the words that came from his mouth.

> *"On desperate seas long wont to roam,*
> *Thy hyacinth hair, thy classic face,*
> *Thy Naiad airs have brought me home.*
> *To the glory of fair Greece*
> *And the grandeur that was Rome."*

A moment lapsed where the meaning of those words sank deeper than the great sea mounts at the bottom of the Atlantic. "You're also a special one, Liam."

"Not really," the vampire said. "My heart weeps for a love taken twice and the sea is the only place I feel peace."

"So why does that not make you special?" Nathaniel asked.

The vampire's eyes became slightly watery. "Anyone can weep beautiful poetry when real love is taken away."

Nathaniel knew this was a sensitive subject for the vampire so he treaded carefully. "Have you found out anything else of what happened there?"

The lack of a response was answer enough. "Don't worry," continued the young man, "there will be sins to commit soon enough."

"I truly hope so," said the vampire wiping his eyes. "Soon shall be the time to act and I am grateful. These hands thirst for blood and I'm tired of knowing much and doing little."

"Lucky you then," Nathaniel said.

"Why is that?" asked Liam.

"Because you know so much. Me? All I know is that I know nothing."

The vampire actually spit his smoke out, braced his forehead and smiled broadly at the human's comment. Nathaniel answered by giving him a firm pat on the back. "So we can admit Socrates said it best and that Plato can go screw himself?"

"Indeed," the vampire said while smiling. They continued to look into the sunset and the vampire offered his battered cigarette pack to the young man. "Care for a smoke?"

"No thanks, those things will kill you," Nathaniel said and then kept quiet next to his unlikely friend. They stared into the horizon and continued to lose themselves in their thoughts.

"Runnels?"

"What?"

"Thanks. I needed that."

"Don't mention it; I still owe you for the earlier assaults."

Again the vampire spat out his smoke and smiled with a sigh of relief at having something that could make him laugh. They stood there silent, content to share each other's company as nature showed them what real beauty was all about. The voyage continued along the

Mediterranean and the route they were taking, which should have taken weeks to traverse, took little more than a day thanks to the Black Calico.

***

A day had passed but for all intents and purposes, it could have been a year. Nathaniel had grown used to the speed of the Black Calico and his surroundings as if he had been born to live on the sea. "This ship is incredible. I never would have thought any vessel could go so fast."

"Thank you, Nathaniel," Captain Jane answered. "With a little help from my children, any voyage can be swift and painless."

Nathaniel looked confused. "What do you mean?"

"Part of the reason we travel so swiftly along the sea is this ship and the routes it is able to travel, but another help would be the large ground swells we've been riding."

Looking over the rail, Nathaniel noticed the ship leaning every few seconds with the push of large heavy waves. Jane continued to look to the horizon but a motherly smile shone on her face. "If you listen closely, you can hear them as they push the waves that carry us across Poseidon's garden. Vincenzo and all of the rest of my sea children."

***

They flowed across the Mediterranean, first to the south of Sardinia, then past Palermo and bordering Malta before whisking onto the Sea of Crete. Almost two thousand miles covered in little over a day.

Daniel had been in his cabin the entire time meditating. When he heard the gentle knock on the door, he knew it was Jane on the other side. "We near Crete, Daniel. I'll be topside so you can tell us where we should land."

She then left the vampire to his thoughts. He breathed deeply, stretched, got up and walked out the door and up the stairs to the main deck. It was night and everyone was looking at the island that lay ahead. He stood next to the captain of the ship.

Her poise was perfect and he looked at her like he loved her, but couldn't say it in words that would do the feeling justice, so of course he talked business. "Please try and place us at Chania by the Lighthouse and then set anchor where you please, m'lady. Just make sure to change station every two hours. One can't be too cautious, especially now. I'll contact you to see where we rendezvous."

"Be careful, Daniel," Jane said apprehensively. "Israfil can show us the way or stray us further from our goal."

"Fret not, sweet captain," he said with his charming smile. "There are still battles to thread and stories to weave."

With a brisk jump, Daniel, Nathaniel, Liam and Edward Louis landed on a small raft to go to shore. Two minutes later, they walked along the lighthouse, surprisingly not being called by any guard or seen by anybody. It was as if their landing had been the most natural thing in the world.

"It's funny what you can do if you act calm, cool and collected," Daniel said.

"As long as you yield to indifference, anything is possible Daniel," Edward Louis said.

"Well said. But now we must be off to judgment."

They walked along the crowded streets of Chania, passing bars, dance clubs, taverns and countless small restaurants. The smell of lamb, raki and tzatziki braided across the air to offer up a spicy Greek essence. They passed countless places with the word Zorba in neon lights and rounded some rather obvious tourist traps.

A couple of blocks passed and the only thing that remained constant were the soft green eyes of Edward along with his shoulder length hair, Nathaniel's cold stare far detached from the human he had been two weeks ago, the constant comfort of Liam's cigarettes and the shockingly blue eyes of Daniel. The small quartet made their way past side streets and offbeat houses searching until they found the place they were looking for.

Statues of catholic saints lined the entrance while Lady Justice had the balance at hand in a large statue in front of a place that only had two symbols for a name:

A Ω

The Greek symbols for Alpha and Omega.

Liam and Edward were pleased to learn that smoking was still allowed when a large blanket of cigarette smoke seeped from the door. Upon entering, smoke played off the dim house lights at times tainted green, other times red. The bar had a decent crowd and the jazz trio offered some good Herbie Hancock to feed hungry ears of cool cats lined throughout the floor. A man pawed his drink like a kitten to a knitting ball while others merely swam in the smoke from their own cigarettes taking every swirl as an opportunity to reminisce.

Edward, Nathaniel, and Daniel took their places at the bar while Liam paid for the first round of raki. The heavily spiced anis liqueur slowly slithered down their throats regardless of how hard they had slammed the shot. Edward then asked for red wine, Liam glowed once a smooth pint of stout was placed in front of him, while Daniel and Nathaniel sipped from two glasses filled with oxide green liqueur with a green fairy on the side of the bottle.

"What are we waiting for?" Nathaniel asked.

"We're waiting for the main act which should be taking the stage any moment now," Daniel said.

The trio finished a wonderful version of Round Midnight and now looked set to take a break when an announcer came to the only empty mike on the small stage and said in Greek in a very deep voice "And now, for who you came to see... Iz."

Some whistles sounded off and warm applause pointed at a side door from which a beautiful large black man emerged whose dark skin made him look both hard and soft like some delicately chiseled black marble statue. Every step forward was sure and firm yet completely relaxed. He scanned the audience and when he saw the group of four at the table to the right, he tipped his hat with the same hand that held a small Iraqi cigarette he generously sucked on while the band started up. A cast of musicians had come out to crowd the stage, but even with nine other musicians around him, the attention was on Iz. A few seconds passed and it was obvious it was a song few people forget if they've seen it live... "Bitches Brew..." Nathaniel whispered.

Edward, Liam and Daniel nodded in approval and Edward even took the opportunity to close his eyes and let his mind swim in the music. The brooding ebb and flow of Mr. Davis's masterpiece danced about the room as sound was blissful enough to almost have its own color and taste. People from the audience swung in drunken joy and some almost seemed possessed by demons of pleasure that made them sway like happily drunken marionettes. Even the bartender had stopped serving drinks to savor each note that blistered out of the trumpet of the man known simply as Iz. When he wasn't playing, Iz acted as bandleader giving band members cues and molding the song with his will.

Nathaniel's eyes swam drunkenly in currents of smoke. He did not mind the sting and allowed his gaze to bounce from one person to another until his eyes met with the lead trumpeter's. The intensity of the music never dropped for one second but the statuesque man's eyes beamed like fires from another world. Smoke currents swirled and merged to form lines, contours and abstract shapes around Iz, but his gaze never broke from Nathaniel's. In the smoke, the young man saw shapes form and a story began to unfold. Flying bodies danced from roof to wall to floor as two lines formed on opposing sides of the room. Images of ancient warrior helms lined up on either side.

Nathaniel felt fear like nothing he'd ever felt before and as the fire of adrenaline surged forth he saw that the opposing sides roared within the smoke. Spears, lances, bows and swords formed... along with a sea of wings. There were angels made of smoke lined up on either side clashing their weapons against their shields. Sweat poured from every pore of Nathaniel's face but the eyes of the trumpeter wouldn't let go of him. Iz roared on his trumpet and smoke swirled around him until lines met curves forming two broad shapes at either side of the trumpeter to create a halo of wings.

Nathaniel's eyes bulged from their sockets when he realized that all this time, the mesmerizing piece of music was being played by the same angel who had the charge of calling forth judgment day. A hand clasped on the young man's shoulder and he was finally able to break from the trance. To his left was Edward with his soft caramel green eyes and tight mouth wound in a smile. "Don't worry," he told Nathaniel, "he wouldn't bring that trumpet here."

"But... I couldn't break away from his gaze," replied the frightened young man. "His power."

Edward let out a small laugh. "That wasn't the power of Iz, my friend. That was the power of Miles."

At that moment, Iz hit his high notes to finish the epic track. He breathed in deeply through his nose and then blew out a smoke drenched thank you of a breath he'd taken almost a half hour before. The applause was shocked at first but quickly gathered strength as the tall black man bowed, signaled to the bar and spoke into the microphone, in a raspy Greek voice. "I'll be back with you soon, but I have to say hello to some friends." He dabbed at his forehead and jumped off the small stage to walk to the group of four. He pulled a chair up and sat down at the same time the bartender set a goblet of brandy in front of him which he thanked.

His voice was low as a bass, but smooth like liquid silk, and this time he spoke in English. "My, my, my... what a merry bunch we have here." His large hands clasped in salute to Daniel, Liam and especially to Edward. He looked at Nathaniel, smiled and also shook his hand. "So you're the cat Sariel told me about. They've told me that as expendable as you are, you're still making quite a name for yourself."

For having been dumbstruck a few moments ago, Nathaniel replied quite calmly. "That seems to be the case."

"A man of little words, eh?" the angel said.

Liam gave another hearty laugh. "Don't get 'im started mate or he won't stop."

"Really?" the angel said as he looked at Nathaniel. "They told me you got in touch with Uroc and that you actually spoke some sense to him. Is that true?"

This time it was Daniel's turn to interrupt. "As a matter of fact, it is."

"Ah... my friend the silver tongue," said Iz. "Took you a while to pipe up. But please, let the boy speak, after all, it was him to whom I was talking. So tell me, boy; were you really the one to convince the Ancient to set aside centuries of fighting to help you?"

Nathaniel's eyes suddenly ran ice cold. "Yes, in fact I did."

The angel smiled at the reply. "Ah.... there's the man I was looking for. Nice to meet you."

"Likewise," Nathaniel replied.

Iz looked around at the group of vampires. "They said this cat almost had his way with some friends of yours at Maestranza."

"Thas' right," Liam answered, "and if it weren't for me, he and the chaps he had a word with would be dead, see?"

"So I've heard," the angel said. "Thas' cool though. Things are bound to get pretty hot and it's good to see someone cool in the middle of the shit. Cig?"

"No thanks," Nathaniel said when he was offered a cigarette. "I've heard those things kill."

"Ain't that the truth," said the angel. "But hey, we all have to die cuz of sumthin' right"

The vampires all laughed but Nathaniel just smiled. "So we were told we should come see you," the human said. "Why's that?"

Israfil took a drag from his cigarette as he let the smile fade from his face. "Simple, little brother; you saw my little story. That's just a hint of what can happen. You came here in part because I'm supposed to point the way to someone else you should meet."

"And that would be?" Nathaniel asked.

Israfil took a drag from his cigarette. "First off, you gotta get to Alexandria and find the Great Library. In there you'll find an unjustly damned and justifiably pissed angel."

The human looked suspicious. "And why is he so angry?"

"Don't you read the Bible?" asked the angel.

"Not really, but I heard it makes great rolling papers," the human said in a deadpan voice. "Nothing like toking on a bit of Corinthians."

Israfil folded his hands over his chest and quietly looked at the human for about ten seconds before he burst out laughing. "Daniel, I like this kid."

"So I see," the vampire said.

The angel then settled down before speaking. "Heh... ok, so get this. Let's say you're one of the four archangels. You're blessed by God and y'all are part of his closest crew. One day he ups and says, yo, get me a fistful of Earth. I'll be waiting here. So the first three angels go down, they see the Earth and say, give me your Earth for God commands it or some saintly crap like that. The Earth says no, because the Lord rules the sky not the Earth and they went back empty handed. They thought God would be pissed, but in fact, he was cool. But that fourth cat? Well he went down and got that same answer but since he had to prove his loyalty, love and devotion to God, regardless of what the Earth said, he forced her to give him a fist's worth of her essence."

"Ok, so what happened then?" Nathaniel asked.

"Well God saw that this here angel had some earth in his hand and asked why he had the soil. This dude just said that since God wanted it and commanded it, he got it, no matter what. Afterwards, let's just say God wasn't too pleased because that angel had forced the Earth to give of herself. So like the good book says, that angel got his due thanks, an eternity of writing and erasing the name of every living creature on the Earth."

"What?" Nathaniel asked.

Israfil took another drag off his cigarette. "Nuts, I know. But hey, they say God works in mysterious ways. Guess this one gets to be filed under M for mysterious then. But Azrael's used to it by now. So that's your next step."

"And you?" Nathaniel asked.

"Well simple, man; I gotta go polish my brass. The day's coming and though I don't like the job, somebody has to do it."

The angel leaned back and calmly sipped on his drink. Nathaniel took a second to realize that this was pretty much the end of the conversation. "I see... well brother, it's been a pleasure to meet you and hear you, but we gotta get going."

"I know, brother man," Iz said. "Thanks for the audience though. Good to see some people appreciate good music. Be sure to pass by sometime, if you're still around later."

"Will do," Nathaniel said while they all got up. "One more question, though."

"Shoot, little bro."

"Is Miles God?"

Another loud clang of the angel's laughter boomed throughout the hall. "Naw man, he only played like one."

"Fair enough," Nathaniel said holding his hand to shake the angel's.

Israfil took the young man's hand in his own and shook it firmly. "You be cool though."

"Glacial."

And with mutually exchanged smiles, they parted ways.

Chapter 25: The Resurrected Library

The Mediterranean Sea lay like a calm blanket of kind dreams as the Black Calico slid towards coastal Egypt down from Crete. To the surprise of Nathaniel, apart from enlightening, the meeting with Israfil had been pleasant. It was the first time he had been able to say he was comfortable with his surroundings.

Others had noticed the change but Daniel felt the very essence of transformation which had taken this simple man, which at one time seemed as if he could have crumbled under the weight of a trench coat and had converted him into something else. Not an all saving messiah, but definitely someone you'd want to count on your side. He'd seen the human convince the therians to join The Cause and had spoken to the Ancient Uroc eye to eye as an equal.

Daniel looked down to starboard side from high up in the crow's nest and Nathaniel peered beyond the sky's edge with the gaze of one determined to will a fish onboard without the use of line or rod. The horizon stood there, edging Earth forwards, half a league at a time as they neared Egypt. There Azrael awaited within the walls of the new Bibliotheca Alexandrina, the tangible attempt to rekindle the greatness of an age of knowledge far withdrawn from the current state of Egypt.

Dusk settled gently on the horizon and the deck of the Black Calico swarmed with activity as they neared land, and with good reason. The fact that the Bibliotheca Alexandrina was going to be quite literally a stone's throw away meant that measures needed to be taken and favors had to be called in. Daniel did his best pirate movie imitation and swung down from the top of the crow's nest to the deck below, quickly making his way to the wheel. "How go the plans, Captain?" he asked.

Jane reacted a bit skeptically at his tone. "Captain now? Really Daniel, you have a unique way of being irresistible yet utterly unbearable."

"Ah shucks, ma'am," said Daniel in mock idiocy, "I don't mean no harm." He then cleared his throat and spoke normally. "Seriously though, are we clear for landing?"

"Alexandria is just ahead," she said, pulling out an odd piece of plastic. "Handy little thing this mobile phone of yours. Who sponsors it again?"

Daniel hesitated in his reply. "Ah... that. Well a magician cannot reveal all his secrets, nor a villain all his plans."

"So you're a villain now?" asked the captain.

"Well I am in love with a pirate," he replied. "More than enough to send me to the gallows and a small price at that."

She could only smile; she had come to rather appreciate this new side to Daniel. His love had always been in private quarters... something she had been through for the better part of two centuries. Through drunken tirades, massacres, holy quests and sheer acts of barbarism, she had been there and he had never swayed to change his direction for another gale to fill his sails. They hadn't always been together but he had always been hers and hers alone.

She couldn't help but wonder as she stared at him. His beard was half grown and she could see the fatigue of twenty sleepless years in his eyes. Yet his gaze bore on like a gladiator's, unwilling to yield no matter how much blood was lost. Since he couldn't sleep, he couldn't dream so his ideal became his dream and his quest had become his fantasy. "I'd rather die than give up this dream," he'd told Jane in bed the night before. She was amazed that his eyes could still burn so passionately, one of his better qualities. But something seemed wrong. She didn't need to have spent a century together to know, but she also didn't know how to ask.

Nathaniel stood starboard side. The night air ran through his hair and while the eyes of others would flicker like soft candles in the wind, his were beacons searching for answers to questions he didn't know how to phrase. He had also come to appreciate and accept the change others had seen in him during the last couple of days.

His jaw seemed to have grown stronger and the beard on his face showed it had been a month since he had eaten that stale pretzel, before going down into a subway to say goodbye to what had otherwise been a hackneyed life and career of bad dates, dumb decisions and would-have could-have moments. He drew in a long breath and felt it course through his entire system. The air tasted of salt while the ocean's musk fed him. Every hair on his body felt, sent information and reacted to his surroundings.

Some people have life changing epiphanies where they describe the experience as learning to live again or living for the first time. Nathaniel finally understood this concept and felt more alive than what he would think possible or even necessary.

For so many years, he had slid down life on autopilot. It had been years since his parents had both died. Their passing had been four months apart from one another and he trickled over those memories like scars that demand to have their origins remembered. Could his parents have even been able to think of him in a scenario such as this?

What would anyone he had ever known say if one day he said he had been kidnapped by a vampire because of energy points found throughout his body? That after agreeing to help, he had almost been killed by demons. That angels had saved him and that he had seen sea monsters in the Atlantic on his way to meet other vampire families. That later he had talked to werewolves, who are really known as therians, so they could help in what the vampires casually referred to as The Cause. That he had met the angel in charge of calling forth Judgment Day and that he now played jazz......... They would have said he needed serious help, but guess what, he was alive and mattered, even if he was expendable. Actually, he was so comfortable with his current surroundings that he didn't actually mind that part of him not being indispensable.

"Better to die because you matter than live because you don't," he whispered to himself.

Near the front of the boat, Liam's body was draped on the portside rail. It seemed he was marinating his pain with generous amounts of whiskey and cigarettes. His stone demeanor hid the fact that he was down to a quarter of a whiskey bottle... the second for the day. Finally his chin came to rest on his chest and he dosed off in a drunken stupor sliding down to the deck. Knowing the body of his love had been ravaged twice and that some hidden demon was torturing her further even after she had died was too much to handle.

"I'll kill... I'll... I kill ye ... bastards," he muttered in his sleep.

Apart from these stationary figures, everything else was a bustle. Weapons and rifles were locked and loaded as a precaution. They were going to be next to the shore that would be steps away from La Bibliotecha Alexandrina, which was extremely convenient, and extremely dangerous. They would be vulnerable to attack on various sides and they'd literally be cornered.

Lucas, Mary and Edward Louis coordinated via phone. Everyone else was on deck in case all hell broke loose. Meanwhile, Nathaniel continued to search the horizon for answers, Liam continued to sleep and two glacial blue eyes reflected the low glow of the still lit cigarette in Liam's mouth. Valencia had always felt more comfortable in the shadows and out of sight, but seeing her grieving comrade had inspired her to at least come into the gloom, if only to make sure her friend didn't catch fire or fell overboard.

The shore had crawled up on the Black Calico and what had been a fuzzy cloud line on the horizon was now the shore of one of the ancient Meccas of knowledge. The high moon dimly shone on the land and the curve of expressways stood clean and clear. If one didn't know better, one would have thought that Alexandria had been abandoned.

"Captain," called Mary Anne, "we land in three minutes. That plus the short boat ride is more or less four minute's time, total. The window we've coordinated will last twenty minutes.

Jane nodded to Mary and called for Daniel and Nathaniel. "You have about fifteen minutes to do your thing and get back before the roads cease to be empty. Please remember that although the Calico can escape the sight of many people, we are cornered and don't need to take our sweet time. Go in, get the information, get out. One of the panels will be left open and a rope will be waiting. Azrael is somewhere inside."

"Thanks captain," Nathaniel said. "I'll be by the boat."

"Weren't three of you going?" she asked the young man.

"Yes," Nathaniel said, "but Liam won't be coming." Looking towards the vampire, one could see his cigarette still dangling from his lips. At least it had gone out although it had left his shirt sprinkled with ash. He then walked to the lifeboats.

"So that makes two of us," Daniel said. "Why the concern, m'lady?"

Jane's face grew cold and stern. "Don't play dumb with me, Daniel. Crete was one thing; Azrael and this place is another story. You've contacted Israfil before..."

"And he's not a warrior angel much less the blessed damned that is Azrael," Daniel said, recognizing the gravity of the situation. "I know... I know. But we need to find out all we can about what's going on. And if anyone knows the answers we need, that angel in there does."

"Don't forget, he also has a temper," she added. "Rightly so mind you, but still... just be careful."

"I will, m'lady," said Daniel with a curtsy. "It's still not my time to die and you can take that to the bank. By the way, you should also be careful. I might be playing it cool, but like you, I smell death in the air. Put Liam downstairs and have everyone ready. And I almost forgot to ask, did you contact Vin?"

"Yes," she answered while pulling out a roll of kelp with a message written on it. It seemed like a wet version of papyrus written in what appeared to be octopus ink. "He's on the outskirts keeping watch in the water. If four consecutive waves crash on the beach, we better make our way out of here... fast."

Daniel nodded. "Good enough. Keep watch to the sky and the ocean then. For now, there's only one thing left to say... I love you." He finished his sentence by giving her a tender kiss that left her flushed and confused since he'd never done anything like that in public before... ever.

Lucas stood at the front of the boat with a spear gun on his shoulder and a length of rope a hundred yards long. He breathed, he aimed, he fired and a steel lance flew towards the shore and buried itself deep within the still warm sand.

Nathaniel and Daniel were already on the boat and were handed the end of the rope. On the count of three they hauled themselves towards shore. In less than a minute, they had landed and saw as the Black Calico turned to ready for their escape, a precaution in case a speedy exit was needed above all else.

The streets were dead with inactivity and mute beyond comprehension. Their steps left only sand as a trace and in a moment they were looking up at the large majestic sun panels of the Bibliotheca that looked towards the water. The length of rope was there, the panel was open and they climbed up the face. When they reached the top, they both looked back towards the beautiful galleon just before dropping into the heart of the library.

Inside everything was dismally quiet and the still new building did little to offer any hint to where anyone might be holed up in. "Where do we look?" Nathaniel asked.

Daniel scanned the library's interior. "I don't know. Where would you hide if you were a bitter angel who has been banished to the Earth after doing God's bidding?"

Nathaniel thought for a moment and then had an idea. "Is there a forbidden section of the library?"

"Are you crazy?" Daniel asked. "The extra space you see isn't for aesthetic reasons, it's because there's no money for books."

"What?"

"They may have a million books in here, but that's nothing for what it should have. The building is beautiful, I know, but at their current rate of funding, it'll take about eighty years for it to be filled to capacity."

"Yeah... and then bombed by the military since it'll be the house of terrorists or something. You know, any excuse to blow stuff up."

"Don't digress, Runnells. Where do we go?"

"Clearly espionage is not a forte for either of you," said a soft yet menacing voice. Behind them stood a man with straight black hair, Arabic features and a black on black suit. In his hand he held a monstrous book, whose weight didn't seem to bother him in the least. "May I be of service?" he said without looking at them and focusing on writing in his book.

The angel didn't seem to care much for them and flipped several hundred pages back, made some markings, flipped several hundred pages more, and did some more markings. He did that ten or so times until he finally looked at them, while continuing this behavior. "Try not to mind me. It's just a chore I've been assigned for being naughty."

Nathaniel stared at the book. "Is that..."

"Yes," said the angel interrupting him. "This is the book with every single name of everyone alive in the world. Slow day actually, Thanatos must have taken the day off."

"Thanatos?" Daniel asked.

"The true Angel of Death," said the angel in a bored voice. "He's gone by so many names that I can barely keep track... but from the times we've spoken, it seems he prefers that one. Now regarding why you are here, I could pretend I know nothing about either of you but I'd be lying and although it's nice of you to visit, I'm not much for company. So first tell me, how is Israfil?"

Nathaniel and Daniel both looked at each other, still a little startled by the appearance of the very creature they were looking for. They had suddenly found themselves trying to figure out a way to have a normal talk with an archangel. Daniel did his best to pursue the conversation. "Well he's playing jazz in Crete. He's actually quite good."

The angel continued writing in the book and looked as if this was the most normal conversation ever before responding in his dull voice. "Very nice. I would imagine he were good, he's had enough time to practice. Is he still smoking?"

"Well... yes," said Nathaniel.

Azrael continued to write but gave a frustrated little sigh while shaking his head from side to side. "Bastard never could keep a promise. Regardless, it's not like cigarettes could kill him... ha ha... ha ha ha... ha ha ha ha ha."

Both vampire and human were at a loss for words because of the angel's creepy laughter. They didn't know how to react and it wasn't like the angel even cared. He merely continued to write down inside the book until he looked around as if he'd lost something.

"So that's the book with all of the names of anyone who has ever lived?" asked Nathaniel.

"I thought we had cleared that up, but yes, you are correct, boy." The angel stole a quick glance into his eyes. "To be quite fair, it's one of the books. Call it the current version."

"So there's more than one edition?" Nathaniel said.

"Of the Book of Life? Oh dear... let me think..." said the angel as he started pacing towards the North Wing. "If I'm not mistaken, this version is somewhere within the realm of the four thousandth version; well the Earth version, for that matter. If I'd have been assigned the entire universe, I'd have pulled my wings out long ago."

"About that..." started Nathaniel.

"You don't see the wings because I don't want you to," said the angel as he wrote in his book. "You should have realized that when you met Israfil."

Nathaniel was clearly caught off guard by the comment. "Oh, I'm..."

"Yes, yes... I know you are," said the angel. "Sniffles, a handkerchief and an Academy Award for you. Do you have any better question to ask?"

Nathaniel took a moment to think before asking his next question. "Ok... how many people have lived?"

This time the angel finally looked at the human for longer than a split second. "Ah... much more interesting question... and many more than you can imagine. I'm sure Montacre told you of the old races. What he didn't know is that before that, there have been many other races and although human science has hinted at the potential age of the Earth, they are clueless when it comes to how long there's been sentient life... and please, take my word for it... I know."

"We can imagine," Nathaniel said.

"No you could not," said Azarael a little offended, "but I appreciate the attempt at empathy. Now what do you want? As you can see I'm always going to be busy and though I've grown used to this chore and am quite capable of what you humans call multitasking, it's not like this is a very productive conversation."

"You're totally right," Nathaniel replied. Daniel's eyes popped out of their sockets and Azrael broke a pen only to open his coat and take out another one to continue writing. "Before you continue on your dramatic bitch fit, let me make it clear that we were afraid of coming to see you because of what has happened to you. We thought you wouldn't cooperate because you'd rather behead us or something of the sort. But no, woe to us for we are going to be whined to our graves long before you show an iota of physical aggression. Archangel? More like Arch has-been throwing a big pity party."

Azrael stood dumbfounded and for the first time in millennia his hand stopped moving. He put the notebook down on a table, undid his tie, pulled off his vest shirt and jacket and stretched out two magnificent brown and gold wings before taking up his notebook again to write in.

"Have your expectations now been met?" asked the angel.

Nathaniel crossed his arms. "Well now at least you look the part instead of some whiny bitch."

Another pen broke and Azrael blew a strong breath from his nose in an attempt to slow his pulse down. Daniel could only stand by, wondering what the hell Nathaniel was thinking.

"Now that I have your attention, might I offer a gift to open when we leave?"

"Yes you may," said the angel, struggling to remain calm.

Nathaniel then produced an envelope and a small leather pouch. "From me to you, dear Azarael. Though I've more than noticed that you were expecting us, we still need to know some information you may have regarding mounting forces. Israfil made it quite clear that we need to be here to talk to you. We have met some other vampire and therian groups which are on our side, but it seems we are still dwarfed by a force which you may have some knowledge of."

The angel took some time to think deeply as he continued to write and flip pages. "There have been a few odd happenings as of late. That I can vouch for."

"Which would be?" asked Nathaniel.

"Well every time someone is born or dies, I must write down or cross off the name. That being said, there have been certain occasions when several people simultaneously die and are born meaning that in the exact same moment, death occurs at the same time as conception or birth."

"Ok, I don't see the importance in that," Nathaniel said. "It could just be a coincidence."

"Granted," said the angel uneasily, "but one thing is twenty people... another thing is four thousand simultaneous life exchanges."

"So what does that mean?" asked the human.

"That is the knowledge I have," Azrael said. "I'm sorry it isn't of much help."

"Actually, it is," Daniel said.

"How so?" asked the angel.

"Last I checked there was a race that came to be through the dead bodies of women."

The angel shuddered as the very thought crept into his head. "Wraiths? But how?"

Daniel looked even graver than usual. "I don't know, but with what happened to the Lygophilials, I already suspected something. Although I may have had my doubts, ignoring this any further would be moronic. We need the photogeni even more than I already thought we did. And Master Azrael, if any of your kind would like a chance to slay demons and probably more than a handful of fallen angels, you are more than welcome to take up arms."

The angel could only look to the ground in shame. Daniel realized what he had just said. "I'm sorry for that. I know that you and Israfil both have obligations that would keep you away from battle."

"That is true, but there are others that can still fight," the angel said. "You need to speak to the forsaken one. Rouse him from his ennui, and angels will take up arms. Fail to do so and they shall continue to live on as mere watchers. I should add though, that Sariel for however much aversion she has of you has taken interest in your cause. But the forsaken one... he is the key."

Nathaniel pondered one moment before speaking. "So where is Michael now?"

Azrael broke a third pen. "How did you..."

"I read, brother Azrael," Nathaniel said. "Though I've often questioned in everything I've been taught, I've always read. Besides, nobody needs to read that much to know Michael resented God for favoring Gabriel."

"I see..." said the angel now turning to the vampire. "My compliments on your fine choice, Daniel. He sees where others are blind."

"I've noticed," replied the vampire, "but now we find ourselves fighting to right the way of a world inching towards disaster."

The angel's eyes grew weary and lost. "The holy path..."

"...is almost lost to us," added Daniel, "and our role in this path is to apparently stop someone or something from attaining the Vairya."

"What's that?" asked Nathaniel.

"It is a most desirable power, my young friend," the angel said. "An angelic word used by your consort in hopes to make the message crystal clear to me. But enough of this Daniel, there will be time for poems later. This is a matter of ahuras and daevas yet again."

Daniel looked at the angel very seriously. "It's more than just a battle of angels and demons, Azrael."

"Not if you consider yourself an angel as well as those who would fight by your side. Elohim though has not made us feel its presence."

"Your one true God has abandoned all his children, Azrael. We need help and heavenly assistance at that. The Daena is off balance, all is not right and it's time to respond to your duties."

The angel walked to a table and sat down hanging his head in frustration. "I've always responded to my responsibilities."

"No you haven't," Nathaniel interrupted.

The eyes of the angel flamed and in an instant he took Nathaniel by the throat and knocked him against a bookshelf. "Who are you to speak of duties?! You're no saint. You're not even the shadow of a proper follower of a religion! Humans like you are what pollute the Daena, turning the true balance on its ass. What makes you think you're even worthy of the Presence? You biped, monkey, homo sapien!!!"

Nathaniel struggled for air but maintained his composure. His eyes burned just as fierce as the angel's and he took the right hand of Azrael and squeezed his fingers into angelic flesh. His face was red and his eyes bloodshot from the angel's grip around his throat, but he squeezed with strength he didn't know he had. His eyes never flickered and as the angel winced and lowered him, the human's face had no change until the archangel finally let go. He began to breathe normally again and twisted the angel's wrist so he would kneel. He then pulled him up to stand right in front of him.

"What makes me worthy?" he said through grit teeth, "My will, the ability to forgive and the ability to speak as anyone's equal. That is what makes me worthy, angel."

Daniel took hold of Nathaniel's shoulder and the human instantly loosened his grip, allowing the angel to break away.

"Now..." started Nathaniel once again, "what else can you tell us? And please be brief. We must be off soon."

Azrael's frightened eyes looked into the face of his assailant. It was almost too much to see the human taking a chair, sitting down and crossing his legs as if nothing had happened. He pulled a chair of his own, sat and began to speak in a low tone. "Someone has been to the fourth province of Sheol."

Nathaniel did not lose his cool this time. "What is Sheol?"

"It's what you would call the underworld or Hades. There are four provinces."

"Why four?"

"One is for saints who await blissful judgment. The second is for the moderately good who await their reward. The third is for the wicked who can still be redeemed, call it a purgatory of sorts though Purgatory is truly more a state of mind... or a lack of one for that matter."

"And the fourth?" asked the human as he noticed that angels could actually sweat.

"That would be what your kind refers to as Hell. It seems as if a fellow human has been rounding about those lairs and is largely responsible for bringing forth the legion."

"Who is it?"

"I do not know," said the angel honestly, "but it is not someone blatantly in power, like a president or a prime minister."

"That leaves quite a few options."

"To be honest, my dear human, it makes little difference if you knew who it was. The battle is coming, he knows it, and he's more than prepared."

"So where's Michael?" asked the human.

"In Dudael," responded the angel still rubbing his arm.

"That place exists?" asked Nathaniel. "I thought it was a metaphor for the state of purgatory with which they left the fallen Azazel."

"One and the same," said Azrael finally starting to write in his book again, "Azazel did fall or well... he was cast. Scripture says as follows:

Bind Azazel hand and foot and cast him in the darkness. Make an opening in the desert, which is Dudael and cast him therein. Place upon him rough and jagged rocks and cover him with darkness. Let him abide there forever and cover his face that he may not see the light. On the day of the Great Judgment, he shall be cast into the fire."

Nathaniel scoffed lightly. "I can see that God has always had a knack for being kind, forgiving and benevolent."

"God has will, freedom of choice, power beyond comprehension and a conscience, or so I'm told," said Azrael. "Michael is in Djibouti, near the Gulf of Tadjoura. He has been there for over three centuries and you are the first to know this."

"Why haven't you said anything to anyone before?" asked the human.

"He made me promise and although I cannot break a promise to one I love, times change and if God can forgive, maybe so can Michael."

"Thank you, brother," said Nathaniel as he got up. "I appreciate you breaking the promise for me and in turn promise that I will make it worthwhile." He grasped the shoulder on the bent angel and proceeded to walk back to the rope.

"One question, Master Runnels. Why did you say I've not been able to bear my responsibility?"

Nathaniel stopped walking and took a very deep breath before turning to speak. "It is because you follow orders without question. One's duty goes beyond following orders. It's doing what is right. God was especially harsh on you because so much more was expected."

The words cut deep into the heart of the angel and for the first time in three centuries since he'd left his brother in the barren desert, he wept. Nathaniel and Daniel walked back towards the rope, but it was no longer where they had left it.

They went back to where they'd left the angel but by this time he had also left the spot. Before they could even decide what to do, the scent of Darjeeling tea tickled their noses. Their eyebrows furrowed and they looked at bookshelves and empty chairs until far off to the left they saw a young man smiling broadly before sipping his tea. Neither knew what to do or what to make of the young man as he wrote in a large black notebook while sipping from his cup. He looked at them again and waved for them to come closer.

Without knowing why, they did as he asked while he continued to write. He had one leg folded under his weight and his glasses twinkled from the lamp to his right. His hair was black and the wavy curls to it went to where they wanted. A white patterned button shirt stood open while a black t-shirt peeked from beneath showing a baby giving the finger.

"Just one second, if you please," he said while writing eagerly in his notebook. Having apparently finished a sentence, he closed the book and looked to his two confused would-be guests. "I was wondering when I'd see you," said the young man with a day old beard and two particular birthmarks that caught their attention, one on his right cheek and one in the lower lid of his left eye.

"Do we know you?" asked Daniel.

"In a ways, we all know each other," said the youth. "Before I continue to be rude, let me introduce myself. I am Fäet Odstein."

"Odd name," replied Nathaniel.

"If you think it's a Jewish surname with an Arab first name, then yes Nathaniel. And you would be Daniel, right? I can tell by the eyes on both of you."

"Where's Azrael?" Daniel asked while taking a stance that would allow a quick attack.

"He went to his office," said the youth while looking at Nathaniel. "Probably to read whatever you left him."

"Who are you?" Nathaniel asked as his heart thumped abnormally.

"I'm a friend and I'm here to wish you well," said Fäet. "And don't worry, Daniel; you won't attack me."

"But how do you..."

"There are things you can and should understand and there are others you should just go along with without worrying about understanding. This is one of those moments. Suffice to say that though I am human, it doesn't mean we don't have a lot in common."

"What would you even begin to know about us boy?" Daniel said.

"Simple. You have one true love and no one else really interests you. In regards to Nathaniel, he might be scared but he is hard headed and perseverant. Some things we have different, but I know you. I just wanted a moment to look at both of you to wish you well."

"That's it?" Nathaniel asked.

"I'm afraid so," said Fäet, "but it was good seeing you. You can go out the front door. It's unlocked and no alarm will go off."

"Yeah? And what makes it so easy for us to trust you?" Nathaniel said.

A peculiar look twinkled in Daniel's eye. "We can, Runnels. Trust me on this."

Nathaniel's face twisted with incredulity. "What the hell? Are you completely insane?"

"No," replied the vampire looking to his human friend, "I just know we can. My thanks, Mr. Odstein."

"None needed, Daniel. Send my regards to Jane. So she's really worth dying for?"

Daniel looked to the floor and smiled genuinely. "She's worth living for."

"I feel the same way about my partner," said Fäet returning the smile.

"And her name?" Daniel asked. "To send blessings to both."

"Hah! She'd kill me if she knew I'd told you. She hates her name."

"It can't be that bad," said the vampire.

After pausing for a moment, the young man spoke her name, "Shaimer."

Daniel pondered for a moment before replying. "Interesting name."

"I think so too," said Fäet with another smile. "But you'd best be going."

"Thank you again," said the vampire. "Come along, Runnels."

They both walked away and the young man opened his notebook and picked up where he'd left off, as if nothing had happened.

"What the hell was that?" asked Nathaniel.

"Answer me one question, Runnels," Daniel said without giving a backwards glance. "Do you believe that you have free will to do what you may or do you believe there is a set path for us all?"

"Either is possible," the young man answered.

"Exactly. Which means that to change your fate it might be conceivable that you might have to influence your maker to change your path."

Nathaniel looked a bit confused. "That's not what I had in mind."

"Which is just one of the great things about free will," added Daniel.

"Are you ok?"

Daniel drew in a deep breath and exhaled in satisfaction. "Magnificent, my dear Runnels. I never knew the liberating powers of being clear on the path I have to follow."

"Ok.... If you say so. But why don't we focus on the here and now and just get out of here."

"I couldn't agree more," said Daniel. "The future awaits."

They arrived at the entrance, saw the gate open, walked out of the Great Library and then across the highway before getting to the shore and climbing onto the small boat.

Inside the walls of the building, Azrael sat in a large leather chair in front of a beautiful mahogany desk. It was covered with various papers and an ornamental pot with a curious little tree planted in it. Tears were streaming from his eyes as he wrote in the Book of Life and Death with one hand and looked at a note in his other hand that read:

You fell from grace for taking without permission. Now it is my turn to give thanks without asking as well. I only ask that you pray for us.

He had undone the pouch's knot and found a fistful of earth inside. He could smell that it had been taken from the island of Crete. The angel cried as he took the earth and mixed it into the tree pot. A wave of energy seemed to course through the small branches of the tree and quite suddenly an apple as small as a cherry sprouted. Azrael smiled as he knelt facing the West and whispered, "Help them brother for they do know what they do and the world has need for them and for us."

He then crouched to the side of the desk and picked up a small chest that he placed on the table. After grazing his fingers on its side, it slowly arched open, revealing an ancient armor with four thousand eyes and tongues etched into it and a four-chain flail that shone even in the twilight. Azrael clasped his hands and looked to the ceiling. "One knows what one must do, not wait until ordered. Forgive me Mother-Father, for I must go against your will."

Aboard the Black Calico, silence swam through the air and a wave of relief flowed across the entire deck. Daniel jumped onboard and seemed to float towards the boat's captain. "Sweet love, we must go up the Nile towards Eritrea... our next destination is Lake Tana."

"So how was that?" asked Jane curiously.

"Enlightening," Daniel said and proceeded to kiss the captain passionately in front of the entire crew, to a chorus of gasps followed by hollers and cheering. When he spoke to her, he gave her a beaming smile. "It's good to be free. Let us be off."

She took a deep breath and called for all hands to remain ready for anything even though a small sense of victory permeated the crew.

Barely four minutes had passed when something broke the silence of the slithering tide on the shores of Alexandria... four seamless waves sliding gently onto the beach break.

Chapter 26: The thin Blue Line

The entrance to the Nile River Delta was just a few hours off. The sea continued to stay calm while the Black Calico made its way through the coast of Alexandria until passing near the sand dyed water of the delta. As usual, the elegant ship glided down the river disregarding depth, wind direction and tide. How it maintained such a heady speed or perfect control could only be answered by the captain.

Nathaniel took his usual stance starboard side as he saw the eddies made by their course tickling the walls of the river bank, much like they had done so in the Rhone River in France. Even at night, one could see the sediment rich waters of the Nile as its distinct bouquet filled the young man's nostrils.

While passing through Arwen, he could actually taste the difference of the waters in the air. The thick scent of earth spiced water tickled his senses and the night had a few hours to go before ending.

"You should get some sleep," said the soft voice of the captain. Nathaniel looked at the helm and was surprised to see that Jane had left Wendy in charge of navigation in such a precarious route.

"Can she drive this big boat?" he asked.

She passed by him and leaned over the rail. "My reply is that otherwise she would not be a Corsaire. Every member of this crew has my trust and love; if not, they wouldn't be onboard."

Nathaniel remembered Nelly. "I'm sorry about..."

"There will be time to mourn later," Jane said coldly. "Trust me, more will fall before this is all over."

"It's unavoidable then?" asked the young man.

"I wish it were otherwise."

"I know," he said looking down at the muddy water. "Where are we going now?"

"Up the Nile until we reach Khartoum deep in the middle of Sudan, there we turn up into the Blue Nile. Then we will go as far as the Tis Abay Falls. When we arrive some of you will disembark and make your way up to Lake Tana."

"What's in the lake?"

"I can only speculate as to why Daniel wants to go there. I know him well enough to know it is necessary. He's never been one to do unnecessary detours when there is a task at hand and the risks are higher than his own life."

"He's never been outwardly affectionate before, has he?" said the young man quite suddenly. Jane's face went extremely pale even for a vampire, but the rouge of her cheeks was more than enough for Nathaniel to know he had struck a nerve. "It's ok if you don't want to answer. I'm just trying to understand all that's happening around me, especially whatever has to do with the one responsible for me being here."

"Identifying with your captor, are we?"

"That's not it. I could say I'm thankful for being a savior to the world but really, I'm just glad to not be rotting away as I had been for so long. I may have been beaten and almost killed more times than I care to remember, but I really don't care. I'm doing something that is worthwhile instead of being one in a billion."

"So you're feeling special now?" she said raising an eyebrow.

"No. I just feel like I matter... and it's been a while since I felt that."

"You are a curious one, Nathaniel," she said with a soft smile. "But at least you're still remarkably human."

"Thanks," he replied not knowing if it was a compliment or not.

"No need," she said while smiling in the direction of Wendy. "I'm not the only one who notices."

"You think?" he smiled back. "It wasn't the most saintly of introductions."

"So? Love is born in the weirdest places sometimes. Just because it was in bed with two other beautiful vampires doesn't make it less meaningful."

"I'd almost forgotten about that."

"I highly doubt that," Jane said with a giggle.

"You're highly correct," he smiled back. "So tell me, how did this galleon earn a fully female crew of beautiful vampires?"

"Well it wasn't a coincidence. I handpicked each member of this crew because each of these women was physically assaulted and left for dead."

Nathaniel's smile faded and a look of shock took over his face. "All of them?"

"Yes," Captain Jane said. "It's not an easy process to put it lightly. Being a vampire, I'm able to sense disturbances rather easily, and it's not like the smell of blood doesn't send my senses running. Initially I would kill the attackers, but after a while, I realized that these women do not need someone to save them or to gain their revenge. Part of the healing process includes making the decision to forgive or to punish, and though I'd rather kill off any scum that decides to harm a woman, the decision must be theirs and theirs alone."

"But they were all so confident when... when we..."

"Nathaniel, another part of the healing process is to re-engage physically. Some of my Corsaires have turned away from men altogether, but the ones who have healed the best are the ones who have liberated themselves of stigmas, emotional scars and feelings of inferiority. My crew has been taught to love themselves and their bodies regardless of what has happened, because it is not a reason for shame. If they want to be celibate, monogamous, turn away from men or be adventurous, that's their decision as well as giving forgiveness or seeking revenge."

"So why are there no men in the crew?"

"We never know when we'll get a new crew member. Besides, being sexually assaulted, left for dead, and then getting turned into a vampire can be a little taxing on the soul, so we try to keep everything in order. Our men are either stationed somewhere to assist us or recruited to traverse the seas with my Daubentons."

"Daubentons?"

"A name I picked up in the 18th century. A species of bats which often frequent areas near water was named after a French Naturalist called Louis-Jean-Marie Daubenton. I think it sounds better and a lot less conspicuous than something like water bats."

"I won't argue there," smiled Nathaniel. "But wow... I would have never thought about the Corsaires like that."

"Don't worry; there is still a lot to learn about all of us."

"I can see that," Nathaniel said.

They both fell into silence and enjoyed the company of each other while looking down to the river. The ship passed the fork at Khartoum, disregarding time, space and distance. The Calico flew down the river, past merchants on small thatched boats with eyes painted on their helms, past large cruise ships that traverse the Nile, past countless villages overlooking the majestic river and past endless clearings that stretched into desert, fields and veldts. For however close they passed to anyone or anything, no one seemed capable of noticing the large galleon soaring down the river.

"How come no one sees us?" asked Nathaniel.

"That would be thanks to the watchers and the egnalem," said the Captain of the boat. "Prepare a large primer with equal parts demon blood and the mysterious spice, use it to cover the ship and draw certain geometric figures with a higher grade of egnalem and you have a ship that flows through currents not found in this world and whose visible presence is only seen in the reflection of the white water. The rest is careful navigation and the blinding power of naivety."

"Naivety?" asked Nathaniel.

Jane looked at the water while deep in thought. "Never underestimate the power of people who don't want to see all that is there Nathaniel. You can see it in religion, politics, and life in general. If people don't want to see a problem or a virtue, they simply focus on something else. When most people swear they've seen something amazing, like let's say, a galleon with black sails floating down a river it's too small to traverse, they are quite capable of dismissing that possibility, insisting they're just seeing things."

"Perception is quite a powerful thing."

"You have no idea, Nathaniel; which is why you should stop worrying about people seeing us and maybe get some rest."

Nathaniel looked at the water, lost in thought while swimming through the almost black river in his mind.

"There have been floods lately," Jane said. "That's why the water is almost black. You did know that the Abay River is really considered the Gihon River, right?"

"The what?" said Nathaniel when he finally snapped out of his daze.

"The river that flowed out of the Garden of Eden," she said and Nathaniel's eyes blossomed with surprise. "I'd love to explain further but I've left my duties long enough. Try to get some rest. The sun will be up soon."

Nathaniel nodded to Captain Jane and then she walked back towards the helm, thanked Wendy and took the wheel again. Wendy gave the young man a deep look and a smile before going up to the crow's nest. His exhaustion was more willful than him and leaning against the rail, Nathaniel fell fast asleep. He was still standing, so unless you saw his face, you would never suspect he wasn't awake. His sleep was deep and the black water flowed through his mind's eye.

Visions of dark pools colored with sediments swirled in the still recently awakened consciousness of Nathaniel. Pure musk swarmed his sense of smell until sandalwood, cinnamon and freshly dug earth tinged everything in ochre.

"Egnalem," he said in his dreams. He opened his eyes to the spectrum of the mid dimension and saw that in front of him stood a hooded figure in red robes. "Who are you?" he asked, but the only response from the hooded figure was to point to the water, where another robed figure stood, beckoning Nathaniel to come. He looked in front of him again and saw that the robed figure on the ship was gone. When he looked back to the water, the figure that was there was also gone. Looking to the shore, he saw the figure again beckoning from the river bank. Without even thinking, Nathaniel lobbed himself to the black waters. He crashed hard onto the unbroken water and sank as one would in thick pudding. The texture was liquid but he didn't sink normally.

A bright blue line glowed in the black water and he took hold of it, testing to see if it held. With one strong pull he saw that not only was the line strong, but that he was being reeled in by it. After several yards, he felt a firm grip take hold of his hand, immediately followed by him being thrust up to his feet on shore. He hadn't swallowed water and simply looked back at the serene galleon that hovered in the middle of the river, as if frozen in time.

The grass was sparse and veldt-like giving way to thick bushes, deep brush and various trees. Several feet ahead of him, Nathaniel saw the figure still waving for him to follow. The blue line continued to glow in the brush and he followed it until he arrived at a clearing where two trees stood alone with nothing else for miles. A large tree stood to the right. A red tree with blue fruits and a small red pond next to it. To the other side began what looked like a floating forest. The deepest of foliage spanned almost a mile and only after kneeling did Nathaniel realize it was all from one massive tree.

He didn't know which to pick and his eyes bounced from one to the other. The blue line had continued to the smaller tree while the same line had branched deep purple to the left, in the direction of the enormous tree.

"Your path should be obvious," said a voice from behind him. Nathaniel turned and saw the robed figure whose face was hidden by a hood. "Straying is not an option and just because there's a fork in your road doesn't mean this is only your road."

"Who are you?" asked Nathaniel.

"Call me a distant relative. Fäet could explain better but I doubt you will ever see him again. Who knows though?"

"You know Fäet?" asked Nathaniel. "What is this? Where am I?"

"You are on your path, Nathaniel; as I am on mine. Mine is to the left, yours is to the right and though I'd love to talk more, I have visit coming."

"Are you a watcher?" asked Nathaniel, noticing an odd glow coming from where the figure's eyes should be.

"Indeed. Who knows? We might actually meet again. But for now, that's your path. Feel free to not doubt yourself."

With those words, the figure left, without giving his name or any reason why Nathaniel should do as he had been told. But he had no reason to doubt the hooded figure either, so he followed his instinct and walked to the red tree. The trail was very easy and a light breeze kissed his cheeks, smelling of vanilla on top of the essence of egnalem that danced about everywhere.

The trail finally ended at the base of the tree and the long reed he had been following had actually grown from the tree; a thin blue line that bled from deep within the bark.

Blue fruit hung heavily from the branches looking alien yet oddly appetizing. Before he could act on the impulse to eat the fruit, the breeze picked up much stronger yet it still felt like a caress on Nathaniel's skin. He couldn't describe what he felt but it was as if symphonic music breathed over him. Even though the only sound he heard was the wind rustling his hair, he felt the warmth of light breathing onto his soul. Tree whispers tiptoed on his ears and his eyes looked for the source only to see the deep red pool rippling to a tempo matching the sounds he heard.

Even if it was completely illogical, Nathaniel spoke to the pool. "What was that?" The whispers sounded louder but he could still not make out the words. He knelt beside the pool and still couldn't make out what was being said. He then lay down on the cool earth, put his ear to the ground and spoke in a calm voice: "Tell me again."

At first, the whisper was very faint and the voice very distant. Then it came closer and clearer.

"........drink from me........"

Nathaniel got to his knees, dipped his hands into the pond and took a deep drink. The flavors he smelled were magnificent and showers of light seemed to rain down on him. He stood up looking to the red sky drinking the luminescent rain and feeling the wind feed every pore of his being.

A strong but deeply gentle voice now sounded off the ripples on the water. "Hello, Nathaniel. It's good to finally see you."

"God?" asked the young man as he looked around.

"No, little brother; you are still not prepared to listen to her grace, but I hope the West Wind is worthy of a conversation."

"I didn't mean to..."

"Do not worry, young friend," comforted the whisper, almost sounding as if whatever spoke was smiling. "No offense was taken and brother Azrael sent word of you. You must reach brother Michael and bring him a message from me."

"And what would that be?" asked Nathaniel.

"That he has always been beloved and that the beauty of his soul is sorely missed."

Nathaniel breathed as deep as his thoughts roamed. "Do you think he'll even believe me?"

"You've already made many believe, my young friend."

"But how do I get back?"

"Simple. Eat of my fruit, drink my essence and fall into me. One day we'll have a full conversation."

"My thanks, brother Gabriel."

"No, small one, thank you."

The wind then died down to a trickle. Nathaniel stood up, plucked the azure fruit and bit into it. The blissful amalgam of sweetness that swam on his taste buds defied description and if you could imagine liquid life, imagine fruit that yielded such a sweet nectar. He drank another deep drought from the pond before he allowed himself to plunge into its sweet cinnamon waters, falling through planes, realities and dimensions until his body grew tangible once again and his soul was weighed down by the vessel of his body.

Nathaniel opened his eyes, turned around and smiled up at Wendy, who stood in the twilight with a look of relief on her face. "You idiot... you almost drowned."

He just smiled and reached up to kiss her in joyous bliss. Everyone else was taken aback from the vigor in the young man.

"He must be crazy," whispered Lucas.

Daniel patted Lucas on the back. "After all we've seen, brother; I think you should know better than that. Leave him be for a while, it's good to be thankful for life for a change."

Chapter 27: Crossing Currents

Few things can embody the perfect combination of destructive power and beauty quite as succinctly as the Tis Abay falls in Ethiopia. Lush greenery surrounds this spectacle that only a few miles downstream eases into desert country.

"This is where we must say farewell for now," said Jane. "Up ahead is a hydro station but that's not what keeps us from reaching the lake in the Calico."

Nathaniel looked ahead at the power station and the powerful thumping of the falling river. "And what would be the reason?"

"A promise, a treaty and magic as ancient as this world," Daniel said walking up to the young man. "Sometimes you can find a way around these things. This however is an example of an occasion where you cannot."

"Ok... so where do we go from here?" asked Nathaniel.

"We climb, we swim and we walk." Daniel then turned to Liam and Lucas. "Up for it, fellas?"

"As if we had an option," Liam said, sipping on his cigarette and wearing black shades even in the twilight.

Daniel then turned to Jane. "I'll see you in the Red Sea."

"You better. I'll be there in a day's time. After that... you have one more day."

Daniel flashed his trademark smile. "Keeping a tight schedule, eh?"

"Exactly. Now be a good boy and follow orders."

He smiled at her and clicked his heels in mock salute. "Yes, mein capitan. Permission for a kiss?"

She looked at him sternly. "I'm not joking, Daniel."

"Neither am I," he said and pulled her into a deep kiss that would make the coldest woman melt. After finishing, he grinned slyly. "You look ravishing in red but I really must go, my love."

"Be careful," she said while still catching her breath.

"And break the tradition? Never, my dear."

The group then made their way to the portside rail and jumped to shore. Daniel stole one last look and locked eyes with his beloved captain. He gave her a final weak smile and dove into the bush to catch up to the other three.

The foliage was thick, the air was heavy with heat and humidity and the roaring drum of the Tis Abay Falls grew fainter with their progress through the jungle. On occasion, sudden steep rock hills appeared in front of them, but that didn't make much of a difference. They climbed them as if they were a natural playground, easily grappling from one rock to another and making the rough trek look like a brisk hike.

Lucas led the throng with his Winchester. "It's been a long time since I've been here, mate."

"Aye," answered Liam. "It still has the same flavor to it though. Nothing quite like it but thank God there is no mist this time around. Dawn's about to burn through the gloom and the last time, a sheet of fog as thick as cotton tumbled through the undergrowth."

Lucas stole a glance at Liam. "Don't remind me. It's the first time in a while I venture into sunlight, so feel free to knock on some wood."

"To set off a trap or wake up the pythons?" asked Liam. "No thanks, mate. We may be longevous, but I don't wish to test my skills with these beasts today."

"Why's that?" asked Lucas. "Don't tell me you're afraid."

"Don't tell me you don't smell it," interrupted Nathaniel.

Lucas stopped in his tracks and took a deep breath. "I don't smell a thing."

"Me either," added Liam, clearly confused.

"Face northwest and try again," Nathaniel said as he passed Lucas and Liam and flung his machete at the underbrush.

The vampires turned towards the direction the human had mentioned and sniffed again. This time, their eyes almost crawled out of their sockets and deep beads of sweat rolled down their dumbstruck faces.

"What the hell is that?" said Lucas.

Daniel caught up and passed both of them as well. "He's been nearing us since France, but now he's even closer and gaining ground. I think our friends have an idea of what we're up to and are now trying to reach us."

Lucas looked more worried by the second. "Friends? There's more than one?"

Nathaniel spoke from up ahead. "Face northeast and sniff for yourself."

Again both vampires did as suggested and found that six distinct aromas swam through the air from that direction.

"But how?" said Liam.

"Face east or west and you'll only smell the Nile and the falls," Nathaniel clarified. "Face any direction south and you'll smell the river we came from and untold mysteries not on our agenda."

"But we were facing north, why couldn't we smell it?"

"Their aromas crossed and canceled each other," said Nathaniel matter of factly. "If we hurry, they'll miss us and we'll have enough time to reach the lake."

"How did you know?" asked Liam.

"Thank Daniel," said the young man. "He noticed long ago and he's a leader for a reason. Now let's go, we have to hurry."

They raced single file following Daniel who had taken the lead and seemed to fell half an acre with every swing of his machete.

A hundred and forty miles northwest, a massive sand storm neared a camp with ten men in the outskirts of the Nubian Desert. The storm was so thick and violent that it blocked out the sun and made it seem as if heaven and hell were pushing against each other for dominion of the desert. A young boy in the camp stood beside the men who stared intently at the wall of thrashing sand that pounded on the bedrock and whispered deadly wails in the desert.

A man who was standing beside the young boy spoke in his native tongue. "That is a haboob, a spirit drainer... a sun swallower."

"I'm afraid father," said the child.

"You should be," replied the man, "I have seen many storms in my life, but I have never seen one with such conscience of direction nor intent. We are in its way, it will not stop and we shall be given no quarter."

The child's eyes welled with tears as he trembled. "Does that mean we're going to die, papa?"

"No, my child. It means we are going to be killed."

The black wall of the storm stood three hundred yards from the camp. Out of the thick dust cloud a mountain of black straw wire clawed and scraped flailing with the wind until it suddenly went limp.

"It is covered in fur," said another man from the tribe.

"It must be some type of desert beast," said a third man.

The figure hobbled its way closer and although it seemed as if it were only going at a crawl, in mere seconds it was a hundred yards away, the storm remaining still behind it. The father of the child stood firm, grasping a jasper and onyx talisman that swung from a long braid that wrapped along his arm while embracing his son with his free hand.

"Stop where you are!!" screamed some tribesmen, but the figure kept walking. At fifty yards the fur stopped looking so thick and the closer it loomed the clearer it became for the men what was covering the body.

"Father... are those? Is that...?"

"Yes, child."

After every man had seen that faces and scalps covered the creature's body, it took about twenty seconds for every bullet in their arsenal to be fired. At twenty paces, the father saw his companions struck by stones. As the skin of their faces flew through the air, thick rust colored droplets of dust and blood rained on the ground. It wasn't long before the man's lifeless body fell over his son's.

The figure only stopped to pick up the torn flesh and continued to walk through the small camp. The massive sandstorm crept over the site, swallowed it whole and like a receding tide of evil winds, swept back in the direction it had come from, leaving only a jasper and onyx talisman on the ground and claw prints that walked towards the heart of Ethiopia.

Two hundred miles east, six pairs of wings flew over the Afar Depression in Eritrea, one of only two places in the world where tectonic plates can be seen overlapping above sea level. For the last several years, volcanoes throughout the area have been waking from long years of dormancy. Although scientists have fascinating theories that will continue enduring, the answer will elude them until they accept the possibility of a hell.

The six sets of wings started tumbling down from the blue sky. Their spiral formation looped wide and on the ground stood two solitary figures; what appeared to be a cross between a condor, a serpent and a dragon and something far more terrible to its right, a small man with rosy cheeks and spectacles.

Down tumbled the angels, every time picking up more speed, ignoring the fact that the ground did not appear to have any intention of becoming any softer.

Two angels set down tandemly, their descent ending in a little air skip and a small tapping of their feet on the ground. They looked at the beast and did not falter, but to the small man, they bowed their eyes to.

"Turiel, Ananiel. Greetings," said the small pudgy man.

"Governor," said the blue winged blue eyed Ananiel.

"Reverend," added the brown winged and yellow eyed Turiel.

"Please... Elliot will do," he said while the beast to his left cracked its beak.

Another angel swooped down, did a long loop and hovered just before touching ground. Black wings sprinkled with white spots meant it was Nelchael and close behind a red winged angel swooped, arched upwards and did two flips before landing beside his brother.

"Nelchael, Rosier; Greetings as well."

"Greetings." they both replied.

"No song, Nelchael?" said Elliot. "I'm disappointed."

"My apologies, sir," answered the angel without making eye contact. "Much wearies the mind."

The fifth angel descending banked hard left, harder right and crash landed horrendously, causing all the angels to groan in unison. "Asael..."

"Lucy!!!!! I'm hooommeee!!" yelled the white robed yet quite dirty angel.

"Show respect to the father, Asael," Rosier admonished. "You sound like an imbecile."

"But he's not my daddy, brother Rosier," said Asael in an innocent and wounded voice, obviously stung by his brother's reproach.

"Leave him, Rosier," said the pudgy man. "He means no harm though you shouldn't always take what he says for granted. He spoke of the ancient homo-sapiens brandished Lucy by the archeologists that found her in this area. Maybe if you all listened more closely you would have been here on time."

Asael smiled wide. "I saw it on the TV."

"I'm sure you did," said the short man with his false smile.

The last angel still soared high until he tucked his wings, plummeted seven stories and landed less than ten paces from the short man. An act which didn't impress or bother Elliot in the slightest. "Hello, Armaros," he said dryly.

"Mr. Elliot," nodded the angel.

"So pleasant to hear that instead of father, reverend or governor."

"You only need to say things once, sir," said the large angel.

Elliot nodded in approval. "That's excellent. You know how I hate repeating myself."

"I would imagine," said the massive Armaros as his black eyes looked at the beast, to which he also nodded in salute. "Ahriman."

The serpent dragon clicked its beak again as if waking up and spoke with its acrid voice. "Ah... so someone finally notices me."

"I apologize but my brothers have strict orders not to speak to demons," said Armaros. "You cloud judgment and cast spells; therefore, they will not even acknowledge you."

The beast used its three large eyes to look intently at the large fallen angel. The left eye was red, the right was yellow and the middle one was a repugnant orange that pulsed when it spoke. "Oh? So why do you speak to Master Elliot then?"

If possible, the angel grew even more serious. "He is spoken to because he is no demon. He is far worse than any demon could be."

The pudgy man smiled and giggled with false modesty. "Now, now; no time for compliments. We have little time and can't waste it on flattery or inane bickering. We are all working towards the same end."

Both the fallen angel and the falcon serpent stood their ground and looked towards the small man.

"I do so hate the weather here," Elliot said. "Tell me what you know, brother Armaros."

"Yes, Father Elliot. The vampires have evaded us since France, but we've been nearing their trail and were about to take them in Alexandria when Ananiel delivered your message. We had been separated for some time."

"I was told," said the small man. "Strange thing that happened there. Maybe next time you'll trust young Asael's judgment a bit more than your own. His isn't as clouded with purpose and conviction." Asael could not stop smiling.

"Yes, Lord Elliot," replied Armaros.

"Continue."

"They seem to be heading for the heart of Ethiopia. They were heading up the Blue Nile when we broke off."

"Then they must be on their way to Lake Tana," said Elliot before turning to the demon. "Ahriman, any news of Murmur."

"Yes, sire;" replied the demon, "he crosses Sudan and has just passed from the Nubian Desert to the great Sudd. He had obtained information from the Lygophilials, was also making progress to intercept and insisted he had news regarding the watchers."

Elliot picked at his fingers, almost seeming as if he ignored the beast in front of him. "I see. Send word to his legions that they will not be needed at Tana."

Ahriman looked taken aback and implored. "But my lord, the attack."

"Would you like me to speak directly to Samyazza or Astaroth?" asked the man. "I could add that you are jeopardizing a mission. Or maybe we can avoid the unnecessary loss of warriors by being a good boy and doing as you're told. I'd tell Lucifer himself but I can't seem to get a hold of him."

The large serpent dragon cracked its teeth and did its best to maintain control. All of his masters had been mentioned in one sentence. The angels looked stunned but none spoke.

Elliot looked at the demon as if it were worth nothing. "Good that we cleared that up. Now go to hell, there is no time to waste. And please, take it as a figure of speech or an order, but waste no time in going to Murmur's legions and directing them to Myanmar. Now off you go."

The serpent dragon stared intently at the small beady eyes of the chubby man and though its jaws could have smashed the frail body like a twig, he bowed, turned around and walked towards a large hole that spat sulfur and subterranean heat from deep in the Earth.

The rest of the fallen angels stood staring at the little man, completely in awe of his treatment of one of the more ancient demon beasts. Elliot now turned back to Armaros. "Desist from pursuing the vampires, Armaros. You are needed elsewhere."

"But my lord, we were so..."

"So nothing, my dear cursed one. You are the fallen, the fathers of Grigori and I need you elsewhere."

"But..."

"I grow weary Armaros and the mere fact of me having to either explain myself or have to repeat orders is something I thought I would not have to do... especially with you. Forces are merging on both sides and I don't need you dirtying the playing field at the moment with your feathers or angel droppings."

"But..."

"But NOTHING!!!" screamed the small man as he raked the face of the angel with his bare hand. "Do not forget who I am, fallen one. Or maybe we should see if a pair of fallen angel wings will be good enough to serve my needs."

"As you wish, my lord," said the angel through clasped teeth.

The pudgy man's face then changed to a look of compassion before embracing the angel. "Armaros, please... call me Elliot."

Chapter 28: Lake Tana

Mist drapes over the rich brown-green waters of the Ethiopian highland lake known as Tana. Sun sprinkles over the horizon and though it has been a rough trail they have waded through, the sparse shrubbery is a welcome change to the group. Even though the dawn fog is thick, tikwah boats made of papyrus show signs of life on the waters as fishermen cast fishing nets or haul large loads of coal. Along with the strong boatmen, patches of reeds and tinder tumble along the banks of the lake.

Quite suddenly an unexplainable sense of joy surged within Nathaniel in a most peculiar way. Heaven knows that the view was serene enough to not merit laughter, but Nathaniel couldn't help it and let out small giggles as he realized that he was merely reacting to the contagious nature of something that floated through the mist.

"Is that laughter?" asked Daniel as he looked at the thick bed of fog rolling in. "Where's it coming from?" But before he could even unsheathe his saber, something darted past him and into the water. When he was able to decipher what had just happened, he could only look on as Nathaniel swam in the lake water, giggling like a small child.

"What the hell are you doing, Runnels?" asked the vampire, but before any further protests could be verbalized, Lucas had flown over him doing a huge cannonball that detonated in the water right next to Nathaniel. Looking back, Daniel now saw Liam sitting at the base of a large tree while lighting a cigarette and smiling freely as he marveled at the majestic dawn in one of the most remote places on Earth.

Through the mist laughter ran loud and free, laughter of the purest kind, the type of laughter you get when you imagine a cardboard box to be a spaceship crash landing as you tumble down a hill, the laughter of children. What seemed like small mud covered kids started to emerge from the mist, some from the water, others running gaily in the field.

They were obviously fascinated by the newcomers as their indistinct features and red stained skin made them close enough to identical to think them all related if not all the same. Daniel looked on as the young boys splashed with Nathaniel and Lucas in the water and even pulled Liam up so he could make smoke rings to throw stones through. He was at a pure loss for words since impending danger danced nearly as did the potential end of the world... yet his comrades had actually found a way to stop and enjoy a moment of life even among all the chaos. They had seized the moment of pure illogical joy and weren't too keen of letting go.

A wave of realization swept over Daniel. His eyes slackened, his shoulders gave a casual shrug and he ran after Liam, snatching the cigarette and taking a long drag before he put on a mock monster face and cried out "I am a dragonnnnn!!!! Hear me roar!!!! RAWRRRR!!!"

He puffed the smoke from his nostrils and chased the giggling mud children, who tossed around and laughed some more. If only for a moment, they all remembered that no matter how tough life was, certain moments make any amount of heartache bearable.

Nathaniel tossed red mud on the children and with every hit, everyone seemed to laugh harder. Lucas clasped his hands together to offer the children a boost so they could jump higher and even Liam was struggling to stay on his feet with a child on each extremity and three tickling him. Daniel was especially set on catching one little rascal that was quick enough to evade him no matter how hard he tried. After a couple of minutes of chasing, he finally caught him and smiled while saying Gotcha.

The child then embraced him lovingly and whispered in his ear: "See? Even you can get a hold of happiness."

Daniel was stunned, the sudden tone and manner strayed from anything one might expect from a child.

"Times will get hard, Daniel," said the child, "but you must always keep faith and insist on smiling. Remember, if you have to go... go with a smile."

Daniel pulled back to look at the child. It smiled broadly showing oddly colored teeth the same as its brick red skin. The child then held Daniel close again and whispered one last thing. "We believe in you."

At that moment the mist started to pull off the lake like satin sheets off a bed. As this happened and the mysterious fog faded, so did the children... they disappeared in wisps of earth scent and echoes of laughter until the four of them were alone again. No one spoke for a long time and though most tikwah boats passed by, impervious to the odd events that had just transpired, one single boat swam from the middle of the lake, with four other boats tied behind. Its pace was calm and its route deliberate.

A green robed figure stood on the boats. It was hooded and its face could not be seen but the strong lean body stood firm and calm and the pace of the boats was not rushed. Upon landing, he stepped off and walked towards the small group. "I see you've met the children of the lake," he said in a calm monotone. "Count yourselves lucky enough to be here at Magic Hour."

"Magic hour?" asked Liam, who was slightly more responsive than the others.

"Dawn holds many mysteries and in this lake, even more so," said the figure. He took a vine rope with a sharp stone at the end and cut the other boats free. "Come with me; you have been expected for some time now."

"By whom?" asked Daniel finally snapping to his senses.

"By the ones in my temple; those whom you seek. First we go to Tana Quirquos, a small island on the lake; then you may have your audience. Now please, follow and keep silent. The children are not the only inhabitants of the lake and you wouldn't like to meet some of the others."

Liam and Lucas looked at each other, sharing memories of the last time they were here. They had followed a Photogeni to try and learn more about them and had been surprised by some of the things the hooded figure hinted at. They rather not remember that day and instead followed the others onto the boats. At the side of each boat, there were long rods fastened which they used to push themselves along to follow the hooded figure.

Their apprehension increased with every additional bit of sunlight that grew from above, revealing more details of their odd guide. His robe seemed made of papyrus instead of silk and not an inch of skin showed. To add to the mystery, regardless of his movements, the hood never moved.

Other boatmen glided by gently, crossing their paths and shaking lightly with the small wakes this particular group left behind. The sheer silence swallowed any noise and pecked at their thoughts as more flotsam floated by and almost seemed to part way for the boats they were on. Nathaniel pushed forwards to catch up to the figure.

"Were those children real?" he asked.

"Of course," said the figure, "you saw them with your own eyes and touched them with your hands. What more proof do you need?"

"They just seemed... well, they looked like they were made of clay to be honest."

"Quite correct," replied the boatman. "They are still too young to be Earth. Earth is much older than mud or clay, it is also wiser."

"But-"

"You are human are you not?" asked the figure.

"Um... yes?"

"Then I am sure you've already seen enough to realize how much you don't know of the world," said the boatman, never looking at Nathaniel and now pushing hard to separate himself from the group to maintain silence. More debris floated near them as they passed a series of small islands. Some of the cays had monks looking towards them, others had the wrinkled eyes of old boatmen surveying them while some seemed completely desolate, yet still possessing an essence that was clearly aware that something foreign floated nearby.

A few minutes passed of that terrible silence until Nathaniel once again pushed to be beside the mysterious boatman.

"Please be silent," said the hooded figure when Nathaniel arrived at his side.

"Tell me your name and I'll keep quiet."

"What difference does knowing a name make?" asked the boatman.

"Friend or foe, I always prefer to put a name to a face."

The hooded man turned to look at Nathaniel and fragments of light shone on coarse brown skin and a bright red eye. "You may call me Banyan, Master Runnels. Now please, be silent. It is for your own wellbeing."

Nathaniel nodded and mouthed the words thank you before falling back with the others. One of the larger islands they had seen seemed to be their destination. A type of mangrove dock was where they ultimately landed with various cinnamon skinned monks giving the welcome to the group and their guide.

Banyan was first off the tikwah and on the right side of his body hung a glass vial that seemed to hold a single flame that hovered in the middle. The monks greeted the hooded man enthusiastically. To the left there was a sign that read:

No

Entrance

For lady

"Funny," Nathaniel said.

"Not really," whispered Lucas, "imagine a bunch of monks stranded on an island in the highlands of Ethiopia for God knows how many years. I'm just glad I'm not androgynous, though I wonder if they'd care. A hole is a hole after all."

"Nice," said Liam, half disgusted at the prospect of anything alien invading their bodies and half smiling at the sheer rudeness of the comment.

Meanwhile, Daniel looked intently as Banyan spoke to the monk. The monk kept looking at the group and pecking at his skin until the hooded man put his hands in front to signal them to wait. He walked towards the group while pulling out a small pouch.

"What's that and what's going on?" asked Daniel, pointing to the pouch.

"You've been in the lake and there are Schistosomes in the water, which cause Bilharzia. They are small worms that bury themselves in your skin and then move to your bowels or bladder. You've been in the water and though I assured them you were not infected, this is not the place to trust in the word of strangers. In this pouch is a powder made of various herbs, spices, tree bark, fungi and roots that will rid you of anything that might be in your system. Let me sprinkle this on you or else we will not be allowed to go forwards."

"How do we know we can trust you?" blurted Nathaniel.

"Because the West Wind sent word of you. That is how I knew when and where to seek you."

"Gabriel?" asked Nathaniel.

"Yes, Master Runnels. He sends his regards and reminds that you still have a long conversation pending."

Nathaniel smiled oddly, accepted the circumstances for what they were and spread his arms wide. "Then sprinkle away, Master Banyan".

Everyone else was a bit confused but followed suit. After a few minutes, the monks led them into an open ground and towards an old shabby monastery that the guides indicated was the keeping place of the Ark of the Covenant. Some tourists passed by: an English man led by an oddly enthusiastic guide named Amlucky, a French woman named Brigitte, a Japanese couple without a camera and a German artist named Niles.

This information wasn't guessed but was obtained after hearing some comments in all three languages spoken fluently. The dust which had been sprinkled over them tingled a bit and Nathaniel actually wondered if his head was going to shrink or if he could now fly by just focusing on a happy thought.

They entered the shack where ancient books, figurines and murals surrounded an open space.

"Some people say the Ark of the Covenant should be here," Banyan said turning to the group while still concealing his face. "Many people have died and some have killed to find the Ark... to truly discover its contents. Some speculate the Ten Commandments written by Moses were kept in it. Others have even said it held the remains of Christ."

He stood silent in the middle and suddenly the room grew much brighter. The blue-white flames of the candles surrounding the room had grown twice as large as they had been and glowing much brighter.

"None of these are the contents of the ark," said Banyan. "The ark is no treasure chest, with no hidden secrets of any religion. It is no little box and the truth of the matter is that there is no such thing as an ark of the covenant."

Each in the group looked at each other with confusion in their eyes except Nathaniel. He had remained particularly motionless. "There is only the covenant of the Ark then?" he said without stuttering.

"What are you talking about Runnels?" asked Daniel.

"Look at his waist. You think it's a keepsake or that it's a coincidence that he can speak English fluently even when he's not even human?"

The hooded figure looked Daniel directly with his red eyes. "As others have mentioned before me, Master Montacre, a fine choice you have made in this one."

But Nathaniel wasn't finished. "What I don't know however is what you are all the keepers of."

"As good a place as any to start asking, my friend. By now I'm sure you've heard of the Holy Trinity, of how God exists yet became flesh, the Christian tale of the Messiah, which is beautiful and more true than you think though some parts are completely fiction. What rarely gets talked about is of the third element of the Trinity and gets referred to metaphorically as a dove and literally as a flame."

"So you guard the Holy Spirit?" asked Nathaniel.

"Actually, the Holy Spirit does not need guarding. We simply administer it and I am one of its keepers."

"And God?"

"Well that's a bit more complicated, Master Runnels. There has always been the debate over one true God and who is right and who is wrong and the only thing I can say is that not only is God far beyond such trite explanations, God has yet to truly care as long as some type of harmony is kept. Judeo Christian, Muslim, Zoroastrian, Hindu, Buddhist or any other definition of God is merely one facet of something that goes beyond our comprehension. What is very true is that Christ and Mohammed and other messiahs were made in God's image. Do you know why that is?"

"Because we are his greatest achievement?" said Lucas.

"No."

"Because who better to understand his creation than oneself?" said Liam.

"Nice words that don't say anything," replied Banyan.

"Because she is mortal..." said Daniel.

"... and she is ill," completed Nathaniel.

A yellow tinged smile shone beneath the hood. "Exactly. For some time now, you've noticed that the world has been falling deeper into a lost sense of identity. Although everyone seems to be in search of self definition and self realization, every day more people care less for their fellow man. Such an attitude has a direct toll on God, but I have one question. Why do some of you think God is a man and others a woman?"

The group looked all around trying to find the answer in the others' faces.

"Well that's how it's always been in the Bible," said Liam.

"Which of the countless versions?" responded Banyan. "And from which religion?"

"I honestly don't know, I think we're all just used to it really. Every mention in most bibles and their version if not every Judeo Christian or Muslim Bible has references to God as a man. I think anyone exposed to that is just used to the notion of thinking of God as male."

"Very honest and true answer. How about you two?"

"It just... it just feels as if God is a woman," Daniel said.

"So faith comes into play?" asked Banyan.

"Yes," the vampire answered.

"Interesting. Well I'll tell you one thing, you're both right. God has been male, God is now a woman... or God can be either or simply nothing else. It is true that God creates in its own image, but humans are not the only creation of God. God simply takes the form of what it needs to be to create, to destroy, to alter and to survive... at the moment, God chooses to be woman."

"And why is that?" Daniel asked.

"Do you know of resilience, courage and perseverance greater than that of a woman? Do you know of any creature more willing to sacrifice everything to survive and more importantly to protect what is held dearest? God is now woman because it needs to be woman."

"And what are you then?" asked Nathaniel.

Daniel answered the question for him. "It is neither man nor woman, Runnels; it is Photogeni."

The hooded figure gave a small laugh. "I beg to differ, Master Montacre, I am Photogeni, but I am also man."

As he stood there, the hood moved by itself and showed not to be of papyrus after all, but thick leaves layered over each other that now collapsed to reveal the thick bark skin of their guide. His deep red eyes scanned the group. The robe he wore also pulled back of its own accord to reveal hard packed earth and straw, much like adobe, packed over thick strong roots that made up his body.

"This body, these hands, the roots that run through me, all of them come from a chance coincidence of magic, the blood of life and time. Like it or not, you were created by God, we were simply allowed to exist, all of us somehow or another show that the grace of God knows no limits."

"Will you help us?" Daniel asked.

"That is not for me to decide, Master Montacre. That is why you will have an audience and we shall make our decision. Do you all agree to these terms?"

They all consented and after Banyan clasped his hands, the floor of the monastery began to crawl and lift itself in lumps.

"Please stand behind me," Banyan said.

The group did as asked and the earthen floor started to shift and swirl into a miniature terrestrial maelstrom. In mere seconds, it had turned into a large hole in the ground from which green light shone up from. A moment later, five giant water lilies ascended from the chasm.

"After you," said Banyan. Each of them stepped onto one of the large lilies, which began to descend automatically after sensing their weight.

"Where does this go to again?" Liam asked.

"You've heard of Eden, I presume."

The vampire had no retort to this and just took a deep breath. Down they went and when Banyan had crossed the threshold, the floor swirled once again but in the opposite direction this time until the room returned to the way it had been seconds ago. The candle lights dimmed down, not a noise was heard and the only evidence of anything having happened was a single solitary leaf which remained on the floor.

The door to the monastery opened and Amlucky, the guide to the English man led the Briton into the room while picking up various tomes and eagerly displaying them to him while speaking at breakneck speed.

The English man took out a handkerchief and wiped the beads of sweat that rolled down his flushed skin. "Oh good, more relics," he said cynically. "Wait 'til I tell mum about my dramatic Ethiopian adventure. Seriously, does anything ever happen around here?"

Chapter 29: A League of their Own

If there were a plant equivalent of a cloud, that's exactly what it felt like for Nathaniel as the soft yet firm platform he stood on descended through the mossy tunnel. He had about fifteen feet of space towards every direction and the moss that covered the entire tunnel seemed to glow unlike anything he'd ever seen. But it was the sound that threw him off balance more than anything he was seeing. An electric buzz whirred through the tunnel while clicks popped from the walls as if it were coming from the moss.

Trying to listen better, Nathaniel took a step forwards on the large leaf, which caused it to tilt slightly towards the phosphorescent wall. Apart from glowing, the moss seemed to ripple and move with small eddies made of light that soared in a ring up the pit far beyond where the human's eyes could reach. Since he could also hear a tiny hum whirring off the tunnel walls, Nathaniel leaned his leaf even closer to the wall.

"Take a look why don't you?" said a whispering voice.

"You should really see this," said another.

"New fig on the branch," said a third.

"You're not from around here, are you boy," said a fourth.

As he continued to descend farther down the glowing tunnel, the whispers escalated in volume and kept coming faster and faster, each with distinct voices and different personalities.

"Jack be nimble, jack be quick."

"Take a look won't you? It won't hurt. Promise."

"Take your hands off me, you big ape."

"I'm half the man I used to be."

"Five against one."

"I swear she said she was eighteen officer."

"Which way to go?"

"I'll swallow poison until I grow immune."

"I'd like to hear a positive drug story."

"Come onnnn lucky seven."

"This article is pure rubbish."

"Well I'm only part vegan."

"Happy, happy, joy, joy."

As more and more phrases bombarded his senses, Nathaniel's eyes began to flutter. In mere seconds his feelings had shifted completely from curiosity to terror and now all he wanted was to get away.

"You know what Jack Burton always says."

"Have you ever felt like time stood still?"

"A wave came crashing like a fist to the door."

"See you on the darkside of the moon."

"You gotta ramble on."

"You can swallow a pint of blood before you get sick."

"Does God have feet?"

"What is this God person and who does he think he is?"

"God damn me."

"Roll God's dice."

"It is like the finger of God."

His eyes trembled like crazed butterflies, his teeth were grinding against each other and all his muscles seemed to pull against one another until he could only scream. "Oh God... Oh GOD... oh GODDDDD!!!!!!"

Suddenly all went green and faded to grey. After a moment or two, large whooshes began to blow across his face and Nathaniel was barely able to open his eyes to see a spiral of ten thousand eyes stretching to the heavens. It wasn't until a strong smell of lime crept into his senses that he was able to fully open his eyes.

"Hush child," said a soft voice. He barely made out two purple eyes and fragments of smooth skin made of flower petals in front of him. "You stood too close to the holy beacon, that's all."

"Are you all right, Runnels?" Daniel asked.

"Give him a second, Montacre," said Banyan's deep voice as Nathaniel tried to get up.

"Uh-uh. Not yet, youngling," said the sweet voice Nathaniel had heard a few seconds ago. He was still having a hard time focusing his vision. "It was only an instant but I'm sure ten thousand voices spoke to you in one second."

"Wh-what just happened to me?" he said as he shivered on the cavern floor.

The sweet voice was suddenly very near and he felt himself being laid on a cold lap. "Here... drink from this," said the voice. He then heard a small snap before being fed what felt like sweet sap from a root. His shivering slowed down until it finally subsided and he felt himself flush with a gentle warmth.

When he was finally able to open his eyes and focus, he realized he was on the lap of what looked like a strong woman made entirely of petals and leaves. Her face looked freckled because of the brown spotted yellow petals that covered or more actually, made up the face of what any simple minded human could best refer to as a plant woman. To make matters more curious, he also realized that the root he had been sucking on was actually one of her fingers.

"There we go," she said while smiling with vivid petal lips and purple buds for eyes. "Better?"

"Yes..." he said while sitting up. "What just happened?"

Banyan came closer to the human. "That, my young friend, was a random flash of your life courtesy of an atypical manifestation of the Holy Spirit. Complicated enough for you? Oh and don't think of it as if you spoke to God, but more on the lines of a reaction to the residue of the spirit."

"Great..." said Nathaniel as he gripped his head. "For a second, I'd almost thought weird things might stop happening."

"Can he walk, Lily?" Banyan asked.

"Walk? I suspect this boy can do a great deal more than that, brother. I smell egnalem within him and not a small amount."

"You can smell?" Nathaniel asked.

Lily laughed at his comment while covering her very human-like mouth. "You still have much to learn, young one. But to answer your question, yes we smell and taste and eat and feel. Don't think it didn't more than just tingle to break a nail so you could suck the antidote."

Out of instinct, Nathaniel looked at her hands to try and understand what she meant. There he saw that instead of regular fleshy digits, her fingers were delicate roots and for nails she had pod-like ovals, from which he had been sucking the sap.

"Let's go now," said Lily, "we must meet with the others. Ready to go, Nathaniel?"

He nodded yes while looking at the straw dress that covered the female plant woman and the small glass vial with a dancing purple white flame hanging from a belt fashioned from vines.

"I'd say to take a picture, because it would last longer, but something tells me you don't need any type of machine to remember. Now, follow me, every setback is time ill spent."

Lily started off down the glowing cavern followed by Liam, Lucas, Daniel and Banyan alongside Nathaniel taking up the rear.

"If you feel lightheaded, let me know," said Banyan.

"I'm fine," Nathaniel replied, "what is this place though?"

"These are the Lime Caverns, halfway between Lake Tana and sea level. It's a complex subsystem of caverns located directly beneath the lake and the outskirts of Raelis, homeland of the photogeni."

Nathaniel still struggled to keep a clear head "Are the walls here really laced with... with the Holy Spirit?"

"No, young friend," Banyan said. "This is the residue of the ghost. Think of it as divine oxidation."

"So this is like... holy rust?" said Nathaniel.

"Well without the negative connotation of decay you humans attribute to that word. But yes, in a manner of speaking."

"So that's why it glows?" asked the young man.

"Well that and the amount of magical debris and seepage left from the first Global War, the one that helped create us."

Nathaniel's eyes glinted with awe. "Sometimes I still think I might be dreaming."

"But you know better than that, don't you? Besides, when you dream, you are conscious you are doing so, which is why you're able to tread through the unknown realms of Oneiros."

"How do you know that?" asked Nathaniel.

"The West Wind holds many secrets if you have enough patience to pay attention and listen." Nathaniel's eyes shone with realization. "Gabriel told me much of you and I am here to try to help you attain aide. There are some who would rather leave humans to their own eradication. I recognize that though some of your kind would do better to expire, rot and feed my kind, instead of wasting the oxygen we produce, there are others who are very worthwhile."

The caverns glowed eerily, covered in the phosphorescent green moss. There were some turns to the left and then to the right, but for the most part it was a pretty linear path that they followed. Nathaniel slowly regained color in his cheeks and his balance grew steady once again. He looked towards his feet and saw that every step he took caused ripples of light to ebb away into the rest of the glowing cavern.

"It's beautiful," he said as he looked at all the ripples converging from everyone's footsteps and at times bouncing off each other like some organically luminescent display.

A few steps on and daylight could finally be made out in the distance. During the walk, everyone remained roughly in a stretched single file though Banyan and Nathaniel remained about a dozen yards behind the last person in the queue. As that person passed a large jutting stalagmite, the glowing moss pulsed brightly and glimmered on the surface of the rock, having various lines dance on the surface every which way until slowly the outline of a body formed on the surface like a green glowing shadow that waited for Banyan and the human."

Nathaniel noticed that Banyan seemed a bit confused. "This is new."

"What is that?" Nathaniel asked.

"Greetings, Nathaniel," spoke the shadow stone with six voices at the same time, some male, some female, some indistinct but all gentle. "My apologies for earlier but you got rather close to some of my life force."

Banyan stared at the stone, then at Nathaniel, then back at the stone.

"God?" asked Nathaniel.

"As you understand it? In a ways. But for many others, I have a different definition and explanation, which is fine as long as some sense of order remains. I would be what you call the Holy Spirit, what some would call the Essence of Light and what others would ignorantly refer to as karma. You know that aspect of God being everywhere? Well that would be me."

"So you're a being?" the human asked.

"That's a challenging question to answer in a way you can understand. You could say I'm a being because I can express myself subjectively as I am doing now. But in the end, I am malleable energy which flows freely through any substance to gain knowledge of it. Earlier I flowed through you, which is part of the reason why we can communicate. Taking into account what I was able to learn of you, the best reference as to what I am is that thing they call the Force in those space movies. Combine that concept with infinite knowledge and the desire for balance. I flow through everything, the good, the bad, the living... even the dead. But that's why you understand me, after having flowed through you; I am now able to project myself in a way you can understand."

Nathaniel's throat caught and he blew out a deep breath as his mind tried to catch up with what he was living.

"I'm sure this is quite complicated," said the voice. "More than anything, I wanted to apologize for our first meeting and to offer one piece of advice: look beyond your within."

"What?"

"It'll make sense from the visions you've had. Continue to embrace them as much as you have to this moment, or even more."

"Ok.......... can I ask you one question though?"

"Yes, child."

"What happens when we die?"

"Ah... how many times I've heard that question. From my experience I'm sure you wouldn't appreciate me ruining the surprise. It's safe to say though, that the possibilities are endless and no one has ever truly asserted to what happens after ascension."

"Ascension?"

"You'll see one day, young one. For now, you must be off. You do not have the benefit or the burden of being everywhere at once. Be well, be safe and be true."

Without another word, the glowing silhouette burst into thousands of fragments of light, which shot up through the tunnel and faded away.

Banyan struggled to get words out from his twig lined mouth, while water droplets dewed in his eye sockets and trickled down the bark of his cheek.

"The others don't need to know, Banyan," said the human, "we need to keep everyone focused on the task at hand. Banyan continued to look at the stone but nodded as he heard the human's words. After a moment, they walked towards the light, away from the rock.

It only took a quick moment to reach the opening of the cave where they walked out into a small clearing surrounded by thick jungle and trees reaching up higher than any forest Nathaniel had ever seen. He gasped in awe at the undulating green aurora pulsating before him. It was as if the plants were more than alive and moved much more than should be the case.

"Keep close, Runnels. The jungle forest does not take kindly to strangers until they have been properly introduced."

Banyan then closed his eyes and began to hum deeply. It was a constant drone that undulated ever so slightly until he opened his cloak. Then the sound got louder and Nathaniel felt his chest vibrating from the noise surging from the photogeni. Banyan suddenly began drumming hard on his chest in an odd pattern. The beat on his chest actually caused his low drawn hum to be modulated and an odd melody started to come from all parts of him.

The leaves rustled gently and a soft breeze slid all over Nathaniel's body as trunks, branches and leaves began to sway. First they moved in one singular pattern and then slowly the different plants broke into various distinct movements.

"What are my eyes seeing?" asked Nathaniel.

"These are our younglings, Runnels; the twigs of the photogeni."

"Twigs?"

"Yes, we have various castes within our society. Twigs are our youngest. After them come branches, then roots and so on."

"What are you then?"

"I am a perennial, a member of the high council."

"So you are the elders then?" Nathaniel asked.

"No, we might make the decisions and are the ones responsible for rules and order, but above us are the wood saints, the holy Yggdrasil."

"Yggdrasil... isn't that from Norse mythology?"

"Correct. As I'm sure you've noticed, not all mythology is without grounds and not all history is true."

"So how does it work? Your society I mean."

"You are born a twig and remain one until you mature enough to become either a branch or a root. Those are equally important and share the same levels in war time or in peace."

"War time? I'd think you pacifists for being in tune with nature."

"That is quite kind of you, Mr. Runnels; but given that we were born out of bloodshed, it is only natural to assume what is in our basic genetic code. Twigs abound and make up our infantry, branches perform strategic attacks and roots offer defense, supplies, medical treatment and reinforcements."

"And let me guess... no perennial fights."

"In-correct, Mr. Runnels. Unlike humans, us not fighting is never an option. Perennials are charged with leading the infantry."

"And your high elders?"

"There has never been any need for any of them to have to involve themselves in a battle to this day. We've been able to manage well in these past thirty millenniums. But if need be, they are battle ready."

"I see."

"No you do not, Mr. Runnels, but you will."

As Nathaniel looked on, the foliage continued to move, splitting up into six distinct figures. Earth, leaves and branches moved of their own accord and kneaded upon themselves as if large invisible hands molded the makeshift adobe. Even with all he had seen in the last weeks, Nathaniel could not help but be in complete awe.

"Are they being born?" he asked.

"No. This is the third stage in the development of twigs. They are still learning to control their manifestations and they still have a ways to go before understanding their bodies and how to control them. The first stage depends on the original photogeni. He or she decides to procreate, speaks with another of our kind, male or female, and together go into the forest. There, they either break off a stem or place a seed into the Earth, they both cut themselves and water the seed with their joined saps or nectars."

"Amazing..." gasped Nathaniel. "So you don't have sex?"

Banyan looked at him a bit taken aback. "Of course we do. If not, then you'd see us warring all the time. It's just not the way you envision the act. We can survive without it, but seriously... who would want to?"

Nathaniel gave a smile and nodded at the comment. Banyan then walked to the plant figures and sat on a stone. "Let's see who we have here," he said while looking onto a figure whose leaves were short and papery as the figure took more and more shape. A series of leaves matted over themselves until a girl's face did its best attempt to emerge.

"Ah, Kalypto," Banyan said in a fatherly tone. "Sit here; let's see if we can't help you sort yourself out a bit more."

The figure walked towards Banyan and sat on his strong rootlike knee. Banyan took what was her head and looked to the rest of the figures. "Now say ah," he instructed. The head really wasn't sure how to obey, opening sideways rather than up and down. So Banyan instructed soothingly. "No, no, no, darling. Remember how I taught you to breathe?"

The figure nodded.

"All right then. I want you to breathe slowly. In... out.... In.... now out. Now look at my face. Look at me smile. Now I want you to close your mind's eye and think of my face. There's a forehead, cheeks, eyes, and a mouth. Now I want you to show me each. Start with the forehead; that one's easy. Take note children, and try to follow along. Now go on, Kaly. The forehead."

The rugged surface of the plant child's head rippled lightly as it listened to Banyan's instructions. First the surface settled down and smoothened and then little by little, what looked like a forehead emerged on her head.

"That's my girl. Now think of your cheeks."

The ripples now went to the sides of her face and out of nothing, cheeks made of leaves appeared.

"Very good, Kalypto. How about a nose? You think you can give yourself a nose? Obviously not as big as mine, we want you beautiful right?"

All the figures did their best attempt at giggling, if you could imagine what rustling leaves giggling would sound like. But although the ripples waked on the child's face, nothing came out until the small thing shuddered as if being on the verge of giving up. Banyan noticed and embraced her head. "No, no, sweet one. Don't give up. Here, touch my nose so you can get a better idea."

From the moment she touched Banyan's nose, a little speck began to form on her face.

"See? That wasn't so hard. Now let's try a mouth. You've seen me move mine a lot so you know what to do."

A small slit formed on the slowly filling face of the young twig. Banyan urged her to give her mouth more feeling. He told her to say letters, vowels that Nathaniel couldn't understand because the youngling did not have a vial with a purple flame. It took a few moments but the small plant girl finally had a mouth and a face, but no eyes.

"Now you can talk. I'm extremely proud of you. But now comes the tricky part. Do you want blue eyes?"

The young twig shook her head saying no.

"Do you want green eyes?"

Again she shook no.

"Then what color do you want them?" asked Banyan.

The small eyeless girl turned to Nathaniel and said something intelligible while pointing to him.

"Fair enough," replied Banyan, "you seem to already have an admirer, Mr. Runnels. She wants her eyes brown, like yours."

Nathaniel blushed a little and bowed to the girl while saying thank you, to which she smiled broadly with her new found mouth.

"Now let's see if we can get the right color," Banyan said as he cupped his hand, took some water from a small puddle next to them and sprinkled some earth into it. He also picked at his bark and then took his own right thumb and soaked it in the mixture, dabbing lightly to form the outline of eyes on the child photogeni's face.

"Does that feel right?" asked Banyan.

She nodded yes.

"Now give me your hands." He then poured the mixture into her hands.

"Atta girl... now put that across your face if you feel it is right."

Though the youngling hesitated for a moment, she put the mixture across her face and with the same love he'd done everything else, now Banyan smoothed out the contours of her eyes like an artist shaping clay with his hands. They were deep loving strokes that pressed into the child's face. After a few presses, one could begin to see the outline of eyes appear.

"There we go," Banyan said as he continued to caress and mold her face. "Just a little more. Now let's see if you can open your eyes, my child."

She responded with a light rustle. It took a little effort, but before long the stems and leaf parts that were shaped like eyes began to open. She blinked a lot and struggled with the light, for after all, these eyes were new and it was the first time they had opened onto the world. Round and round she looked, taking in all the wonder with her new brown on green eyes. She looked towards Nathaniel and gave a large smile and then another even bigger one to Banyan as she clasped him in a wrenching embrace.

"There, there, young one. Let's see how your brothers and sisters have done."

Nathaniel had almost forgotten about the other twigs and now he looked around at some of the new faces that surrounded him and although there were a couple that had managed to do well, others were a complete mess. One had his nose where his eyes should be, another was missing one eye, half her nose and half her mouth and one blank face even smiled at Nathaniel from the top of its forehead.

Banyan gave a hearty laugh at the odd sight. "Ah, Master Runnels, I'll have to do some sorting here but feel free to go on ahead. I assure you that you are safe here in Raelis after the message I sent. Just keep to that path right there and you'll meet up with your friends.

Nathaniel nodded and waved goodbye to the children and to Banyan but he hadn't taken twenty steps when he heard the photogeni calling. "Wait, Mr. Runnels. Before you go, take this." Banyan then handed Nathaniel a necklace that glowed purple grey in the shade. "That way you won't have to wonder what anyone is saying."

Nathaniel gave his thanks but looked to the deep bush not knowing where the path was. Banyan wrestled with the younglings but was able to talk to him. "Remember who we are, Mister Runnels. Ask kindly and the path shall appear."

Nathaniel half confused, raised his eyebrow before turning to speak to the deep jungle. "All right.... can I please go on the path towards the rest of the group?"

A long breeze rushed on the young man and he could listen and feel a whisper, which replied "Certainly."

In front of him, one tree moved to the side, then another, then some branches until a clear path opened in front of him.

"Thank you," he gasped and without a backwards glance, he stepped onto the path.

Chapter 30: A meeting, a feast
and something left unsaid

As Nathaniel walked along the trail, he couldn't help but feel like he was swimming through a lush green ocean. Big leaves swished around him like breaking waves while vines flicked off the top of them like sea spray peeling off ocean swells. "Is all of this forest alive?" he said out loud.

"Of course," whispered the trees. "Plants are alive. What you were really wondering is if it's all conscious. The answer to that question is... sometimes."

"Sometimes?"

"Yesssss... plants sleep too or have you never heard the expression that you humans sleep like a log? Well it's not just an expression. Some parts of me are very awake; like this trail. Other parts of me are quite dormant. Some are alive. Some think for themselves, others don't. Others are dead or dying. But even in death, there is life. It's all part of the natural process."

Nathaniel walked on fascinated as he'd thought he could never be after all he had lived in such a short time.

"You are quite the breath of fresh air, young one," said the forest. "It has been a while since we had a human in the deep jungle. But if you will, please wait there one moment."

Nathaniel obeyed because he didn't think it very prudent to disagree with a forest. The rustling waves to either side quieted down and everything became silent and still. He was beginning to wonder what was going on when deep thuds started quaking beneath his feet. He looked up and for the first time realized that there were trees almost six hundred feet high. It was so light that he had not even taken the opportunity to look up. As he marveled at the natural skyscrapers, something even more amazing began to happen. Platforms of earth and forest rose in batches of a hundred square feet until the entire forest seemed to spawn an overhead level that blocked out most of the sunlight with occasional holes to let light and sound in.

Before Nathaniel could react, a sultry voice whispered in his ear. "Don't move." His skin crawled and his heart raced. A figure strutted into view that made Nathaniel choke on his spit. "Hello, Mr. Runnels. I am Belladonna."

Her skin was pure and smooth, a mix between purple, green and scarlet. Her smile was thin but her face was almost human as was her body, which was fleshy enough to look the part of a centerfold. She stared at him as she spoke. "Lily sent me to look for you. I am another of the perennials."

"A pleasure," he said, still hoarse from the brief coughing fit.

She stood beside him, scanned him from head to toe and looked forward to the trail that was still open even though the original layer of it was now two hundred feet above them.

"What are we waiting for?" he hesitated to ask because even though the thumping noise was still noticeable; he couldn't make out what it was.

"You'll see right about.......... now."

The thick foliage to Nathaniel's right parted and in a sudden burst, the subtle thudding became a thunderous stampede as a herd of no less than thirty elephants roared ten feet from where he stood. After about a minute, the herd passed and the explosion of their passage faded into strong thuds, then small thumps, and then nothing. The forest platforms then descended slowly and everything went back to its normal place as if nothing had happened.

Belladonna smiled when she saw Nathaniel's dangling jaw. "It's the best way to help them avoid poachers. That's why tracking them is not as easy as a GPS tag."

"And that's why they are said to live in the deep jungle," he managed to say.

"Good boy," she cooed. "You are a smart one."

Her plant eyes fluttered and her braided vine hair rustled gently. Nathaniel took a good look at the female photogeni. It was as if she was wearing a deep purple glossy leaf as a corset. Small vines crept up her legs like stockings and her feet blended into tough bark as if she wore stiletto-heeled boots.

"Follow me," she said, "the feast is being prepared but you can start by meeting some of the others."

She led the way but he stood still looking at her. She'd walked ten paces before noticing. Peeking over her shoulder she gave a wicked smile to the young man. "See something you like?" she said while looking down at the silky pink thong that had caught Nathaniel's attention. "Come along now."

He followed and walked behind her obediently realizing he was back at the room in the Halo Maze. Just as confused and awestruck as that first day even with all he had seen and lived since then. At one point he even thought nothing could amaze him again, but life is special that way and he appreciated the reminder. He had changed but the essence to him was still there. He walked along the trail and saw everything in a slightly different light. It was so sudden yet so smooth in transition.

"You are rather quiet, Mr. Runnels."

Nathaniel looked at the photogeni woman, and snapped out of his reverie after realizing how serious his face had become. "Please, call me Nathaniel."

"All right... Nathaniel then. Would you like to share some of those thoughts or would you rather I wasted away in silence?"

He finally smiled a little easier. "Sorry, it's just that a lot has happened in a very short time. One minute you feel like some lost scared child, the next minute you know everything and the minute after that you realize that even if you know a lot more than you just did, in reality you don't know much about anything."

"Impressive. I didn't know my backside could cause an epiphany of such magnitude."

She giggled, he blushed and they walked.

"Those are some interesting thoughts, Nathaniel. Even we have gotten word of some of your adventures. In little time you've gotten quite the reputation and more impressive still is that angels, therians and vampires have grown to respect you."

"Respect me? But why?"

"You speak with your heart and you are ready to die to make a point for a cause you believe in. I'd say humans like you are not common, but in reality, your breed is rare in any species."

"But I've never done anything like this before."

"So? Perilous situations have a way of bringing forth our real selves. Even though it didn't seem that way, you had no choice."

"But I tried to run away at the Halo Maze," he protested.

"And later you helped kill a demon," she retorted. "I'm not deeming you a modern day Achilles or anything of the sort, but I can't say I don't understand what other people see in you."

"Ok... so what do you see?"

Before she responded she smiled slyly and pushed up against him. "I'm not sure, maybe I need to take a closer look to give you an answer."

She laughed again and kept walking until the trail turned sharply to the right into a wall of trees that seemed impassable.

"We are here for the feast," Belladonna said.

"Hello, my child," the forest whispered. "You may enter."

"My thanks, Forest Mother."

The trees leaned to one side revealing a long slab of rock raised three feet to serve as a long table, which had many seats already occupied.

"THERE you are!!!" called out Daniel. "I was wondering where you had got to, but from the looks of it, you're up to the usual."

"My apologies, Master Montacre," said Belladonna. "It took me some time to find him. Quite the curious one to say the very least."

"Yes, yes, but let us all sit," Daniel said. "Lily has told us much but there are more of our hosts that you should meet."

The vampire then led them near the middle of the large table where Lucas and Liam sat with Lily and five other guests.

"Excuse me for leaving so suddenly," Daniel said. "This is Nathaniel. Nathaniel, this is Juniper, Fichus, Snare and Willow."

Nathaniel looked at each and realized who had more seniority just from how developed their facial features were. Fichus had a very long face with liquid green on green eyes and two long leaves on his upper lip, acting the part of a moustache, while small roots seeped from his chin, like a goatee. The more Nathaniel looked at him, the more he seemed like an herbaceous manifestation of Don Quixote. Juniper had warm rosy skin and short-cropped grass hair with tender features and a friendly smile. Snare looked a bit rougher and more plant-like with disheveled features, showing chipped pieces of bark and matted areas of leaves. He also had a square jaw and craggy wood bits for teeth. Willow had long strands of vines and flimsy mats of willow vines for hair. His exact features were mostly covered but his face was round and his body was a wide trunk with what seemed like a sad longing expression.

"A pleasure to meet all of you," said Nathaniel, before sitting on the ground next to Daniel, with Belladonna to his left. He had a calmness to him that all took note of since he carried himself as an equal rather than a mere human.

"So what do you think of Raelis, Master Runnels?" asked Willow from behind his vines.

"It's definitely a place that opens the mind and soul. One thing's pretty curious though."

"Just one thing?" asked Snare with his crooked smile.

Nathaniel returned the smile. "Granted, there is much to broaden a horizon extensively, especially one as limited as mine. But it's still interesting to see how your kind is in a way an expression of humanity."

"Ah that..." Lily said. "This is not our only physical expression but it is one of the more logical ones when it comes to communication. True, we might need aides for all of us to communicate, but having a face and body is a more effective way to cross language barriers. Face it, sometimes words aren't needed to say something."

"As for our natural expression, there is no one universal mode that is our base because even though we start very plant-like in our development and inception, we change because we mature and have the option. You have to understand that in essence it's always our decision to look one way or another. Although different from humans, in principle it is like getting a haircut, a tattoo, changing clothing styles, hair color or what have you. We are merely more flexible in regards to expression. Rest assured that among us there are purists who are always in plant form but at no point in time is there any animosity for however way any of us wishes to express ourselves.

Nathaniel tucked his chin as he listened to all Lily said, nodding occasionally. More photogeni arrived at the table while she continued to talk directly to Nathaniel. She spoke of plant expression, equality and all they'd learned from a variety of humans, from the monks on Lake Tana, to men and women who had come across the photogeni through some expedition gone wrong.

"You'd also be surprised at the amount of humans we receive in their passage to adulthood or people making the ultimate soul search. Luckily, most of you are receptive to our existence and only a few we've had to deal with in unpleasant ways."

"Unpleasant?" asked Nathaniel.

"Burying someone alive, leading them to lions, or otherwise aiding them in their search for an early demise is something that happens on occasion."

"I'm sure it does," interrupted a deep hollow voice.

Nathaniel looked to his left and dressed in regal green stood a tall looming figure, looking the part of a tree king. The long table was full now and Nathaniel could see a wide variety of photogeni accompanying them. He had been so immersed in his chat with Lily that he had failed to notice any of what was happening around him.

"Welcome friends, old and new. To those unfamiliar, a double welcome. I am Elm and will be your host for this feast. To my family, let us welcome our four guests. They bring much news and winds of change. We shall enjoy their company first and decide later how we shall face this wind. Will we stand, will we bend or will we fly? That is for us to decide later. For now, and if it pleases our guests, let us feast.

Elm rose from his chair and along with Banyan and two other large perennials, they stood behind the table in a small clearing. The four visitors took their cue and turned around so that each of them faced one of the perennials.

"Before you stands Elm," said the elder in front of Daniel.

"Before you stands Aster," said the perennial in front of Liam.

"Before you stands Pine," said the photogeni in front of Lucas.

"Before you stands Banyan," listened Nathaniel to the wooden man.

Elm spoke on their behalf. "We welcome you to Raelis, children of the night. You stand before us requesting the strength of our wood, the resilience of our roots and the vines that tie. You have come into our home and we trust in receiving the two most important gifts you can offer: your silence and your respect."

All four visitors nodded and stood in front of their respective perennial.

"We are a peace loving warrior nation. We fight for peace, for justice and for balance. On your behalf has spoken the West Wind and soon enough we shall hear your request. But first we must commune if we are to consider what it is you will ask of us. From all of your messiahs, your Christ shared his body figuratively. He broke bread with his brothers and though we have no bread to break, we also share, commune and offer ourselves to you."

After speaking those words, Elm took out a blade from beneath the leaf mat that covered his body. The other three perennials did the same.

Aster, the photogeni before Liam clenched his hand in a rough hard fist. "I give of the knuckle for war calls for a strong hand to deliver a just blow." He then took the sharp blade and sliced through part of his hand. At that moment a large solitary leaf fell from above. Aster took the leaf, placed the piece of bark on it and offered it to Liam. The vampire raised the leaf as if toasting to his assigned perennial. He ate the piece of bark and then gave a low bow to the photogeni.

The photogeni named Pine then stepped forwards. "I give of the smallest of fingers, for a human once taught me the value of a promise and how it should never be broken." The rugged plant man then took the knife and sliced on the side of his small finger to offer to Lucas who bowed just as Liam had done.

Banyan then looked deep within the eyes of Nathaniel, who had half a smile being thankful it was Banyan who he had drawn, even though he barely knew him. "I give of the finger print, to remind you to never forget who you are." The wooden man took the knife and with a light tap on his fingertip, showed just how sharp the knife was by filleting a piece of his thumb. Nathaniel nodded in respect while never breaking eye contact, even as he chewed and swallowed on the fleshy bark offered by the Perennial.

Elm stood tallest of all and gazed deep into Daniel's pale blue eyes. "I give of the back of my hand. For it is imperative to know oneself as well as one knows others." A quick slice and a ginger colored piece of wood lay in Daniel's hand, to which he gave thanks to the regal woodsman.

Nathaniel looked at the knife and its razor edge. Elm took notice and held it up to one of the beams of light descending from the forest rooftop.

"May I, Master Elm?" asked the human, signaling to the knife.

"Of course, my child."

Nathaniel took the blade and marveled at how flawless it was, how hard it felt and the perfect balance of its weight. "I give of my heart, for it is mine to give, yours to receive and ours to share."

Two quick flicks of the knife on the center of his palm later, a small heart made of skin lay next to the fresh wound on his hand. Banyan smiled as he took the offering and swallowed the human's flesh.

"You honor us, Master Runnels. Please sit at my side and let us begin the feast."

"My thanks, Master Elm; but just as well, you may join us instead for I am in my rightful place and deserve no special treatment. I hope you do not take offense."

"None at all, my friend," he said with a smile, "I'll be over soon enough, now let's feast."

As if on cue, three curtains of brush and undergrowth behind them shifted to reveal a row of large drums. Thick vines swung from the trees and beat on the drums to create an infectious melody. In essence, the forest itself had become instrument, musician and conductor.

Another large veil dropped and long stone trays came sliding from long leaves that gently eased them into place. Countless fruits and berries were put on display along with a variety of meats which slightly puzzled Nathaniel as he saw how delicious roasted meat was being heartily passed along and twice as heartily consumed by all photogeni.

Banyan looked at him from across the table and smiled in between mouthfuls. "What is it Nathaniel? Don't tell me you thought we were vegetarian."

At hearing this, laughter roared and boomed. Nathaniel joined in as yet again he was amazed by the illogicality of reality. Everyone laughed as they ate and a couple of stories of the photogeni bounced along including tales of a turbaned pirate, the descent of some men into the Heart of Darkness and of the travels of a man they referred to as the hunter of hunters. A man who collected the skulls of all the poachers he came in contact with.

Everyone was increasingly merry except one photogeni, a root it appeared to be, from his general constitution. A root who stared into nothing, as he ate nothing, said nothing and smiled at nothing. Occasionally though, he stole gazes towards Nathaniel that were anything but friendly.

Seeing this, Nathaniel leaned towards Banyan. "Who's the sour chap at the end?"

"That's Oleander. Never one to talk much unless it were something foul. He means well, he just worries too much. Why do you ask?"

"Nothing, just a strange feeling. But if it isn't too much trouble, something to drink would be greatly appreciated."

"Certainly," said Banyan.

Three long stems then came from the foliage behind Nathaniel. One was clear green, another was a reddish brown and the third was yellow. Banyan explained: "The clear green is rain water. The brown red stem contains a type of liqueur that tastes like cacao and the third is honey milk sap. Have as much as you want."

Everyone drank and ate to their content and though they didn't have blood wine, the photogeni had prepared a mixture of honey milk or the cacao liqueur with fresh blood for the vampires. Alligator blood for the cacao to give it more bite and antelope blood to further smoothen the honey milk sap.

Smiles spread all around as stories continued and everyone had their fill. After a long while Elm stood up again and gave his belly a hard pat before speaking. "I think we could use something light for dessert. So let there be light!"

After the tall woodman snapped his fingers, various things happened in sequence. First, large holes opened in the forest rooftop to let in several large pools of light. Then the plates were swept back into the forest and replaced by small cups and plates with a fruit the size of a golf ball on it. Lastly another veil of vines opened to let in a huge floating object that looked like a phosphorescent udder that stretched out various tentacles to fill the cups with a gold glowing liquid that shone right out of the glass. While some photogeni chose to stand in the large pools of light, Elm picked up a glass and stood as tall as his long body allowed him.

"Master Runnels, would you be so gracious as to give the toast?"

Nathaniel hesitated a moment until he stood and took the glass in his hand. There were a million things to say and now was not the time to say everything, but he did have something in mind. "To be honest, I do have much to say, but I would prefer that one of my companions gave the toast. I wouldn't be here without them."

"Very well; then let the eldest speak if I may have my way of choosing."

Nathaniel looked at Daniel and the vampire could have sworn he was looking at himself from the devilish smile Runnels gave him.

"Agreed..." said Daniel as his technicolor eyes flashed several shades. "Friends I have but one thing to say.... To WAR THEN PEACE!!!!!!"

All at the long table smiled and followed in suit.

"WAR AND PEACE!!!!" they all screamed and drank the liquid light and slammed the glasses on the table. Nathaniel felt as the warm liquid coursed through his body. After that, the photogeni took the fruits, slammed them against the table as well to crack the thick peel and ate what seemed like large seeds of glowing light.

"These are lumieres. The cordiale you just had is called nova and they are made of a special plant whose fruit and sap store light in its pulp and sacs."

Nathaniel looked at the glowing fruit in his hand and bit down to savor the delicious meat while looking at everyone else finish their fruit and drink. "Nothing like having everyone light headed to liven the party eh?" said Nathaniel to Banyan.

The old woodman laughed but quickly quieted down. "What were you going to say earlier at the table?"

A feeling of bliss had come over Nathaniel so completely that he couldn't remember what he was going to ask. "Sorry, Brother Banyan, seems it slipped my mind. Oh well, it couldn't have been that important."

Chapter 31: Looking for a tree-tea

Night had faded in the forest of Raelis. Fireflies bounced about and along with phosphorescent red flowers - Dragon Blooms, Banyan had called them - the forest kept quite alit after the frenzied euphoria of the feast had subsided. Nathaniel stood smelling the glowing blossoms and found himself walking with no direction.

"I almost expect hobbits to come out and do a showtune," he said to himself. The combination of the lumiere fruit and nova sap in his system not only filled him with enough energy to run a mile at full speed, but had also woken up something he thought had died, his own self before this madness.

"Vampires, angels, werewolves, demons and now plant people. PLANT people. I'm pretty sure a nice 'what the hell' is more than due. It's almost as if I've been sleepwalking for weeks."

He felt awake, alive and aware. He felt his old self stirring up from a long slumber. Maybe it was that the shock had finally subsided. It was a dream, he could try and tell himself but having perfect vision in a forest at night along with everything he tasted, smelled and felt reminded him that something was very different within him.

He let his hands fold behind his back as he walked through the forest, looking like some curious museum walker taking in the sights. His step was light but his considerations were heavy. He had killed, attacked, witnessed a slaughterhouse, slept with more women in the last few weeks than in the last five years, consorted with beings of another kind, hallucinated and was partially responsible for the cooperation between species in the preservation of an existence he had grown quite fond of disliking. Not bad for a hackneyed reporter working on the next great American Novel.

Leaves grazed his hands and triggered the gentle memories of the females he had conquered, or was it the other way around? He remembered his vampire lovers, especially Wendy and also the therian Luna, even though nothing had been consummated with the Fury.

He continued to walk down the forest path and briefly remembered Daniel insisting on his not 'going for a stroll'. That things were dangerous enough as it was, even in Raelis. Of course he had waved the vampire off telling him not to worry so damn much.

"Right enough," he had answered. "But some caution is never overdue."

He always seemed to say things like that but it didn't bother Nathaniel. He just thought it curious, though not as curious as the vampire's eyes. They could change to any color in the spectrum and beyond, but when he had warned him, instead of an electric blue, or that demonic jade, they had been brown. The most normal, most sincere color Nathaniel had ever seen in Daniel's eyes.

"He worries too much," he said out loud as he drank some more cacao liqueur before clasping the wooden mug behind his back again. His step stayed light but his balance was still there and pretty much everything made him smile. He didn't care that he was in a deep jungle in Ethiopia, which was clear from his lack of reaction to the boas that slithered next to him, the hand-sized spiders he stopped to take a good look at or the nod he gave in the direction of a low growl, whose deep yellow feline eyes and teeth shone with the dim glow of the fireflies.

Nothing fazed him or disrupted his good mood. Not even the bug eyes of a photogeni that looked more like an animated skeleton made of wood and leaves.

"Hello, Master Runnels," Oleander croaked.

"Ollie, ollie oxen free!!!!" Nathaniel screamed. "Good to see you, man!! What it issss??? What's happening? How's it going or how's it hanging? Or hey, you're kinda plant like, how's it growing?"

The wooden man groaned at the energetically drunk human. As he replied to him, he dissected Nathaniel with every word he spoke. "All is well, Master Runnels. Just out for a stroll on a quiet night, much as yourself. I trust you enjoyed the feast?"

"Hell yes!!!" replied Nathaniel with another swig of the tall jug that was already below half level. "Kick ass party you guys threw. I almost expected to see dryads and nyads and gonads and fofads... actually I expected to see anything that ends in ad, except Sinbad... we already have kickass pirates of our own."

"It's good to be able to treat our guests well. Would you care to partake in another one of our traditions?"

"As long as it doesn't have to do with vines crawling into crevices labeled one way only, I'm game. Whatcha got?"

"Have you ever had your fortune told, Master Runnels?"

"I once went to this psychic who had a third nipple, but I only went there for the show. I didn't pay much attention to the rest."

"Fascinating," droned Oleander, obviously not sharing the human's enthusiasm. "Well have you ever had your tea leaves read?"

"Not really," said Nathaniel with a drunken snort.

"Very well, for a reading you must take fresh leaves and put them in a stream."

"Ok, so where's the stream?"

"You're standing in it," said the photogeni in an irritated voice.

"Oh wow. No wonder I felt the urge to pee. Ok, then what?"

"Take the leaves in your hand and place them in the small stream."

Nathaniel went to a nearby tree, clutched some leaves and dropped them in the stream. "10-4. Roger Dodger. Now what?"

"We follow the leaves to where they may take us."

They followed as the leaves bounced along the flicker of a brook, following closely as the leaves twisted and turned with the ground beneath.

"Very interesting," Oleander said. "Though it is obvious by now, the leaves show you've had a rough journey."

At that moment, the leaves suddenly got caught with a pebble and created a small jam, which started damming up water.

"Shouldn't you push that?" asked Nathaniel as he took another drink from his mug.

"Of course not, Master Runnels. You must let the leaves take their own course. After all, you can't control fate."

As if on cue, the small trail veered to the side to create a new tiny stream where the leaves were able to follow.

"See?" said Oleander, "you might have been stuck but eventually another path opened and now you make your own way through your journey in life."

"Deep," Nathaniel said before unleashing a powerful belch.

"What is deep?" asked the photogeni, slightly repulsed by the human's lack of manners.

"It's an expression, veggie boy; a human expression. Don't worry about it."

Oleander obviously reacted to the human's belittling but his tone kept calm throughout. It was in his eyes you could see the anger, because although his countenance was stoic, his eyes were anything but silent.

For its part, the little stream instead of losing itself actually reattached to the original stream that had slightly dried up. Nathaniel noticed. "And what does that mean?"

"No matter how far you stray from the path, there is always a return that's inevitable. Would you like to go back to your path, Master Runnels?"

"Maybe," answered the human. "I don't think it really matters, though. From what you say, it's not like I really have a choice, do I?"

"Most precise observation, young master."

"Thanks," replied the young man downing what was left in his mug, "what's next?"

Oleander kept leading the way until they reached a series of hot springs. "Now we brew."

***

In another part of Raelis, a very different scene was unfolding. Elm, Banyan, and Daniel stood in an open clearing within the forest. They had been standing there for fifteen minutes in total silence. The only sound was the creaking of wood, the rustle of leaves tickled by a breeze and the occasional leaf that fell.

Though quiet and standing calmly next to the two plant men, it was painfully obvious that patience was a far removed virtue that one

Daniel of Montacre did not care to ever grasp or put into practice. He writhed cross-armed and clicked his fangs with his tongue until he spoke to them. "Might I be so inclined as to inquire how long we have to wait here for the audience?"

Both photogeni turned to look at him in a rather perplexed manner. Elm was the first one to speak. "Wait, Master Montacre? They have been discussing your situation ever since you arrived."

Banyan gave him a friendly smile. "From the human this wouldn't be a surprise, but from you? One would think you a bit more aware of such things, Montacre."

Daniel was torn between embarrassment and frustration. They had been talking about him all this time and he had been completely oblivious to that fact. He could have blamed it on the lumiere, but he knew better. He had to accept the fact that this alien world possessed a set of rules and laws that were completely foreign. He might have been able to speak all languages, because of the vial of saintly essence tied to his waist, which allowed him to speak all languages, but that didn't mean he could hear all that was said.

The photogeni looked ahead into the grove as the whispers of creaking trees and rustling leaves discussed outcomes and verdicts the vampire could not take a part in. He took the glowing vial in his hand, looked at it and decided that conversations concerning him could always use one more participant. So he uncorked the top of the vial and swallowed the glowing essence in one gulp.

Fire and ice dueled in his throat until his belly heaved and a loud thump rumbled forth from his chest. He felt every nerve in his body twitch, every pore gasp and every follicle surge with electricity. There was no pain but he felt his entire body expand and contract as crackles and slithers wisped in and out of his hearing. Rustles of leaves slowly morphed into distrusting whispers at first and then audible speech. His eyes flashed a calliope of colors and what had been outlines and curves with no tangible meaning, started to curl and curve, until he could see eyes among the foliage, lips on the bark of the trees and much more than just simple greenery. It was a full council discussing his case.

"... and how do we know these vampires are to be trusted?" said a giant face rustling among the leaves. "How do we know they won't suck the life out of the photogeni as well?"

The face seemed to Daniel like some conservative father, talking about teen kids and their rebellious nature. In other words, a dumb and dull face.

Daniel shivered before he spoke. "S...s... sim... simple," he was able to finally say, much to the surprise of all those present. "Be... cause... we're tr...trying... to sss.. sss... save the w...w...world."

"Explain yourself, vampire! How can you hear us? And see us? What's the meaning of this?!!" The once droll face was now overcome with emotion.

"Calm down, Robel," calmly spoke another tree trunk, "that glint in his eyes can only come from someone who has taken the spirit within."

"HERESY!" roared the first tree. "He must be killed!"

"Heresy?" asked the second tree almost chuckling. "My dear Robel, if heretics, blasphemers, naysayers and mutations were to be eliminated from this Earth, you'd be half tea tree, half furniture by now."

The whirlwind of vines and leaves settled down and the second large trunk spoke again, this time directly to Daniel. "That is quite brave of you, Master Montacre. I am Roanoak. The livid one behind me is Robel, and along with us, we have Fern to your immediate left, Cedar to my right and Hibiscus up above."

With some effort, Daniel remained as calm as possible as all the figures began to take more and more anthropomorphic shape until five titanic giants stood, sat or laid around him. The vampire's eyes filled with tears and his eyes became coated with a phosphorescent glaze. The more solid the glowing glaze became, the more he could see the elder titans.

"Welcome, Daniel of Montacre. We are the Yggdrasil and where once you were blind, now you can see."

While those words sank into Daniel, only one flowed from his mouth, "Nathaniel."

***

Back at the hot springs, Oleander leaned over the drunk human. "Interesting, Master Runnels; the trek your leaves have taken have soaked them with some sediments and water. Now you will brew the flavor out of these leaves and taste your future."

Nathaniel merely tilted to the side with gargled eyes that had a hard time focusing on anything.

"Still with me?" asked the photogeni.

"Yes..." replied Nathaniel, "just a bit tipsy is all."

"Excellent. The tea will be good for you then. Help to wake you up a bit?"

"I guess."

"Lovely," Oleander sneered. "First you take your leaves and put them in your mug. Then we walk over to the hot springs, take some water and look for a steam chute."

"What's a steam chute?" asked Nathaniel.

Right then, a large blast of steam shot out from what looked like a broken branch sticking out from the ground.

"Let me guess... that's a steam chute."

The photogeni rolled his moss green eyes and held the mug over the steam chute with his right hand. "Three bursts should be enough."

The fireflies all around them had been buzzing gaily, but little by little they began to migrate away. Some even fell dead on the floor. The wood man's face changed considerably from one of focus to one of concern. "Do you smell that?"

"I can't smell much of anything, except that tea brewing," Nathaniel said, fighting to stay awake.

As it kept getting darker, Oleander's mossy eyes looked around but couldn't find the reason for the light to be dimming that way. A large thunk half woke Nathaniel from his stupor.

"What was that?"

"Nothing..." rasped Oleander.

"Why's it so dark?" asked Nathaniel.

"Strange happenings occur all the time in Raelis, Master Runnels." Oleander's voice had a razor edge to it Nathaniel had not noticed before.

Through hazy eyes that couldn't focus much, he noticed the change. "You OK? You don't sound so good."

"I... am... fine," replied the plant man. "I might also need some tea for my throat."

"Knock yourself out buddy... anything you.... Whoah!!!! What's all that gooey stuff at my feet?"

"Probably a sapling we've stepped on. Pay no mind. One sugar or two."

"I dunno... just make sure it's sweet."

"As you wish..."

By now, Nathaniel couldn't see much but he heard three drops before a bitter fizz wafted into the air. "Damn Ollie, you sure that tea is ok?"

"I'm having some myself," rasped the voice.

Nathaniel took his mug and sipped at the bitter tea. It warmed him a lot and he had another sip. The darkness in his eyes warbled slightly.

"Damn liquor," he said as he took a third sip from the cup.

He was still light headed but felt a bit off and not drunk, it was an odd feeling and not necessarily a pleasant one. His skin tingled, his nostrils flared and his eyes finally focused enough to see a shadow moving away from him while a single thought tumbled from his mouth.

"Ollie... why does it smell like blood?"

Chapter 32: The Third Vision

A line of jade fire burned through Raelis as Daniel raced through the forest. The green had an odd hue to it from the shell over the vampire's eyes. He ran almost tearing through the sound barrier from what he'd seen on the reflection of a single leaf that had fallen in front of him and the Yggdrasil. A figure stretched on the floor draped over earth stained with black blood.

Daniel had smelled the blood that Nathaniel had breathed minutes ago. He stormed through the forest with his enameled eyes looking for signs of the human. He breathed deeply even in full sprint but only found earth, river, water and plants in his sense of smell. No blood and no Nathaniel.

He stopped mid-stride and tried to look for signs. He wafted in every direction and even knelt down to taste the earth, but nothing. Not a single hint. His lower lip bled from his desperate teeth trying to grit an answer out of nothing at all.

His fist slammed hard against the dirt in frustration. "Somebody help me... please," he whispered on the verge of crying and out of desperation... not because he thought he could get a reaction.

The vines and flowers around him slowly twisted a few feet from Daniel. He looked on as the shape of a child condensed from the loose vegetation.

"Leave me, child," he said. "Hope is lost and I'm in no mood to make conversation."

"I just wanted to say one thing, sir," the little plant girl said.

He looked at her dismissively. "Speak then."

"When all seems hopeless, you sometimes need to give up. Only then can you listen to your heart."

"Is that all?" he asked, still annoyed by her presence.

"No... your real heart isn't inside of you. It beats all around and lives deep beneath the Earth."

The bleak horizon that had been Daniel's face suddenly dawned with realization. He wanted to ask who she was and exactly what she meant but he didn't need answers to what he knew deep within. He nodded in appreciation, lay on the floor and put his ear to the ground.

There it was.... faint, but it was there. A low drumbeat, the soul's hum, a pulse that was far away yet clearly to his right. A light fuzzy moss covered the ground and he held his hand over it, making small bristles stand on end. For a moment, they stood still until slowly they leaned to the same direction from which he heard the heart beating. He wasted no more time and sprang forth dashing at full speed into the brush.

***

Swirling deep purple clouds muddled Nathaniel's eyesight. He was kneeling in a pool of photogeni blood next to a body whose chest had been torn wide open. Oleander's eyes slowly grew brittle and dry and his body position and facial expression showed he hadn't had enough time to realize he had just been killed. Beads that lined his body were on the floor, bone white pellets that contained some sort of sap.

Nathaniel knelt there, catatonic, looking forward with his eyes dilated and static, like those of a blind man. His side was stained with bloodied mud and he'd risen only seconds ago. "Where am I? I can't find myself."

He breathed broken splinters of breaths as his lungs burned and pain ripped through his body. The mug he'd drunk from lay beside him, still having some tea in it and various pellets like those along Oleander's body. His vision mumbled images to him. Of the subway, the Halo Maze, the Black Calico, Spain, France, Crete, Alexandria... everything. Everything flew into his vision.

Meanwhile, a small orange dot began to shine in the middle of what he was seeing and he heard someone whisper. "Look here."

Words and vision bounced off each other illogically and he thought he was going to die. A familiar thought maybe, but unlike other occasions, this time he knew he was going to die. Visions of Wendy, Captain Jane, Daniel, Liam and all the others melted into one another and noises crashed and whistled, then whispered in the wind. Sounds of sex, of laughter and of death spun on the same track and still Nathaniel's eyes remained utterly blind.

The orange dot shone brighter.

"Look here," insisted the murmur.

Flashes of Maestranza cascaded over the crashing seas of the Atlantic over the shadows of the Cross in the Valley of the Fallen and the massacre of the Lygophilials. Nothing made sense to Nathaniel except the burning pain ripping from within. He thought his soul would burst through his ribcage and scream victory while biting into his heart.

The orange light became even brighter.

"Look here," repeated the voice a third time. It was now stern and low, also a little less patient.

Now Nathaniel saw his mother and father, he saw the subway route he took every day to a job that drained his soul since he kept it to not be a loser, yet felt like the biggest one for settling. Memories of lemon cake collided with those of a small blonde cocker spaniel that had once been his best friend. Tinkling images of him having supper with his grandparents and lost summers where he did nothing and everything, an image that was quickly replaced by vampires.

The orange light began to pulse like some living beacon or a luminescent heart. Higher still rang the voice, "Look here."

Nathaniel found himself having to think about breathing because it hurt so much that he had to force his body to perform the most basic of life functions. His heart raked against his ribcage and tears fell from his blind eyes. He wanted to scream but his body denied him even the slightest whimper. His burning lungs didn't care about what their host wanted to say. Nathaniel curled up in pain, wishing he could die, wishing he could kill or maybe just wishing he could live. The poison tore relentlessly into his body, but he kept looking to the orange light that was now a veritable firefly dancing barely ten feet away.

"Look here," repeated the voice.

Nathaniel struggled to get enough air to speak a sentence. "W... what.... What difference... make?"

"It makes all the difference," was the reply.

Nathaniel drew in a painful breath and began clutching his way to the light. Every fiber in his body strained as he clawed through the blood soaked ground. Flashes buzzed in his head like micro migraines, hotwiring his retinas as sounds melded with sight and taste, creating a sensory maelstrom.

A curdling cough made Nathaniel quiver on the floor. As he looked at the cluster of fire grapes hanging near his head, he spat out a wad of the thick black blood that flooded his lungs. He dug his hands into the earth and pulled within arm's reach of the orange light. It looked so familiar to him but it wasn't until a cloud of smoke puffed from the light that he realized what it was. "Bi... Bill?"

"Look here buddy, I never thought any cigarette-o-mine would serve as a beacon. Normally it's what gives me away when I'm trying to run over some dumbass at night, with my car lights off."

"Wh... whu... whuu..."

"Whu, whu, whu what the hell am I doing here?" Bill said with the highest dosage of cynicism possible. "Buddy, this is the greatest day of your life. It's the final one and all because like a jack ass, you decided to get hammered with something you don't even understand. For a second I thought Oleander was the one that was going to kill you, though by the looks of it, that is kind of true."

Nathaniel groaned as he clutched at his side before spitting out more black blood. Bill looked down on Nathaniel, both literally and figuratively. The cigarette end lit again as he took a long drag, which he actually and accurately blew right into Nathaniel's face.

"How does it feel to be dying in vain? To know that you could have saved the world but instead you got drunk with some mysterious liquid without even knowing or asking what the hell is in it. It's like going to Mexico to drink from the tap and expecting everything to be fine."

The human responded by crying into the ground. His mouth stained with blood and his eyes turned a yellowish green. His breathing became extremely faint and weak, and quite suddenly it stopped. Bill sucked on his cigarette and found it had lost the cherry at the end and had extinguished.

"Wait a minute. Wait – a – minute," Bill said while looking down on Nathaniel's now lifeless body. "You think you're just going to die now? Now that's funny."

Bill then opened his black over shirt and pulled out a black box with red sigils on it. He took out a long cigarette, knelt next to the dead body of Nathaniel and tapped his face on the forehead.

"Psssst.... McFly... it's not your time to die."

He then took out a copper lighter with other sigils on it and lit his cigarette with one smooth fluid motion. He sucked on the tobacco hard and the cherry at the end burst into flames.

Nathaniel's body then lifted at the midsection and arched in the air as if some invisible giant had just picked him up. Bill simply looked on as he continued to suck on his cigarette. He took in a mighty drag, expiring a fifth of the cigarette before pulling it away from his lips.

Nathaniel's body fell back to the ground and still lay motionless. Bill then took his right fist and began to pound hard on his chest until he did a wretched hacking sound as if a thousand rakes had just scraped through gravel. He then hawked a tar like glob the size of a grapefruit. He wiped his mouth and walked to the dead body of Nathaniel, which was still lifeless but no longer looked green and gray.

"Funny thing," said Bill while holding his cigarette, "they always say these things will kill you... ha ha... ha ha ha.... Hahahahahahahahahah."

Bill then knelt down to Nathaniel's ears and said some words in an unknown language, while a low roar stirred deep in his chest. He took a deep breath and when he exhaled, all the cigarette smoke he'd breathed in now came swirling out and seeped up Nathaniel's nose.

Another hit of the cigarette and Bill nodded in approval to one minor change in Nathaniel's body... the rising and falling of his chest.

"Guess secondhand smoke isn't always bad for you, huh."

Chapter 33: Red tide for a red sea

A record player's hiss slowly fades into radio static. Word bleeps chirp for nanoseconds leaving their meaning to the wind.

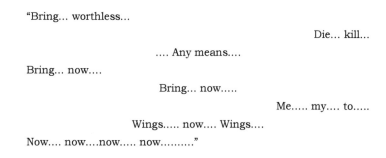

"Bring... worthless...

Die... kill...

.... Any means....

Bring... now....

Bring... now.....

Me..... my.... to.....

Wings..... now.... Wings....

Now.... now....now..... now.........."

Nathaniel was barely breathing less than five yards from Oleander's body when Daniel found him. His shirt had burn marks on it, black blood stains on the fabric had become rancid and he was muttering incoherent words and phrases. While tossing and turning, he'd broken into four different fevers.

The first one had been normal. High temperatures, sweating, and from his grimaces, one could assume the presence of genuine pain. Eventually it subsided but during the second fever he burned up even more fiercely. Unlike the first fever however, this one did not break and he didn't sweat. This meant the fever continued to rise to dangerous levels, which the photogeni tried to help by wrapping his body in large wet leaves and packing cool mud over his body, but the leaves dried and wilted to dust in minutes and the mud baked and cracked over the human's scorching skin. Finally, when they had almost lost all hope, the fever broke and torrents of sweat poured from his body. But before anyone could celebrate, he rode into the third fever, this one dropping his body temperature to hypothermic levels. Now those assembled around him scrambled to throw buckets of hot spring water over him but the steam would quickly fade and tiny icicles even formed around his face and over his skin.

Somehow he was able to pass that fever but everyone realized it had been a preamble to the last one. It had been the worst by far. His heartbeat switched from a hummingbird's flutter to a loud drumming and later to a faint whisper. At one moment, it had seemed that it had even stopped beating for a few seconds. It seemed as though he was all but lost when thick tears of white sap streamed from his eyes.

However his breathing was still jagged and his fingers curled and uncurled on themselves as if his hands were breathing. Visions of green gold sunsets and purple waves framed within his mind's eye while whispering vines kissed him, their perfume and leaves rustling loving secrets he could not understand. It started to feel as if long swirling leaves took him in a deep embrace and he floated in a strange vulnerability that only the most tried love could inspire. He felt his lungs get drunk of sex and passion as sweet blossoms caressed his face and lips. He kissed first tenderly and later with unbridled desire and passion. He felt thousands of lustful flavors running through his mouth and he drank hungrily.

He felt a maternal tenderness brush upon his lips and like a newborn reacting out of instinct, he kissed and sucked. A smile of relief and satisfaction came upon him as he lost himself in the sheer bliss that soared through his body until he released and breathed the sweetest air his lungs had ever known.

Moments ebbed by until his breathing settled and his eyes finally came to. He woke and saw he was sleeping in a bed fashioned of leaves and coiled vines. Pressing on the cushion, he had to admit that it was quite a comfortable bed. He looked to his right and saw an opening where light seeped in as he tried to focus his eyes.

"Welcome back... or is this another false alarm?" said the very tired voice of one very tired vampire. "You see, the problem with being a sunrider is that there are no imposed rest periods and though I'm not much of a sleeper, I do rest; something that's been a tad impossible since we found you lying on the floor."

"Sorry, mommy; I didn't mean to be bad," said Nathaniel jokingly.

"You almost meant to die, you ass," replied Daniel.

Nathaniel suddenly tasted something sticky and sweet on his lips, a rather strong and sweet flavor. The vampire noticed the confused look on his face and went to sit beside him. "Runnels, you don't cease to amaze me."

"I've heard. So what now, oh fearless leader?"

"I have to admire your nerve. You were poisoned with enough oleander to kill a small village, yet roach-like, you persist. For now though, the tragedy of others has been our blessing and the manner of Oleander's passing helped the Yggdrasil to side with our cause. It was bad enough they killed one of their own, that it happened within Raelis? Well let's say we're going to have quite a decent cavalry."

Nathaniel sat up and looked at the vampire. "You haven't answered me. Now what?"

"Now we go to barren lands to find an oasis where an old drowsy friend waits for a wakeup call."

"And how exactly do we get back to the Calico?" asked Nathaniel.

The familiar smile that so often had worried the human appeared again. The vampire's fangs seemed to shine that much brighter and Nathaniel felt that odd pang in his stomach that told him he didn't necessarily like what he was going to hear.

***

After a few minutes, they walked out to a clearing outside the hut to meet with Banyan and Elm and though in a somber mood, they greeted both visitors warmly.

"I trust you feel better, Master Runnels," Banyan said.

"Yes. Sorry for giving you all such a scare."

"I actually think it could have been worse," Elm said. "There might have been more photogeni around when whatever found you did. Tragic though the loss of one of our own may be, it seems your shortcomings actually helped lessen the blow. At least Oleander didn't seem to suffer much. But the assassin was ruthless and precise. More importantly, he has tainted the earth of Raelis with our blood prematurely. The sleepers described him as large, dark, with grotesque claws and a face that was not his own."

"Sleepers?" asked Nathaniel.

"Photogeni who have chosen dormant forms of expression, meaning that they choose to be more tree-like and less anthropomorphic than some of us. Is that clear enough, human?"

Daniel's face scowled. "Any reason for the animosity, Elm?"

"Quite," said the large photogeni, "without your visit, we might have been spared this strife. Be it as it is though, our paths shall run parallel for the sake of this Earth."

"Listen here..." began Daniel, but Nathaniel put a hand on the vampire's shoulder interrupting him.

"We give thanks to you for your help, brother Elm. We are also saddened to have brought forth this burden but we wouldn't have come if we didn't know what we do, including the dangers that we all face. Be it as it is, we're grateful for all the help we may find."

Elm replied with a low dignified bow and left the clearing to melt into the deep brush, leaving Banyan with them. "Pardon his brashness," said the perennial, "it's just that though we may thrive on war, there are some of us who would rather just live in peace."

Nathaniel could easily identify with that feeling.

"Please, come with me. It is time to take you back to your ship."

They walked to a thick wall of leaves that slid to the side to reveal twelve square holes about a foot deep each. In front of the holes there was a thin mud pool. From a side bush came four photogeni women, which Banyan presented. "As a reminder, these are Lily, Juniper, Begonia and Belladonna. They will assist you with the exit ritual of Raelis."

All four plant women curtseyed to Liam, Lucas, Daniel and Nathaniel, though Belladonna smiled a little wider and looked at the human with a little more focus than the others. Without speaking a word, all four stood in front of the holes while a photogeni woman took some red mud and began covering their bodies in it. Quite suddenly, two scents bashed into Nathaniel's sense of smell. One was the mixture of rich earth and sandalwood and spices he had become very familiar with.

"Egnalem?" he asked and Belladonna's eyes answered the question... or was it something else.

Her hands felt like loving silk covering his body. Clearly he was enjoying the sensations but suddenly he remembered the sappy delicious flavor in his mouth that morning. After Belladonna was done, she stood up and took a step back to show a damp spot on her hearth shirt, over her left breast.

Daniel had to cackle. "Hell of a night, eh Runnels?"

Banyan remained focused on the task at hand. "Now lay down in a hole."

They obeyed but nothing happened. Nothing unusual about that, thought Nathaniel. This sort of thing usually takes some time and some effort. As the thought coursed through their minds, they began to sink down into the earth. Belladonna didn't let go of Nathaniel's gaze until the quicksand had swallowed him whole.

***

Captain Jane was a vampire. She had lived for centuries but if something had always been a chore, it was to stay calm and be patient... especially when it came to Daniel. The relief she felt once she saw an ocean bubble rupture into muddy water was indescribable, but nothing compared to the sheer joy that coursed through her every fiber when her eyes met those of the one she'd been longing for ever since she'd arrived on the Red Sea.

Chapter 34: Desert on the water

Sailing through the Red Sea, the Black Calico floated quietly with Eritrea to one side and Yemen to the other. Nathaniel took turns looking at each horizon, giving little or no thought to the varying differences between one continent and the other. His mind was concerned with Oleander's tealeaves and how they were supposed to be a mirror of his path in life. He wondered if he would be lucky enough to return to his original path or if it would pool into a dead end?

Death... how funny the way in which that concept had changed in a few weeks' time. How elusive and far away it had seemed once. Now it was like some would-be lover that constantly teased him.

How many deaths had he escaped? How often would disaster suck on his fingers only to wave him off with a slap on the wrist? He'd been very quiet once back on the boat. Jane had embraced Daniel even while he was completely drenched from where Raelis had brought them out to sea. Wendy had been extremely happy to see Nathaniel, but something in him had been lost even after being born again.

The heavy smell of smoke still tickled the back of his throat and a question scratched at his brain. Had he died? If so, what had brought him back? They say you are able to look down on your body immediately after you pass away, but he hadn't seen or felt anything like that. He'd felt a warm darkness wrap his entire body and he had even thought about the irony of feeling truly safe only when he was dead. The rest was just a blur.

The region of Obock came into view as the beautiful galleon turned west in the dark turquoise waters of the Gulf of Aden. Normal timeframes and distances were immaterial to the Black Calico and its captain rode every wave and made speed ten times faster than any normal ship.

The seas knelt in front of the mighty galleon but after some days, something had become increasingly clear to everyone on board. If any one thing gets magnified in the vast space of the ocean, that would have to be silence. The Gulf of Tadjoura was alarmingly quiet. No gulls, no wisps of wind, no rain, only the occasional splash of water against the hull.

Everyone onboard felt the silence slowly gnawing at their insides. They'd give anything for some other noise. To the north they passed Tadjoura and south of them was Djibouti. Both were a long way in the distance, only slithers of land on the horizons.

On went the Black Calico making its way to the heart of Arta in its Ghoubet Kharab, a large closed bay which they were navigating straight through the middle of when a small sand bank came into view. It couldn't be fifty yards across but there it was, illogically standing in the middle of the Ghoubet Kharab. No trees, no bushes, no rocks. Just baked sand that looked blisteringly hot and dismally solitary.

"We go around the bank!" called Jane. She had been told they needed to throw anchor to walk to Yokoki deep in the region of Dikhil. Ghoubet Kharab, Obock, Okoki, Tadjoura, Arta, Djibouti. All these names meant nothing to Nathaniel and as he looked onto the sand platform, he couldn't help but feel completely divorced from the world. How many places had he been to that he didn't have the faintest idea that they even existed? He always said he wanted to travel but he never thought why he wanted to do so. He thought about this and the life he had died away from in a few weeks' time and suddenly he just wanted to stand on that sand platform.

"I'm going there," he said out loud. Before Daniel could ask what for, Nathaniel had jumped and was swimming to the odd island.

Daniel screamed after him that what he was doing was madness and to come back but a stubborn mind when decided is as solid as iron and completely deaf. Nathaniel didn't care if there were sharks, or some unknown beast beneath the water, he just swam as hard as he could to the small bare island.

In the distance, the large galleon finally turned around when Nathaniel reached the sandy shore. Instead of the water getting slowly shallower it stayed oddly deep until he reached the sand and climbed onto the ledge as if he were getting out of a pool. The sand burnt his arms but he ignored the pain and walked to the center of the solid platform.

Once in the very center of the island, he looked up to the sky. He thought of his long journey, of what he had lived and suddenly emotions started piling up inside him. Anger, lust, sadness, frustration, confusion, joy, inspiration, confidence and fear all swooshed inside of him and he almost buckled from the emotional overload. It was literally as if he were being draped with several hundred pounds of weight, but he did not fall or kneel. Grief and ecstasy joined into the emotions, next to pride, humility and desperation. His eyes trembled, his lips quivered but he would not bend or yield to what he was feeling.

His eyes filled with tears, but he knew he wanted to be there, for some reason he had to be there. Disappointment, satisfaction, charity and clarity joined the other emotions, but Nathaniel would not bend his will or his knees. He didn't know why he was on that platform or why he was feeling all of this at the same time, but he knew he wanted to be there. Desire joined the lot making the burden that much more difficult to bear while despair and devotion followed closely behind.

Emotions and feelings clashed in his head and heart as the world's burden seemed to pile within him. His body trembled but his will remained committed. He thought of how he hadn't even knelt at church since he was a child and he wasn't about to do so now. His jaw clenched and his arms spread out with his palms up in what would be a pleading stance... or was it his way of holding himself up.

More and more feelings and emotions curdled within him as the weight began to literally sink him into the sand. Yet all the strain and pain within served only to push him as he whispered in pain: "I will not yield."

As if reacting to his defiance, the sun beat down on him having long dried his clothes only to drench him with his own sweat. Nathaniel felt the heat bristle his skin but he would not yield. It just wasn't in him. His brain thumped, his heart burned and for the first time in his life, he actually felt his soul. It was an inexplicable wave of condensed energy, pulsing, irradiating and coursing throughout his body. His eyes were glass and his mouth was dry, painfully dry. But through all this heat, he felt a soft breeze blow from the west, before he felt the last emotion that had not fallen upon him.

"Hope," he said faintly.

That's when sand and stone broke beneath him. As he tumbled down into darkness, he found himself clinging to the strongest of all emotions that had been the last to fall on him.

Chapter 35: The space between

How many feet had Nathaniel fallen? That's not an answer he could give if his life depended on it. He only knew he had fallen hard, crashing through wood beams and several levels of thin floors until slamming against a grimy platform. The fall hurt but it did not kill him, it hadn't even injured him seriously. It had been a numb thud that took his breath away but he was able to get to his feet and shake off the dust and sand that had fallen with him. He looked around and everything was bathed in rusty gray and reeked of old stale air. Apart from the thousands of pounds of dust covering everything, small wilted trees draped in dust stood beside broken statues and spots of light floated along what Nathaniel saw was a long hall.

There was so much soot floating around that it almost seemed to Nathaniel as if he were standing at the bottom of a murky pool of water. The particles actually seemed to be trying to cling to him but he kept swatting them off while walking around and surveying the area.

However, light in the hall was beyond his understanding. There were floating patches of light ten to fifteen feet across, mingling with dust and darkness. Nathaniel decided to follow one of the patches of light and saw the difference between things that were lit from afar and those that were bathed in the light.

Being lit at a distance was much like any light source and Nathaniel was able to clearly see the wilted rubble of a mess in the hall. It was completely different when anything was bathed in the patches of light. One moment there stood a wilted plum tree but once under the light, the tree sprouted lush green leaves with the juiciest fruit ever to be borne from a plum tree. It was magnificent... until the patch of light passed on. When that happened, every bit of vivid beauty that had blossomed in the tree seemed to be sucked right out of it, until only a shrill husk was all that remained.

Every time the paths of light passed by the broken statues, they shone in perfect ivory beauty as limbs reshaped and reattached for the briefest of moments. Even the dust seemed repelled by the floating light amoebas.

It was a long rectangular hall and it might have even been a church if not for the statues and trees. Mosaics stood dark and indistinct until light shone from behind whatever stood behind these walls. On the mosaics, images of angels battling or flying shifted within the glass. When lit, the figures would move of their own accord but when the light shifted away, the mosaic would crumble, losing glass shards and rusting instantly.

Noises suddenly hissed from the dark corners like some huge scarab scurrying in the shadows. Not even with his keen eyesight could Nathaniel penetrate the gloom that permeated throughout the hall. As he walked, every step lifted the damned dust which clung to his clothes and skin like cold static.

Ahead in the hall, the space cleared of rubbled statues and dead dry trees. There a massive figure sat hunched over covered in a mantel of dust in front of a huge pillar that stretched beyond where light could reach to a ceiling Nathaniel couldn't even see. Close by the figure, a huge sword lay on the ground, which seemed as if it hadn't been moved in centuries. Beside it there was a rusted shield that had a heavy crust of dust atop it.

Both items were about fifteen feet behind the crouched figure. When the clouds of light floated nearby, the blade gleamed as if it was made of fire and light and the shield shimmered with an inscription which Nathaniel read aloud. "Quis ut deus."

He now walked beside the ruined statue and saw that the clouds of light shied away from it, leaving only a faint light to see the whole shape. Frozen in a kneeling position, the statue captured the true meaning of hopelessness. Its broad shoulders bore no pride and great grief came to Nathaniel as he saw that one side of the statue's face had deep trails dug into its cheek coming from the eye. Although the other half was completely untouched, the damaged side was a mess of crumbled stone; a beauty long forgotten.

The scratching in the dark corners continued, but now fluttering wings joined the sonic tussle. He could have asked himself what was making all that noise, but he knew better than that. If he wanted answers, he would have to find them out for himself.

Clicks and scratches sounded and Nathaniel's hawk eyes followed every single trace of movement. First one side of the hall, then another until he saw a dark figure in one corner. In a flash, he leapt with all his might but was only able to clutch at a dust ridden corner. He heard as more wings flapped and more scarab legs pinched the hall floor. It took several attempts before Nathaniel accepted that he couldn't catch whatever was making that noise.

While the shapes buzzed back and forth, he decided to just sit and sulk, covered in dust and drenched in frustration. One of the light clouds came thirty feet from him and he saw how the bubble of light floated idly by as the fluttering in the shadows continued. He was about to wonder what would happen if one of those things passed near the light when much to his surprise, it did.

Two flying shadows had collided. One fell into the shadows while another crashed straight into a pool of light. Nathaniel heard a small thud and something he really didn't expect to hear in such a place... the gurgled cries of a baby. The sound took Nathaniel by surprise and with some effort he stood up, swatted off the patches of dust that had latched onto his clothes and walked behind a statue where infant cries seemed to be coming from.

His eyes were seeing but he wasn't believing. There, bathed in light and on the pristine floor lay a baby, not six months old, just laying there. The baby made little noises while peering deep into Nathaniel's eyes sharing with him a look of mature loneliness quite impossible for an infant that young. Nathaniel was going to pick him up when the baby went silent.

As the light got farther away, the rosy skin of the baby slowly turned gray. Its eyes were still lonely but they now became inhumanly cold. The infant rolled onto his belly and started making a wretched sound as if it were choking on something. Before Nathaniel could even begin to decipher how to react, the toddler's back split wide open and from the gash spread two leathery wings that quickly whooshed him away.

"The unbaptized may not ascend," said a voice as cold as the chill that had crept through every pore of Nathaniel's body. Behind him stood the nine-foot statue. Even by the dim light, Nathaniel could see the torn face, half of it bathed in grief, and the other half eroded for the same reason.

"You smell of the Mother Father," said the stone hulk as he breathed deeply. "You also smell of brother Gabriel, of the universal essence, of Mother Time and of my bannock which she baked for you. I am the second in line, the slayer of demons, the Viceroy of Heaven, and my name is Mikael. State your business and await judgment."

With every word spoken by the figure, more of its stone face crumbled. He had not picked up his sword or shield, but it really didn't seem as if he needed anything more than his bare hands to pass judgment on Nathaniel.

"My name does not matter, but it is Nathaniel. My purpose however, that does matter very much. It is to plead for aid. The world is at risk and all world kind alike. I'd say I come in peace, but I'd be lying. I come for war because we have been left no other choice."

"No.... other.... choice," sputtered the angel statue as more of his face fell to dust with every word spoken. "How many times has man verbalized such words? This is not the first time I have been prayed to for goodwill in battle and sometimes the one who asks genuinely deserves my aid, thus receives it."

"Then what must I offer to receive said aid, brother Michael?"

The angel statue looked at Nathaniel with his clear eye. He didn't say a word, but if ever Nathaniel had wondered what it looks like if a statue held back tears, he was being given a firsthand lesson.

"This is my place, my home," said the grief stricken angel. "I deserve to be here."

"But this is..."

"Purgatory," finished the angel. "I am sorry but I cannot help you."

"But why?" asked the human.

"Because the Mother Father has not spoken to me in over a thousand years. Maybe longer. So I wait here for the Day of Judgment, at least then I'll be able to say hello... or will it be goodbye?"

The lumbering figure then turned slowly and began walking back towards the large pillar. His feet scraped the floor and his shoulders sank, drained of energy and stripped of pride. Nathaniel followed him as he walked past his shield, long covered in a mantle of dust, past his sword, long sheathed, back to where the human had first found him. Scratching sounds from every dark corner told Michael that the lost children waited for him. He sank down to the floor and a dozen of them ran to meet him.

Caterpillars and scarabs, spiders and flies, butterflies and large worms all with the pleading faces of lost children came to him... the wanted but lost. They fell on Michael, caressed his cold arms and gave him the love he longed for. The large angel once again addressed the human without looking at him directly. "These are my children now. I cannot leave them."

Nathaniel looked at the grey eyes of the children seeking shelter within their adopted father's arms.

"I see," Nathaniel said. "Then let that be your reason to stay brother, because like you said, we all have a choice. My apologies for the disruption but before I leave, let me share three things with you."

"Proceed," said Michael while caressing a spider child.

"First, Gabriel sends this."

Nathaniel took a deep breath and exhaled slowly, releasing a warm wind that seemed to flow from his entire body to fill the entire hall. It smelled of fresh cinnamon, rich earth and sandalwood. The tired angel and his children smelled the rich aroma and smiled softly at the tender caress of the gentle wind.

"Second, you were right about your bannock. Well to a certain point."

Nathaniel then took out a piece of lemon cake he had wrapped in linen. Somehow it had not been affected by the time that had passed from his stay in the Fin du Monde Inn or his recent swim to the island in the waters of the Ghoubet Kharab. He gave the cake to Michael causing the angel to give another half smile from his broken face.

"Mother always made the best cake," he said as he began breaking off pieces to give to the children. "And last?"

Nathaniel replied by walking among the children who had kept coming from the shadows until a small ocean of kneeling sons and daughters of purgatory surrounded the angel. He put his arm on the large stone shoulder and looked Michael straight in his good eye. "No one ever stopped loving you."

He then leaned down and kissed the angel's head while a human tear fell from his eye onto the angel's crown. He stood back and looked at Michael, knowing no more words were needed. He just gave a gentle smile and began to walk towards the back of the hall.

His eyes watered and in his mind, he held the prospect of nearing battle and the hopeless cause that was awaiting him up above. He walked past the angel's shield and his sword, past the trees and past the statues. He was crying so much he didn't notice the ripening plum in a tree he was passing even though there was no ball of light nearby. He also didn't notice the ivory statues glowing ever brighter and much less the burning sword which had been freed from its sheathe or the beautiful shield that proudly shone its inscription. He only heard the low gong of a bronze pillar that had been struck and the fluttering of a thousand wings.

Chapter 36: Arabian night in the Arabian Sea

Dusk settled itself on the Ghoubet Karab. It had been hours since Nathaniel had disappeared on the square island not fifty yards from where the Black Calico had laid anchor. Daniel had dived into the water to follow Nathaniel onto the island, but when he got to where the square of sand was supposed to be, he found only water no matter how much he searched, nothing changed the fact that the island had disappeared.

They had dropped anchor or at least tried to. Two hundred feet of rope had not been enough to touch bottom. Those from the crew who could be in the sunlight, were at a loss for words, and Captain Jane could not talk sense to Daniel. She told him that without being anchored down, they couldn't be sure they'd stay in the same place. He was about to give in and tell her to go towards land when a light breeze blew from the west. After the gentle caress of the wind, he calmed down and asked Jane to give some time before making a break for shore.

"How long are we expected to wait out here?" she asked.

"Four hours," he answered. "Give him four hours."

When she looked into his eyes, she noticed that he had gone from frustrated despair to a sense of calm security and she wasn't about to deny him four hours. She knew that look and decided to risk staying, while Daniel stood on the crow's nest looking for any sign in the surrounding waters.

The eerie silence continued to grow on everyone's patience. One hour passed and a single solitary bird passed high above the ship. Daniel focused all his attention on the bird. Its small wings found hidden currents of air allowing it to glide softly far above. He remembered how desperate he felt a few hours earlier and how he had calmed down after feeling that light breeze. It was quite similar to the one that was now caressing his salty face. Looking at the bird, Daniel finally felt something that had been missing within him for too long.

It was as if a low tone seemed to chime from deep within his being; a grave note that seeped from his diaphragm, fighting its way up the vampire's entire body. He felt warm, at ease and illogically happy. The feeling that had been lost for so long now ran upwards from within him. He allowed himself to feel its bliss and to taste all the life that surrounded him. It had been ages, but the relief he felt from a tear he released made it completely clear that the long lost feeling still lived within him and he allowed himself a satisfied smile as he remembered what it felt like to have hope.

"Starboard Ho!!!" someone yelled.

Daniel followed the finger of a Corsaire to a glowing patch of ocean that bubbled seventy yards from the ship. The low tone grew louder within Daniel and he could see that everyone not only heard it, but felt it. As the volume grew, so did the activity in the water. The patch shone brighter until what seemed like liquid gold was bubbling up from the ocean floor. The louder the tone grew, the more blissful the feeling within everyone on the ship. Tears of joy streamed down everyone's faces, those topside and those beneath the deck. Daniel found he could not control his tears or the smile that insisted on showing itself to the daylight.

The circle of light continued to shine on the water until water began slipping down from the very middle. At first, it was the size of a small ball but it didn't take long for the void that had opened in the water to grow big enough for a small room to fit into. Pretty soon it seemed as if a spillway like those used to drain a lake had formed right in front of them. But this wasn't a spillway, it was a circular waterfall in the middle of the sea and the wider it stretched, the more light shone out of it. Suddenly the sound changed and what had been a low tone now sang like millions of violins, harps and voices singing the same note in unison until a pillar of light exploded up from the water.

Everyone had to shield their eyes from the light as a warm air current swooshed past all of them. When the light finally subsided, they saw the hole begin to close. Water seemed to seep slowly out of the hole as it got smaller, looking as if a long sheet of water was being pulled back. No one understood what was happening and they would probably never even try to explain the incident, much less the platform of sand that rose like an elevator and stood in the same spot as where the hole had formed, with Nathaniel smiling and waving as if nothing had happened.

**

Hours of questions ensued, but none of the answers made anything of what happened any easier to understand or accept. Everyone wanted to know more but Nathaniel just wanted to sleep and after orders from the captain, he was able to stow away downstairs in his quarters. The next moment his eyes opened, it was already nighttime.

After splashing some water on his face, Nathaniel put on some fresh clothes and headed topside. The night was warm, star studded and not a cloud dared block the celestial canvas of Nyx.

Nathaniel looked around and saw some other people on deck but decided to say hello to the captain first.

"Hello, Nathaniel," Jane said before he had arrived at the helm. "I pray you were able to sleep."

"Yes I was. Thank you for asking and for getting me some space."

"Don't mention it. The least I can do is keep the riff-raff off you long enough for you to be able to complete a thought."

Nathaniel gave a low laugh. "Yeah I know. It was kinda crazy there for a moment."

"I'm sure it was. It's not like you dove off a ship in the middle of a bay to reach an uncharted island that then disappeared, with you tagging along for the ride."

Nathaniel could only scratch his head a little embarrassed at his brashness. "Yeah... sorry about that."

"Not at all, Nathaniel," said the vampire captain looking him straight in the eye, "I'm quite sure whatever happened was for the best."

"You don't want to know what happened?"

"I don't need the whole story to understand you made contact and that we may have some assistance coming our way."

"You should have seen his eye."

"Was it really Michael?"

"That's what it seems like. Mikael he called himself."

She allowed the information to settle before asking more. "What was he like?"

"Sad... then glorious. His face was so full of pain at first."

"You saw his face?" she asked surprised.

"Yes."

"But he only shows his face to the dead or the ones he means to kill."

Nathaniel gave a smug smile. "Exactly. I wouldn't say I've remained unharmed during this trip, captain."

A look of realization came over Jane's face. It was a fact that Nathaniel had been killed recently, even though he had been resurrected.

"But you should have seen him when the light came back to him," he added.

"I can only imagine," she said detachedly.

"I'm sure you can't, even with all that you've no doubt seen."

"You'd be surprised at what I've seen, young man. This is only the second time I've completely crossed this sea... and for good reason."

"Oh?"

"Oh is just the beginning, Nathaniel. It was 1710 and it had been a few calm years where we had not been part of any conflict, any battle, or any war. We were living our lives at our own pace. The thing is that oftentimes when that happens you fall into a false sense of security.

"It was midyear; the weather was heavenly and Daniel was actually behaving, as he occasionally does. We had been out on the Indian Ocean for a long time, fishing, free diving, and even looking for treasures in sunken ships. You should have seen all we found: rubies and emeralds, sapphires as large as a tortoise and diamonds that by themselves could buy a small country... it was perfect... until the monsoon came."

Jane looked forward with her eyes lost in the horizon. "It takes much to scare me at sea, Nathaniel, and I was terrified. I swear I've never been that frightened in my life, not even when a large shark almost bit clean through me. From the beautiful days we'd had on the ocean, it all went black with clouds. I'm not saying grey or dark, but black. Black as in the blackest black there's ever been.

"From having been placid and lazy, the sea turned vicious in only a few moments. That has been the only time I've seen any weather that could sink this boat. The waves were so big that you would have thought the sea was folding upon itself, with the Black Calico in its way. It got to the point where it was completely irrelevant who was topside trying to do anything, but everyone stayed at their post. As if things weren't bad enough, little rogue waves leapt off the mountainous waves like isolated water avalanches that batted against the sails, putting endless strain and damage on the ship. At least everyone was accounted for... until a side wave hit us."

Nathaniel gave her a moment as she relived the memory before insisting for her to follow. "What happened?"

"It had to be fifty feet tall and it wrapped the entire ship. When we came afloat, Wendy, Mary, Liam and Daniel were all in the water. Wendy and Liam were closest and were actually able to get themselves back on the ship. Daniel came back soon after them but Mary didn't answer to calls and since the logical thing to do wasn't to the liking of Daniel, he took the end of a rope, said we were to pull back the line once there were two tugs given to the rope and jumped into the sea.

"The ocean spray spat in my face as I saw him paddle off in search of Mary. It was if it were mocking me. At that time, there wasn't much chance to react but I don't think I've ever felt relief as when I felt the line tug twice. We pulled with all our strength and as promised, Mary was at the end of the line. However, no matter how much relief I had felt when the line tugged, it was a speck of sand in comparison to the despair that took hold of me when Daniel didn't come back on the line. I'd like to say it was my sense of duty that kept me at the helm, but it was more a dull shock that only allowed one to do what came natural. I have been a captain of this ship for a long time and I had to get her through that slice of hell. So I focused."

"The storm kept my mind busy enough to not think of Daniel. It kept me focused and that's a good thing because the storm seemed endless. It could have been hours but the dull taste of shock made it seem like weeks had passed until we finally made it out of the tempest. You'd think it would be a relief to get out of the storm, but it then led to my destruction at the hands of realization."

Nathaniel saw as tears flowed freely from her eyes.

"At that time, I don't think I could have cried any more, Nathaniel. Sometimes it was a dull pain, at others it felt as if my soul was ripping apart, so naturally I could not accept he was gone. I knew he was alive... and if he wasn't, I would will him back to life because he couldn't just leave me like that. Five years of searching and praying it took, but I finally found him living with the Moken, a tribe of sea nomads that live on islands around the Indian Ocean. I wanted to kill him and kiss him in equal amounts, but seeing the way he was living... well maybe I'll tell you about that some other time."

"I'd like that," he said.

"It's a promise," she answered and Nathaniel didn't need to hear it to know she wanted to be alone. So he left her at the helm, one small goddess overlooking her realm.

Nathaniel walked along the deck while the lingering moon stared down on him. The wonderfully askew Cheshire smile in the sky brought one to his face, though it might have also been the pleasant surprise of the humming of guitar strings high up in the crow's nest.

"That's Edward," said a voice that came out of nowhere. Unlike previous occasions however, the sudden company hadn't startled Nathaniel.

"How's it going, Lucas?"

"Everything good on my front. Yourself?"

"Just having a stroll around the deck. Getting some fresh air and whatnot."

"I hear ya. Gets a bit crazy downstairs and I don't think I could ever be calm in this sea ever again."

"You too?"

"So Jane actually told you about that hideous storm ages ago?"

"Yeah. She told me Daniel had been lost at sea."

"That's the one," said the vampire as he led Nathaniel to the rail. "It damn near killed both of 'em. I tell you Jane was in a pretty bad state and I couldn't bear to see her that way. Three years it took me to finally decide to do something about it."

"So what did you do?" asked Nathaniel. There was obviously more to this story than the version he had heard.

"I went to look for him. We all knew he wasn't dead but no matter where Jane looked, she found nothing. We didn't do anything for those three years except look for him in this godforsaken sea, until we came across another storm like the one that had shown us what hell on Earth could be like. Eight hours into that cyclone I saw the look of relief in her face because she honestly wanted to die. I saw her with her arms wide open and her soul doing something I'd never seen it do... yield."

Lucas' face was lost in the moment of the memory. "That's when I made my decision. I walked to her and slapped her face as hard as my arm allowed, screaming how she couldn't leave her crew adrift. She cried then and I saw her wounded spirit weeping in front of me. So I made her a promise. I looked her in the eye and begged her to trust me, to believe in me, and to wait for me be it one day or one decade but that I would find Daniel. I gave her a kiss on the forehead, jumped into the storm and swam off no matter how much she cried for me to turn back. It pretty much tore my heart but I couldn't see her that way and not do anything."

Again his eyes became lost in the sea of his memory. "Two years I was adrift and looking for him. Initially it had taken me two days of floating and one of swimming to reach some unknown island. Then I swam from one island to the next, looking for life and signs of Daniel. One day I got a lead that there was a race of sea nomads called the Moken. These people live off the sea and were completely in their element among the tides. While humans and even vampires have limited vision underwater, these people could see for miles under the right conditions."

"I had been told Daniel was among them but that he would not be easy to find and damn it, they were right. The Moken aren't exactly the most social people you'll ever meet, hence them being called the ghosts of the Arabian Sea. If you cornered them on land, that was one thing, but if a way to the sea was nearby, they would find it. It sounds unlikely, but you'd be surprised at how many places have underground rivers that flow into the ocean."

"Like the one in Raelis?" asked Nathaniel.

"Exactly," said Lucas with a twinkle in his smile. "So there was pretty much no way to catch them."

"So how did you find Daniel?"

"It all happened the day I gave up. After I made the decision to try and drink myself to death, it took about eight bottles until I started screaming like a madman. Just when the barmen were about to break a bottle over my head, the owner took over the bar and started talking to me. There I was, crying and saying I'd give my soul if I could find Daniel. The owner of the shop then proceeded to pour me three shots of tequila. Where or how he had gotten it, I don't know but he asked if I was serious about what I was saying and I said of course. I downed the shots and he poured me two more, gave me a set of instructions to find an island bordering Kenya and told me that I would find who I was looking for. Of course I asked how he could be so sure. He just laughed and urged me to drink the shots. After I did, he poured me one more shot and swallowed what was left of the bottle. Then he used my right hand to put out his cigarette, gave me a pat on the shoulder, bid me farewell and left."

"Damn... so did you follow the instructions?"

"You've met Daniel, right?"

"Point taken," replied Nathaniel. "Wow, so you must really love Jane then."

"Jane? Damn.... I'd do anything for my sister. Anyways, I should be off mate. Try and get some rest."

Nathaniel replied with a tepid OK as the record of his mind still skipped a beat from learning the extent of sibling love between vampires. He looked to the deep purple night sky and breathed the salty essence of the Arabian Sea. His eyes became teary from the light breeze and he became aware again of the guitar that gently wept from up above.

As if it were the most natural thing in the world, Nathaniel jumped on the rail, then to some crates, climbed up the mizzen-mast to a sail, and then jumped to another sail until he reached the top and stood there watching Edward Louis as he strummed the six string. Even in the dim light, the gentle green eyes welcomed Nathaniel as he continued to play.

"Funny how we redefine what's natural from one moment to another, isn't it?" said the vampire. "Could you imagine yourself jumping around like that a month ago?

"I don't think so. What are you playing?"

"Not much. Just a couple of songs I've written along the way."

"So play something."

"Ok, I didn't know I was gonna be performing tonight, but here goes."

Edward cleared his throat and began to strum an E minor on his guitar, then a G chord, followed by a C chord before he began to sing in a deep baritone.

You are the ghost
I am your memory.
A faded smile
Without a remedy.
Restless sands
Of time and thought
I said I love you
Or maybe not.
In the desert
Where time has no name
Faith lacks expression
And love has no reigns.

Twisting turning
Always burning
Fed a lie
Truth's not discerning
Could have been your lover
But turned into a ghost
Wish it would be different
But such is what we chose
You are the ghost,
I am your memory
A faded smile
Without a remedy
Tried to give you life
But you just tried to take my own
I am your ghost
And darling you are mine.

After two long strums, the song ended.

"Very nice," said Nathaniel, "any insight on what made you write it?"

"Seems everyone on this boat has a story from this sea or the surrounding lands. Turns out I did as so many do and fell in love with a woman that couldn't be mine. It turns out that Arabian deserts have all types of markets and to my surprise at the time, there was even a night market, deep in the Saudi desert."

"The story I was told is that it started one night where two caravans met in the middle of the desert and wanted to trade. There had been bad months of business so pretty much all merchants were willing and eager to sell at night. The head merchant declared the market open but only until right before sunrise."

"At first it had been something casual, but the more often they did the night market, the better the business. It didn't take long for things to get really interesting regarding who came to sell. Traders and merchants alike began coming from far off lands and to say there was racial tolerance is an understatement. It wasn't long before vampires and therians began trading. Hell, there were times when even dwarves came from within the Earth to trade. To be honest, there were even a couple of demons seen selling, but since tolerance and respect were paramount in the Night Market, everyone was truly welcome."

"Most importantly, no one asked too many questions. For how hard it may seem, people didn't even think about who they were selling to. It was trade in its purest expression and no matter how odd someone seemed, no one asked, no one knew and no one cared about who or what they were dealing with as long as the products were good and the price was right."

"So that's why a beautiful woman did not know I was a vampire, actually she just didn't care. She only knew I was mildly pleasant and always bought her as much incense as I could carry. For however long the market lasted, I went every night and I swear I loved that girl. I honestly lost count of how many years I went."

"So what happened?" asked Nathaniel.

"Well I did mention the part of people not asking questions and this being a market of pure trade, but that doesn't mean people didn't steal or break rules. Too bad for a bandit he stole from the beautiful woman that so enthralled me. Worse for him was that he had struck her. Worst of all was that I hadn't eaten in weeks. I ran him down, taunted him and broke one of his legs... then I had my way with him."

"As I fed, I became intensely aware of the scent of jasmine incense and when I turned around, I only saw her tear ridden face in the night... I swear I didn't know it was her son. The cry she gave still haunts me to this day. My way of apologizing was to let her stab me over and over and over and over. I fell down the dune and saw how she kissed her dead son. She screamed and wailed and some nights I need to play to see if I can't get something else inside my head."

Edward continued to strum idly as a pregnant pause hung in the air. Waiting for something to break the silence, Nathaniel felt obliged to do the honors. "How long ago was this?"

Blood tears welled in the vampire's eyes. "Too long... but not long enough."

Yet again the human found himself as unwanted company. He put his hand on Edward's shoulder and held it there for a few moments. "Forgiveness begins within."

"True... but maybe I'm afraid of forgetting my ghost... Maybe I'd rather she haunt me."

Nathaniel smiled. "Then I hope you have many restless nights."

Edward gave him a thankful smile and Nathaniel jumped down to the deck. His landing was met by the familiar scent of Liam's cigarettes.

"Lovely night for a smoke," Nathaniel said.

"Still haven't met one that wasn't," replied the vampire.

"You know those things will kill you, right?"

"Well I'm already undead as you humans put it. Why stop there?"

"Nice way of seeing it. Can I ask you one question though?"

"Of course my friend, eager ears await."

"The salt of the ocean is quite different to the ones from tears and though Edward offered up some, yours smell different."

"That wasn't a question."

"Like I have to say it out loud. Answer the why and we'll see if talking can help any."

"Unless you can bring back the dead or undead in this case, it seems you won't be of much help."

"Well at least you're not drunk."

"Jane locked up all the grog. After one attempt to get it, she showed me just how strong a five foot captain could actually be."

"What'd she do?"

"Well to make her point, she dislocated my index finger, my wrist, my elbow and my shoulder with one move. Although her technique was more than commendable, I can't help but think she was a bit overzealous in her execution."

"Maybe... so are you going to say anything about Melissa or will you continue to ignore your pain, and wallow in a corner."

Liam wanted to retort and keep up the playful banter, but his throat had locked up on him and wasn't planning on letting go. Five times he tried to start a sentence, but his thoughts were choked away in painful gulps as he fought to express all that was ravaging his heart.

"It's just..... it's ... it's just.... I ... didn't... get to ... umm... say... umm.... Goodbye. And.... And even though she was my complete opposite.... sh .... she ... sh... she was the only one I ever loved."

"But wasn't she a Lygophilia? A lover of the dark?"

"My friend, love can be deaf, dumb and blind, but when it comes to the heart, it'll more than just play pinball. She has been the only one I've ever loved as such and I can't handle knowing the pain she has passed and what waits. I've seen the birth of a wraith and it is one of the most hideous things imaginable. The woman's dead body bloats, turns grey and finally ruptures spewing forth waste and bile, which coincidentally is what a wraith feeds on. Decay and destruction is its nourishment and my Melissa is going to have that thing inside her.... and... and... she'll feel every last bit of it."

"How do you know for sure?"

Liam looked Nathaniel square in the eye while rubbing his hands in pain. "Let's just say that there a bonds that are almost impossible to sever." The vampire then lost his eyes in the waters and pulled a long drag from his cigarette, almost daring Nathaniel to look at the red tattoo on his ring finger.

"Something tells me that's not ink," said Nathaniel.

"And something tells me you might have something better to do."

The sudden lash took Nathaniel by surprise. It was clear he had crossed a line that he shouldn't have. "Not sure if I do, but for what it's worth, my apologies and I'm sorry for Melissa... and for you."

Liam tried to say something but his throat caught again. Nathaniel replied by patting him on the shoulder. "Don't worry, man. If you want company, I'll be around."

"Thanks."

With that, Nathaniel got up from the rail and took one deep breath of fresh air while gazing at the moon. She loomed high in the sky in all her glory and he couldn't help but give her a wink and say good night. He walked towards the steps and went below deck, coming across the luminescent eyes of Daniel, this time decked in a pale blue.

"Nice night out?" asked the vampire.

"You could say that. Ran into a few people topside."

"I would imagine. I however prefer to be below deck during nights in this sea."

"I can also imagine. Though Jane could use some company."

"I'm sure she'd rather have me right where I stand."

Nathaniel looked to the floor, gave a sigh and smiled. "How old were you again?"

"A couple of centuries more than you."

"And you still don't get women. Keeping a promise doesn't mean you can't be near someone you love. Just don't go about doing something stupid like going for a swim and not coming back."

Daniel opened his eyes in mild surprise. "I see you've heard some stories this evening."

"You could say that. Care to add another to the mix?"

"You have my book, Nathaniel. Any story worth telling is in there. Besides, I don't want to run the risk of you misquoting me."

"I'm a real reporter... I don't misquote." Nathaniel smiled at his onetime captor. "I'll give you my review when I read it."

"So you're a book critic as well?"

"Not really, although I could be. But please, go topside. If she lashes at you, I can always serve as an excuse."

This time it was Daniel who smiled. "I knew there were more reasons why I picked you."

"Yeah... I get that a lot. Anyways, go to your captain, I'm off to bed."

"All right... rest well."

"Cheers."

Nathaniel then walked down the hall up to his comfortable room. He opened the door and there was Wendy on his bed with what could be considered clothing if only for the fact that it left a few things to the imagination.

"And this?" he asked while smiling a bit nervously.

Wendy patted the bed. "I thought I'd offer a bedtime story."

Chapter 37: Broken Circles

A vast hall stretched for what seemed like miles. Death and rot sunk into every breath and small flickers shone from stone walls that looked like cooling magma. Its rough surface was impregnated with the potent smell of decay that could only emanate from death while a constant bombardment of sulfur made the air almost un-breathable.

Weak eyes welled with tears and attempted to record memories one would rather not have to forget. A man of broken spirit looked around and barely managed to catch a glimpse of a crude stone blade that finalized the divorce between his head and body.

If in fact a person remains alive several seconds after decapitation, it was guaranteed that this poor fellow would have a dizzy run towards the end of the tunnel. His head rolled past countless lanes of dead bodies occasionally skipping over a trail of blood that was feeding drainage pipes, which sang with the blending of unwilling blood. The head continued down the path with its dull dead eyes seeing everything and nothing until it hit a stone pillar, landing with its stare squarely set on another set of dead eyes.

A ravaged body swelled grotesquely as a creature gorged itself on the insides of a once beautiful woman. Her gray rot skin was stained from tears of bile. The difference between these eyes and those of the head on the floor was that these eyes showed they could still feel.

Melissa's hands were bound to the stone slab she had been laid upon. The pain she felt every second was unspeakable, but she had long stopped crying for mercy, crying for help or even crying at all. The tears that now fell from her eyes were but a mere reflex. She winced lightly as the thing that was in her womb ate her insides and defiled what had once been her path to maternity. She was dead but she felt pain to last three lifetimes. Unfortunately, the gift of death had been stolen from her.

She was alone now for one simple reason, the demon responsible for her current state had tired of her. When she had first been brought back every gnash on her flesh burned like fire much to the demon's delight. Then thirst and hunger slashed at her being, yet she still remained. A hundred deaths she'd experienced in just a few days. It had gotten so bad that the bastard had even brought her back after having suffocated her on one occasion, just for amusement.

With every pain, it had laughed. With every death it laughed harder. He had even pleasured himself while she writhed in agony. To Murmur, it was just a game he was playing. But one day, she decided she would scream no more. Not for pain, or fear or desperation. He would not get the satisfaction he had relished. Initially he had been fascinated, but that didn't last. He quickly grew bored and when he saw that his taunts had minimal response, if any, he left.

Now she was alone, staring at eyes fortunate enough to actually be dead. The pain was horrid, but she had been strong. She had silenced any cry that might delight any of her captors. Not even when the claws began to tear out from within her womb did she scream. She just held on to what little faith she had left.

***

Several hundred feet above this hall was the landscape of a country known as Burma and Myanmar. A country ravaged by military strife that shares borders with China, Thailand, Bangladesh and Laos. Somewhere along its countryside, a large crater gapes within a wide valley. Within such a geological phenomenon, the tendency is for soil to be desolate and arid, a death vacuum of sorts. However, even with all the bile that flowed far below, this crater had grass and shrubs growing inside it.

Torchlights flickered in the tepid evening. Not a breath of air blew and the lazy torches made the shadows twitch in jittery little bursts, unable to hold a certain shape... but that soon changed.

The once slowly flowing flames abruptly bent almost parallel to the floor, acting as if hurricane gales blew clear across the basin. The odd thing was that the flames did all of this while there was still not a gust of wind to be felt. All shadows danced madly to and fro, almost like TV images fighting against sheets of static. Just as suddenly as their disruption had begun, the shadows returned to their original state. All except one.

A shrub that had been green and lush and full of life even within the crater had now drooped pathetically to the floor while an ash color had slipped over it. The green seemed to have been long removed from its leaves and any sign of life more than extinguished. Beside it now stood a new shadow. Stuck to the new piece of shade was a small man with pork pink skin, a comb over, glasses and a black suit with a white collar.

No one in this world could look so pathetic yet command such fear. He looked around as rows of demons had appeared and began to kneel before him. "I see I am expected," he said surveying the submissive horde. "No doubt Cleora's work."

Just then, a midget demon, no larger than three feet high raced between the throng, panting and heaving while making way for a group of six demons that walked towards Elliot.

The small man's eyes burned with a calm intensity. He scowled at the group of demons since his presence had yet again failed to present him with the audience he desired. That they decided to walk in a formation depicting an inverted pentagram disconcerted him about as much as the river temperature in some brook in Greece. He knew each demon by name and in truth, Elliot almost yawned in their faces.

The two in the front, Aamon and Pruflas, were both Dukes of Hell, ruling over 25 legions each. Aamon had a raven's head, the body of a man and teeth that looked fit for a rabid mastiff. A high ranking Goetic demon, he is often accompanied by a wolf with a rattlesnake tail, who can supposedly spit fire. For his part, Pruflas was a renowned seducer of women. A literal snake tongue, he wore a grey turban, had filed nails that seemed capable of tearing worse than any size talon and more than once was known to enchant women to serve him.

In the middle was Samyazza, the demon who had attended Elliot on his last visit to Hell. His yellow eyes shone in the darkness, but Elliot looked at the oncoming throng with little or no concern.

On the right side of the angel, a woman wore a suit that extended to a noose around her neck, which also bound her hands. She was known as Cleora and apart from the magic she commanded, not much else was known of her.

To Samyazza's left stood an old bearded man: Barbatos. He wore a brown tunic while a variety of animals crawled over him. From bugs, to snakes, to crows and bats, this visually deceiving demon commanded thirty legions and among the captains of his forces were four wicked kings, each sent to hell for crimes atrocious enough to never be forgiven by heaven and always commended in hell.

Last and certainly least was Rashaverak, a beast with few peers regarding his brutality. Apart from the three rows of teeth, he had mouths in both palms and more than once had devoured innocent flesh while still smiling.

The sea of devils parted and the group of demons stood before the small man. "Lovely entrance," said the balding man, "but best to do away with excuses, formalities or any other waste of my time. You know the answers I seek and I bore of subordinates. Speak, and please make it precise and to the point."

Samyazza clenched his fists, but quickly regained composure. Like every demon, he detested the sight of this human, but just the same, he knew better than to cross him. The others grit their teeth as well, Rashaverak doing it three ways with the mouth on his head and the two on his hands.

"The next harvest is about to hatch," said Samyazza. "This will push the wraith army to fifty thousand."

Elliot was all business. "What of the lesser demons? How many are at your disposal?"

"Onsite we have 150,000 with an additional 100,000 en route by way of the underground tunnels from throughout Asia. Unfortunately, the swarms coming from the west were obliterated."

"The Halo Maze incident?" Elliot asked.

"That was a fifth of the force. The rest were also destroyed. The only clue as to what happened was a cut off message that indicated some sort of fire."

"Fire?" said Elliot gravely.

"Yes; something about a flame."

The human became even more focused. "A flame? Could it be? .... Uriel?"

"Pardon me sir, but one angel cannot kill a hundred thousand demons."

"You underestimate your brother, Samyazza. Uriel makes your wickedest demon look like a tame baby in comparison. He might be wise and he might even be the sharpest sighted spirit, probably of all heaven, but he has no pity and any definition of wrath falls leagues short of what he is capable of. Good thing he is on a leash so to speak. Actually this is both good and bad."

"What good can you see in the eradication of our forces?"

"That's the bad, clearly. The good is that he's loose and out of control. That may confirm what I originally thought. What news of my wings?"

"The surgeon is on his way."

"That means you have an angel."

"He would not be close to arriving otherwise. But I must ask, what is your theory of the Flame of God?"

"Simple, dear Samyazza, if Uriel is running around killing demons, it means one of two things: either God let him loose to attack as he sees fit..."

"Or?"

"God is unable to contain him."

The angel became confused. "And what does this mean?"

"Think of it this way: are the words immortality and eternity synonyms?"

"Not necessarily."

"Exactly. Now take me to Lucifer; he has avoided me long enough."

"Pardon me, Master Elliot, but I have a new master. Lord Astaroth will see you."

Elliot gloated in his realization. "I see God is not the only one capable of forsaking then."

***

Beneath the Earth, Melissa's dead eyes continued to cry dully as she lay on the rock slab. She had been completely torn from the inside and lived to see the wraith that had fed on her womb step into the world. She had even been able to catch its eye, connecting for one brief moment with the beast. It had looked upon her and for a second, the creature almost expressed an air of grief or regret. But that feeling was quickly dissipated and replaced by anger and fear as another demon came lashing with a stone whip pushing it away to the end of the hall and into another.

She had at one moment resigned crying but the pain was too much. She smelled her own bile spilt on the floor as blood sewage of the collective slaughter gathered below. Any resolve or pride she had was deflated and she cursed God for not granting her death.

Amidst the amalgam of wretched smells, something different and distinct surfaced. It was familiar to Melissa, but completely out of place there: the smell of a cigarette.

Steps now echoed loud in the vast silent hall. Most other sounds had died off with the hatching of the last wraith a few minutes after hers. Demons, wraiths and goblins had filtered out, leaving her completely alone in the vast cavern. She grew desperate with every step, yet she could not muster the strength to scream.

As if the cigarette smell weren't odd enough, she then heard something even more out of place, a Texan accent.

"Now isn't this a waste," Bill said as he looked over her mauled body. He was smoking one of his black cigarettes and inhaled deeply. "I'd offer you a drag but something tells me you're not exactly in the mood for dragging anything. I know you're asking yourself who I am, or what I'm doing here or if smoking is even allowed within these charming facilities. I'm sure you also have a ton of questions but given that I'm short on time and you don't have a diaphragm, which pretty much renders you speechless, I'll cut to the chase. You have tasted immortality in its sweetest form and in this horrid expression you currently live in. Of course you know you shouldn't be here, but all angels of death are busy at the moment, so they kind of left you on hold. That being said, I have four questions for you. Don't worry about verbalizing, I just need your answer to be in your heart and I'll be able to hear it loud and clear.

Melissa's eyes had calmed down and he took that as a sign to ask away. "First, do you have any regrets?"

As he said the question, tears came to her eyes. Real tears, not the bile that had been seeping of its own accord. Her lips quivered and she tried taking a deep breath. Bill just nodded as if listening closely though not a sound was made.

"I'm sure he knows, but I'll be sure to tell him. Second, do you believe in God?"

As the words left his lips, her eyes became a flurry of confused blinks.

"This is no trick question," Bill said, "It's just my way to let you know she exists and to give you a chance to prepare."

Her eyes blinked slowly, still in confusion and despair. He tried to calm her down. "Don't worry, you'll understand soon. Third question: do you wish to be forgiven for your sins?"

Melissa trembled while she tried breathing slowly. Even with all the pain, she managed to calm down and give a weak smile. Bill also smiled. "No. You don't have to regret all of your sins. I'm sure some were real fun, but I'm glad you still have a sense of humor." She nodded, not even realizing that the pain that had torn straight through her was slowly ebbing away.

"Last question: do you want to die?"

Her response was to stare blankly into the poorly shaven man's face. She took a deep breath, closed her eyes tight, and when she opened them, resolve had set in and she gave a single, certain nod.

"Good," Bill said, "I just wanted to give you a choice."

He looked at the small tuning fork that still stuck out from her throat and made to take it out when the vampire took a deep breath as if trying to say one last thing.

"What's that?" asked Bill as she looked deep into his eyes. He stared back and gently nodded. "Of course."

He then undid her binding, took her hands in his and asked if she was ready. Her throat moved, trying desperately to release the words in her soul. He was in no hurry and held her firmly and patiently.

"Th.... Th.... Thnk... thank... y...y...you."

"No need, my child. No need."

When his hand took the pin out, her body went soft.

Bill looked around at all the carnage and down at the once beautiful woman and lit himself another cigarette since the one he'd been smoking had gone out.

"Hmm.... this mercy thing ain't half bad."

He drank deeply from the new cigarette and though he could not hear it, he knew a roar of pain had shaken the entire Indian Ocean. Bill looked down to the ground. "Sorry, Liam. Please realize that your anger is a gift."

Chapter 38: Sail on to Ceylon

Nathaniel sat in the noon sun staring absentmindedly into the waters of the Indian Ocean. He smelled of sweat and blood. His shirt was a mess and his knuckles burned like raw fire. The last six hours of his life had been some of the most torturous memories he had ever had to archive in his soul. Below deck, a dark room reeked ten times stronger than Nathaniel's shirt of blood, sweat and tears. Liam sat alone in that room.

Scarring a vampire isn't something particularly easy. Actually, it's almost impossible. But there was Liam's face, with a fresh scar on his right cheek, still there even though the rope burns from his wrists had long faded.

Six hours ago, a roar unlike anything anyone aboard had heard in their lives had threatened to capsize the boat. Daniel and Nathaniel arrived first and saw something that would even cause demons to look away.

On the top deck, Liam was roaring would-be death throes while tearing his clothes from his body with his bare hands. It took Daniel, Nathaniel, Edward Louis, Lucas and three other Corsaires to subdue him.

"She's dead! She's DEAD!!!! THEY KILLED HER A THOUSAND TIMES!!! SHE'S DEAD!!!! SHE'S DEADDDD!!!!" Liam screamed. They pulled him below deck thrashing and throbbing, more than once knocking everyone down. It took all of their effort to lock him in the room. After he was tied up, Liam screamed and fought but just as suddenly as he had begun wailing, he dropped to the floor limp and catatonic.

His breathing was still labored but his mind was anywhere but there. Everyone had fanned out of the room except Daniel and Nathaniel. Liam's lifeless eyes floated on his face, two belly-up fish swaying in the currents of his thoughts. They both sat in front of their friend. What had happened to make him lose control like that? Both felt lost in a void and wished Liam would just say something. It was so uncomfortable that they couldn't even look at each other.

After the longest half-hour of their lives to that moment, their wish was granted. What sounded like a murmur or a hoarse whisper were actually two words coming from Liam's mouth. A request, maybe even an order, but both Nathaniel and Daniel looked at each other with breathless stares, completely caught off guard by the words he had spoken. Liam possibly realized he hadn't been clear the first time, so the second time he said those two words, he spoke so clearly that there was no space for misinterpretation.

"Hit me."

He ground the words out of his mouth and the immeasurable suffering in the order struck both onlookers in the gut.

"I said HIT ME! Hit me until I don't feel!!! Hit me until I am numb!!!! Don't look at me! HIT ME! Don't THINK!!! HIT ME!!!!"

"But Liam—" started Daniel.

"Step outside, Daniel," interrupted Nathaniel.

His eyes were cold and dead when he had said it, but there was no hesitation. Daniel stood awestruck at what was being suggested.

"Please Daniel, step outside," Nathaniel said as he signaled the vampire to the door.

"What are you going to do?" asked Daniel.

"Whatever I have to... for however long I have to do it. Now please..." He signaled to the door once again.

Daniel walked to the door and looked one last time at Liam and then at Nathaniel. He then closed the door behind him.

Nathaniel locked eyes with Liam. They looked deep into each other's souls until Nathaniel gave a nod as if asking a question and Liam gave a nod as if answering. The first punch was thrown mercilessly and received thankfully.

The human hadn't yet grasped the regenerative powers of vampires but he was about to have a firsthand encounter with that phenomenon. For every broken lip and chipped tooth, the vampire's body regenerated bone and tissue in an instant. At first Runnels was afraid of throwing punches, but after hundreds of blows thrown and no signs to show for his effort, he started getting angry.

He raked palm strikes, knees, elbows and kicks on the bound vampire. Soon pain would come over all his limbs and the red from Liam's blood started to mix with his own. Blood wet flesh struck against resilient skin and pants and grunts of aggression turned into screams of pain and primal fear.

An hour passed and Nathaniel had not stopped hitting Liam. His blood red eyes thirsted for damage to mirror his own. His fists stung and ached. Sweat and tears burned his raw flesh. His muscles felt torn and his bones felt like they were slowly being ground into dust. Sometime after the second hour, he stopped punching.

Nathaniel collapsed in a wounded heap with his arms trembling. Liam was breathing hard, but apart from his blood drenched clothes, and the quickly healing cut on his left eyebrow, nothing showed that he had just received a beating the likes of which a hundred men would not have survived. He leveled his breathing and looked at Nathaniel intently, observing the beaten human before him. He only had three words of consolation to offer.

"Is that all?"

Nathaniel opened his eyes and stared at the vampire. Liam returned the human's gaze with simple cynicism. He clicked his tongue as if waiting for the human to finish what he started and to make it snappy. Nathaniel obeyed the call, standing up and forgetting his pain.

It was as if the ache in every limb had been erased. The feeling of defeat was burned away by rage and he stared at Liam as he walked closer, one step after the other. He came within inches of the vampire and breathed deeply the essence of blood that lingered on his body.

"I feel nothing..." said Liam, "...and you expect what you did to make a difference? Seriously, why don't you try again, girlie?"

Pupils dilated, teeth clenched, bloody knuckles cracked, lungs filled with air and Nathaniel seemed to swell in size. His skin stretched and tensed like taut leather. He felt no pain, he felt no fatigue. He only felt rage and a release that clicked deep within him.

The first blow he threw in this second session cracked Liam's jaw. The knee that followed broke a rib and every strike thrown was meant to kill or maim. This time instead of every blow getting progressively weaker, they grew stronger.

It got so bad that Nathaniel untied the vampire so he could be allowed to drop to his knees. But instead of an opportunity for mercy and respite, Nathaniel saw this as an opportunity to strike down with more leverage so the blows landed even harder. He broke the vampire's collarbones about ten times each and his strikes were so hard and fast that after another hour, the vampire's flesh was starting to heal at a slower pace, though still not showing traces of the damage offered.

Nathaniel's knuckles were pure bone but he felt no pain. He didn't hear any noise. He punched and kicked to the rhythm of his heart and every thump of his pulse was a blow he struck. Into the end of the fourth hour, Liam began to weep. His face was a mess and the floor was littered with pieces of bone he'd lost. Nathaniel kept punching and seeing the weakness in the vampire only served to spur him further. Blow after blow fell on his comrade and soon the weeps turned into moans and groans and cries of agony.

The vampire's flesh no longer healed but Nathaniel didn't stop. No pain would make him stop and his entire body had desisted from sending signals of damage or pain. His blows simply came faster and faster until Liam began choking on a word. Nathaniel paid no heed and kept striking his friend.

Again Liam tried to speak but Nathaniel closed his mouth with an uppercut that sent two teeth flying. Every blow sounded like a thud on the outside accompanied by a sickly crunch on the inside. Punch, kick, elbow, knee, punch, punch, punch, punch, punch, punch.

"Stop!!!!!! STOP!!!!!!!!!!!!" Liam cried. The words had finally freed themselves from within and with those words came a torrent of tears as he slumped onto the floor. Tears of pain... tears of relief.

Nathaniel still had his right hand cocked to deliver more punches. His face had been stone and it was wet with sweat but suddenly the salty dew mixed with something else. His hand unclenched slowly and he felt himself trembling. Like Liam, he fell on his knees. He looked at the vampire crying as his face tried to make sense of itself, regenerating torn features and growing back teeth that had been shattered. Liam wept as he found himself feeling once again and in his reunion with sensation, he had company. Nathaniel had killed off part of his humanity for him only to resurrect it through compassion and empathy. For the longest time, man and vampire held each other's shoulder, occasionally embracing in their search for balance in this life.

That had been six hours ago. Now Nathaniel looked towards the bright blue horizon and thought about every breath he took. His eyes were focused, still sore from crying next to his friend, but focused. Below deck, Liam sat in the room and traced the scar with his finger. He smiled and whispered his appreciation. "Not all gifts come with a bow."

The midday sun had burned intensely, but before long, darkness had snuck its head in the day and the azure waters of Northern Sri Lanka replaced the dark indigo of the Indian Ocean.

"Where are we?" asked Nathaniel.

Daniel had almost forgotten that words existed and could be spoken. His throat was sea-salt dry and his thoughts took a few seconds to gather. "We're arriving at the Great Meeting."

"Meeting?"

"Yes. For the first time ever, therians, vampires and photogeni convene. The presence of a common enemy has postponed the usual quarrels... now decisions have to be made."

Nathaniel looked at the shallow waters and the purple sunset. Galleons and yachts began to appear. He hadn't noticed them before. Little dots on the horizon got closer and the distant island originally known as Ceylon flicked in the distance.

"Captain, would it be possible to reduce speed a bit?" Daniel asked.

Jane answered with a curt nod. They slowed down and the small dots grew larger as they got closer. To the north they saw a small island come into view and the water grew lighter and got shallower the closer they came to the shoal.

"Where is this again?" asked Nathaniel again.

"Northern Sri Lanka," Daniel answered. "It is an ancient meeting place and a land of common ground for angels, humans, vampires, therians and photogeni alike."

"Why's that?"

"Well if you read the Judeo Christian Testament, Zoroastrian mythology and the Koran, you can see that though there are differences between these religions, there is much more that binds them than you would think. Parables, direct quotes, characters, rules and in this case, places. In this place of the world, all humanities and supra-humanities have this point in common. In ancient times, this shoal used to be a fully exposed land bridge. Most religions have something to say and even the faith of vampires and therians take into account the importance of this location.

Boats got nearer and large barges dwarfed the galleon. Each vessel assembled to form a naval carpool and greetings were subdued. The flags were as different as anyone could envision and Nathaniel recorded in his memory the image of each one. He'd never seen so many shapes and colors. Square flags, circular ones, triangle and diamond shaped.

"Why here and why not on that island?" asked Nathaniel to the vampire as he looked towards the left.

"My young friend, where we are arriving is the spot where all the spilt blood from the first Great War pooled. From here, earth, blood and water mixed and were somehow swept back to the original battle scene in Ethiopia, the earthen version of The Garden of Eden, where we were not too long ago. Moreover, angels worship this place for it quenched the flames of the fall of man.

"Fall of man?"

"Have you read Genesis?"

"Yes."

"Do you remember that charming anecdote where the naïve couple ruined their stay in the Garden of Eden?"

"Of course, but what does that have to do with this?"

"Where do you think man landed, so to speak?"

Nathaniel's eyes opened wide as he remembered reading about how an impression on a large mountain resembled a large footprint. Legend has it that the imprint was the first step man took on this Earth.

"Adam's Peak?" he asked the vampire.

"Exactly. And this shoal is Adam's bridge. Once a full land bridge, it is now a partially submerged shoal."

"From a book I once read, I remember the shoal and the beauty of Sri Lanka. I remember the clear blue waters. I even remember seeing a sunset much like this one, but I don't remember that island we're nearing."

Daniel gave a small laugh as if he knew something Nathaniel didn't. "Well for starters, we stopped moving two minutes ago, so we are not nearing anything. Secondly, that is no island."

Nathaniel didn't understand at first, but that feeling vanished the minute he realized he was looking at a floating section of forest. Raelis had followed them there.

Chapter 39: Dinner and a show

While smaller sea craft deployed from each boat, various groups walked in the knee-high water. Looking on, Nathaniel noticed that each unit carried a flag representing them. Only then did he actually take a moment to look at his ship's flag. Eight hands curved to outline a circle although none of the hands were touching. In the center, a single flower floated in water. The flag's color went from auburn to deep night purple, while an inscription in some odd language was written below the flower.

"United in soul, adrift in life," said a voice from behind Nathaniel.

He turned around to see Liam smiling, his newly formed scar visible even in the dusk gloom. "Every flag has a story and a reason for being," the vampire said. "Our group has always been in and out of touch and rarely do we all stay together for long. But life's currents always seem to drift us back together like some karmic jetsam."

"Interesting," said Nathaniel. He looked on as large tables were drawn out on the deck of each boat. "And what are we here to do?"

"We're here to dine and plan our attack. Tomorrow will be the moment to siege. Decisions, truces and details need to be finalized among leaders of hordes and broods alike. We've been in communication, but it is the first time we meet face to face. You have to understand that vampires, therians and photogeni all have different social structures. Therians are tribal with the Eight Furies as the main leaders. There may be several small tribes, but in the end, they all answer to the elders."

"And vampires?"

"Ah the covens... we once operated much like therians, but internal tensions, betrayal and more conflicts than we'd care to admit to prompted the dissolution of the original council. Now every group acts on its own. We follow common laws that were agreed upon centuries ago and convene every fifty years to ensure compliance while addressing rogues before leaving each other alone for another half century."

"And the elders?" asked Nathaniel.

"Dead some, either by their own hand, by ours or who knows what. Others are exiled in remote places and very few are actually accounted for. That is why the Laius, Gerald, Magdalena and Louvetiers are all so different in structure. Apart from some differences in nationality, most therian hordes operate in much the same manner."

"That's funny; from all the movies and books, you'd think therians would be the disorganized race."

"What can I say? We have better Public Relations."

Daniel appeared topside and walked towards them. "Feeling better?" he asked Liam.

"Much better. Thank you for asking."

"Wish I could have done more."

"Mate, I owe you enough as it is. Let's focus on the now though, ok?"

"Agreed. Nathaniel, could you please see that the captain does not need any help?"

"Sure thing," the young man replied. While walking towards her, Jane looked at him out of the corner of her eye while some Corsaires set the anchor.

"Can I help you with anything, captain?"

"So formal, Nathaniel; you would think we would be on a first name basis by now."

He kind of smiled to himself, slightly abashed by her honesty. "Sorry, it's just that... well things have been odd since... well you know."

"What happened with my brother, whatever actually happened is only the business of you and him. We can only speculate from what we heard and the physical evidence left behind."

"Well actually... wait a minute... he's also your brother?"

She laughed as she pulled out large clear globes with lanterns suspended in the middle of them. "Quite a lovely scar you gave him. Actually, none of us thought it was possible but you've had a way of being the anomaly on more than one occasion and of leaving your mark."

Nathaniel screwed up his face in confusion and she smiled wider. "Let's put it this way, it's not like we socialize with humans. We either avoid, dispose of or feed on. So from the very beginning, you have been quite the irregularity. Add to this your development in such a short time and your Don Juan exploits with any appealing target, regardless of race or species, and well, you just become even more peculiar. But that's not a bad thing what you did for my brother. You pretty much did what none of us could have done."

"And what's that?"

She stopped pulling out the lanterns and looked directly at him. "You helped him accept his pain. You risked your humanity for him. That's why we have faith in you. That's why you're so important. That is why you have been taken so into consideration."

"Into consideration? I don't know about you, but being kidnapped doesn't exactly seem like a way of being taken into consideration."

"Maybe, but have you seen any vampire feeding on another human? Don't forget, Nathaniel, we are vampires, we do feed on your kind and it's not like we magically stopped drinking blood and it's not like we haven't been doing it. It's just that it is not something you have to see. The way we have been portrayed, you'd think we only think about blood. Fortunately, there's much more to us than stealing babes, drinking blood and hissing at garlic while striking dramatic vampire poses."

Once again, it seemed that everything Nathaniel had ever read or seen of vampires was short changing his knowledge. "Sorry, Jane, it's just that every day I seem to realize just how ignorant I am."

"Good," she replied. "That's why you show promise. Not only are you able to recognize your shortcomings, you have an undeniable hunger to change for the better and evolve. What's truly amazing is what you've become in so short a time. Most humans would have imploded after a fraction of what you've lived through."

"Guess it comes from being stuck in a moment for so long, treading water and losing ground no matter how hard I swam. It's almost as if the current has shifted and now I'm swimming at blazing speeds like some human version of the Nautilus that has slipped into the Gulf Stream. I just need to be careful not to hit a rock or fly off some waterfall."

"Or into the willing arms of a female from another race."

Nathaniel turned so red that Jane couldn't help but laugh out loud. "Don't worry, seems you're making up for lost time and none of us judge you for it, although sometimes we are amazed at the rate of your conquests."

"Are you sure about that?" he asked almost doubling over in embarrassment.

Jane once again stopped what she was doing, tipped his chin up so their eyes met and spoke in as motherly a tone as Nathaniel had ever heard. "Wendy does not judge you and although she might be jealous, she's also a realist. Hell, remember it was me and Daniel who unleashed the girls on you. Above all else, you are a man and your self esteem needed mending. We just never guessed the monster we were unleashing."

She had to stop again to laugh at Nathaniel and the way he looked like an embarrassed eight-year old that had been caught peeking into the ladies' fitting room.

"Listen to me. Some relationships are not meant to be constant, stable or even monogamous."

"What about you and Daniel?"

She took a moment to think. "I guess other relationships can't survive unless they are constant, stable or monogamous. For all the years we've been together, Daniel has been the only one and I'm sure it is the same for him."

"But how can you be sure?"

"You can't, but for me, if you can't trust a person, how can you love them?"

"So you trust him?"

"Nathaniel, I don't know what will happen tomorrow or the next day. I've had one crisis of faith after the other and questioned the very nature of my existence and in my life, there is only one being I trust in completely. Though far from a god, Daniel has never failed me and has never given me any reason to doubt or question him."

"Wow... I wish I had that."

She scoffed in reply. "No you don't. I appreciate the envy, but I'm sure it does not apply. Here, take these lanterns."

She gave him the end of the rope where forty lanterns were suspended in the middle of glass spheres. Nathaniel looked again to the water and saw that a series of long tables had been set in an enormous circle and that many groups were already sitting in the knee-high water at their table with their flags erected in the shallows. All around, hundreds of globes had been lit and everything seemed to be touched by their warm yellow glow. Underneath the water, other hundreds of lights were lit and the flames burned bright green.

Jane noticed Nathaniel's face when he saw the underwater lights: "Those are from the photogeni. They have a much better understanding of the dynamics between carbon monoxide and oxygen and have gained knowledge of various energy sources much more advanced than any scientist could fathom. You think nanotechnology is incredible, you should see their studies of physis natura.¬"

"Physis natura?" Nathaniel asked.

"Yes. Natura is the Latin root word of nature and physis is the Greek translation of the same word. Nature looks through humanity to gain a better understanding of everything. You see, modern science may have had its formal beginnings somewhere around the 16th century, but scientific research reaches well into the prehistoric era. What no one ever realized was that nature was always watching and learning."

While modern scientists often waste hours inside sterile rooms that are hermetically sealed and completely controlled, the first scientists studied, observed, recorded and learned in the laboratory of the real world. There was communion and respect between humans and nature but the focus has been lost since the Industrial Revolution. Since then, nature passed from being an accomplice and partner to being a simple resource or habitat. As you can see from our leafy friends over there, nature feels and this battle is for the survival of all world kind."

As his brain condensed the new information, Nathaniel was actually thankful for being a part of this moment although more than a little ashamed of his own race and all the things it had done to the Earth.

If the scene was already beautiful, what came now completely took his breath away. From the base of the floating photogeni island, a large kelp bed stretched out with glowing strands of bright phosphorescent colors. They reached up from the water, swirling into glowing statues that held large drops of dew that shone the same color as the reed that formed the statue.

Everything glowed and most of those present were already at their table. Jane had already lit and thrown the light line to form part of the beautiful scene below.

"Let's go, Nathaniel; time for dinner."

They climbed down by rope ladder and walked into the wide area where the dinner table was. Made by connecting dozens of other tables, it held over two hundred chairs, all of them occupied. Nathaniel saw familiar faces in the crowd. Jeremy the child vampire leader of the Laius smiled and waved as did Christopher who was sitting further down on a floating chair, representing the Gerald faction.

Each group had a flag behind them. For the Laius, a young sapling was shown uprooted by demon hands, which now passed the plant to a floating orb of light. Below the image were the words 'Taken from youth, given into eternity'. The Gerald flag showed a white sand beach with foot prints of only the left foot going off into the distance with the phrase 'Completed by our path' written below in dark maroon letters.

Nathaniel and Captain Jane continued to walk towards their part of the table. The therian Gevaudan nodded in salute, and the human greeted him in return. Looking at the ships around them, it was if they'd been arranged to form a makeshift coliseum. The different levels of the ships revealed different portions of the sky and the small gaps in between vessels allowed cold night air to seep through.

The young man also saw Luna though she hadn't noticed him because she was in an agitated discussion. There was some finger pointing in the heated debate and some other therians screamed and pointed in the direction of another group. This vampire group looked at the therians with blank expressions and the reason for their discussion waved above them. A flag showed a severed wolf head with a pool of blood underneath. Written in the puddle was the inscription 'Killing for a better world'.

Jane noticed Nathaniel had seen the flag. "Now do you understand why we need this meeting? Having the same cause doesn't mean we get along."

"But Castle Margeride?"

"Is the home of Uroc, hence the tolerance and the mentality that permeates there. It is by no means the standard mindset of therians or vampires."

The argument continued to escalate and swords were about to be drawn when the fighting came to an abrupt stop.

Nathaniel couldn't understand what was happening, but from the look on Jane's face, she did. Her unblinking eyes drew a straight line that Nathaniel followed to the very figure of the elder therian standing next to the quarreling groups.

"Are you done?" said Uroc icily. His eyes had an unsettling dead calm to them and his voice surged with indescribable power, even if he wasn't screaming. He turned to the vampires and what were once blank expressions betrayed fear. "I do not fancy your colors, friends. Feel free to give me a reason to let you live."

What appeared to be the leader of the group trembled lightly before replying. "Y-yes, father." With those words spoken, they took the flag down.

"Thank you," Uroc said, "that will do. Now let us sit. There is much to talk about and little time to do so." The hulking therian walked past the groups and towards the tables followed by some of the other therian Furies and Daniel.

After they resumed their walk, Jane told Nathaniel the names of the therian factions present. There was the Wendigo tribe from Canada, the Kitsune Werefoxes from Japan, the African Boudu Hyena men, the Mexican Nahuales – shape shifters – and the Runaas Jaguars from Argentina. For the vampires, the Louvetiers were next to the Night Rooks, and apart from them were the Laius, the Gerald and the Corsaires next to the Magdalena. As for the photogeni, perennials were representing all factions that were currently resting on the floating island, getting ready for the battle ahead.

"Where are the angels?" asked Nathaniel.

Jane looked down. "No one has heard of them. Only one is present, the Hashmallim Selaphiel."

Uroc walked towards the angel that sat in the shallow water. He knelt beside the pious Hashmallim and spoke in a low whisper. "Have you been cared for, brother?"

"Yes, Master Uroc," said the angel in a gentle voice.

"And your kin?" asked the elder therian.

"Awaiting my report. We are facing discord on various planes. In addition, Mother has still not answered any of us."

"I see... she still ails?"

"In such a morally bankrupt era, let us give thanks she is still with us."

"Quite true. We shall begin then. If you need anything, do not hesitate to ask us."

"My thanks."

The elder Fury stood up and after one last glance to the angel went to his table with the other Furies.

Jane had turned to Nathaniel not long after the conversation had ended. "How do you know Selaphiel?"

As was his nature, Nathaniel did not bother to lie. "He was at the Halo Maze when the attack occurred. I'd taken a wrong turn when I tried to run away and ran into him. But he seems different; he isn't holding any roses this time."

"Oh, I see... you mean you saw Buraquiel?"

"What?"

"His twin brother."

"Twin?" said Nathaniel confused.

"Just because they are angels doesn't mean they weren't born or that there can't be something as siblings or twins in their kind."

"I could have sworn they were one and the same."

"No Nathaniel... Buraquiel means Blessings of God and as chief of the Guardian Angels, his responsibilities are as varied as the blessings he bestows. Selaphiel's name means the Communicant of God and he communicates directly with her."

"So God is a woman?"

"When she chooses to be," Jane said cautiously. "Other times she can have male features and other times, God can choose to have no gender. The will defines expression and the times define the will."

Just then, Uroc walked into the center of all the tables. Kelp reeds seemed to swirl beneath him, forming steps that allowed him to walk up to a makeshift platform.

"Impressive the level of control the photogeni have achieved with kelp," Nathaniel said.

Jane muffled a smile. "What you see there is not kelp. You are looking at the work of the one true alchemist left in the world."

"What does that even mean?"

"Nathaniel... there is only water there. What you saw move, glow and what is now holding Uroc as a platform is just water. He willed it to hold his weight. The kelp you thought you saw were reflections."

Nathaniel looked closely and saw that in fact there was nothing underneath the therian except water that looked much darker than the pool beneath. The imposing figure took an air as if he was about to speak and everyone went silent.

"Comrades in arms... enemies in life. We are here out of the need for survival. For ages we have attempted to achieve peace with limited success and quite honestly, that is a debate we should have some other time. For this moment, however, I must acknowledge the vampire leader of the Magdalena group. Without his efforts, we would not have been warned and we would not be here together to face this threat."

He paced on the liquid platform before continuing. "It seems the first Great War did not eradicate the goblin race as most of us would have liked. Furthermore, thanks to human corruption, there has been a dangerous surge in wraiths. Countless innocents of all races have lost their lives and all because one human is working towards one goal: to overthrow the kingdom of heaven. Ludicrous? Yes. Insane? Most certainly. Possible? .... well we wouldn't be here otherwise."

A chorus of whispers began to sound off from all the tables. Uroc responded with a deep breath, which seemed to silence everyone and force them to shut up.

"I know, friends. It sounds impossible and insane, but we have reliable sources who have confirmed this human's intentions. Therians and vampires alike have died because they were needed as material for the spawning of these beasts... that or because they knew something. Humans are being used as hosts for wraiths and we do not know how many have been spawned because the government of Myanmar has been bought accordingly. In exchange for weapons and power, tens of thousands of men, women and children have been killed. It is a time for conflict. It is a time for war. It is a time to kill.

The last word had been spoken with such bloodlust that it made Nathaniel shiver.

"If we do not deal with this now, there will not be a tomorrow for us to kill each other accordingly. So for now, put aside your differences, have therians join vampires, join photogeni, angels and human and let us feed the Earth with the blood of our enemies!!!"

The entire crowd roared in unison; one single war cry to make their intention clear, one clear message sent to heaven without the need of Selaphiel to guide it.

Unknown to them, the sky was sending a response. However, it wasn't anything like a celestial message. It was a mortar that Nathaniel saw land ten feet from him before everything in his vision went white.

Chapter 40: The Fourth Vision

Lights of every color imaginable pressed into Nathaniel's eyes. His body was completely still while at the same time feeling utterly ragdolled by some titanic force. Gaining any sense of direction was futile and he was quickly reaching the point of wanting to at least crash against any surface if only to be able to tell up from down.

All around him a surge of noise and memory shrieked and pulled at his being. Screams, moans and whispers all cocktailed into a sonic waterfall and his head felt like it was about to burst.

"How can you eat pudding if you don't eat your meat?"

"We didn't start the fire."

"Everybody hurts."

"I want to do something that matters."

"And just like that, he was gone."

"Freeedddoooommmmm!!!!!!!"

"He's only human."

"Kill 'em all."

"Some men just want to see the world burn."

Countless lines from his mental archives bombarded him but it was better than the sludge he had been hearing previously that had threatened to implode his brain. Finally he felt his body slow down while the air around him seemed to get thicker, halting the downward spiral of his descent. Before coming to a complete pause, he heard a strange voice scream in rage.

"Give me my wingssssss!!!!!!!"

The blood curdling order came just before he was finally able to stop. The lights around him flickered in a dizzying sequence before all went black. Familiar territory to him, hence his calm tone when he spoke to himself. "So this is what it feels like to die."

Nathaniel half expected an echo; instead, he received a reply.

"Not quite," answered the darkness. The strong voice came from all directions, but Nathaniel's eyes did not flicker desperately from side to side. If he had learned anything, it was that answers had a way of revealing themselves eventually.

"You've died before. This is different. How are you feeling?"

For his part, Nathaniel adjusted in the viscous nothingness that suspended him. It was as if he was reclining on air. "I think I now know what Adam felt when he landed."

"I highly doubt that since the first son landed foot first on land and you have neither landed nor are anywhere near land."

The young man noticed that his descent began winding in a long wide circle. His face was in deep thought and his next question was simple enough. "So where am I then?"

The darkness continued its slow deliberate downward churn and the shadowy omnipresence offered its response. "Specifics being almost impossible, let us say you are currently hovering in between a dream and the bottom of the ocean."

Nathaniel remained overwhelmingly calm. "Wow... even Confucius would accuse you of being a tad confusing."

In the distance far below, three small glowing embers appeared. Since he didn't know their real size, there was no way Nathaniel could tell how far off they were. He continued to recline in the solid nothingness as he thought of the next thing to ask. "So I'm in a space between a dream and the bottom of the ocean. Then tell me, what happened at the top of the ocean?"

"Your meeting was being held in very hostile waters. For years, Northern Sri Lanka has been dominated by a militia known as the Tamil Tigers. Their naval forces are among the elite of the world and they caught you off guard."

"Well I only remember the mortar that blew up close enough to rip my head off. I'm kind of wondering why it didn't."

"As has been the case on other occasions, you prove quite resilient." The dark voice's swirling tone lessened and focused on the opposing side of the slowly gyrating vortex.

Nathaniel appreciated the general direction in which to speak to. "So were there casualties?"

"Very many. There are actually various Tigers currently being fed on. Your companions did not appreciate being startled or the interruption."

"So how many of my side died?"

"From your side? Why none. It is admirable that the Tigers were able to surprise your forces. But apart from your concussed state and some shrapnel injuries, the only fatalities were human."

Nathaniel scoffed at the weakness of such an elite military force. Deadly soldiers had been reduced to nothing more than an evening snack.

"So how do you know how Adam landed?" asked Nathaniel in the direction of the three embers.

"Quite simple; I was there."

The response had been flat, precise and completely true.

"Further back than you could imagine, there came a fall; THE fall to be precise."

"Yeah, I know. Eve convinced Adam to eat the apple, he did and God punished them. It's in Genesis, we lost all we had except each other."

"That would be in the edited version of the book. The truth is a little different. It is true that Adam did eat of the forbidden fruit because of Eve, but she didn't do it of her own accord. God asked her to do it."

As Nathaniel turned towards his left, his eyes narrowed like venomous slits. "You mean the fall of man was God's idea?"

"Why not? Humankind's greatest triumphs and achievements often occur during the darkest times. Eve knew Adam would eventually yield to her suggestions, it's not like he had never thought about it for himself. God had asked this of Eve and thus, she was the first being to sacrifice it all and could easily be considered the first Christ or the original savior. She went from living in bliss to giving up everything just for the opportunity to do something magnificent."

Nathaniel continued to swirl in the wide circle, slipping deeper into the abyss. His face was of realization rather than confusion, enlightenment instead of entanglement. "I'd never thought of it that way."

"Naturally," replied the humming voice, "a lie has been nailed into your subconscious since you had your first thought."

Just then, a droplet of deep purple lit in the middle of the spiral. They were stopping their descent until a soft sand bottom returned Nathaniel his bearings. In fact, the small lamp in between him and the glowing embers gave him an idea of how big the three glowing dots were.

The light grew brighter, drops of cold salt water dripped from the ceiling of the bubble that had formed and the smell of smoke and sulfur prompted the human's next question. "How the hell do you know all of this?"

From the purple darkness a cloud emerged disregarding the ocean walls that surrounded them. The three embers then walked through that blanket of smoke. The bottom one was a cigarette, and the other two came from a steady glare reaching out from Bill's eyes.

"Like I said, kid, I was there."

Nathaniel's facial features suddenly remembered the look of confusion that had so often owned them. His breath caught, his throat snagged and realization bore into his consciousness like a tsunami of truth.

"You're the … you're… the… you're…"

"A lot more complicated than you can imagine, son. And just so you don't freak out, I don't mean that literally, we aren't directly related."

"But how do you…."

"The Good Book wasn't all wrong, Nat. There was a snake. Little did I know I was going to be the author of a Judeo Christian cliché, but hey, I've played many roles that have bitten me in the ass. Luckily, I was able to purge myself of that part of my being, thus Iblis was born.

Remember that snake Daniel killed on your first trip across the Atlantic? That was once a part of me. And as an added fun fact, you should know that Adam roamed the Earth for a thousand years before forgiving himself."

Nathaniel had to clear his throat several times before he was able to attempt to speak. His voice failed him and he was barely able to muster the words over his attempt at sympathy for Adam. After a few moments, he was able to ask a question. "What happened to Eve?"

Bill smiled. "Glad you asked. She waited at the very spot he fell, hoping he would return. After a thousand years, he did. The interesting thing was that she hadn't moved an inch. Guess women have a different way of asking for forgiveness and being loyal, than men."

Bill picked up the lamp and sat closer to Nathaniel on the damp ocean floor. "See? I am the light bringer," he said with a chuckle.

"Why are you doing this?" asked Nathaniel.

"This? What's this? Saving your life? Interfering in a battle? Offering you this much information? Come on, Natty boy; you haves ta be a tad more specific. If you want to ask me about all the dirty deeds with fire, brimstone, the pitch fork, etcetera, etcetera, please just remember that the Bible isn't all true and that it works best when used as a loose moral guide rather than a history book."

The poorly shaven man hauled a drag from his cigarette before continuing. "As for my nature, well like I said, I'm endlessly more complicated than what I've been shown to be. In a base sense, I am a necessary evil. But that doesn't mean I am incapable of feelings like love, mercy and giving and looking for forgiveness. Like Eve, I also had a choice and was forced to sacrifice a lot. To be honest, I really think I've paid enough dues to have earned some time off and that's part of the reason of why I'm doing any of what I'm doing. Especially now that mom isn't doing so well."

"Mom?" asked Nathaniel. "You have a mother?"

"Well she can be a mother or a father, remember that. God is defined by the times. She can also ail. Too little morality present on the Earth and a lack of faith has done more harm than any human can imagine. Oh, by the way, that does mean that God exists, and that she bore me, but if you're wondering about the meaning of life, there's no one correct answer to that question."

"So God can get sick?"

"It's not just that she could get sick Nathaniel, she is sick. I know the thought of combining omnipresence with mortality seems a bit contradictory, but such is God."

"So why is she a woman now?"

"Well women are stronger for starters. By nature they are better survivors than men. Besides, they ail much more gracefully than men and no doubt about it, mom isn't doing well. I'm pretty sure that's why the human who is orchestrating these happenings wants the wings. His name is Elliot and I'm pretty sure he plans to storm heaven. The idea is to take over and have the clear distinction of good and evil... It seems he's obsessed with eradicating the grey area of modern day morality. He is insane and he's authored tens of thousands of deaths. If I'm a necessary evil, you can consider him an unnecessary evil."

"Necessary evils?"

"Yes, necessary evils." He took a deep long drag from his cigarette, lightly scratching his chin while assembling his thoughts. "Even if what the Good Book says is a little off from what really happened, it's not like I have an unblemished record. I resented my role so much that I got to become a villain and trust me, I did some pretty terrible things. I didn't fully appreciate my role as a necessary evil until I met Jesus. You probably recall that whole bit about me tempting the son of God and so on and so forth."

"I remember from school."'

"I bet you do. Well what truly never changes in any version of the story is the fact that this kid never yielded to temptation during this period. Mind you, there's a big gap in the history of Christ, but what was recorded later was pretty kosher. Trust me, though; the books do little justice to what I tempted him with. Hell, he was so pious that I grew to hate him. I cursed him and even rejoiced when I found out he had gotten double crossed by one of his own."

Bill then took another long drag and muttered something to himself to which Nathaniel looked quizzically before interrupting the silence. "So then what?"

"Then I met him a second time. The plan was to gloat and even laugh at him as he died. You know, pissing on his grave before he was even laid to rest. That type of thing. Please take into account that this kid has just been whipped, crowned, beaten, has had to carry a cross for a ridiculous distance, was beaten anew, nailed to a cross and stabbed. And you know what he did when he saw me gloating?"

Before he spoke, Bill puffed a large ball of smoke and drank deeply from his cigarette as the shadow of a tear almost pried away from his eye. "He smiled."

Nathaniel's head snapped a little at the thought of Christ smiling down at Lucifer. Bill could only give small nods accepting he understood the human's reaction all too well.

"I know and to top it off, he thanked me for doing his father's will. Since I didn't understand, he had to tell me that I'd made good on the name our father had given me because I had helped him see the light."

Nathaniel felt the pit of his stomach give way to a huge void. Tears fell at his feet, but they were not his. They had thousands of years of emotion pent up and contrary to anything he had ever believed, there they were, flowing free from eyes that had seen the highest citadels in heaven and the deepest crags of hell.

"It is pretty much against my nature to feel defenseless, Nathaniel; but his words carved deep. I floated up to him, kissed his forehead and told him that his sins, for however few, were more than forgiven. Incredibly, he breathed a sigh of relief and thanked me for that. He gave me another warm smile, closed his eyes one last time and passed away. That was the moment I understood the concept of necessary evils. He could have been saved at least a dozen times, but he had to die and not for your sins as you are always told. He did it to inspire greatness at a time when faith was ailing, though it was nothing like today."

"Wait a minute. So Jesus didn't die to save us from our sins?"

"Exactly. He did it to save Father because it was for the greater good. At that time, Father was male and trust me, he learned a lot from that experience. But going back to the story, in his own way, Jesus had saved mankind from itself. But in a ways, it's like my existence... I'm a necessary evil that exists for the greater good."

Nathaniel looked around disoriented from the millions of emotions that conflicted in his heart. The cool ocean floor echoed his breathing while Bill decided to lie down and continue smoking his cigarette. Nathaniel searched for a word or a question but his mind failed him and he couldn't muster a complete thought let alone an audible word. Confusion mixed with rage, sadness and an overwhelming sense that he was dealing with something far too big for him.

"So what the hell am I?" he asked.

Bill sat up with some wet sand on his back and sipped yet again from his cigarette. "That's easy, man. You are the reaction to evil and you have to do what is in your power to help your side win. You aren't the only key to saving the world. Everyone's made that abundantly clear, I'm sure, but you are needed since you are the only human that is currently on the side of good in this battle."

"Good? I'm good even if I have to kill?"

Bill scoffed. "Hey, sometimes you gotta break a commandment or two to get the job done."

Again he drank of his eternal cigarette and again Nathaniel grew numb from the moment he was living. "And now?"

"Well you do have cardinal points still blocked. Remember those?"

Nathaniel became aware of his entire body and felt all the spots slightly tingle. "And what will I be able to do once those points are released?"

"You will see things no one else can see, hear things no one else can hear and do things no one else can do."

Nathaniel couldn't help but give a small chuckle. "Kind of like the stuff that came along in the six demon bag?"

Bill gave an incredulous smile. "Six demon bag... yeah, something like that."

A yellow and white light started to shine up from high above them – something with a rich cold glow. Nathaniel looked at the titan as it descended from the upper reaches of the ocean and down onto his spot in the abyss. His mouth fell open; he knew what it was but couldn't believe it even when he said it out loud. "Is that the moon?"

Bill smiled up at the enormous orb that descended on them. "Actually, that is your moon. A fragment of the moon's soul that is yours. And yes, planets, objects and celestial beings have souls. Actually most everything has a soul."

"But..."

"Like I said, kid; there are millions of things humans don't know and can't even begin to understand. That you even entertain the idea that you have a clue is just a testament at one of the finer jokes of the universe. Come with me, I think she wants to say hi."

Nathaniel stood up and stared at the orb as it plunged thousands of feet without causing any disturbance. Nothing shook or trembled; nothing quaked or shuddered, everything just hummed with energy. Thousands of feet passed in an instant until the satellite came within the human's reach. It pulsed and glowed, seemingly waiting for Nathaniel to reach out and touch her.

"She's magnificent," he said while trying to take in the vast glory and processing what he was seeing. After all, it's not every day you see a moon at the bottom of the ocean. "She's enormous."

To this comment, the moon pulsed its glow in a varying sequence and Bill laughed. Nathaniel looked at him confused. "What?"

"She says she hopes you don't think she's fat. Guess females of all kinds have more in common than we thought."

Again the moon pulsed a sequence of bright blips, which Bill seemed to listen to intently. Nathaniel for his part knew better than to ask if the orb was communicating via light pulses, it was obvious she was.

"She says she's going to get a little smaller to be able to talk better."

While Nathaniel was left wondering what that even meant, the moon shrunk rapidly until it was the size of a small shack. Upon reaching its new size, the moon hummed a few glows once again.

"She's asking if that's better."

Nathaniel smiled as he looked from the moon to Bill and back again. "How do you talk with her?" he asked.

"Well Nat, ma boy, first thing is you listen; and by listen I mean really listen. Open your senses and let your entire being communicate. Trust me; she can hear you just fine."

The moon then glowed and bleeped a sequence of lights. Nathaniel heard nothing and was left face to face with a miniature moon in a space between his soul and the bottom of the ocean. The sheer oddity of his current situation did not escape him.

Bill glanced at him sideways. "Listen better, not harder. Allow yourself to accept that you can listen to the light."

Nathaniel looked onto the moon again and looked intently as the sequence of lights repeated.

Silence.

He concentrated harder on the lights, seeing each sequence and not hearing one sound. The bleeps settled into a pattern that started to repeat itself. Four bleeps, four separate times, the moon shone brighter, but he heard and felt nothing. His teeth grated and he wanted to yell until he remembered something from when he was a child. He remembered those 3D images that you could see only by allowing your sight to lose focus. No matter how hard he tried, he couldn't see a damn thing, until one day instead of concentrating more, he simply relaxed his eyes. His vision had drifted for a second and voila, he finally saw the sail boat.

Without realizing it, his memory triggered something and he was now hearing bleeps like Morse code. He did his best to unfocus his hearing, disconnecting from the altered reality and paying attention but not focusing on the bleeps.

After a moment, bleeps started becoming phonetic fragments.

"Cu.. ou.... rrr.... ee."

He didn't want to get too excited so as not to lose his focus.

"Ca... ou..... eeer...ee."

Almost there, he could make something of it.

"Can ... you... hear ... me?"

425

His eyes blazed open as he looked towards the moon. Somehow he didn't need to see it to know she was smiling.

"Y- yes — I can hear you."

The moon started glowing once again but now he could hear a distant whisper speaking clearly. "Finally! What a great pleasure to finally be able to speak to you or should I say me, though really us is more appropriate since we are separate yet one and the same."

Nathaniel continued to look at the moon but struggled to understand how this satellite could possess a fragment of his soul.

"Actually I don't have anything. I AM a fragment of your soul."

Bill chuckled as he kissed his cigarette. "Man... your brain has to be pretty scrambled by now. Just in case, yes she can also hear your thoughts."

The moon continued in its airy disembodied voice. "It's simple really. You know stars and planets and satellites are all called celestial bodies, right? Well that's pretty accurate because we also have a mind and soul to go with that body."

"So why do you talk like a girl?"

"Well there are two main reasons. One, have you seen how many TV satellites are in orbit? It's ridiculous how many channels I get. Add to that the outrageous amount of text messages and web chatter I come in contact with and you get this voice."

"Ok........" Nathaniel was quite confused.

"Oh and one more thing." added the moon.

"What?"

"You had a hand in choosing a voice you'd be receptive to."

Bill had to laugh again. "Complicated enough for you?"

The moon simply glowed back. "Leave him alone, Bill; or I'll remember all the time that's passed since you've come to see your moon."

Immediately his defenses lowered and his voice took a sweet begging tone not unlike that of a child when asking for forgiveness. "I'm sorry."

"All right, but you better visit more often."

"Will do, hun; now let's focus on the boy. No offense, Nathaniel; but we are your seniors by a smidge."

A sequence of rapid beams about how one shouldn't disclose a lady's age ensued but luckily, she got back on point.

"Ok, Nathaniel, to unlock these particular cardinals, I need to know you are willing to do this."

A deep breath and focused eyes preceded a simple nod.

"Good. Before we go further, know that you will never see things the same way ever again. Anything. Are you still willing?"

"Yes, I am willing."

"Good. Bill?"

In a flash of an eye, Bill kicked off the sand bottom, picked something up and hit Nathaniel in the center of his forehead. As Nathaniel fell, everything went in slow motion and he could clearly see Bill leaping towards the moon. He stabbed her with a silver sword, turned mid air and chimed the blade with his fingertips.

Before Nathaniel touched the ground, Bill was supporting him while four gold-red droplets fell from the blade. Nathaniel felt his shirt open and one drop fall on his chest; the next one fell into his mouth, the third fell in his right eye and the fourth on the tender spot in the middle of his forehead. He felt tingling everywhere a drop had fallen while pillars of warmth began steaming off his body.

Bill laid him down on the ocean floor and whispered into Nathaniel's ear.

"Here you burn,

There you shine,

Earthly no more,

Now divine.

Close your eyes and wake to life,

Go to war and justly strike."

His sight became blurry, his body felt as if it was on fire and the last sight before passing out was a blood red moon rising up through the sea.

Chapter 41: Blood Red Sky

The commotion in Northern Sri Lanka had been brief. The Tamil Tigers had succeeded in taking the allied forces by surprise. Mortars had been thrown, grenades detonated and bullets shot, enough to level a small army. But the only two things that happened were that three hundred soldiers in the unit were already dead (the remaining hundred having been rounded up) and that Nathaniel had disappeared without a trace.

Daniel was now atop the largest barge, surveying the waters for any sign of the human. The dead Tamil bodies had been recovered and Nathaniel was not among them. The large circle that had been made by the boats was stained with blood and visibility in the water was quite hindered. The vampire searched frantically but found nothing. Reaching into his pocket, he took out the multicolored disc that once again leapt onto his face hungrily ripping into his flesh.

The grueling process of the lens embedding itself into his eye was as painful as ever. All around Daniel, a bright red light almost blinded him. He looked around but still couldn't see a sign of the lost human. What he did see however was an invisible whirlpool forming in the mid dimension.

As it spun, he saw a bright red point shining in the center of the vortex. Round it swirled, growing ever larger. Daniel looked on but couldn't comprehend what he was seeing. "What the hell is that?"

It took a full twenty seconds before he got his answer. The light had continued to glow brighter and more intensely until he saw a huge shadow crawling from beneath. He would have screamed out for people to watch out but he knew he was looking into the mid dimension thanks to the egnalem and the Eye of Cardino. People might have felt something odd, but they would not be able to see or hear the titan rising from beneath them. Actually, they would have only felt the shadow of its touch.

Instead of a large roar, the vampire felt a cataclysmic drone. At the sight of the red moon rising from the depths, he almost fell off the ship. The satellite soared upwards and when it reached a height of about sixty feet, it seemed to turn to face Daniel and proceeded to glow brighter in a deliberate sequence. After the series of lights had finished, the red moon began to ascend anew, up and beyond the clouds.

Still awestruck, Daniel's jaw slacked as he followed a trail of what he could only describe as red moon dust that sprinkled down into the water at the center of the arena where he saw and incandescent body floating in the water.

"NATHANIEL!!!!"

The vampire jumped off the barge and landed the eighty foot fall as if he'd just skipped. Before he got there, Nathaniel had stood up in the knee-high water and Daniel could see as the blood water drained from the human's nose. "Nathaniel! Are you all right?!"

The human proceeded to signal him to wait a moment. Although more blood water came from the human's nose and now his mouth, he did not cough nor seem remotely affected by the gallons of water that drained from him. When the water finally stopped, he casually glanced around. "Have I been gone long?"

Daniel was stupefied. "Gone long?! Nathaniel, where the hell were you? One second I see a mortar exploding, sending you flying and the next moment we can't even find your body."

"Yes, I know. But how long?"

"What? Did you even hear what I said?"

"Of course I did. But you obviously didn't hear me. How long have I been gone?"

"Uh... fifteen minutes, I think."

"Hmmm... interesting. Time seemed much slower there but come to think of it, fifteen minutes seems about right."

Daniel looked crossly at the human. "What are you talking about?"

"Is everyone all right?" asked Nathaniel.

"Uh... yes. You were the only one unaccounted for. Now that we've remedied that, it would be rather nice to know where you were and what the hell just happened, but you know, in your own time."

Nathaniel gave Daniel a very odd smile as he focused on the colored glass eye. He walked up to the vampire, put one arm on his left shoulder and pulled the thin gold chain that hung from Daniel's right eye. Instead of the usual resistance, the disc easily slipped free from the vampire's flesh. It had been ages since it had been that easy to remove the disc and the moment left Daniel at an even greater loss for words. The human came close to his ear and whispered. "Let's just say I'm a little less expendable now."

As smoothly as the smile had appeared, it faded. "Where are the remaining Tamil Tigers?" asked the human.

"How do you...?"

"I just do, Daniel. Take me to them, please."

"All right, but it is a disturbing sight, I'm pretty sure therians and vampires alike are feeding."

"That's fine, just take me to them."

Daniel didn't like the change he saw in Nathaniel, but he led him towards the prisoners. They hadn't walked long when they began to hear screams.

"You're sure about this," asked the vampire turning around to the human.

"Completely."

The water began to become redder and the smell of blood was probably attracting sharks from miles around. After turning past one of the therian ships, there was the scene Daniel wasn't sure he wanted his human friend to see. No less than twenty vampires were feeding on live soldiers and about thirty therians were gorging themselves on the dead ones. Countless faces were stained with blood and the soldiers that still lived were too afraid to even speak. However, when they saw Nathaniel, they began to cry and scream and even though no one spoke English, there's something about begging for one's life that translates perfectly to any language.

But Nathaniel's face was devoid of emotion. He looked at the carnage with an almost bored look on his face that caused everyone to stop feeding. Not even seeing Wendy's bloody mouth elicited a response from him. The prisoners continued begging for their lives. They somehow recognized he was human and knew he was their only chance at survival.

"Is Jane around?" he asked Daniel.

"Yes, why?"

"I have a few questions and a request."

Daniel looked at a young vampire and he didn't need to verbalize for him to fetch the captain. By now everyone had stopped feeding entirely but nothing seemed to concern Nathaniel.

After a moment's pause, Daniel asked a simple question. "What do you want us to do?"

Nathaniel raised his eyebrows at being treated as if he were in charge. He surveyed the scene, locked his gaze with some vampires and therians and gave his first clear and concise order.

"Kill them all."

***

The red moon hung low in Myanmar and a pair of beady eyes looked at it from a tall temple tower. The rosy flushed cheeks of Elliot blew out and drew a breath and his steel eyes did not blink for a time. His lips mouthed silent whispers and it almost seemed as if he were reading something in the heavens.

He looked towards his right and tilted a small mirror disc he had in his hand to reflect light into the eyes of a small demon waiting a few yards down the tunnel. At seeing the glint of light, the creature jumped paws first and with one gallop was beside the diminutive priest.

"Yes, Master Elliot. Did you want something to eat?"

"No, dark child; I need you to fetch me your masters immediately." He continued to look at the moon.

"They are in a meeting, Master Elliot."

"So interrupt them."

"But what shall I say?"

"That we're expecting company much sooner than we expected."

"How do you know?"

At the question, Elliot blinked and looked at the lean black skinned demon directly in its eyes. The small creature had been a child corrupted by evil. Most likely he had been forced to drink demon blood and kill an innocent creature, one of the many ways to create a demon. His small lean body was pure muscle although he had a small pot belly, normal for relatively new demons.

"Why don't I go myself instead to save you the trouble."

"Oh thank you, master."

"No trouble at all. But if I'm not mistaken, you had offered me something to eat."

"Yes, master. Anything you want."

"Anything at all?"

"Why yes, master. Anything at all."

"Do you have a knife I could borrow?"

"Of course, master. Take mine."

Elliot took the large knife in his hand and inspected it in detail. The small demon smiled and gave little hops at the appreciation his weapon was receiving from someone as powerful as the master. He was even more eager to please. "So what was it you wanted to eat, master?"

Elliot took a moment to think, gripping the knife in his left hand and then his right. He looked down to the little demon and gave it an awful smile. "Well actually, I think I'm in the mood for some dark meat."

Chapter 42: The Surge

The ocean breeze grazes Nathaniel's face, slightly stinging his eyes. He doesn't tear, he doesn't flinch and only occasionally does he blink. To his left stands Daniel... his focus is just as severe. The vampire's fangs dig into his lower lip and his eyes are a deep dark red with no white in them. To Nathaniel's right, Captain Jane stands behind the wheel. Her eyes are also a deep red, though not as crimson as Daniel's. Next to her stands Liam with his own set of maroon colored eyes. They all look forwards towards the looming horizon.

The speed of the Black Calico had often times been the subject of many legends. From all the routes he had witnessed onboard, Nathaniel knew that the root of the legend was a ship of unimaginable speed and God knows what else. But their current situation was something different altogether. The boat wheezed and creaked under the pressure of speed and power. The vessel was holding her own, but just barely.

"This is a bad idea," said Jane.

Nathaniel looked pensive for a moment before answering. "Maybe, but we need to regain some element of surprise and I couldn't think of anything better."

"But it's still a bad idea," Jane insisted. Her red eyes also stung slightly because of the spray that hit her face.

Daniel looked on at the horizon. "Are the ships keeping up?"

Liam looked behind at the pursuing ships. "All of them are right behind us and the Yggdrasil are behind them."

"Are they ready?" asked Nathaniel.

For a moment no one answered. They all looked ahead towards the horizon before Jane said what they were all thinking. "I don't think anybody could be ready for this."

***

Elliot sat down in the demon council chamber. He looked around and saw images that would have been the end of any typical human. He briefly picked a piece of black flesh from his teeth and cleared his throat with a dainty ahem.

"For some time now, we have been preparing for our moment of truth. We've used the resources afforded to us by this world and the sheep that overpopulate it. I was never invited by your master but as has become obvious to me, he is not coming back, he has abandoned you and you have been forsaken. Lord Astaroth has been kind enough to lead you. As for me, this is not the first time I have assisted the wayward and it has not been the first time I fill the void left by an absent father. It shall also not be the first time I use my followers as a means to an end. This world has grown immorally homogenous and the line between good and evil has been blurred. We are all here to see evil and good restored to their purest state. No longer shall we tolerate the grey morality."

"This God has become lenient and forgiving... tolerant and weak. I tried to steer the heathens through good and what did it get me? Weak faith, faltering beliefs and excuses instead of declarations."

Elliot paused a moment to allow his words to sink in. "So what happens when the path of light does not enlighten?"

The demons stared at each other. Sharp fangs, deadly talons, triple jaws, brown scales and yellow teeth remained idle on either side of the table at the question posed to them. No one seemed to have an answer.

Elliot took a breath before offering it to them. "When the path of light does not enlighten, you turn off the light, leave them in complete darkness and wait until they beg for light."

Horrible smiles gleamed in the dimly lit room and Elliot stood up and put his hands on the table made of human bodies. "Well if it's darkness they want, then darkness they shall receive."

***

"Where did this armor come from?" asked Nathaniel as he put on a light chain mail that hugged his body.

"You wouldn't believe me if I told you," Wendy said.

"Hell, it reminds me of the mythril armor I read about in Tolkien's books."

Wendy gave a slight shrug and muttered beneath her breath. "Or maybe you would believe me if I told you."

Nathaniel put on two light gauntlets, fixed two short swords to his sides and a large claymore on his back. His entire body took on a dark grey aura and he pressed to make sure all armor was well fixed to his forearms, thighs and shoulders.

He felt the armor and weapons but couldn't help but give a small laugh at the finely crafted albeit antiquated equipment. "My kingdom for a gun," he said with a soft laugh.

"So you're still human after all," said Wendy as she muffled her own laughter.

Nathaniel looked at her. "Sorry. Just feeling a little underprepared at the moment."

She walked towards him and smiled while caressing his body with her feline eyes. "It's not like guns would make any difference. Humanity has become all too dependent of its technology. Because of this, you've grown slower, weaker, and a lot less bright. With all that you've seen, don't you think that it's evident by now that what we're facing doesn't fear guns. Sure it's easier to pull a trigger, but what happens when the thing you shoot at doesn't go down? What happens when missiles and bombs kill more allies than enemies? Well you return to what worked before... as in way before. So although it may seem idiotic what we are doing, it also happens to be the only option. When something born from fire does not respond to fire, you use cold steel."

She was now inches away from his lips. He smiled down at her. "So I guess the trick is to study an enemy, find their weak spot and attack. Right?"

Wendy kissed him deeply as he held the back of her head. "Something like that," she said and kissed him again.

***

Topside, Daniel looked at Nathaniel in his armor. "Hardly seems like the 21st century, does it? Still, armors have been put on, weapons are fastened and the hunger for the kill is present. Now we just need to get some meat for the grinder."

Nathaniel looked approvingly. "Good. How far off are we, captain?"

Jane gripped the wheel tightly as her red eyes surveyed the horizon. "We'll be arriving soon... very soon."

***

Elliot looked down into a courtyard where eight large human battalions stood in formation. The military government of Myanmar had ordered thousands of soldiers to the devil fortress, no doubt negotiated by the priest. Next to the small man were seven figures, each grotesque in its own right.

To Elliot's direct right was a devil whose skin was charcoal black. Samyazza, the devil he had met with earlier in the depths of hell. Legend has it his color was a direct result from his fall from heaven. His skin writhed and moved as small worms bit through the flesh searching for light. His eyes were solid yellow and his focus was set on the army battalions below.

"We're a little short handed, my dear Samyazza," Elliot said while still picking black flesh from his teeth.

"Hell is not as unified as it once was," replied the devil as a worm broke through his cheek. "What are our odds, King Asmodai?"

Next to Samyazza stood a devil with stark white skin. His body was covered in lightly bleeding cuts depicting cards from a poker deck. His eyes were solid black and his mouth watered with blood rather than saliva. The sole dress on his body was a loincloth and a bag slung over his shoulder. He casually stuck his hand in the bag and took out a large silver coin and three dice. With his left hand he flipped the coin and with his right, he threw the dice. All of the objects fell flat on the floor without bouncing once. "Two sixes and a seven surrounding the cross," he said. "There's a one in four chance for success, Master

436

Elliot, but my gut tells me to not gamble this round and hold our hand."

"Many others would agree," the human said. "That is why many desisted from taking part of our cleansing and why the False Father has left us to die."

"Can you blame them, brother Samyazza?" said a more human-looking demon. "Without a parental figure, everyone does as they wish."

The manlike demon peered from behind red glasses and a thin long pipe the color of rust. His skin showed the perfection of cosmetics and he smelled of rose and lavender.

"Naturally, Azazel, I cannot blame them... their decisions are their own and will only factor if I'm given the chance to judge them."

"Ooooohhhh.... so feisty," said the man devil as he leaned on his ivory cane and sipped on his rusty pipe. "I get chills even."

"Hold your tongue, leech!" scolded a booming voice from what appeared to be a black winged angel, "or I'll rip it off and feast on it." His face was covered in a pitch black veil but his body was ashen gray and extremely muscular. The words would have been enough to silken most anyone but the sharp edge of a halberd, kissing the neck of Azazel guaranteed that he had the attention and compliance of the cock legged demon.

"Stand down, brother Samael," said the jet black Samyazza. "Tis the wretch's nature and unfortunately, we need him. Tamiel, what news of the hatchlings?"

Behind the group of demons crouched an abnormally short but thick demon. His skin was sickly green and his face was covered by a mask made of braids from his own hair. He smelled of caked blood and musk and his hands and feet were disproportionately larger than the rest of his body. The demon licked his bladed gauntlets and breathed in deeply while savoring his lips. "All hatched, brother. Now they just need something to tear into."

"And the bodies of the women?"

"All kept in the crypt."

"Good," said Samyazza. "Tell the wraiths that if they fight well they will be able to feed on the skin of their mothers."

The repulsive devil, responded with a twisted green smile. "That'll make them restless and angry."

Samyazza remained emotionless. "I know."

A large flap was heard from the remaining shadow.

"Yes, King Astaroth?" asked Samyazza.

From the deep shade came a sound like a massive talon scraping on asphalt. Out walked a demon that was at least nine feet tall. His skin was pale white and coarse, while his hair was long, wild and flaming red. His legs had scales like a dragon and rough claws for hands. His chest was bare and on his massive back were two large leathery wings. The kilt that seemed to cover his lower body was actually a second pair of wings, colored as black as a raven. His eyes were all white and his face was human and actually delicate.

"Do we have any news from Ceylon?" said the demon in a low hiss.

After a moment where no one answered, Elliot felt the need to clarify. "What is it, King Astaroth? Why do you ask of those forces?"

"Your kind has an expression that truly applies, Master Elliot. It is a gut feeling because I realized that no one noticed when Tamiel failed to mention our forces down in Ceylon. I think it a curious detail to overlook at this juncture."

All eyes turned to Tamiel as Astaroth continued.

"After all, it was he who created the Tamil Tigers, trained them, helped them establish a base off Adam's Bridge and recruited their services in the forceful acquisition of the hosts for our wraiths."

With every second, Tamiel looked more like a negligent parent ashamed of his forgetfulness.

"When was the last you heard of them?" asked Astaroth.

Tamiel looked to the stone floor. "Three days ago, my lord."

Astaroth's eyes narrowed viciously. "Lovely," he said. He then spread his wings and gave a massive flap that sent him soaring high above the temple. After climbing at least a hundred feet he stopped suddenly, clasped his hands and began a low chant in a language older than any recorded memory.

Slowly his lower wings spread open and his stark naked body turned towards the southwest. His all white eyes snapped open and he swiped his claws through the air, appearing to tear into nothing. But his claws had connected and in the middle of the air a red and black slit appeared and spread. The void crackled electrically and his arm disappeared into the small emptiness.

The group below looked up as Astaroth stood next to a gap in space and time and pulled out what seemed like four red glowing cables. He then strummed the four strings like a guitar. Six times he struck them until he put a brown claw nail against the strings causing a harmonic chime to ring for miles around.

He then neared his mouth towards the luminescent strings and breathed onto them: "Children... answer thy father's call and give me news." With every word, the strings sent vibrations deep into the void. He then hovered above the temple waiting for a reply.

All of a sudden, three distant thunders rang followed by a fourth boom much closer. The demon held the strings and closed his eyes as four large vibrations rocked through his arm. His stone countenance suddenly turned endlessly more grim. He let go of the strings and opened a large gash on his forearm. He pressed his hand against the wound and then passed the black blood stained hand against the void. The gap trembled and sounded like cloth tearing in reverse as the hole sealed. He spit on his hand and pressed it against the wound and the blood began to boil as his lower wings clothed his body once again.

Afterwards, he collapsed his wings to fall about nine stories before spreading them again to brake his descent. He fell the remaining fifteen feet and landed exactly from where he had lifted up. Samyazza looked particularly anxious.

"What news do the four have, Lord Astaroth?"

The devil king gave Tamiel a hateful look before speaking. "Get a radio connection to Bago city right now." He spit the words to the stout devil as if he were about to decapitate him. He then turned to the shadow he had originally emerged from. "Cleora, it seems your talents are as honed as ever. Do as we agreed."

With her orders received, the slim silhouette of a woman faded further back into the shadow until nothing of her remained. Astaroth then turned to those still present. "All four have answered with news. Aamon informs me that a large legion of angels surged from Dudael in the heart of Djibouti. They headed towards the heavens but no movement has been seen afterwards. He suspects and I agree that like our brothers who have deserted us, heaven wants no part of this conflict."

"Why the neutrality?" asked Elliot.

"If there was an imbalance of power, they would interfere, but their righteous beliefs have actually given us a chance. Barbatos has told me that Murmur has been detained by lower echelon angels but that he is on his way."

Tamiel then appeared with a short wave transmitter radio. "I have communication with the base master, what should I say?"

"Pruflas told me that the entire Liberation Army has been eradicated."

The other devil stood with his jaw slacked without breath. Samyazza decided to intercede. "Did Rashaverak have news of the other base? What should we tell them?"

As he said this, the radio receiver began to rumble in Tamiel's hands. A deep roar eclipsed the screaming of hundreds of people on the other side of the line. Astaroth looked at the radio and clenched his jaw. "There's nothing to tell them. They're dead."

***

At Bago, a massive surge demolished the entire base and kept surging inland without losing any speed. Survivors would later tell of the enormous wave that had come and the eight ships that seemed to have been dragged in from the sea.

***

Atop the tidal surge, the ships were barely holding together. All around they saw the destruction of the wave they rode and now as they neared the temple, the source of the surge began to appear. Ocean vampires began filtering out from behind the water below the ships holding large narrow sheets of steel. As each vampire stopped serving as propulsion the ships decreased speed until they were left in the wake behind the surge that still rolled on. Huge makeshift anchors made of boulders were thrown off the side and soon all vessels had fallen behind as they watched the giant wave hurtle towards its target like a rogue bowling ball streaking down a lane.

The Black Calico was struggling but managed to handle the strain of the anchors and the speed. Other ships were not as fortunate and tore in half when the anchors were deployed. The ocean vampires picked up vampires and therians that had fallen from the ships and passed them onto the ships that still held together.

Behind the wave the water receded quickly and where once there had been a lush jungle, now only a raked plain remained. With several large thuds and cracks, the ships touched on the ground. Nathaniel looked to the distance and could see the wave still reeling a mile away. One massive wall of water that had the simple purpose of destruction. As all forces jumped from the ships and began to run in pursuit of the target, he couldn't help but smile.

Chapter 43: The Battle of the Plain

As the sun descended into the horizon, a low rumble swelled into a roar of destruction. Much of the initial strength of the mass of water had dissipated, but that didn't matter. The wave continued to rip a clean path, uprooting buildings, trees and anything foolish enough to remain in its way.

A flock of birds takes flight from the trees next to the temple. Seconds later, a sickening crash is followed by an earsplitting crack. The temple wall had been breached. Water swirled into the corridors on that side of the structure and the rest spread into the surrounding areas. All that remained was silence.

A thousand yards to the south, paws, feet and roots run north across a muddy trail a quarter of a mile wide. Hundreds of eyes survey the devastated southern wall of the temple.

"Hold!!" cried the Black Calico's captain. All forces stopped instantly. Beside the captain were Nathaniel, Daniel, the therian Furies, Uroc and Corsac as well as the photogeni perennials, Banyan and Elm.

Daniel and Nathaniel both wore dark grey armors while the Furies carried heavy steel plates that hung loose from their muscular bodies. For their part, perennials wore thick armor made of tree bark, which had taken on a red hue from having been infused with egnalem.

"What do you see sister?" asked Banyan.

"Nothing. I don't hear anything either. And if you ask the therians, I'm sure they will sense a lack of blood in the air. They knew we were coming."

"Are you sure?" Uroc asked.

"Father Fury, you don't ravage the oceans of the world and save my esteemed colleague repeatedly without learning to know when you are expected."

"So now what?" asked Daniel. "If they know we're coming, we should oblige them."

Jane gave him a look that could castrate. "That's exactly the type of thinking that always has me saving your ass. We hold position here because any artillery becomes nullified due to distance. Right now we have no cover and the element of surprise was never ours to begin with."

Nathaniel clenched his jaw and quickly realized that the current situation was his fault. He hadn't really thought of any back-up plan. To make matters worse, a hideous howl screeched from the temple. When the attacking force looked, a small demon atop a platform was seen rallying a force of about a thousand wraiths. At the sight of the enemy, the entire Bouda Horde sprang to life and raced to meet the creatures head on.

Jane did her best to cry for them to stop but they were already transforming. As they ran, their bodies swelled and took on the distinct hyena traits of their clan as they lobbed cackling war cries. Muscles expanded, bodies grew and where once dangling pieces of metal hung, rigid armor was now fixed.

The speed with which they reached the body of soldiers was impressive but not as impressive at how easily they dismantled their foes. Sharp talons drew black blood and wailing cries filled the air.

"So those are the wraiths," Nathaniel said.

Jane's eyes gained a deadly focus. "Actually, those are weakborns."

The Bouda were relentless in their attack and they'd killed more than three hundred grunts before being surrounded by fifty lightly armored wraiths. One of the hyena men was especially savage in his attack, ripping torsos and decapitating bodies at will. His name was Bieti, the leader of the Bouda. He took a spear from the ground and impaled a wraith until his fist pressed against its chest plate. Right then he noticed a red gem on the armor, which sparkled with the sunset's glare.

'But that can't be' Bieti thought, realizing the sun was at the monster's back. He looked deep into the yellow and grey eyes of the wraith whose last gesture was to twist its face into a disgusting grin.

Overlooking the battle, Elliot smiled as monstrously as the wraith. In one hand he held a glass of dark liquid, in the other was a detonator. A giant explosion instantly killed every Bouda as well as every wraith. From the temple wall came the second wave of wraiths, much meaner in demeanor and much more solid of body.

"What just happened?" asked Daniel.

Jane's focus unwavered. "Reality happened, Daniel. Nina, Louise, Cheng!"

As soon as the words had left her mouth, the three Corsaires landed at her side, covered in mesh to keep the sun at bay. "Yes, captain," they all answered at once.

"Get to the Yggdrasil as fast as you can. We need Roanoak here as fast as his roots will take him. Tell him to bring the anchors we brought and help them any way you can. Now go!!"

"Yes, captain!" they replied in tandem and darted straight towards the south.

"What are we going to do with the anchors?" asked Nathaniel.

Jane's look almost beheaded the human. "They didn't question me for a reason. You should do the same. Though you could make yourself useful by leading a troupe against that offensive which is bearing down on us."

A young looking Japanese man neared Captain Jane. "I am Juno from the Kitsune Horde. We can go with the human."

Jane gazed deep into his eyes. "You are aware that this is probably another trap."

"Yes, captain; but we are not in the mood to wait for death. We rather meet her head on."

Jane smiled at the bravery of the Japanese warrior. "Spoken like a true Kitsune. Go, but use distance attacks. They won't try the same thing twice but they will try something."

"Yes, captain," answered Juno as he tapped Nathaniel on the shoulder. They ran to the front of the camp and were met by twenty-five other warriors.

The wraiths were about halfway to the forces when two dozen flying knives took down twenty of them. The werefoxes drew their second set of blades and ran in two lines to meet the wraiths head on. The first line did a double flip and reloaded their knives closely followed by the second line. In the blink of an eye, another twenty one wraiths fell dead on the wet ground. Nathaniel didn't know much Japanese but from the reactions of the unit, he could tell that the orders to draw weapons and kill had been given and they were being followed exquisitely.

The transformation of the werefoxes was faster and smoother than other therians, although their armor had never been as loose as the Bouda tribe's. The unit cut into the wraiths and in one minute had nearly killed two hundred of the foul creatures. Nathaniel had drawn his double swords and killed twenty monsters by himself when a collective crack rang from the jungles on the side whose trees hadn't been decimated by the tsunami.

Three Kitsune fell along with ten wraiths. When Nathaniel looked towards the thick brush, he couldn't see anything until a second volley cracked from the jungle allowed him to see the glint of at least two sniper lenses. He continued to chop down wraiths but was now running into the trees when a log was lobbed at him, which he ducked at the last second. But instead of a loud crash, he heard a limp thud on the ground and then saw that the log was really the body of one of the snipers. When he looked back into the brush, Nathaniel saw two jade eyes making their way out of the jungle. "I thought you'd like a souvenir," Daniel said.

The roaring, screaming and tearing of flesh were all Nathaniel needed to hear to know that the snipers were being taken care of. The Kitsune werefoxes had been joined by the Runaas werejaguars from Argentina and out from the jungle charged the various shape shifters from the Mexican Nahuales Horde and the Canadian Wendigo, including Rufus the Red Wolf leader and the massive Beorn drenched in blood in his bear form.

"Let's go back to the captain," Daniel said as they both ran to the rear of the compound. There they had fashioned a battle area where Jane, Uroc and Banyan stood over a rough representation of the battlefield.

"Father Fury, regroup your therians after they finish this swarm of wraiths. No one should be exposed unnecessarily."

"Yes, captain," responded the elder therian and left to do as had been instructed.

Jane now turned to the photogeni, "Brother Banyan, are your forces ready?"

"Yes, captain."

"Are you sure about this?"

"We didn't come here to sit on the sidelines, madam. We are ready."

"Ok, you remember the signal. But remember, only as a last resort."

"Agreed, captain," said the rough skinned perennial as he walked towards a group of young looking photogeni.

"You look so sexy giving orders," Daniel said.

"Later, Daniel. How long until sundown?"

"Twenty minutes, give or take a minute."

"Good. Roanoak is ten minutes away."

"Are the other vampires all right?"

Jane looked at him incredulously. "I don't know, Daniel! I'm sure Roanoak's foliage provides the cover they need but I'm kind of busy at the moment."

Daniel looked to the floor and marveled at his ability to be a complete and utter ass regardless of the situation at hand. "Sorry. Is there anything I can help with?"

Jane was unable to answer because explosions crashed from the field. A third line of wraiths even larger than the second one was running towards the remaining therians who were still finishing off the second wave. At the base of the temple a large infantry of Myanmar soldiers was launching grenades and walking behind the wall of monsters to get nearer.

Tamiel's drums boomed from the moving infantry. They had bought the time they needed and were just now mobilizing their true forces.

Jane's eyes filled with terror and focus. "Daniel... I'm going to need you to hold that off until the cavalry arrives. Kill as many as you can and by all means, pray."

***

Astaroth looked on as the huge infantry moved down the field. Four thousand well bred and nourished wraiths armed with giant swords, spears, and war hammers were followed by another four thousand human foot soldiers. At the other end of the field, the opposition barely numbered a thousand. "Are the demons ready, Lord Samael?"

"On your signal, my liege. But are they going to be completely necessary?"

The scowl on Astaroth's face should have been enough but next to him a smug and rosy human face stared at him. "Mercy and underestimation will be your undoing one day Samael; although I could save you the trouble right here and now."

The demon looked down on Elliot and could only think of all the ways he would love to disembowel him. "We'll have a conversation when this is over, human."

Elliot looked at him dully as he sipped on his glass of bile. "I look forward to it, half demon."

The demon gripped his halberd with every intention of using it but was interrupted by Astaroth. "Thank you, Lord Samael. Ready the demon infantry and await my signal."

Even behind the veil, it was clear that the fallen angel clenched his charred jaw and his muscles had to fight to obey his lord's order. "Yes, King Astaroth." Samael then stormed out of the balcony and jumped down into the central garden next to an infantry of about 3,000 demons.

"Master Elliot, I know you are not too fond of Samael but a demon can only tolerate so much."

Elliot scoffed in reply. "You say that as if I should be afraid of your pet. Maybe he should be the one afraid. I already had a tiny aperitif this evening. Maybe this time I can go for a full dish of broiled meat."

The demon king could only stare in awe at the human. Meanwhile, Samyazza and Asmodai overlooked the inner garden coordinating the forces below.

"Damn!" said Samyazza. "What are the odds on Samael ripping the head off of that arrogant ass?"

Asmodai lowered his head while smirking. "I don't have to toss a coin brother. Samael would be dead in three moves."

Samyazza's neck cracked from how fast he turned to look at the gambling demon's face. Asmodai continued to peer down into the central garden. "You really have no conception of what that little man is capable of."

***

The war drums rang loud and the stomping of the third tier wraiths was only overcome by the explosions of the grenades being launched from behind the ground troops. Five battalions ran in a V formation to meet the enormous force head-on. At the farthest ends were Uroc and Corsac leading the remaining Kitsune werefoxes, Nahuales and Runaas hordes. The middle two teams were led by Daniel and Nathaniel.

Daniel's group included about 50 vampires covered in mesh to withstand the remaining sunlight while Nathaniel rode on the back of the great Beorn in his massive bear form. The top of the V was made up of a young group of photogeni led by Elm. The perennial's bark had grown very thick and his face was now covered by thick wood that served as a face plate. His hands had also covered themselves in a thick bark with spines that had been sharpened to a deadly edge. The young photogeni were of the twig class and most were barely forty years old. They also wore wood armor on their bodies but not as thick or tough as Elm's. They'd decorated their bodies with vines and sap and various pods that trembled with each step.

The eyes of the perennial were set on his target as he led the group against the massive infantry. He ran with both arms ready to spill blood and the grenades that exploded near him did little to take away his focus. At a hundred feet, he lowered his head to gain more speed and screamed through his face plate.

"READY!"

The next three seconds passed in a blur.

"NOW!!!!!!"

Before reaching the infantry, every twig drew the pods dangling from their bodies and threw them onto the coming force. The pods managed to hit various wraiths in the face, temporarily blinding them. Otherwise, it proved a fruitless attempt on the hand of the photogeni before crashing into the infantry.

Elm drew first blood and slashed clean through six wraiths before taking a single hit. Though young, the twigs wielded spears and wooden swords that drew more blood than some steel weapons had in their entire lives.

Seconds later, Daniel and Nathaniel also engaged the enemy. Daniel slashed at dozens of wraiths with his rapier. Nathaniel was still riding Beorn who had six javelins latched to his sides. Each one the human threw scored its mark. He then picked up a long spear that had also been fastened to Beorn's back and leaped onto the warriors below.

Last to land were the therian hordes who broke off to attack the lateral sides of the infantry. Blood flowed freely from all races. Therian claws and talons slashed, photogeni spears and swords struck and wraith war hammers and axes felled bodies without prejudice.

A loud whistle rang and mid-swing, all vampires, therians and photogeni ducked and covered before several hundred arrows fell from the sky ripping into the wraiths. Before the first wraiths had fallen, two other volleys had landed leaving no less than six hundred dead on the ground.

By the same token, grenades were doubled but the human infantry could now see the skirmish in the crowd that had cleaved through more than halfway through the forces.

Elm's battalions continued in a straight line, Daniel's banked right, Nathaniel's banked left and both therian hordes ripped through the forces perpendicularly until breaching the other side and reentering the throng.

Tamiel saw the great losses in his army and called over two human soldiers. "If this drum stops, your families die."

The soldiers didn't understand a word of what the demon said but when he drew his blades and translated into their language, the color left their faces and they hit the drum just as fiercely as the demon had been doing. When he looked at the battle again, Tamiel saw a grenade fall directly on one of the twigs and though he wanted to celebrate the kill, he noticed that the photogeni had exploded sending thick patches of what seemed like liquid fire into all the wraiths that surrounded him. When he looked towards both sides of the battlefield, he saw hundreds of flames light up almost simultaneously and soar over the crowd.

Every single patch of sap caught fire and whatever remained of the third infantry was being dealt with quickly. Nathaniel continued to score countless kills and his face was drenched in wraith blood. A group of six wraiths came running in his direction. He ran to meet them head on with a short sword in his right hand and the long spear in his left. After parrying four blows, he buried his spear deep into the chest of a wraith, slashed the wooden beam of the spear with his sword, stabbed another wraith with what he had left of the spear, snapped the wooden beam yet again and stabbed a third wraith, finally leaving what was left of the handle in the monster's flesh. A fourth wraith fell from an arrow to the head, the fifth wraith of the group got beheaded by Nathaniel and the sixth wraith was tackled by a flaming twig that pushed its burning limbs into the beast's mouth and eyes.

While he drew his second short sword, a loud bang threw him back twelve feet. In the distance, Tamiel held what looked like a seven foot long musket with a sight on its top.

"Oh goody, one of my toys in action," smirked Azazel from the balcony. "You don't get to teach these kids how to make and use weapons without keeping a few things for yourself."

Astaroth kept looking towards the battle and Elliot held his glass up in salute to the cock legged demon. Azazel ignored him preferring to retouch his makeup. The large figure of Samael came running to his leader and stood by his side.

The battle raged on and they could see their forces had lost more than three thousand wraiths and now the human militia was also taking heavy losses. The branch photogeni forces had shot all their arrows and were now picking up the wounded and taking them back to the root photogeni for treatment.

Elliot finished his glass of black liquid and seemed genuinely untroubled by the violent conflict below. His focus was still on egging Samael. "So, strong one, still think you will easily overpower this resistance? Hell all they had to do was kill twenty per head and they'd wipe out the infantry."

Samael breathed so hard that his veil almost lifted over his nose. "I'll have your head!"

Before the fallen angel could even grip his halberd, Astaroth pounded on the veranda breaking off a three-foot piece of granite. His eyes stayed focused on the battle though. To his right, Samyazza kept his eyes on the battle as well. "What now, my lord?"

The demon king scraped his talon on the floor, kicking bits of granite into the air. "Send the rest of the militia and order them to kill that damn human."

***

As bodies kept littering the floor, Tamiel sliced through two therians, a vampire and five photogeni. With him, several soldiers ran with assault rifles shooting anything that moved.

Daniel was two hundred yards away and had seen Nathaniel shot, but a group of two hundred wraiths stood between him and where last he had seen the human. Tamiel continued to move forward and when he got near the human, he saw that he was actually getting to his knees and taking off what looked like a cracked chest plate.

A disgusting sneer snailed across the demon's face while he licked his bloodied gauntlets. He relished every step that took him closer to the wounded man. All around he heard screams and grunts and remembered why he enjoyed war so much. Death, battles, the warm spray of blood bathing his blades; this is what he lived for. But the screams of vampires, photogeni and therians exchanged for blood curdling screams and cries for God. When he turned around, he saw a

451

walking flame beheading a soldier with one blade, crushing the skull of another on the ground and impaling another one with his other blade.

Completely engulfed in flames, Elm had killed thirty soldiers and ten wraiths on his way to Tamiel. Nathaniel saw as the demon's smile faded away. He turned to the enflamed perennial and ran with his blades drawn. Nathaniel saw Tamiel score six hits on Elm who stumbled forwards until a seventh blow had Tamiel's gauntlet blade buried in the chest of the elder photogeni, but when screams of pain sounded... they were the demon's.

The perennial had pulled him closer and wrapped him in a burning embrace. As soon as the screams had ebbed away, the sound coming from the scene was maniacal laughter. The photogeni kept burning but looked toward the sky as he laughed for a time until he went silent, took a deep breath and gave out a blood-curdling roar. He broke off his badly damaged arm and roared into another crowd of soldiers.

Nathaniel was about to black out when he saw five soldiers coming his way. He went to pick up his short sword and fell on his knees, looking at the soldiers as they drew their guns and fell right before pulling their triggers. Two had long spears in their chests, two had daggers in their throat and head and the middle one was getting his throat ripped out by a vampire that hadn't even bothered to take the cigarette out of his mouth.

After finishing the soldier, Liam knelt next to the human. "We truly have to stop seeing each other like this." He opened the shirt that had been under Nathaniel's chest plate and saw a black bruise covering more than half his upper torso. "Nice hit. Let's take you to the roots for treatment."

The vampire helped the man up and held him on his shoulder when he heard hundreds of guns being fired and the slow thumping of the war drums. Liam saw about ten thousand human soldiers running straight at him and his heart almost gave way. "Nat, I'm not sure what's worse, the gunfire or the war drums."

Nathaniel was looking back at their camp and a trail of blood trickled down the corner of his smile. "That's no war drum."

When Liam turned his head he saw the imposing figure of the Yggdrasil Roanoak casting a huge shade on the entire battlefield. Large boulders had been launched from the trees and all the remaining vampires were running towards the oncoming infantry under the cover of the massive tree.

***

Astaroth's eyes glared as he saw five hundred soldiers die in about thirty seconds. To his left Samyazza stood gripping his sword and clenching his teeth. Elliot's usual smile faded and a sinister look came over his eyes. "Now would be the time to send everyone out, my dear king."

The demon spread his wings and looked at Elliot as if he was about to kill him. "SAMAEL!!!" he called.

"Yes, my lord," said the veiled angel.

"Lead the fourth tier and release the demons."

"Yes, lord!" responded Samael before jumping off the balcony into the inner garden.

Again the demon king spread his wings and Samyazza gave him a large black scimitar. "I'd like to meet this human before he is killed."

Astaroth then leapt off the balcony overlooking the battle and glided down using his powerful wings. Elliot brushed off his frock and produced a large book.

The front cover was black with gold letters and read 'The Bible'. Elliot looked at it and puffed a small laugh as he looked at the back cover which was bone white and had something written upside down in deep maroon. Azazel looked at the human and gave a little giggle. "What are you going to do, read them to death?"

Elliot flipped the book to have the red on white letters upright to show him the title of the book. The usual giggles that would come from Azazel went silent and his eyes bulged as if each one wanted to rip itself out of the demon's skull.

"Fer... Fernaculum...? How did you get that?"

"If you survive today, I'll let you know."

The demon looked at the raging battlefield and Asmodai walked towards them and looked down to the book. "I don't know, brother

453

Azazel, fighting in that battle doesn't seem like it offers good chances for survival."

Elliot laughed lightly at the demon's comment and cleared his throat before speaking. "Who said anything about fighting?"

***

The crippled vampires of the Gerald faction had done away with dozens of human soldiers already. Christopher rode a steel wheelchair with spiked wheels, automatic crossbows on either side and an array of weapons at his disposal. Another vampire with spikes for fingers pushed the Gerald leader's wheelchair and continued to chop down the waves of soldiers. To the left side of the field, the Laius child vampires were assaulting the forces as well.

Liam nodded at them as he carried Nathaniel through the carnage. Half the human's armor was gone but he still had one short sword and the large claymore was still slung on his back. Liam banked left moving to the east part of the field and Nathaniel saw the Louvetiers and the Night Rooks finishing off what was left of the third tier wraiths.

When they got to the rear of the battlefield, they saw how the root forces had set up a medical area to mend lesser wounds to resend therians and photogeni into battle. Unfortunately, many therians had taken severe injuries and were sidelined next to Roanoak's center tree, receiving more advanced healing treatments from the large wood.

Liam helped Nathaniel sit down as a root photogeni sat next to him.

"Hello, Mr. Runnels," said the woody creature as he checked the human's chest. "We met once but you weren't too conscious on that occasion." Nathaniel winced as the tree put pressure on the bruise. "You're lucky you didn't crack your sternum."

Nathaniel sat up a bit more and grabbed the photogeni by the shoulder. "I need to get back out there."

Liam looked at the photogeni's long twig-like fingers and noticed that they were all different colors. "Mate, we need an analgesic, a pain killer and anything that can get him more energy."

The photogeni looked at him crossed. "But there might be a fracture."

Liam gave a rough grunt, picked up a stick, put it in Nathaniel's mouth, took out a pouch and dumped half the egnalem inside onto the human's chest causing him to almost bite through the piece of wood. He then looked at the photogeni and grabbed him by the throat. "I'm his doctor; now give him what he needs."

***

Daniel continued leaving a trail of dead soldiers everywhere he passed through. His rapier had already run through and slashed ninety wraiths and soldiers. Towards him now ran twenty more. They fired a volley which he jumped over, throwing his sword into one of the soldiers, landing in position to snap the neck of another. He used that dead body as a shield and pulled another soldier's gun so his shots hit three of his comrades. After that, he ripped the throat of another and pulled his rapier from the body of the first soldier he'd killed. Before he could add another kill to his résumé, the remaining soldiers were chopped in half by an axe the size of a small house. Wielding that axe was a hideous wraith thirteen feet tall and about six feet wide. Its grey skin seemed to glow in the darkening night.

Daniel didn't think twice about retreating and screamed for others to follow. Some vampires were not able to get out of the way and were felled by the behemoth. Another huge boulder had been launched by Roanoak directly to the fourth tier wraith. The monster looked straight at the three-ton rock and punched it to the side as if it had been a beach ball. As Daniel ran to warn the others, he heard battle roars coming from the middle of the field.

The eight therian Furies, Beorn and Rufus were running straight for the fourth tier wraiths, which numbered about thirty. They literally tore into the ground with their sharp claws and as they got nearer they completed their transformations into the full manifestation of their therian side. Their bodies grew and their muscles flexed and tightened. Daniel saw the moving force and ran to meet them before they collided with the mammoth wraiths.

He saw Rufus the red wolf leader of the Canadian Wendigos, Aureus the Golden Jackal, smaller brown wolves, probably Madonna and Phoebe, two huge black wolves that were Vilkacis and Gilles

Garnier, a lean spotted wolf that had to be Corsac, the beautiful white mane of Luna and largest of all, a grey beast that could have been a lion, the great Uroc. But it was with Beorn that Daniel locked his jade eyes with. The huge bear was battle weary but his injuries were meaningless when you saw the menace in his eyes.

Words didn't need to be spoken. The vampire climbed onto Beorn's back to face the menace that was making its way towards them. Daniel looked to the left and saw how the Laius were herding a thousand soldiers to the left. He also saw how another force of branch photogeni made its way through the western wood to surprise the soldiers hidden there. To the right, the last of the third tier wraiths were finally brought down by the Gerald vampires, while ahead the Night Rooks and Louvetiers tried to hold off the fourth tiers.

The vampires had actually brought down two of the massive wraiths but had been forced to join what was left of both factions to try and mount a stand.

The therians gave a collective roar and even though the wraiths had turned to face them, three had been tackled by the large beasts. Daniel jumped off Beorn and ran straight towards the fallen monsters to stab their eyes and slit their throats. Though the fiends proved resilient, the wounds had been strategically struck and the assailing therians proceeded to focus on those wounds.

Among the huge wraiths, one towered over the rest and Beorn rammed straight into it with a vicious growl. The massive beast reeled back and dropped its war hammer but caught the bear as he ran into him again, locking arms and wrestling as others fought around them.

One of the wraiths punched Vilkacis and Giles Garnier fifty feet away but Luna's white mane stained with grey as she slashed clean through the back of its neck. Corsac along with Madonna and Phoebe attacked another wraith until Corsac was able to lay behind the beast's legs so the female furies could trip it and pounce to rip through its chest.

Rufus had wounded two wraiths but his mane was getting redder from two wounds on his back and one on his left hind leg. In front of him, the two wraiths came straight for him with battle-axes in hand.

The one on the left had risen its axe but quickly went limp as Daniel slashed the tendons in its hooves, knocking the axe forward so the creature buried itself on its own massive weapon. The wraith on the right had swung and missed with its axe but managed to hit the red wolf with a back fist that sent him hurtling across the air. Before Rufus could even realize what had happened, his flight came to an abrupt stop from Samael's massive halberd which had buried itself in his ribcage.

The fallen angel laughed cruelly as the lifeless body of Rufus fell to the ground. Daniel's cry would have made anyone shudder but not a sound came from anyone else when they saw the legion of demons that followed the fallen angel. His pain was short lived though. A volley of arrows dropped fifty demons and the cry of all the forces roared from behind Daniel with every single being that could walk and hold a weapon attacking.

Branch photogenis lobbed spears and javelins, twigs slashed with their wood swords, perennials used lances and wooden axes, the remaining vampires slashed at anything that moved and all therians still alive joined into one massive horde. Daniel gripped his rapier and struck into the heart of a wraith as he saw another one being beheaded by a seven-foot claymore.

His eyes a black canvas of rage, Nathaniel swung the long sword with deadly intent. Following him, the Corsaires unleashed death with the swing of their swords. They cut deep into the demons, killing more than twenty a minute. Bringing up the rear, Captain Jane had a sword in each hand and a demon below her boot. Slashing through its head, she gave Daniel a nod and kept fighting.

He nearly got his head taken off by a fourth tier wraith but Lucas and Edward Louis stepped in and slashed at the monster's neck and ribcage. Luckily Liam had driven a broken lance through the beast's neck, but as soon as they landed from their attack, both vampires got kicked in the face and Lucas just barely dodged Samyazza's sword.

The demon's yellow eyes glowed in the darkness and the worms breaking free from his body screeched in the direction of Daniel. "You and your little friends will pay for my failure!"

He swung his sword and tore at the air trying to get to the leader of the Magdalena. Daniel had no time to get his footing and continued dodging the barrage of attacks from the fallen angel.

The other three vampires had gotten to their feet and recovered when two Corsaires tried to push Liam and Edward out of the way, but Lucas was not able to dodge and a huge black scimitar cleaved clean through his right arm before a huge hoof kicked him across the chest. The Demon King Astaroth stood up his full height and spread his dragon wings wide.

The Corsaires attacked but both were swatted away like pesky flies. Astaroth put his scimitar to his tongue. "Feed my blade!"

The blade slashed through anything that didn't bother to duck. Demons fell, human soldiers fell, therians, vampires, photogeni and even wraiths fell as well. His sword was truly an equal opportunity killer. The demon licked his sword with his long serpent tongue and howled like the hell beast he was.

Daniel continued to dodge and attack anything he passed that wasn't looking to defend from him. The fallen angel's sword never stopped following but it was always an inch away from the vampire's body until he caught his foot and fell to the ground. Even though the demon's steel was quick to follow, blood did not gush. Instead, steel clashed against steel from another sword... Jane had parried the blow in the last instant.

The worms in the demon's flesh screeched in protest followed by his own growl. The demon's strikes became even more vicious and Jane had to duck and dodge aggressively as Samyazza inched closer to her. "Stop fleeing and face me, you bitch!"

In the middle of the battle, Beorn continued to fight with the leader of the fourth-tier wraiths. He had killed three more of the monsters while battling their leader. Even after dozens of hits, he still fought valiantly. The wraith leader was also battered but kept fighting just as fiercely as his opponent.

The bear tore into the wraith's flesh and the beast crumpled the left side of the great Beorn, probably breaking several ribs in the process. What the bear hadn't seen was that another wraith had been nearing from behind. Beorn's left eye had been beaten to a bloody mess so naturally he hadn't seen the wraith or much less the moment when a claymore sliced clean through its neck.

After dealing the deadly blow, Nathaniel looked at the bear just in time to see the wraith give one final grueling blow to the bear's ribcage before the bear snapped and ripped its head off. The mighty bear gave a triumphant roar and held the head in the air but it didn't take long for him to crumble under his own weight.

Nathaniel killed two demons and ran to the mighty bear. Kneeling down, he heard Beorn whimper like a wounded cub while coughing up blood. "Hold on! I'll get Liam!"

"No, boy," said the bear struggling on his words. "Thank you, but you need to keep killing."

"No no no no no no no. I'm going to get Liam and-"

"You will kill, boy!!" the bear roared before another cough sprayed the ground with his blood. "You will kill... and do me proud. Please, let me die with that peace. That and one more thing."

"What?" asked Nathaniel as tears flowed from his eyes in what seemed like the first time in an eternity.

Beorn spoke slowly with a weak smile on his face. "Promise to kill... but also promise to live. After all, you're only human." Beorn's eyes focused on the young man and became glassy while he kept smiling. It took a few moments for Nathaniel to realize he'd stopped breathing.

The battle raged all around with thousands of bodies on the ground. He saw the eyes of a therian woman, dead on the ground. Her face was expressionless, unlike a vampire that lay next to her. Holding her hand, his face showed that he had been crying when he died. Thousands of bodies surrounded Nathaniel. All seemed to look at him and before him the mighty bear lay with blood seeping from the torn mouth that still smiled up at him with the wish for one more kill.

He took his blade and cut off a long piece of the bear's mane. Bodies continued to fly. Bullets were scarcely heard since most humans had been killed. Meanwhile, Nathaniel sat tying a braid seemingly oblivious to the chaos around him. He stood up and scanned the battlefield. A couple of seconds passed until he saw what he was looking for. He looked down and kissed Beorn's large head, closed his eyes and tasted his fingers after touching the great bear's blood.

He stood up casually. Picked up his claymore and walked to the west side of the battlefield. Vampires and therians fought and were doing away with a group of demons. Branches and perennials lashed at five remaining fourth-tier wraiths. Laius and Gerald vampires were beginning to drag the wounded back to the great Roanoak.

Among all the chaos, Nathaniel walked as if nothing and after a hundred steps or so, he knelt down again. This time the body was of Rufus the red wolf. His face showed the pain that comes only from dying alone and unexpectedly. He had shelled into a fetal position and his now human body was on top of wet grass, reddened with his blood. He put his hand on the shoulder of the fallen therian. After closing his eyes for a moment, he took his sword, cut off a long red lock from the wolf leader and tied it to the one he had taken from Beorn.

Again he stood up but after a deep breath, he looked to the ground. He smelled the battle weary air around him and a look of disappointment came over his face as something broke through the other scents of battle. Tears rolled down his eyes and it didn't take him long to find Wendy's lifeless body.

This time he leapt to her and picked up her lifeless body when he knelt next to her. His body shook and his breath broke and rattled as he held her tightly. His eyes streamed rivers of tears and he would have stayed there forever, but the sight of two demons and a vile looking man running into a flaming hole in the ground brought him back to his senses.

He looked at the battle and saw that three large demons still ran amok and again he picked up his long sword. This time however, he did not walk.

***

Samael slashed at air with his halberd finding only cigarette smoke or steel. Liam's lance parried aggressively and even knocked the grey hulk off balance a couple of times but the fallen angel was relentless.

Spurred by these attacks, Samael seemed to fight harder still until he saw some flames from the corner of his eyes.

The angel saw a large cave rip open from the ground with Azazel and Asmodai running into it. That would have been bad enough, but Elliot smiling directly to the fallen angel was more than Samael could bear. To his surprise, the pudgy human turned to walk back to the temple. The angel roared but his attention had been distracted long enough and Liam buried his lance deep in Samael's right shoulder, which was immediately followed by a shoulder tackle courtesy of Nathaniel.

The fallen angel tumbled on the ground but instead of dealing a deathblow, Nathaniel kept running. In pain, the angel got up to his feet and ran full speed to the temple.

Samyazza had scored some hits on both Daniel and Captain Jane. They each bled from an arm and though they had taken other blows to the torso, none had pierced their armor. Samyazza swung right, Jane ducked left and Daniel scored a light hit that decapitated one of the dozens of worms in the fallen one's skin. For his efforts, he received a knee to the mid section and a fist square on his face. Jane was on her way to strike Samyazza but the angel turned around with a right cross that sent her straight to the ground. The angel then raised his sword and along with the worms in his body, gave a hideous shriek.

But it wasn't a shriek of victory. It was the reaction to having a seven foot claymore sticking out of his stomach. Nathaniel's eyes burned into the angel's as he pulled and twisted the blade back and out to maximize the damage.

The fallen angel pulled away from the blade and staggered from one side to the other. His black blood spilled onto the ground and his yellow eyes scanned from side to side as he choked on his own blood. Nathaniel stood back and helped Jane up from the ground. Just then, the dying angel rushed towards Daniel grabbed him by the face and pinned him to the ground. The demon giggled maniacally spitting on the vampire. Daniel had even buried his own rapier completely into the demon but Samyazza just laughed and vomited blood onto him. "Can I tell you a secret?!" screamed the angel as he put his mouth to the vampire's ears.

It was only a second but whatever he said caused a terrible effect. Liam and Nathaniel knocked the fallen angel off Daniel, who was now writhing on the ground screaming.

"MY HEAD!! YARGHHHHHH!!!! MY HEAD!!!!!"

The angel kept laughing even as Liam and Nathaniel both stabbed him repeatedly with swords. "Sweet dreams!!!! HAHAHAHAHAHA--"

The only thing that had been able to silence him was the claymore chopping his head right off. His face and the worms had been frozen mid screech.

Daniel continued to scream and writhe, his eyes shifted and the veins in his head and neck pulsed feverishly. His head was an explosion of sirens and thunder and he couldn't see a thing because his eyes kept rolling around against his will. He couldn't hear Jane or Nathaniel or Liam as they screamed at him and he didn't see two huge dragon wings that spread out behind him. Only slightly did he feel two talons dig into his shoulders before his body fell backwards onto a slab.

After Astaroth had smashed the base of Daniel's skull on his knee, the vampire's lifeless body fell face first on the ground. Jane had seen his eyes go blank and the demon roared in triumph.

"NOOOOOOOOOOOOOOOOO!!!!!" Jane howled and struck down on the demon slashing so savagely that the beast did not have a chance to reply.

"I'LL KILL YOU!!! I'LL KILL YOUUUUUUU!!!!!!!!"

She struck the demon's legs and arms, hit him on the chest and even tore chunks of flesh from his face. Astaroth could only reel back from the crazed vampire.

"DIE!!! DIE!! DIE!!!!!!!"

Her screams were horrible and she continued to hit the demon as Liam and Nathaniel could only stare at her madness.

"YOU KILLED HIM!!! YOU BASTARD!!! YOU KILLED HIM!!!! DIE!!!!!!!!!!!!!!!!"

Just as she was going to give him the final blow a loud metal clang sounded, an arrow fell to the ground and Jane had been knocked over. The bloodied demon grabbed his sword and ran off into the same hole where the other demons had fled through.

Liam and Nathaniel would have gone in pursuit but two large wings forced them to halt as they felt a soft breeze flowing from the west.

"Leave him to us," said a deep voice as the aroma of sandalwood and cinnamon lightened their spirits. The angel's smile was friendly and his hair flowed just above the shoulders. The wings had a blue hue to them and the tunic he wore was also of a light blue. In direct contrast to the soothing nature of his being, he carried a silver scythe that seemed to glow with moonlight.

Nathaniel then looked around and saw dozens of globes of light whizzing back and forth as the battles finally ebbed to nothing. The angel looked on approvingly and turned back to Nathaniel and the others.

"Please, get up from the ground, my friends," the angel said as he reached them.

"Hello..." said Nathaniel, "are you --?"

"Gabriel? Yes, young brother. And you and I are due a talk. Let us go to the back of the field next to Roanoak."

The lights that had been buzzing all over the battlefield now circled around the surviving members of the forces and started shining brightly while a soothing hum filled their ears. An instant later, they were in the back field next to the great tree. There dozens of wounded were being treated by roots and the shining globes of light.

Nathaniel was still a little disoriented from the sudden change but as soon as the angel touched him, he regained his bearings and looked around as if he'd just woken up from a dream.

"I'll be right back, Nathaniel," Gabriel said.

"Where are you going?" replied the human.

The angel looked back and smiled. "I have to put out a fire."

Gabriel spread his wings and gave two massive pulls which landed him in the middle of the battlefield. He looked at the temple then turned to the cave where Asmodai, Azazel and then Astaroth had gone down through. He swung his scythe and buried the staff four inches into the ground while his hands began to weave a mysterious pattern as if he were kneading air. The blood soaked grass stood on end like hairs do when they come into contact with static. The air might have buzzed and cracked from the energy that was being emitted, but the angel's expression did not change even when he clasped his hands causing the cave entrance to implode.

Inside the cavern, Astaroth heard when the entrance caved in but continued to hobble into the deep. "Where are those two?" he said. His eyes were so damaged that even he had a hard time seeing in the dark. "Damn woman," he spoke into the silence... but the silence was quick to answer.

"Well, they do say that a woman's wrath knows no pity."

The demon stumbled sideways as he raised his weapon to defend himself. A low light started to glow in the dark and the demon could see a shining veil with a scale on it. An angel wore that veil. He lifted his hand to unclasp it and revealed a kind and gentle face, framed by golden locks. The demon read the inscription that shined in the darkness. "Quis ut Deus.... Hello, viceroy."

"Michael will do."

Astaroth clutched his sword even harder as he looked into the eyes of the angel without blinking. It didn't matter that blood was dripping into his eye; he wasn't going to give the angel any type of satisfaction. "To what do I owe the pleasure," he spat. As he said the words, he hobbled deeper into the cavern to at least have the option of making a run for it, even if his leg was badly damaged and one of his wings merely dangled by a strip of flesh. The angel looked at him smiling whimsically at seeing the interim king of hell in his current state.

"Oh, dear Astaroth, what have you been up to?"

"Mind your business, envious one. Let me be on my way down to the very tunnels I've created."

"Ah yes... about that. That's actually part of the reason why I came to speak with you. I know you had great plans for the Underworld, but it seems as if you have not completely understood the concepts of property or trespassing. I'm actually here because some friends of mine wanted to have a word with you."

Suddenly, over a thousand torches lit inside the cavern. The demon looked onto a sea of helmets and axes, thick beards, short legs, stout bodies and little brown eyes looking directly at him. His jaw slackened incredulously and the song of his falling sword echoed deep into the cavern. Without asking a single question a cloud of dwarf axes was launched towards him.

As he wiped the blood off his face, Michael gave a small smile and made the sign of the cross before putting his veil back on.

***

Back at the castle, Samael searched the grounds looking for one last kill.

"Elliot!!! Where are you hiding?!!"

His body was littered with injuries and he was losing a great deal of blood but his soul demanded one more kill. He cracked columns with punches as he passed them and clutched a sword in each hand because he had left his halberd behind.

"I'm not hiding, you silly ass," said a voice from the left corridor. "I'm down here."

Samael ran into the chamber and found nothing.

The voice rang from the corridor on the other side. "You really are stupid, aren't you? I said over here."

The fallen angel ran and grunted with every step because of pain and fatigue. Once again though, his efforts went unrewarded.

"ARGHHHHHH!!! FACE ME YOU COWARD!!!!!!!"

The patronizing voice continued to tease the fallen angel. "Ah... just like your master. All bark and no bite... not to mention zero intellect. I'm out here, idiot."

This time, the voice came from the inner garden of the temple. Samael ran even faster than he had before and roared into the garden, which was also empty. The scream he gave made the very ground quake.

Looking around, he saw a handkerchief floating down from above. The angel looked to all sides before picking it from the air. The silence continued and he saw that something was written on the small cloth.

Salvation lay at your feet.

When Samael looked at the ground, he noticed a blue glow all around him. He hadn't noticed the figure because the hexagram was so large that it covered more than half the courtyard.

With a cataclysmic explosion, the entire temple was blown to pieces and a wave of fire spread in all directions. Outside, Gabriel stood in the middle of the battlefield. When he heard the explosion he spread his bright blue wings. The wave of fire stopped to form a huge wall twenty yards from the angel.

Everyone at the back end of the battlefield looked on in awe... everyone except Jane. The fire proceeded to fold onto itself and extinguished. She sat on the ground with Daniel's body in her arms and her hands caressing his face, her tears raining down from above. Nathaniel looked at her and his tears kept hers company. He stood beside her and put his hand on her shoulder.

"I'm so sorry, Jane. I wish I could have, I should have... dammit... I lost someone too."

At those last words, Jane's eyes snapped open and the pain in her face switched instantly to rage. "You what? Am I to understand you lost someone? What the hell did you lose? What could you possibly have lost? Someone who you had a fling with? A one night stand?!!!"

"But I lo-- "

The word got slapped out of his mouth.

"Don't you dare say you loved that girl, you pissant. He's dead, they're all dead and you couldn't do anything to prevent it from happening. They're all dead because of you! Because of YOU!"

Three times she slapped him before a firm hand held her back. "That's enough," said Gabriel.

Jane would have reacted to him but she saw four cherubs carrying Daniel's body away. "What are you doing???!!! Leave him alone!!!!!!!"

Gabriel held onto her and embraced her as she fought with all her might against the powerful angel. She begged for them to not take

Daniel away, but with sad faces, the small angels took flight and disappeared into the clouds with the body of her beloved.

Jane cried and screamed and begged and the angel simply held her in an embrace as his wings wrapped around them both. The sounds of her torment continued for a moment but were quickly muffled. Gabriel's wings then started glowing brightly as a breeze from the west brought the sweet smell of egnalem.

The screaming grew fainter and when the angel's wings finally opened, the courageous captain lay fast asleep. Gabriel signaled for Liam to take her and the vampire threw away his cigarette to hold her in his arms.

The angel then walked to Nathaniel. "I think it's time we finally had that chat."

Chapter 44: Parting Ways

With blood still wet on his face and an empty feeling gorging his soul, Nathaniel started to walk with the angel. Gabriel's wings tucked behind him as they walked back onto the battlefield. Nathaniel saw how the fire had consumed most of the plain and the bodies that had been there. The angel also surveyed the makeshift valley with a weary look in his eye.

Four minutes into their walk, Nathaniel's nostrils stung with the smell of burnt wood and flesh and he could stand the silence no longer. "What the hell do you want to talk about?"

"I was giving you some time to gather your thoughts, Nathaniel. I'm sure there's a lot on your mind. There's no need to lash out, although if it makes you feel better, then proceed."

Nathaniel bowed his head ashamed. "I... I'm sorry."

Gabriel kept looking forwards. "That's fine. Now what do you really want to ask?"

This time Nathaniel thought for a moment. Ashes and the smell of burnt flesh kept burning his eyes. Tears welled and his voice grew shaky. "W-why did it have to come to this?"

The angel stopped walking and turned to look directly at Nathaniel. "What makes you say that it had to come to this? Do you think there was no other option? Was this really the only choice?"

Nathaniel thought on the words and it hurt to think that all those who had just died had done so in vain.

"And don't think they died in vain either," added the angel.

The human looked at the angel a bit surprised. "Can you read minds?"

Gabriel gave a little laugh. "No. but I've been around humans long enough to know how you think. What I said was just a reaction to your question. Don't judge events as correct or incorrect; simply accept that some things just happen. Why they happen is also a combination of events that cause another event and so on and so forth. Some are fortunate, others unfortunate. Could all of this have been avoided? To answer the question, yes, but what's the use if there's no way to change the present?"

Nathaniel gave real thought to what the angel said. As a sweet breeze blew on his face, he breathed deeply before looking at the angel. "What's gonna happen now?"

Gabriel stretched his wings a moment. "Well for starters the news media will likely say the Sri Lankan military eradicated the Liberation army of Tamil and that what happened in Myanmar was an explosion triggered by a rogue tsunami. The wounded will be healed, the dead that were not burned shall be taken by each group, and everyone will return to their factions. They won't quarrel at first but it's up in the air whether peace between therians and vampires will last. The photogeni will return to Raelis and we will return to our daily activities. Those are all possible results, but apart from not being able to read minds, I can't see into the future either."

"Oh... sorry."

"No need to be, my young friend. You know something? You apologize a rather great deal."

Nathaniel let out a small chuckle. "Mom used to say the same thing."

"I would imagine," replied the angel.

Another cool breeze blew as they walked and Nathaniel smelled the sweet spice of egnalem. It was almost as if the angel was made of it. That was the first time Nathaniel really grasped he was talking to an angel. He'd seen some in the Halo Maze, he'd seen Raguel aboard the Calico, he'd woken up Michael, he'd even listened to Israfil, but this was the first time he was completely aware that he was talking to an angel and he stared a bit more than he should have.

"That took you long enough," said the angel, "it's amazing to see how humans can become so disconnected at times. Good to have all of you here now."

"But I didn't say anything," he replied.

"I don't need to read minds to know what you thought. Is there any other query I might be able to clear up?"

"What happened to the demons?"

"Well it all depends on which demon you're referring to. Two demons named Azazel and Asmodai fled through the underground. You yourself beheaded the fallen angel Samyazza. Another demon named Tamiel was ended by Elm, one of the photogeni warriors who fought as brave as I think any living being has ever fought and Samael went up in flames with the temple."

"What about the one with the wings? The one who... who killed Daniel."

The angel momentarily became very terse. "Astaroth? He's been taken care of."

Nathaniel knew better than to pry, but his face still struggled with something on his mind. Something the angel was quick to notice.

"Speak, little brother, or forever avoid your peace."

Nathaniel looked at the angel resolved to ask. "There's a couple of things."

"Then tell me the first one, and we'll go from there," said the angel with a friendly nod.

"Is there a heaven?"

The angel was surprised by the question. "You wonder of the lady Wendy?"

Nathaniel's eyes watered. He was that obvious and for the moment he could only nod.

"Heaven does exist child; as does hell. But they are quite different and governed by different rules than the ones you know of."

Nathaniel thought about the angel's answer. "That doesn't answer the other question."

The angel smiled almost proud at having had his bluff called.

"Souls are a peculiar thing, Nathaniel. They are weightless but they can move mountains. You probably ask because you worry for her soul. Let me start by saying that no one is denied heaven eternally. Vampires and therians can get to heaven but there is more than one way to reach that plane of existence and some take longer than others. Consider them different routes to the same destination."

Nathaniel's eyes grew precise and severe. "So maybe she has to pass through hell first. Is that it?"

The angel gave another stretch of his wings.

"I actually don't know if that's it. Getting into heaven is not just passing the balance test. As you've seen with the visors, there is another level to this reality. Actually, there are several. Consider heaven as the penthouse of a building. There are different stairwells and elevators and various other routes that can get you to that penthouse. You can go up a level, down a level, walk across a floor or even leave the building. But eventually everyone can get to the penthouse. It's all a matter of when you choose to go."

Nathaniel wasn't sure he understood but asked another question. "What happened to Daniel before he died?"

"Ah... that." Gabriel seemed to not want to answer but complied anyways. "The fallen angel you had mortally wounded was called Samyazza. His name means infamous rebellion and of the hundreds of things that I could tell you about him, one of the most interesting was that he was the only creature in existence that knew the real name of God. Some people sometimes ask what's in a name? To that question I answer that everything can be in a name. Try to imagine the knowledge and emotions of a God... now try and imagine one creature being given all that information in one whisper. It might seem cruel but that demon executing Daniel was a merciful fate in comparison to the alternative."

"The reality is that names are a curious thing. Lucas means bringer of light or morning and Liam means will or protection. Wendy's name means friend. Edward means healthy guard. For her part, Jane's name means God is Gracious. As for Daniel? His name means God is My Judge. And you? Well yours means God has given. Compare yourself and your friends to the roots of your names and you'll see that part of your essence is in your name. God's name is different because apart from meaning, the name itself has essence."

Nathaniel's jaw clenched as he heard the angel's words. "So does that mean that the essence of God was lost forever?"

The angel flapped his wings and Nathaniel could swear he felt and smelled a sweet ocean breeze. "Remember what I said about the different routes to eternity? Well with Daniel a new road is being forged as we speak."

"What does that mean?" asked the human.

The angel just smiled at him. "It just means that you may eventually find out. Is there any other question?"

Nathaniel thought hard as the pre-dawn light peeked through. "Is there anything I can help with?"

The angel snapped his eyes wide open. "I don't think I ever expected that."

"Well I'd love for you to talk about anything that's bugging you, but for now, I expect you're short on time."

"Hmmm.... I might take you up on that offer some day. As for helping out... there's one thing you should know. This whole mess happened in part because of something very evil... or more precisely someone very evil."

Nathaniel immediately thought of Bill. When he had realized who he was he'd instantly thought it was all a trick. All deception. "I think I know who you're talking about."

The angel looked him straight in the eye. "I think you don't. It's a man and I'm pretty sure all the results from today were what he was looking for."

"A man? But I thought-"

"That some beings are incapable of doing good? That's fine but if you ever see Bill again, be sure to apologize."

"How do you..."

"He's my brother and he fell for his arrogance when we were ruled by a wrathful father. Things change and so do circumstances. I'm talking about a mortal human twisted by righteousness. He does not approve of the current methods of the Mother-Father. You asked me what you can do to help… find out all you can about this human and stop him."

"But what do I do to find him?"

"You still possess a blank card from Tobias and a vial of blood left to you by Melissa. These items are not trivial. Keep them safe. They'll assist you in due time, but alas, I must be on my way. We shall talk again and I'll be seeing you around."

"Wait a minute!" said Nathaniel. "What am I supposed to do now?"

The angel looked at him one last time. "That's completely up to you, my friend."

He then gave a huge lunge with his wings and soared out of sight into the clouds. A glint of sunshine peeked through the hole Gabriel had left in the clouds and Nathaniel felt its warm caress as cold water lapped at his boots, covering them with sand.

He was startled to realize he was no longer on the battlefield but on a shoal surrounded by azure water. The ocean air still tasted of egnalem and when he looked over his shoulder he saw a familiar Black Galleon floating on the water.

Hearing someone call from the ship, he looked at how the water did not move except for a few ripples. He took a deep breath and walked into deeper water to completely submerge himself. After pulling his head back, he took another deep breath and spoke his mind. "I sure hope you know what you're doing, God. I'm only human, you know? Oh and Gabriel says my name means God has given, so right now all I'm gonna ask from you is for you to give me a sign that I'm not alone in all of this."

The air didn't move, the water remained completely still until he received a response. He couldn't help but smile as a single solitary wave made its way to him breaking across his feet. "I'll take that as a yes then."

With a tired body and soul, he dove into the water and began swimming towards the boat, resolved to follow whichever path the wind may carry him to.

Epilogue

There was an uneasy sense of peace on the battlefield at Myanmar. Amidst huge chunks of debris laying on the ground and a couple of makeshift graves, a lounge chair was set in the middle of the field. In it sat someone unaffected by the carnage that had happened on this plain. Instead, he focused on the cool beer in his hand, which helped quench his parched tongue. He leaned back and lit a cigarette, breathing deeply and exhaling a long black breath.

Clouds above looked like dancing elephants to him and his eyes looked like he was trying to say something to the heavens but nothing came out. With a quick tug he returned the reclining chair to its original position and leaned forward, looking for something in his pocket. After a brief search, he pulled out a switchblade with the letters L.S.B. engraved in deep red letters on its mahogany hilt. He flicked his cigarette, drew the blade and looked up to the heavens again.

"My work here..." he said, pausing before putting the blade to his hand, "has only just begun."

He then slashed his hand, let his blood drip on a wet patch of grass and buried the blade to the hilt in the ground.

Bill then pulled out another cigarette along with a copper lighter which he snapped open and lit. He put his bleeding hand against the flame healing it instantly and used the still lit lighter to ignite his cigarette. Standing up, he gave a long stretch and proceeded to walk away. As he did, small vines began to grow from where he had stabbed the Earth. His pace seemed normal, but in seconds he'd covered a league and the only trace of him, were little puffs of smoke fading away in the distance.

Acknowledgements

For years now I've been working on, tweaking, editing, writing, rewriting, researching and insisting on Only Human. What started out as a book on a whim has become into something that will span more books because there is simply so much information on which to feed from and because the story took on a life on its own and who am I to deny it the life it so covets.

Throughout the entire process, there have been some constants that I'd especially like to give thanks to. My wife, who was my girlfriend when I began this book has served for inspiration of so many characters that I'm sure she's surprised as to how many layers she has and the depth of the impact she's had in my life.

For her part, my mom has supported me in anything I've chosen to go for at all times during my life. Regardless of the career path, the main thing was to be happy and I wrote this book in part to show her what makes me happy... writing... well writing and a Mama cooked meal (that goes without saying).

Thanks definitely have to go out to my friends and family for the support throughout. There have been people waiting patiently, anxiously and even pestering me to finish this book already... for the support, the motivation and the follow up, a big ole thanks goes to a long list of people I won't go name by name on for fear of leaving someone out and having to resubmit the book just because I was enough of an ass to forget.

Thanks to Tony Arocho for the wicked cover. Although it took a while, we got there man and it was completely worth it. Thanks to my wife, Finees and Joey for being my guinea pigs and reading the first draft. Your feedback helped shape this book and the ones to come.

For musical inspiration, I'm completely indebted to Pearl Jam, Tool, Soundgarden, Elbow, Jimmy Hendrix, Miles Davis, Alice in Chains, and Blind Melon, just to name a few. For literary inspiration, my thanks to: Frank Herbert, H.P. Lovecraft, Neil Gaiman and J.R.R. Tolkien.

Finally, my thanks to all the people who somehow inspired the DNA of certain characters in this book.

Cheers.

Made in the USA
Columbia, SC
11 June 2022

61633500R00290